# The Rootless

Original title: Ontworteling

Translation from Dutch by Donna Berkle & M.K. Altena

Front cover image by Hakan Aker

Front cover and book design by M.K. Altena

ISBN: 9798385660902 (Hardcover)

ISBN: 9798378969609 (Paperback)

Printed by Kindle Direct Publishing / Amazon

First printed edition: 2023

ContactTheRootless@gmail.com

M.K. Altena

# The Rootless

Translated by

Donna Berkle & M.K. Altena

SOUNDTRACK

The Rootless has its own soundtrack!

Listen to each song
and every musical piece
that is mentioned in this novel.

For the playlist, go to Youtube
and search for M.K. Altena.

# PART I

*NOTHING MAKES US SO LONELY*
*AS OUR SECRETS*
Paul Tournier

## 1

FLIGHT


*Amsterdam Schiphol Airport, February 2009*

*"Mind your step" said a metallic voice from the speaker above us. I was so caught up in conversation with Claire though, that in spite of the speaker's warning, it failed to grab my attention. Suddenly I therefore found myself lying upside down at the end of the travelator... and although I was vaguely aware of startled voices of the people scrambling to avoid tripping over me, I barely had time to feel embarrassed, as a figure that appeared to the left of me grabbed me by my shoulder and pulled me up in one fluid motion. It was the same man who had caught my eyes earlier at the other airport, and he said "Happy Valentine's Day!"*
*This all happened in less than five seconds.*

Out of all twenty seven February 14s that I had experienced in my life, this one could easily go down in the books as the most strange. But when my travel alarm clock woke me up just now, too early for my liking, I could not yet have known this. After all, this morning routine was no different than any other: get up, get dressed, pack the suitcase, unpack the suitcase, pack it more efficiently, a rushed breakfast and then the anxious wait in the hotel lobby for the airport shuttle bus. This had happened to me before, here in Reykjavík. If you missed your connection you had to transfer at the bus station with major hassle. Grabbing heavy suitcases from the luggage compartment by yourself and hauling all your temporary worldly possessions to a bigger and almost certainly totally packed alternate bus. Or did having to transfer buses depend on what hotel you were picked up from? I honestly didn't know anymore. The one thing that I did know was that I wanted to delay being among Dutch people for as long as possible... which was just wishful thinking, of course.
Claire and I were lucky to both find aisle seats near the back of the bus between two Icelanders who were silently staring out of the window, but the slow yet harsh drawl of a Dutch guy a couple of seats in front of us, was impossible to ignore. The way in which he described his all-night binge drinking in full detail to his fellow countrymen and listed which dance clubs in town hosted the most leggy chicks, made me wish I was still in bed so that I could bury my head underneath the largest possible pillow.

After the usual fuss of going through customs, with jackets, bags, laptops and even our shoes, there was a brief moment of freedom. One hour to kill by doing some last-minute shopping for perishable delicacies, like dried cod and as much chocolate as the remainder of spare change in my wallet allowed. Next, down the long corridor with people waiting to the left and the right, outside the windows you could see the occasional tail or wing in the signature blue and yellow of Icelandair. And inside, on the walls, there were the photos: advertisements with images that triggered hopeful excitement upon arrival, but instilled such melancholy while you were making the way towards the gate to return to your home country, that they almost made you burst into tears.

Pictures of the Blue Lagoon. Sceneries of gray-green moss overgrown lava fields and of its vast expanse... We have seen it all these past two weeks. And this time even from a rental car, no less! I really should be thankful to that magazine's editorial staff for that. In thinking of our living situation – I wondered how many household chores I could make Claire do as a trade-off for all the free tours along natural wonders that, until now, she had only seen in books and on the internet. From her comfortable passenger side of the car, my flatmate had gawked at all the literally jaw-dropping beauty that flew by. Lava fields as far as the eye could see on the Reykjanes peninsula. The geothermal springs of Seltún with its boiling hot, dark-gray bubbling mud... At one point we had spent all day driving around lake Thingvellir in one big loop, from the slightly snow covered hills on the southwestern shore to the spectacular vista that unfolded before our eyes as we drove downhill and then from the south up the east to return back north. But the one thing that Claire was not gonna recover from any time soon was when we actually went ice climbing on the glacier of an active volcano. Although I was rather blasé about it all day – after all, I had to stay focused on my photography – I was not completely indifferent to seeing us, all geared up with crampons and pickaxes, walking over this fire mountain that was several years overdue from erupting. The Eyjafjallajökull... an unutterable and unforgettable experience.

I was going to miss it, this island, with her rotten shark, brandy and Viking vibe, her incomprehensible language and that quaint accent with which her inhabitants spoke to us in English... and, if I could say so myself, the editorial staff should feel lucky to have me as a photographer, since I had even been able to capture the northern lights, on one of our final evenings. Albeit not entirely without effort. It had been freezing cold and the wind had been relentless, but back at the hotel, scrolling through the results with frozen fingers, I knew I had captured something special: the aurora borealis set against the backdrop of a romantic, white lighthouse. Claire would beat herself up if she saw what she had missed that night. Her fault for getting engrossed in conversation with those nice, Christian Faroe Islanders in the lobby...

"Did you hear about that wedding event, just now?" Claire asked as we dragged our feet to the gate.

"Heard about what?"

"Well, at that shop someone said that our plane, after landing in Amsterdam, will be converted into an actual chapel. And on its return flight to Iceland, a wedding ceremony will take place for a whole bunch of couples all at once, with a Lutheran vicar and everything!" she rambled on.

"Nice publicity stunt by Icelandair," I mumbled. "Will probably get them a lot of new customers."

A wedding event, in the air of all places, things shouldn't get any crazier. I could not bring myself to feel the same enthusiasm that my flatmate felt about novelties like that. Way too much romanticism this early in the morning... oooh, why not admit it: I was in a bad mood. Being in airports on my return trip home never had a good effect on me. The impossible departure times, never enough chairs in the waiting areas at the gates and, as always, the much too heavy carry-on containing way too many books, camera lenses and foreign delicacies. Was I ever going to learn? And then there were the stares from those types of people to whom subcultures were completely alien, who seemed to frown upon my alternative style. How could I make it clear to these people that having a different look was not the same as wanting to stand out? Yes, I knew my hair was red. I also knew that it was not the standard redhead henna color, but a cyclamen-red. And if they could not deal with that, then why did they not just look the other way? Whoa, my mood was really foul this morning...

Obviously the man who was sitting on the floor across from me could not read my mind and it was clear that he was indifferent to the defensive look on my face. He observed me as though I were some scientific object. Until I locked eyes with him on purpose, and his trailed off. Only briefly, by the way, because within a few seconds his eyes were on me again as he continued to judge my appearance. Whatever! Just imitate him and shamelessly return the favor. Hmmm... auburn hair, a face that portrays a chronic lack of sleep, gray or light-blue eyes below distinctive eyebrows. His age somewhere around mid-thirties, a sexy body, sharply dressed... he was not bad looking at all. Actually, he was downright attractive. Too bad though, about that standoffish arrogance with which he looked away again...

After the airplane had left the Icelandic soil Claire and I first discussed the division of the household chores for the next few weeks. After that I took out my camera to walk through the stack of photos that I had accumulated in the last fourteen days, starting from the beginning. Together we assessed which ones were suitable for the travel magazine and, as expected, my roommate was insanely jealous over my unplanned evening of northern lights. She asked me to describe in full detail how I had experienced this natural phenomenon and whether it really did make a sound, as some people had told her, and how quickly it changed shape and color... "Man," she sighed after my detailed, but also slightly romanticized explanation, "should anyone have doubts about the existence of a Creator, they need only look at something like that."

"Let's keep God out of this, shall we?" I snapped back, after which I apologized immediately, a bit flustered.

"Yeah, yeah, I know, you're going through your atheistic phase..." she said mockingly.

"If that's alright with you." I rolled my eyes at her.

Only Claire could get away with saying things like that to me. And even if she could not, she would anyway. Apparently, that was part of 'being best friends'.

I nudged her shoulder to indicate that I needed to get past her. Quickly stretch my legs, go pee...

I barely made it halfway towards the back of the plane when some turbulence made me lose my balance and I had to hold on to a random headrest next to me to catch myself. The rumble did not last long, but was strong enough to grab the attention of one person in particular who was sitting close by. And there I was, back into the game of staring and looking away with that most interesting male person I saw at the gate at the Keflavík airport. Only this time his gaze was so piercing that I had to remind myself to continue walking. Good grief. What was that all about, what did I do now? He seemed surprised about something, the way he looked at me, as though... nope, don't fall for it. It's probably some 'man thing'.

After my visit to the restroom I thus walked right past him with smug confidence and returned to my chair without even giving him a single glance. The remainder of the flight was as unremarkable as any. Conversations settled down and were replaced by periods of quiet with an occasional comment back and forth, and finally, silence. We ate the breakfast that was distributed by the flight attendants, drank coffee and tea, drifted in and out of sleep... and for the longest time, the only thing that I was aware of was the high pitched, steady humming of the airplane's engines.

A chime followed by the characteristic tone of voice of a flight attendant brought me back into the here and now. I yawned and my ears popped, looked at my watch, looked around me and as soon as Claire seemed awake enough, started talking to her. From the corner of my eye I noticed how the Dutch guy, from the bus this morning, held his head in agony. A hangover, most likely. I, on the other hand, actually felt rather good. I had slept exceptionally well and, miraculously, completely lost my bad mood.

Some twenty minutes later, with refreshed courage, I stepped out of the plane while chatting away with Claire as we entered gate F-something at Schiphol. Perhaps my optimism was nothing more than bravado. Either way, my mind was so focused on my flatmate, myself and fourteen days of wonderful memories that I forgot to watch my step...

And there I was the next moment, lying upside-down on the travelator. It barely even hurt. And even if it did, I would not have noticed, as mesmerized as I was by *him*. I could not imagine anything more romantic or old-fashioned... a strange, attractive person had come to my rescue and wished me *Happy Valentine's Day*.

Now I just had to get to know him!

So I tried my best to catch up with him as we made our way towards the baggage claim area. Finally, walking next to him I asked in English, just off the top of my head: "You're not from The Netherlands, are you?"

He briefly glanced to the side but did not slow down his rapid pace. "I am of mixed heritage," he replied. His tone was flat and gave away his relentless unapproachability. I could not think of anything else to say and, with that, our fleeting encounter came to an end in exactly the same way it had done so at the airport in Keflavík.

I let him continue his path and slowed my pace to wait for Claire. I had made a fool of myself again. I knew I was known for misinterpreting situations, but this...!

As we arrived at the baggage carousel my mysterious lover-for-a-minute was just disappearing through the sliding doors and into the arrival area.

2

## DUNGEON

Back to real life. After all, life was not only about taking stunningly beautiful vacations to remote destinations – there was work to be done. Therefore I spent the whole week transferring all Iceland photos to my computer, deleting failed Iceland photos and editing Icelandic visual gems for the magazine that had given me this job.
I only ran into Claire on the stairs or in the kitchen. She had gone straight into a night shift the day after we got home...

On Saturday I was on a photography assignment at the Dungeon to shoot a concert. The Dungeon was a *dark* venue. They said things could get a little wild in there, that it was youth center with a dubious reputation, but feeling awkward or out of place was not my experience of the Dungeon. I was quite comfortable here, most likely due to the band that was playing and the pale skinned artists who were masters in cloaking their existential lyrics in a divine haze of ethereal sounds. As I was looking through my camera, my imaginary eye could almost see their messages crawl like slow moving reptiles, down the stage and onto the dance floor. They were luring each individual person into a cocoon of peaceful isolation. Yet, at the same time they managed to create a sense of togetherness that you could not find anywhere else.
Lolita girls dolled up in pastel dresses dancing side by side with cyber goths dressed in black latex with brightly colored accents. Hand held glow sticks whizzing by purple velvet and crisp white lace of the classical Victorians with their incessant black eyeliner, blood-red lipstick and – sometimes even – fake vampire teeth. Fangs that were prone to dislodge most awkwardly from time to time, say, in the midst of drinking an exquisite glass of red wine.
After shooting for an hour and a half I called it quits. While I waited at the bar for a drink I did some stretches.
Grim Reaper, the bartender, watched me in amusement and asked: "Massage my dear?"
"No," I replied sounding as offended as possible.
He left me alone and continued his work. Grim Reaper, with his lanky limbs... For as long as we had been vaguely acquainted, I had wondered about whether he suffered from a serious illness: Marfan, or something similar. Although I had never dared to ask.
A little later, as he was standing near me washing some glasses, he tried to connect with me again: "Probably been standing in the same position for too

long, huh?"

"Sitting" I replied, "behind my computer. Had a deadline..."

"And now your neck is stiff?"

"No. Sore shoulder."

Grim Reaper smiled, this time with a little twinkle in his eyes. "I'm sure there's something we can do about that," he said, and with a little more emphasis than before: "Massage my dear...?"

The staff at the Dungeon's coat check obviously was really trustworthy! A little dazed I stood there staring at the total, disorderly contents of my jacket's pockets that I had just emptied out on my desk. It was Sunday morning and about time to finally unpack my suitcase. I thought it would be a good idea to wash my jacket along with my dirty clothes but when I saw how I had forgotten to secure my valuables before checking it for safekeeping, I was a bit shocked. Literally everything was still in there: my bike keys, debit card, bus pass... Well, at least nothing was stolen. I shook my head as I moved towards my suitcase.

The vacuum sealed, dried fish was in the fridge. I did manage to recover that on Tuesday. The hand cream and facial scrub from the Blue Lagoon went onto my nightstand, and then there was the *Draumur*, a ton of Draumur: that typically Icelandic, thick, salted licorice buried deep inside disgustingly sweet chocolate bars. Afraid that Claire would steal them accidentally-on-purpose, I hid them in a drawer within reach instead of bringing them to the fridge.

On to the debit card, keys, candy wrappers and other trash. Oh the things one collects during two weeks out of the country... incomprehensible notes scribbled on torn-off pieces of paper that you had written down there for some important reason or another and thus had kept. Even though you were almost always certain that you would never use them, until they ended up in the garbage anyway a year later.

A distinctive rock I had found by Lake Thingvellir, no wait, along the edge of the Eyjafjallajökull. Pieces of paper with addresses and a couple of business cards of new friends. Where that note with just that email address had come from, however, I could not remember for the life of me...

3

CONTACT


Just an email address, in a handwriting that was unfamiliar to me, not very helpful. Why wouldn't I have written down a name below it right away? And of all my acquaintances who in the world did those capitals, written with such mathematical precision, belong to? After racking my brain for several minutes I decided that this kind of pondering was useless. This called for a different approach. So I turned on my laptop, created a brand new email address and wrote a polite note asking who said person was and where I had met him or her. Both in English and in Dutch. There, problem solved.
Then I went outside to go for a walk to try to get rid of this Sunday drag.

The clear voices of children playing in the neighbor's garden downstairs sound lively. Noises that feel right at home in the light of the late morning sun trying to find its way into a darkened bedroom in the shape of a narrow stripe on the wall.
There is movement underneath the sheets of a king size bed. At first the man just rolls over, away from the noises that reach his ears through the open window. Then he opens his eyes anyway. He looks at the alarm clock and groans. After snoozing for a few more minutes he gets up sluggishly. He closes the window. His arm reaches behind the heavy curtains, as he stands there for a moment without moving. Then the man's hand touches the brown-purple velvet again and slightly opens the curtain. A column of sunlight transforms the dust in the atmosphere into tiny sparkles, floating on currents of air in a dreamlike manner. Absentmindedly the man runs his hand over the stubble on his chin and through his hair. He pulls out a single strand and wraps it around his finger, thinly but tightly, a dark-brown contrast to the whitened skin on either side. His fingertip begins to turn purple and he studies this phenomenon. Finally he slowly unwinds the chokehold and restores his cut off circulation.
He pulls out another strand of his hair. This one he drops just above the narrow beam of light that pours into the room. Dark-brown turns into golden-red...
In the living room the man starts up his computer. He opens his email. Then he walks to the dining table. He sits down, leans a bit forward, rests his hands on his knees and stares off into space.
After a while he takes out a piece of paper, no larger than half an a4 sheet, from a drawer and lays it on the table. He also takes out a knife that looks like a surgical scalpel, with a sharp tip, and pricks into the tip of his index

finger. He presses the drop of blood that forms into the paper. He squeezes now, but the finger remains dry.

He pricks himself again, into the exact same finger. This time he drags the blood across the paper into a slightly curved line that runs from a scarlet-red to a color that is nearly indistinguishable from the white. He repeats this. He repeats it again. Until a number appears on the paper: *three*.

Then he stands up and walks to the kitchen. The man takes a chocolate muffin from the fridge. He removes it from the paper liner and places it on a pastry dish. In a cabinet he finds a box of small colored candles and a lighter. Once returned to the dining table the man inserts one candle with meticulous precision into the center of the muffin. Yet again, without flinching, the man pricks his index finger and smears the blood onto the paper. Pricks. And smears. Until a bright red circle appears. The number *zero*.

Finally it is time for the muffin. He slides the paper aside and moves the saucer with the sweet pastry right in front of him, almost with ritualistic reverence. He lights the candle. For a moment he sits there staring at the flickering of the flame, but then he resolutely pulls his artwork towards him. Another zero appears next to the two numbers drawn in blood – *three hundred* – and after licking his finger he gets up and takes his creation to the book case. He tries to let the piece of paper stand up by itself, but when that does not work, he folds both ends and traps them between some books.

Back at the table the man raises the muffin towards the slowly drying numbers, the way one raises a toast by holding up a glass with some sort of beverage inside.

"Congratulations, asshole," he mumbles, and after blowing out the candle, he begins to eat. The muffin is stale and crumbles between his fingers, but he continues. With stubborn resolution he chews and swallows it until it's all gone, including the last crumb that is carefully swept up from the pastry dish. Then the man picks up the candle and puts it in his mouth, burnt wick and all.

When he is done eating he leans back in his chair, arms folded behind his head. A smile – or rather – a grin appears on his face.

Then he jumps up and goes to the bathroom. There he kneels down in front of the toilet, opens the lid and sticks his finger down his throat.

At that moment a sound emerges from the computer in the living room. An alert of an incoming email...

As soon as I got online around seven that evening a pop-up appeared on my laptop screen. A friend request from an *Aeolus,* whoever that could be...? For a brief second I considered deleting the notification, but I knew myself better. Would the day ever come that I could control my curiosity? After I added Aeolus he appeared in my friends list. He was online.

*Rhona says:*

*'hello'*
Aeolus says:
'Goedenavond.'

Ah, Dutch after all. But wait! This could be the person behind the strange email address that I had found...

*'are you the person from that note with that email address'*
'That's correct.'
*'do we know each other?'*
'Not yet.'
*'but you have seen me somewhere?'*
'Yes.'
*'and you want to connect?'*
'Isn't that obvious?'
*'but, um, I have no idea who you are.'*
'That's the charm of online contacts. Or do you feel differently?'
*'not sure about that... I'm not in the habit of chatting with strangers'*
'Ever heard of capitals and punctuation?'
*'?'*
'Your writing is unclear. Use capitals, commas, periods. It looks better.'
*'Well pardon me, but chatting just goes too fast for that.'*
'That looks more like it.'
*'tsk tsk, you're not a very shy person, huh?'*
'A sloppy use of language shows a lack of respect.'
*'and sticking your hand down someone's pocket to leave a note, how would you call that then?'*
'You're offended easily, aren't you?'
*'only with good reason'*
'And so you thought: let's email this complete stranger.'
*'oh shit...'*
'An open door.'
*'Who are you?'*
'I enjoy the anonymity of the internet.'
*'that was not what I asked'*
'If you don't mind, I won't disclose my name.'
*'and your nickname is not your real name obviously...'*
'Nicknames will have to do for now.'
*'this whole thing seems strange to me. you want to connect, but at the same time – where do I know you from? are you a model?'*
'A model. As in, fashion model?'
*'do you work in a pub, are you a bartender or something?'*
*'do you live around here?'*
'If I were to answer that...'

'are you worried that I would be able to trace you then?'

'Of course not. You don't know enough about me.'

'what makes you say that?'

'I make observations.'

'you make observations, and exactly how much time do you spend observing?'

'People who are more knowledgeable on this subject would never have sent an email to an unfamiliar address.'

'oh of course, stupid of me. but it does mean that you have taken advantage of me'

'If you look at it that way...'

'at least there is one comfort: you can't track me down. my email address and profile on here are brand new. made just for the occasion, so to speak. do you know a lot about computers?'

'Sensible, very sensible. However I must ask you politely, yet seriously, to not challenge me on this.'

'what do you mean?'

'I feel more comfortable not knowing who you are nor where you live.'

'ehhh whatever you prefer. I think. but you haven't answered my question yet.'

'Whether I am computer savvy... I know a thing or two, yes.'

'okay... and is it your field of work as well?'

'IT, you mean?'

'yes'

'The field of IT is quite broad. But yes, I work with computers.'

'Well well, I learned something about you, though we've been chatting – for how long now? I have to be honest with you, I find all this a little bit pointless. chatting with a stranger who has a practically empty profile, just like that, without a clear reason to be talking... I don't know.'

'Then let's switch things up. Time for a little game.'

'I'm not the game-playing type'

'I say a word and you respond with one word only.'

'ugh, do I have to'

'Aww come on...'

'hahaha, you big sulk. fine, whatever. but only if you respond to my word immediately as well. because I'm not in the mood for a one-sided interrogation. do you get what I mean? we keep replying to each other's words, so we end up with a word chain.'

'So you caught on to me. Alright, we'll keep things in balance. This is my first word: white.'

'snow'

'Storm.'

'glass'

'Shards.'

'blood'

'Donor.'

*'kidney'*

'Heart.'

*'membrane'*

'Sack.'

*'pericardium'*

'That's Latin.'

*'I know that'*

'The rule is: no foreign words.'

*'pericardium is a loanword and is used often enough'*

'In the field of medicine it is. And it means sack, so you basically just repeated my last word.'

*'sorry, I will never do that again.'*

'Something tells me you don't mean a word you're saying.'

*'hahahahaha!'*

'Okay, let's continue. Hit me.'

*'no'*

'Why'

*'I had started already. "no" was my word'*

'And "why" was mine.'

*'ooh... alright, hold on. OK, this one follows your "why": guilt'*

'How'

*'injustice'*

'World'

*'overcrowded'*

'Logically'

*'desire'*

'What'

*'peace'*

'Soul'

*'pain'*

'Is your soul in pain?'

*'stop. forget "pain". let me try to come up with a new word'*

'That's not going to work. I would like to know what's going on. Are you sad or troubled?'

*'would you discuss private issues with a complete stranger? over the internet?'*

'It may be liberating.'

*'perhaps, but for all I know you could be someone in my circle of acquaintances and...'*

'Rhona, I can assure you that that is not the case.'

*'and you just expect me to trust you on your word. excuse me, but that's just not me'*

'You display a strange combination of recklessness and distrust, do you know that?'

*'oh, never crossed my mind. but stop distracting me. I want to ask you a question. do you think you can answer it without making a fuss?'*

'What's on your mind?'

*'oooh, you are so arrogant! I just wanted to ask you how your week has been so far. nothing dramatic, just out of interest'*

'My week? Okay... well, without getting into too much details: I worked on a project that was delayed unexpectedly not very long ago. That comes with the necessary amount of tension and conflicts and because of that I have tried to give my mind some space in my spare time.'

*'and how did you do that?'*

'By diving head first into a highly intricate musical composition.'

*'you're a musician, then?'*

'Viola da gamba.'

*'what's that? some kind of violin?'*

'It is a string instrument that can originally be traced back to the guitar. It is played with a bow and sometimes with your fingers. To the untrained eye it resembles a cello the most, but without the pin that rests on the floor and the bow is used in an underhanded fashion. In addition, there are more strings at your disposal: 6 or 7. The viola da gamba's timbre closely resembles the human voice... it sounds a bit rusty, with a lot of depth. Quite a rich sound, in my personal opinion.'

*'it's not as one might call it a conventional instrument! what made you choose that instrument over all others?'*

'My father played it and I learned it from him.'

*'is he a professional musician then?'*

'No.'

*'I see... you were using the past tense... is he still alive?'*

'No, my father is not with us anymore.'

*'sorry, I should have been more sensitive'*

'Don't worry about it. Aren't you going to ask me what I get up to with that strange instrument?'

*'ah, yes. tell me'*

'I play renaissance, baroque – Mr. de Saint-Colombe, Marais, Forqueray... But also rock, metal and some of my own compositions.'

*'huh? rock?'*

'It's not uncommon, although usually done with cellos...'

*'what songs do you play'*

'Among others Behind Blue Eyes by Limp Bizkit and Ohne Dich by Rammstein, as modified arrangements.'

*'yesss, something like what the guys of Apocalyptica are doing with Metallica's music, right?'*

'Something like that, yes.'

*'is that a smile I see?'*

'I'm not sure what you mean...'

*'well, to be honest, up until now I got the impression that you are the kind of person that doesn't smile often, if ever. but now I thought I detected something. as if you were amused by something I had said.'*

'Am I this transparent or are you that sharp? It looks like I should watch what I write.'

*'no, please just be yourself. I should not be the only one enjoying herself here.'*

'So you've changed your mind about this chat? That comes as a surprise...'

*'uh, yes, I guess I don't mind this kind of chatting as much as I thought I did ;-) not like I trust you completely now, but...'*

'But what?'

*'if it's alright with you, can I tell you a little bit about my week?'*

'I would like that.'

*'okay, let me think. yes, my week basically started with the ending of a two-week trip abroad. I was in Iceland to take pictures. did you know I'm a photographer?'*

'Please continue.'

*'uh, right, that's how my week started. And when I got home I had a ton of things that needed to get done, like doing groceries, editing photos and getting them ready for the magazine'*

'Don't say anything about the magazine or the genre of your photos! We must remain anonymous to one another.'

*'wow, you sure are strict, man! do you have things to hide or something ;-)'*

*'hello?'*

'I'm still here.'

*'I won't give myself away, okay? And I'll stop making lame remarks about your personal life.'*

'So you did the groceries, your photos – what else?'

*'Well, then I took on another assignment. Barely made any money on it, but I have no regrets. The venue was fun with an interesting audience... I was asked to take pictures of a band that performed there.'*

'Iceland, hey? Did you enjoy it there?'

*'yes, I am to-tal-ly crazy about Iceland. And this time there was even some snow!'*

'Do you like snow?'

*'Very much so... everything outside becomes nice and quiet, it changes the lighting during the day and even at night, it makes everything so... intimate! Don't you think?'*

'No, I'm not very charmed by snow.'

*'Oh, that thing about the intimacy was just my daydreaming, of course. You see, I'm still not over what happened during the return trip.'*

'Oh?'

*'Yes, it was Valentine's Day and Icelandair was going to perform an actual wedding ceremony for a bunch of couples in our airplane later that day.*

*While in the air on the way to Iceland!"*
'The airplane that you had just traveled on? Interesting...'
*'And then something happened to me as well. But you have to promise not to laugh. Cause I must warn you, it's really crazy.'*
*'I had some exciting eye contact with this man, it had started at the airport in Iceland in the morning, and when we got to Schiphol I tripped and fell on the travelator and he came out of nowhere and helped me get up and then said "Happy Valentine's Day".'*
'That is so... fifties!'
*'My thoughts exactly.'*
'Well, at least someone thought about your Valentine's Day. I had to make do with a lot less this year.'
*'But that man disappeared as quickly as he had appeared. So it was of no use to me after all...'*

Right at that moment my phone's ringtone sounded so suddenly and loudly right next to my keyboard that I jumped up a few inches from my desk chair.

4

MASON

Suddenly I was aware of my surroundings again: my always messy workspace, the bright desk light above my head and... yes, I was thirsty. I could really go for a cup of tea. But first let's see who was calling. The display showed Claire's name and I picked up. "Hold on," I said, "I'll be right with you."
I quickly sent '*brb phone*' to Aeolus and picked up my cell phone again. "Yesss?" I said.
"I'm bored. Can you think of something fun?" my friend complained.
I counted how many days she had been on the night shift... three, I think. Or was it four...? As I got up to go the kitchen I asked: "Is there no one who needs a band aide on their little booboo?"
"No. At the moment we only have model patients: sleeping and breathing exemplary. What are you doing?"
I picked up the kettle and held it underneath the tap.
"I was online, chatting," I said.
"Oh? With whom?" Claire asked.
"Nobody. Just someone I met on the internet..."
"Yeah I got that. But who is she? Or is it a he?"
I turned on the kettle and grabbed a cup. My free hand reached up into the cupboard and impatiently rummaged through the box with the bags of tea, which caused it to fall and land on the counter with a soft thud. "It's a he," I said reluctantly.
"Yes... and?" Claire waited. Claire always won.
Cussing on the inside I began to reorganize the tea box while giving her the highlights. I told her about the note with the email address and the resulting chat conversation.
"And how are you going to find out whether he's not some kind of creepy pedophile?"
I rolled my eyes. "Fine, let him be a pedophile. He'll find out soon enough that he is about ten years too late. I am an adult, remember?"
"Ten years, twenty years..." Claire said under her breath.
"Yeah yeah, you will always be one year wiser than me. I know. Bitch." We laughed. And I reassured her that it had been Aeolus who was the one who had pulled the brakes as soon as things got too specific when it came to identity and things like that...
Strange actually, how panicky he had been about the magazine and my photo assignment... I felt the sudden urge to check if he was still online.

While holding my cup of tea I sat back down behind my computer.

I opened the chat window and typed: *'Are you still there? Sorry it took so long, but my best friend phoned me...'*

Aeolus says:

"Check your inbox – I have written a little story in the meantime, and sent it to you."

*'Wow... you've been productive, hehe... hold on, I'll open it.'*

*'We were talking about snow, right? Well, keeping in the spirit of...'*

*'Huh? That's not just a short paragraph, that's a whole piece! How on earth could you have written that in such a short time?'*

*'Does that matter? Just read it while I continue my work.'*

*'Oh right, oops, I totally didn't realize! It's already who-knows-what-time and we're just chatting away, but I might be keeping you from doing more important things...'*

*'Don't you worry about me, I'm perfectly capable of managing my time. You just go and focus on my email...'*

What a character. Should I think of him as nice or authoritative? Either way, I unplugged my laptop and brought it to bed with me. I quickly undressed and crawled under the covers. As I began to read an unsettling chill came over me. I was starting to get tired...

"Rhona,

In light of our conversation about your love of snow I would like to tell you a story. Therefore...:

It is the year 1709, the year of 'Le Grand Hiver', the long winter that crippled all of Europe and covered it with a layer of ice that literally reached the rock bottom of rivers and lakes. What should have become the harvest, that would have fed many, was ruined. Seamen wasted away on their ships in the Gulf of Genoa. The homeless perished by the dozen despite the public fires that were lit on street corners and in public squares. Because of the major shortage on food, the wealthy in the cities in France were forced to open up their kitchens to the poor.

In this France, or in Lyon to be exact, lived an architect. We shall call him Raphaël. He came from a well-to-do family of Czech-Italian descent, was married to a beautiful wife and had two children, a girl aged ten and a boy aged twelve. Raphaël adored his wife and children, although there was a constant source of stress among them: his employment and membership with the masonic guild, which was later to become the Freemasonry. Being invited to become a part of this brotherhood was an honor and not seldom lucrative. It brought him close to the fire, to the people who were his direct subordinates and to every person needed in order to speed up his career. As such, his work took him all over Europe and his network grew, but the strain this had on his home and family life weighed extremely heavily.

Raphaël was a man who knew what he wanted, even though his whims were not always as clear to the outside world. It so happened that one day he outplayed the head architect – even though he was only twenty five and had barely finished his education – by acquiring a commission to build a country house just outside of Prague. A project that from a technical perspective was less than challenging. Nobody understood why he had gone above and beyond to build this particular villa, however the clients did see it as their very own prestigious property in which years later even Wolfgang Amadeus Mozart would become a regular guest. He consorted with the people who owned the villa at that time and it is said that he finalized his opera Don Giovanni there.

Now back to 1709. In the first days of that year another situation arose that challenged Raphaël's loyalty to his family. A fellow architect and friend in Venice needed his specific expertise and despite pleas from his despairing wife he could not say 'no' to that request. This time she had fought tooth and nail to keep her husband at home, but the architect was mesmerized by the honor and glory that this job would bring. He left, not knowing the impending disaster that was to befall upon him and his family...

In those times a trip to Lyon to Venice could take days and days. There was nothing more at your disposal than a horse-drawn carriage. And around the sixth of that month, only halfway down our trip, the temperature dropped drastically. I should have seen this coming. After all, I had meteorologists within my circle of friends. One could say the gods must have favored Raphaël, because he safely arrived at his destination. Completely frostbitten, but safe...

He hadn't been with his colleague longer than three weeks. He has always remained discrete about what happened, but a few facts remained: one night after a muted but intense argument inside the house he was staying at, Raphaël had suddenly left in search of an inn. In addition, he had promptly lost his masonry guild membership. Rumors of breaching trade secrets were to circulate, but only a few knew the finer details of what had transpired. One thing was sure: this was the end of what could have been a glorious career.

Raphaël took the first break in the weather to search for a coachman immediately. He had to return home at all cost, especially considering all the disturbing news about the devastating consequences of the harsh winter. Both his worries and longing for his wife and children had grown by the day and was made stronger by the negative circumstances under which he had left them. And for what? These last few days he had come to realize that his entire life had come to a crossroad, not just his career.

Raphaël, still an *enfant terrible,* now called upon this energy in an attempt to persuade the coachmen at the inn, until one was foolish enough to drive him to Lyon for a considerable amount of money.

The bone-chilling temperature was not as noticeable to Raphaël as it was to the man who drove the carriage from the perch. Nevertheless, in his heart there was the longing for a warm place by the fire, in combination with the familiar scent of lavender... lavender, his wife's favorite scent, that saturated the entire house: the furniture, the linen, her gloves... he used the sleeve of his coat to try to partially clean the window so that he could look out. The snow had started to fall again. Thankfully the largest part of the trip was behind them, but there was one dangerous obstacle still ahead: the Savoy, a mountain range west of Turin. By now the landscape had turned into rolling hills and – an unexpected jerk to the right and a loud bang disrupted his daydream. Suddenly all hell broke loose. The vehicle swerved violently, the driver screamed, the horses let out a shrieking neigh and then everything came to a stop in a ditch by the road. Raphaël was vaguely aware that the carriage was not in the upright position anymore and he felt a sharp pain in his head. The last thing he saw before he lost consciousness was the empty eyes of the coachman fixed on his from an illogically close distance, but with the broken glass of the side window between them. And a pool of blood that slowly expanded around the poor man...

Visions of gardens with spring blossoms and children dancing in white dresses alternated with flashes of confusion and panic. The shivering had seized, but by instinct he searched for objects with one hand, for clothing, for just about anything to cover himself. His arm moved slowly and uncoordinated and could no longer do what Raphaël's brains wanted it to do. Then everything became numb and peculiarly peaceful.

It did not seem like his own reality in which he heard a soft thud above him. He briefly blacked out. Then, far off in the distance, something that sounded like the opening of the carriage door. And suddenly close to his left ear, a sound as though someone was squeezing a half-frozen bag of water...

To be continued.

Signed, Aeolus."

It took a moment for me to return my thoughts to the present. Being careful with my laptop I sat up a bit more and placed the pillow behind my back. With the computer on my lap I began to write:

*Rhona says:*
*'What a strange ending...'*

Aeolus says:

'Be patient. You will get to hear the rest in due time.'

*'You've piqued my curiosity. Where did you get this story?'*

'I told you I had written it myself.'

*'Oh right, you mentioned that. It is really good, man! You've got talent...'*

'Thank you.'

*'But I noticed that once you got so deep into the story you switched to the first-person.'*

'No, that's impossible.'

*'Do you need me to quote you? Hold on, I'll copy/paste: "I should have seen this coming. After all, I had meteorologists within my circle of friends."'*

'With displeasure I must admit that you are right. How careless of me. But I noticed something about your writing as well. You took my advice and started using capitals...'

*'Uh, yes, now that you mention it... humph.'*

'That was a blow below the belt, I believe. Sorry. I tried to take the attention away from me.'

*'Why?'*

'I'm dreading what I'm about to tell you.'

*'?'*

'Let's go back to what happened to Raphaël as he lay in the crashed carriage. As I said, he was aware of some sounds, one of which was that half-frozen ice being crushed. That ice was the frozen skin of his neck.'

*'Ah gross!'*

'In a panic he began to throw punches, assuming a wolf had found him and was about to shred him to pieces. If only it had been a wolf that had found him...'

*'But?'*

'The figure that had sunken its teeth into Raphaël's neck appeared to be that of a man, but was anything but human. It was a vampire.'

*'Dang! That's a surprising plot twist... and then??'*

'Not right now. But the partial point of this story was to illustrate why I don't like snow.'

*'As I said: you really identify with that character, huh...'*

'That's because I am that character.'

*'Uhhh, now you've lost me.'*

'I am Raphaël, although I've chosen that name for the occasion.'

*'Wait. You'll have to explain that to me.'*

'I'm a vampire, Rhona.'

A feeling of unease sank into my stomach. Disappointment. I thought that I had met an intelligent and interesting person, but here I was, chatting with a loony!

Aeolus says:
'Are you still there?'

And now? Hightail it out of here? Save my sorry ass? But what if I didn't feel like doing that, because in and of itself there was nothing wrong with this communication. And I was sure there was a perfectly good explanation for such a statement… oh wait, why hadn't I thought of this sooner!

*Rhona says:*
*'Sang or psy'*
Aeolus says:
'What?'
*Rhona says:*
*'Are you a sanguine or psychic vampire?'*

If you knew where to look you could find people who called themselves vampires. Not those types of people with fake fangs at dark parties, but individuals with a very specific lifestyle. The sang-vampires, or *sanguinarians,* drank blood and had found 'donors' for this within their circle of acquaintances. These were people who willingly allowed small amounts of blood to be tapped, to satisfy the vampire's thirst. Many of which claimed to literally become ill if they weren't served on a regular basis. But in my opinion, this was simply about people making their own personal choices. The psy-vampires, they were a different story altogether. I had never quite understood which of the abilities that they claimed to possess, were real: due to a leak in their field of life energy they needed to look for emotional, or so-called pranic energy elsewhere and they found it by taking it from other people, leaving them exhausted. This story always seemed a little strange to me, although I had experienced dealing with people who mentally completely drained me…

Aeolus says:
'I am neither. My sire, my maker, has bitten me and I've been both alive and dead ever since. There is no more delicate way to tell you this and I realize that you will have difficulty processing my claim.'
Rhona says:
*'Oh get off it…'*
'Rhona, I really don't expect you to believe me. It would even be better for us both if you didn't. But I cannot and will not keep up this facade if our communications are to be maintained. So take this information any way you like, but respect my wish concerning mutual anonymity, for your own good…'
*'So basically you're implementing rules of conduct for us…'*
'Is it okay if we continue to discuss this tomorrow? It's already late.'
*'Yes, we'll see if we can find some time tomorrow, okay?'*

After a brief goodbye I went offline and turned off my computer. But I did not want to, nor would I be able to sleep. After brushing my teeth I therefore dove back into bed, pulled the cover over my head and called Claire. At that time I could not care less about what her reaction would be – I needed some feedback...

5

RESEARCH


*Sunday, 28 September 2008.*

'Are you done yet?'

'take it easy, on my way. 5 more mins.'

'Where are you?'

"Yeah, whatever..." I thought. I was just enjoying the sunshine and was not intending to rush by any means. So without texting back I put my cell phone into my shoulder bag and looked to the left and to the right of the street that I was about to cross.

I strolled along the sunny side of the road, past the Pakistani phone house, Turkish takeout and coffee shop. I passed a post office, luxury furniture store and another Turkish place, but this one a little fancier. Only during the last stretch, when the white plastered facade of Grand Café Wester Paviljoen came into view, did I slightly pick up my pace.

"Five minutes..." mouthed Claire with slow emphasis, as I took off my jacket and sat down across from her. "I did not bike down here like you did..." I said and shrugged.

We looked over the lunch menu. Ordered something to eat and to drink and watched everything around us for a bit. The interesting loners at the reading table, with magazines, macchiato and weekend editions as their company. Academics sitting opposite each other engaged in quasi heated discussions about anything or nothing in particular, and trendy young families having a good time juggling with pancakes and baby formula.

And out on the patio the sun lovers had gathered. Here behind the window it was warmer and the view of the intersection was just as good, with the cars and the trams and everywhere the colored leaves of the defoliating plane trees.

"How was church?" I asked.

"Oh, good, nice... we received the Communion."

"The Holy Communion..." I thought out loud. "Yours is still done with real wine, right?"

"Yes, it still is."

"And you still got here before I did..."

"The service lasted forty five minutes longer, I believe. We finished around noon. I even stayed for coffee... after."

"Our church could learn a thing or two from yours," I grouched... "You Protestants church so much more efficiently... 'churching', is that even a verb?"

Claire chuckled. Then she asked: "How were things at yours this morning?"

"Meh."

"Meh?"

"We had a guest speaker."

"Anyone I know?"

"Yes, I've mentioned him before: that tiny overly enthusiastic little man that bounces up and down the stage while ferociously flailing his arms."

Claire looked puzzled.

"Sure you know him. He's that preacher who hopelessly misses the mark every now and then with the things he says."

"Oh wait, don't tell me it's the one with the Jesus vitamins...?"

I grinned and mocked: *"Hey you there! Why are you still slumped in that chair of yours like a couch potato? It's about time you get blessed with some Jesus vitamins!"*

With a perfectly straight face my friend asked: "And, did he have any exciting messages for today?"

"Oh, who knows... something about riches and poverty and Jesus' salvation on the cross. But when he claimed that that salvation was really only meant for the poor and not so much the rich, he completely lost me..."

Claire raised her eyebrows. "Did he say that literally, about the poor?"

"Yes, word for word."

She stared out the window, seemingly oblivious to the ambulance making its way up Nieuwe Binnenweg with screaming sirens, and mused: "That's one way to go about it... being creative with Bible verses..."

I grinned. "*'Blessed are the poor in spirit'*, I did hear him say that at one point, yes."

"What Bible do they use in your church? King James?"

"Yep. Unless the NIV serves their message better."

"TLB, NKJV, MSG... don't you just love that code language."

"ESV, RSV..."

"Darby."

"Holman."

"Amplified."

"RAM."

"Huh?"

"Random Access Memory. To remember it all."

"Good. And what else?"

"What else? This morning?" I sighed. "Well, nothing out of the ordinary, I think. Yes, the usual *'give and it shall be given unto you'* just before collection. Naturally it went along with those archaic doctrines of tithing and such..."

... Immediately my thoughts drifted back to this morning in the great Hall, and I could hear the muffled voices and the jingling of pocket change. The 'transparency-above-all-else' collection baskets were passed down row by row as my neighbors on either side clumsily attempted to fill out authorization forms by using their knee or purse as a writing surface. And in the meantime, over all the soft whisperings, there was the happy sound of stimulating songs from the hymn book. Claire woke me from my daydream. "Isn't there anything positive to report about this morning?" she asked.

I shook my head. But then something came to mind. With my index finger pointing upwards and a mysterious look on my face I said: "Something *did* happen today. A miracle. Quite a big miracle, in fact," upon which my flat mate was not sure how seriously to take me. "Someone took a liking to my gothic outfit," I declared and she burst out laughing. "Must have been a not yet converted," she said, but I replied that they were not and told her that it was a child, a boy no older than ten. "After the service he was standing somewhere near the outside doors and when I walked by in my purple dress he stared at me with big eyes and told me that I looked like a real princess!"

"That more than makes up for the *blessed are the poor in spirit.*"

"Or, better translated as *the innocent of heart...*"

A coffee and a cola were placed on the table for us. As soon as the waitress turned around and walked away Claire took the pack of sugar from my saucer. She tore off the corner and emptied it into her cola. Immediately things began to foam and she started drinking, with hurried gulps, against the rising of the erratically frothing mass and today she actually won and saved herself from ending up with a brown, sticky mess on the table and on her ivory-white blouse. As she burped silently she looked at me with a mischievous sparkle in her eyes. I looked right back, refusing to show any sign of annoyance. Then she asked: "Was it the petticoat that made him like your dress so much?"

"Partly, perhaps, but he mentioned the tree branch pattern and all those flying black birds in particular." I randomly ran my hand across the smooth fabric of my dress.

"But weren't his parents near him?"

"How so?"

"Well, they would have known that those cute little birds really represented sinister ravens and what they stand for in the gothic scene."

"They are crows, my dear, not ravens."

My friend began to play with a light-blonde lock of her hair and mouthed: "I don't believe you," but I said "No really," and: "I can prove it, you know. Across the internet it is advertised as 'Purple satin halter dress with *crows*'."

With a look on her face that said ' yeah yeah, whatever' she stared into space and I crossed my arms.

After a few minutes it was Claire who broke our silent standoff. She contemplated: "Going back to that 'poverty and riches', hey... do the people at your church even know with how little you have to get by? That you haven't accepted any financial help from your parents?"

I inhaled. "I don't think anyone there knows how much money my family has. Perhaps I should come out and just tell them one day. Maybe then they will accept me 'for who I am', haha!"

Slowly my friend shook her head. "My dear child. You're laughing about this now, but if we look at it carefully you do have a problem. Because – where do you really belong now? Definitely not with the rich, although we can't exactly call you poor in spirit. And the sorority... well, let's not talk about that altogether..."

"Yeah. Let's not," I sighed.

"Whoa, sweetie – that *was* a joke, you know!"

"A joke – perhaps, but in reality it is the truth. Cause, let's be honest, I am strange, stubborn and I follow my heart. No wonder I keep shooting myself in the foot."

"If you look at it that way... By the way, do you ever see anyone from the sorority?"

"No. Yes, Mathilde, every once in a while."

"Oh right, Mathilde... and what was she doing again?"

While our lunch – a falafel burger and meat croquets – were placed in front of us on the table and we picked up our knives and forks, I answered: "She wanted to work with people, so she went into psychiatry."

There were a few possibilities. One: Aeolus was a psycho after all. Two: he was an actual vampire. Yeah right. Or three, an explanation that Claire had come up with, that did not sound all that bad: Aeolus was into *Life Action Role Playing,* LARP. And instead of pretending to be vampires, chasing each other through the forest as part of a club, he had set up an experiment in which he persisted in his online character towards a random 'victim'. If that were the case, it would be up to me to decide whether to continue this way or to break our contact. Because... was it at all possible to have a meaningful conversation with a man who acted mysteriously for no apparent reason?

*Rhona says:*
*'You're online I take it...?'*
Aeolus says:
'Yes, just now.'
*'Long talk last night.'*
'You can say that.'
*'So, what now...?'*
'Don't we have plenty of conversation topics after last night's three hours and forty-seven minutes?'
*'Yeah, we do...'*
'But you don't know how to see me, let alone handle me, which is understandable.'
*'Do you have more online contacts like this? To whom you tell the exact same*

*thing about who you are? And how do the others respond to that?'*

'Do you think that I see this as a game??'

*'Oh I'm sorry, I'm just guessing here.'*

'But what do you think? That I'm rolling on the floor laughing leaving traces of myself all over the internet by making random "friends"?'

*'Well you were the one who thought I was so ignorant about how things work online! Then don't get mad if I ask a stupid question.'*

'My apologies. There are no stupid questions. Only painful ones. You must understand that much of what I do comes with complications. A person of my kind has practical concerns that a mortal person would never run into...'

*'I'm listening.'*

'Interaction between vampires and humans have always contained an element of danger. Not just for you, but most certainly for us as well: avoiding being 'discovered' is a matter of life and death to us. For that reason we live by a very strict code of secrecy, for example. Partly because of that we are able to live a somewhat normal life, it makes it possible to, say, find regular employment and lets us participate in society without too much difficulty. Even so, our contact with mortals must remain superficial under any condition.

Therefore we can only find more meaningful relationships amongst ourselves, as couples or in groups, the so-called 'covens' or 'houses'... alliances that sometimes last for centuries, but most often only for short duration.

And then there are also rules about not living or operating too close to each other's territory and making sure you don't get a criminal record... as I said, being exposed must be prevented at all times and having a run-in with the law is one of the worst things that could happen to us.'

*'Question: why the law?'*

'Think, Rhona, think...'

*'Are you saying that you don't want to be arrested because you can't 'eat' in prison?'*

'Very clever. And because escaping, while very easy for us to do, often goes hand in hand with violence, is not an option. It draws too much attention, especially in this day and age in which information technology continues to advance. All of this results in a relatively lonesome life being a vampire. And should a coven develop, you often quickly end up with a mix of young and old undead, who came from all walks of life. Which can be quite exhausting. After all you're stuck together for eternity and even if you leave the relationship or coven, you're bound to run into each other somewhere or another.'

*'Sounds like my former church.'*

'Now you've surprised me. Please explain.'

*'If I really think about it, a church community has many problems similar to what you just described: there are younger and older members, newly converted Christians and people who have been of faith for many years, and*

*everyone has a different background... laborers, students, doctors, lawyers, housewives etc.'*

'And they all have eternal life.'

*'Exactly... Well, so to speak, that is. For vampires eternal life is literal, obviously.'*

'Oh? Have you lost your faith in God and His message?'

*'I've seen too much for that.'*

'Is this about the pain in your soul you mentioned before?'

*'Your words, not mine.'*

'I'm not here to attack you. And I am capable of listening as well...'

*'Okay, fine: in my opinion the church is a system fabricated by humans, overflowing with xenophobia, prejudice and hypocrisy. And I want nothing to do with that.'*

'Nothing to do with that *anymore*. What happened to you there?'

*'That's not important. What's worse is that these things are still going on. And that people still are getting damaged by the carelessness with which they are treated.'*

'As though common courtesy has lost all meaning...'

*'It seems as if they think that as soon as you belong to their 'club', they have the right to constantly meddle with your affairs and 'set you straight' left and right, even if it hurts you.'*

'Why do to you think this happens?'

*'If you've got the answers, then by all means...'*

'I think there are two issues here:

1: As soon as people get together, regardless of the context, there will be interpersonal relations. Within Christian circles they even continuously refer to the concept of being a family. But simultaneously they forget that if you become a family, you have to invest energy in how you treat and care for one another.'

*'And factor 2: Christians believe they have eternal life, so it is in their best interest to maintain good relations, because they will meet again, either in heaven or somewhere else. And even if it's true what the Bible says about grievances among each other disappearing over time by the power of Jesus' blood, right now they still have a big responsibility as well as being role models. But even that is lost on many.'*

'The fact remains that you are alone now.'

*"I'm not alone. I still have friends, you know.'*

'Including a total stranger who won't divulge his real name, but with whom you've now been talking for over an hour already...'

*'Not a total stranger anymore. Although I think you are a bit peculiar ;-)'*

'Even so, you seem to agree with the code of conduct that I enforced.'

'Hold on. I'll send you a picture. The title is 'Anybody out there?"

I clicked on *My Documents – My Pictures – Reims* and then on one of the photos that I had taken on a day trip to this French city while on a recent vacation in the Ardennes. I had visited the cathedral back then and I had shot this image in the front part of the building right after I entered: from an upwardly tilted point of view, to a high angle in which two dark gray stone walls met. Walls with gothic-like alcoves that contained artistic statues of human figures unknown to me, a part of an incredibly massive pillar and finally a lot of stained-glass windows in blue and other colors.

Aeolus says:
'Aaah, Reims! Le Cathédrale des Anges...'
*Rhona says:*
*'You know that cathedral?*
'I certainly do – did you visit the museum in Saint-Remi's Abbey? It's situated right next to it.'
*'I believe so.'*
'When the medieval ship of this abbey was replaced under the supervision of Le Tellier, just before the year 1700, I was busy studying Architecture. I traveled with my mentor from site to site. As such, I have received part of my education in the Saint-Remi.'
*'Very funny.'*
'I'm not asking you to believe me. But going back to the title of your photo: why 'Anybody Out There?''
*'That's how I feel towards God. All my life I thought I would find him in church, but now...'*
'You have perfectly combined your feelings of desolation with the first impressions that visitors of this building get. I myself needed a minute to shake a feeling of disappointment the first time, to then discover the magnificent colors and play of light among all that 'bombastic' and 'gray'.'
*'This image is part of a book I'm making...'*
'Stop!'
'Take a minute to consider what and how much you will tell me about your book.'
*'That's not that difficult: I'm a photographer and I'm assembling a photo book with my own pictures that have depth and meaning. Is that vague enough for you?'*
'Vague enough, yes. Thank you.'
*'You are welcome...'*
'Perhaps you don't realize, but it isn't a small deal for me to have these kinds of conversations with a mortal human. To talk to you in this way... to be able to be this open, protected by the anonymity of the internet... it's a completely new world to me.'
*'Haha, I'm sure it is. Well, good for you, right?'*
'Definitely, absolutely. Although I feel like I should restrain myself a little. You've got your own life, your daily activities and I need to respect that. For

that reason I would like to end the conversation for tonight. Is that alright with you?'

*'Uh... if you think that's necessary. So you're not mad anymore about my comment at the beginning, earlier?'*

'Again, my apologies for that – I was in a bad mood. It's about time for me to look for something to eat. As you can see: nothing human is alien to me ;-)'

*'Heyyy, Aeolus uses a smiley! How... human!'*

'Goodnight, Rhona.'

*'Bye.'*

Adrenaline. All through my body... We were having such wonderful conversations... this man possessed so much knowledge.

Or was all that knowledge just for appearance's sake? Because a historical tale like Raphaël's could be made up easily enough. But still, if you wanted to make it sound somewhat believable, you would have to do background research first. However little amount, something like that is prone to inconsistencies after all.

Let's see. Google... *Le grand hiver...* oof, that did not get me anywhere. Way too much French. How about *Winter 1709?* Yes, that was much better: *The year Europe froze.* When I clicked on the link a painting appeared of a row of old-fashioned houses and to the left of it was a crowd of people. The people were scattered across a frozen plain and in the description I read something about the frozen lagoon of Venice. Okay then, that was one thing that he had looked into... but the villa that Raphaël had supposedly built, what was the deal with that?

*Prague Mozart...* the immediate result was a screen filled with references and with the link appearing *Meet Mozart in villa Bertramka* I knew that I had found what I was looking for. Bertramka turned out to be a museum in Prague completely dedicated to Mozart. The year of construction was around 1700, so that was another accurate fact – hats off to you, Aeolus – now to find the name of the architect...

I searched again, and found it. A sentence in the text about the history of the villa: 'History – It is not known who built Bertramka'. Shit.

And nowhere, absolutely nowhere on the internet could I find the name of the architect of Villa Bertramka. For some reason that did not sit well with me. Why this building out of all others? Why would Aeolus even resort to using his story just to emphasize his anonymity? Did he really do have a secret? A terrible secret, perhaps?

I laughed at myself. A vampire... sure, why not. Um, not.

He had claimed that Raphaël was of Italian-Czech descent and had grown up in France. But Aeolus himself spoke Dutch, in proper, fluent sentences... No, LARP. Live Action Role Playing. That was my final answer. And Aeolus was not Raphaël; he had just studied history.

When I turned off my computer, his status was still set to 'online'.

6

CHURCH

The morning glow warming my face slowly awoke me from my sleep. A ray of
light that peeked through the curtains initially made me squeeze my eyes
shut... I turned my head away, stretched and looked at my watch.
Startled, I leapt out of my bed It was eleven thirty and I had an appointment
at noon! How stupid, how terribly stupid of me; I could not afford to mess this
up – especially not with a corporate client of such high profile!
Completely frantic, I therefore picked an outfit, got dressed, applied my
make-up and parted my hair into two little tails. I briefly glanced in the
mirror. A short black skirt, purple leggings, flats with exaggerated tread...
good enough. Quickly grabbed a bagel, my leather jacket from the coat rack
and – oh shit, of course, the camera case! – and then down the stairs like
rolling thunder.
Once there I only managed to get my bike down from the hook on the left side
of the stairs after three impatient attempts. A lack of space meets practical
ingenuity... sometimes I hated this house.
Exactly four minutes to twelve I entered the office building on Weena
Boulevard panting heavily. Practically right after checking in at the reception
desk I was met by a secretary, who was well-groomed from head to toe. As we
walked to the boardroom, while keeping up with her pace, I tried to fix my
hair one last time. Unsuccessfully, of course.
"Ah, our photographer!" said a middle aged man with graying hair. He got up
from behind his desk to shake my hand.
"I'm pleased that you arrived perfectly on time," he said, "Not many people
are that diligent."
And as I stood there staring at his furiously bushy eyebrows I almost forgot
to answer the secretary when she asked me if I would like a cup of coffee.

If I still believed in them, I would have definitely labeled the remainder of the
day as a miracle. My mind constantly had to switch between two
mechanisms: the 'business as usual' mode that allowed me to successfully
finish the photo report and had got me walking through the supermarket
right now in search of my evening meal. The second mode completely
revolved around the mysterious man with whom I had now been talking to
for two days in a row. Two chat sessions. That wasn't a lot. But this contact
had a deep impact on me. Deeper than I had expected...
With a hot plate of food on the desk in front of me I set my status to 'online'.
Hoping that he... was it even possible to sound nonchalant on the internet?
Like someone who was not waiting for someone in particular, shall we say?

And were there ways to blatantly express this? Like, look for songs on YouTube, or something – a pop-up notification told me that Aeolus had logged in. And the wave of excitement that came over me almost made me nauseated.

Aeolus says:
'You are online.'
*Rhona says:*
*'Hi, yes, I'm having dinner.'*
'Oh, should I leave you to it then?'
*'No no, don't worry about it. I always do this...'*
'How was your day?'
*'Hectic... I overslept and almost fucked up a photography assignment. Everything barely worked out.'*
'Looks like my day. I had just begun to play when a fret broke off...'
*'A fret?'*
'Frets are those thick stripes on the neck of the viola da gamba next to where you place your fingers. You can find them on guitars as well.'
*'Okay...'*
'I've searched the entire house for material to make a new one, but could not find anything. A hallway mirror got hurt in the process.'
*'Oh...'*
'Rhona, I got too emotional yesterday and that should never have happened.'
*'But that's no reason to get so worked up.'*
'You know so little about me. So very little...'
*'There is something you can do about that, I think.'*
'How?'
*'What if I'd ask you some 'safe questions' from time to time? Ones that won't make you worry about our code of conduct?'*
'And how do you envision that?'
*'Well, I could ask you something like this: what happens when someone leaves or is kicked out of the masonic guild?'*
'Haven't I told you about that already?'
*'You did, kind of, but you only told me Raphaël's career was over when it happened.'*
'Peculiar question of yours. Anyhow... I can only tell you what the implications were in the eighteenth century. At that time studying Masonry automatically ensured membership: first you were a student, then an apprentice and finally a master. The privileges increased with each masonic level. I may not have been a mason or master builder, but my skills as an architect were welcomed by the guild with open arms and this really helped my career progress. I had done a lot of traveling and I had made a name for myself before not too long. Until that name was erased. The guild was thorough and successful in doing so. You have to remember that information

and technology were still a world apart in those times.

I tried to swallow the lump that had formed in my throat. I could not. Why did everything Aeolus tell me make so much sense?

Aeolus says:
'You tried to do a background check on me?'
*Rhona says:*
*'Sorry.'*
*'I just wanted to complete the picture of your story in my mind... Three hundred years ago – how could that possibly be a threat to you?'*
'What did you find out?'
*'Nothing in particular...'*
'And that is all you will ever find, Rhona. Nothing in particular. Nothing on the truth about my life and nothing on my current location. I could be sitting in the house across from you, but I could also be in Abu Dhabi or Timbuktu.'


*Summer 1953. Communist Prague.*

Mister Štěpánek was a somewhat quiet, not strikingly conspicuous man, although he had one trait that stood out: he truly never appeared to be in a hurry. While waiting in line endlessly in front of the shops to get milk, meat and bread – the perfect place in which stress, but also passive boredom could be seen on everyone's face – his practically always expressed a moderate smile. In the early hours of the weekend evenings you could often see him strolling leisurely through Grebovka Park, or just sitting on a bench for long lengths of time without a book or a newspaper or any other preoccupation. And during the week, early in the morning, he usually was the last person to start walking at the crosswalks in the City center while hordes of people around him tripped over their own and each other's feet, as they hastily rushed to get to the factory before the whistle blew. It was not a surprise then that he almost always arrived a few minutes late at the construction site of the Bethlehem Chapel.
In spite of this, Mr. Štěpánek was not a careless person and even more so when it came to his work. It just so happened that more often than not at the end of the day he was the last person to leave the now almost renovated house of prayer, and when he gave instructions to a student or apprentice, as part of his function as master mason, you could hear in his voice how much he loved his profession. Yes, his ability to speak with such enthusiasm had to come from the love for the trade, because Mr. Štěpánek did not really maintain meaningful relations with any of his colleagues.
It was therefore nothing short of a miracle when one day he suddenly accepted Jakub's invitation to have lunch together. You see, up until now he

had habitually left the site around noon like clockwork briefly saying "everyone, I'm going for a walk. See you in a bit," and at first people had occasionally suggested they should join him on his walk. But the way in which he then answered with a "maybe tomorrow" with that look in his eyes had, as time went on, resulted in nobody considering to ask the same question twice. And thus they all just let him be...

Mr. Štěpánek and Jakub had worked side by side on the scaffolding several times by now. Initially it had appeared that the reason that had brought this on was that Jakub could work very efficiently. He was at least fifteen years younger than Mr. Štěpánek and not yet graduated as a painter in the fine arts, but his talent was unprecedented and he was able to apply large sections of the fresco onto the wall that was freshly plastered with mortar, faster than anyone and in one stroke, long before the base layer had dried. Along the way conversations had developed between them. At times these conversations were of a light nature and loud enough to be overheard by others, but sometimes they were conducted in a quieter tone of voice. And carefully formulated comments in passing had grown into conversations that were as open as the communist society in Czechoslovakia allowed them to be.

The two of them found a place to sit down on a stack of bags filled with lime protected from the afternoon heat in the shelter of the chapel. Jakub had made Mr. Štěpánek laugh with a remark on something or other and after a few minutes of simply resting, the tea, bread and the cold dumplings were brought out. They shared the food and talked...

"Why haven't you told me you were ill?"
"Because I'm not."

The lunch break was over and Jakub looked at his colleague, who had just returned from the lavatory, with a look of concern on his face. "But I did hear it clearly," he said, "you had to vomit. Everything you have just eaten was expelled."
"That was not vomit, that was..." Mr. Štěpánek sighed, "I'm not in the mood to discuss this, actually."
But Jakub made an unyielding face and commanded him to follow. "You look even paler than you normally already do. There is no shame in having an upset stomach, and acting as though everything is fine does not make it go away. Ah, Mr. Fragner just stepped in, we'll make use of that."
And just as Jakub had predicted the head architect was in the same good-natured mood today as he was known for among his colleagues. The site manager on the other hand looked less friendly. Nevertheless he minutely registered the sick leave in the big logbook: "Štěpánek, Ilja..."

"Those couple of days of sleep have done me well. Thank you for that."

"So you *were* ill. Then I was right after all."

Mr. Štěpánek smiled. "But please be more careful next time. The site manager wasn't particularly happy with my sudden absence." But Jakub dismissed those worries with a simple shrug and helped him carry the heavy tub filled with mortar into the white, square main hall of the chapel. On top of the scaffolding, while the mason picked up his trowel, half a yard to his left the young painter began to draw the phrase *veritas vincit* on a banner attached to a flag. Below that the partial outlines were visible of knights in battle, armed with sword and bow and lance, and a head that evidently was to become a horse. "... It's a backwards world we live in," he muttered under his breath, "here we are painting scenes from the Jena Bible on the walls of what once was a house of God, but what will it end up being used for? *Propaganda.*"

The mason smiled and remained silent...

And the friendship between the two colleagues grew. It matured into a rapport in which the young painter in particular felt more and more relaxed. Something that frequently resulted in remarks such as: "Hey Red, are you late again or is your watch still behind?"

The usual reply was something on the order of: "No," (a little surprised) "I have moved it forward a bit just yesterday," which then prompted Jakub to grin and say: "As I did mine."

Or: "Say Red, where did you leave the – "

" – My hair is brown, not red."

"It is, when the sun hits it..."

*Friday morning, 14 August 1953.*

"You missed a spot." Jakub pointed at the thin second layer that Mr. Štěpánek was meticulously applying onto a portion of the wall. The mason briefly glanced aside, though withheld a response. Then Jakub said: "Did you know I will turn nineteen next week?"

"No, I did not. Congratulations."

Again silence.

"I've invited a few friends over for tomorrow evening."

Mr. Štěpánek nodded.

"If you would like to join us..."

For a moment the mason lowered his trowel. But just as quickly continued his work. He said: "Thank you. I would be honored to attend."

And so it came to be that Mr. Štěpánek wound up in the Podoli district around seven thirty the next day and rang the bell of a door in a block of poorly maintained apartments.

The following Monday he did not show up at the construction site of the Bethlehem Chapel. There was some complaining and a few wondered aloud where he could be. But when Mr. Štěpánek again made no appearance at work the next day the site manager phoned the police...

*Tuesday evening, August 18th, 1953. Klosterneuburg, Austria.*

In order to determine the emotions behind the man with the silver-white hair it was of no use to look into his eyes. Because they always looked the same: dark and devoid of expression. Therefore any spectator had no choice but to interpret his body language and to pay attention to the movement of his face. At the moment, for example, the man's eyes had narrowed into small slits and he sat at the table slightly hunched forward. He asked: "Should we be worried?"

"Not in the least," came as a reply from across the table.

"But you did have enough reasons to disappear, apparently."

The other person looked away. "It was time," he said. "Some things just have to end."

The man with the white hair leaned back in his chair.

"May I ask what happened that night?"

"It was a set-up, by Jakub. He wanted to introduce me to his friends and couldn't tell me at work that in actuality the occasion was his grandmother's Name Day."

"Please explain."

"His grandmother plays a prominent role in the anti-communist movement, even though she is severely disabled. She is only able to use two fingers, but with those fingers she relentlessly types up manifestos, pamphlets... And in certain circles she finds a greedy audience. Jakub decided her house to be the most appropriate for his party."

"Thus you were introduced to her and some others."

"Yes. Jakub called me a great thinker, with inspiring ideas..."

"I presume you made sure you weren't followed?" the man asked. He kept his head facing the side, but nonetheless his eyes were locked with the other's.

"The secret police has no idea. It is only because she is in such poor health that the woman does not raise any suspicion."

"Hmmm, so fragile, yet so dangerous at the same time...for sure there are fascinating people walking this earth. Or should we say: limping?"

The next second the other stood over the table with his right hand around the man's neck. "Jakub was a *friend*! I hold no grudge against him," he growled.

"Oh my, a *friend*..." he sounded raspy, "exactly how much did he manage to find out about you?"

"Nothing. Absolutely nothing." The grip around his neck loosened. The man with the white hair coughed a few times.

"You realize of course that this Jakub will be subjected to an investigation."

"Naturally. But I can guarantee you that you won't find anything of interest."

For some time the man stared at the figure across from him. Under the light of the lamp above the table the skin of his face had a peculiar, pearly sheen. Then he asked: "What really intrigues me is why you managed to continue under that regime for so long. Why not have escaped it in 1948 already?" The other made an exasperated gesture. He walked to the book cabinet and briefly glanced over it.

His voice sounded soft, broken even, when he said: "How can I expect you to understand it, when you have never experienced that sensation... 'Not standing out' means that even you must wait in the long line in front of the shop for bread and other necessities. And if you have nothing more to sit on, the choices for buying something new are even for you – to put it simply – limited.  But those *are* the moments that make you feel like you're becoming part of a collective memory. The concept of a 'chair' or a 'bed' brings to everyone's minds the exact same image. And I haven't even mentioned diplomacy and lies yet, how it is vital for *every* individual in that society... Tell me, Fabian, can you say you have ever felt that united with your surroundings?"

For a brief moment, a split second, the muscles around his mouth showed a certain tension. Then the man got up. In front of the mirror he brushed back some locks of his hair with his fingers. Then he picked up his coat.
"Come," he said. "Let's get something to eat."

*Rhona says:*
*'I seem to have hurt your feelings.'*
Aeolus says:
'This is not about feelings getting hurt.'
*'Then what is it about.'*
'You would not understand.'
*'Try me.'*
'The problem is you. You are inquisitive.'
*'Tell me something I don't know. That's old news.'*
'Nevertheless, curiosity is your every right.'
*'Boy, am I ever relieved...'*
'I have offended you?'
*'Oh, not at all. That's not how these things work. After all we hardly know each other.'*
'Rhona, I'll be more careful with what I say from now on. I'm sorry.'
*'No problem...'*
'Are you still in the mood to talk?'
'Rhona?'
*'I'm back. Had to go lick my wounds.'*
'If you like, you can start a new topic.'
*'How about music?'*
'I believe that is a good idea.'

'Okay. So you like classical?'

'Which was contemporary music in my time.'

'Yes. Well, I don't know much about any composers, but I think Bach is amazing. Because of the St Matthew Passion, primarily.'

'Perhaps this is not such a good idea after all, this topic of conversation. The Passion just so happens to be the one piece I cannot bear to listen to.'

'But isn't it brilliantly composed? Everybody thinks it's a masterpiece…'

'Clearly you have never looked into the text.'

'I'm pretty sure I know what it's about.'

'Do you really? Then what does the final chorus, no. 68, say?'

'Geez… I didn't say I knew it by heart.'

'Ruht, ihr ausgesognen Glieder!'

'Oooh… I see…'

'Precisely. I take it you can read German?'

'Well enough to understand what you mean. 'Rest peacefully, thy drained limbs…' You probably feel guilty when you hear that!'

'Guilt is both an enemy and a companion to a vampire. It is a predator that's always lurking in the background. Nonetheless that predator needs to be tamed, because every once in a while, often unexpectedly, it raises its ugly head, looks you straight in the eyes and bears its teeth…'

'That's a beautiful description. And also, totally understandable. I can't imagine having to wander the streets at night and completely drain people, leave them for dead.'

'I thought that you of all people were so against preconceptions. How would you know that in order for us to feed, we kill people?'

'Isn't that what all the literature says? Isn't that the essence of being a vampire?'

'Have you ever seen any of us going at it? Have you ever been present at one of those killing frenzies?"

'No. Of course not.'

'Well then.'

'I'm waiting…'

'Are you saying that Anne Rice was right when she wrote about the blood of rats…?'

'…'

'No. Big game??'

'Shady deals with staff from the blood bank?'

'It's not a part of your world and so I'm not going to tell you about it. Although it is important, in my opinion, that due to your lack of knowledge you do not have the right to judge me.'

'The victim of prejudice has become the perpetrator. Ouch.'

'A hard lesson learned, indeed.'

'Would you like me to stop asking questions on this topic?'

'I don't think that would be fair. Ultimately it was I who burdened you with the knowledge of my identity…'

*'Gee, then I don't know anymore. Then tell me something about, oh I don't know – teeth, eyes, coffins, the sun, mirror images… what, if anything, about that is true?'*

'Not much.'

*'Great.'*

'People let themselves be misled by all the stories that circulate. Stories that even contradict each other: Bram Stoker, for example, makes Dracula sleep in a coffin, but Stephenie Meyer claims that vampires stay awake all day and night. Which one of them is right? Stoker, because he was there first and is generally recognized as *the* authority on the genre? And what else do we have here? Right, our eyes. Their color changes with each book- or television series. It is quite entertaining, because all that disinformation only works in our favor.'

*'How so?'*

'A little while ago I came across a statement about us in a television series that was not only clever, but also closer to the truth than those screenwriters will hopefully ever realize: allegedly over the centuries vampires themselves have leaked all sorts of myths into the world, in order to prove when need be that they were "simply human" '

*'Oh really?'*

'Picture this: we spread the fable that we are not visible in mirrors. What do you think will happen if we stand there washing our hands right next to other people in public restrooms?'

*'Nothing.'*

'Exactly!'

*'And what about the fangs?'*

'Which type? Single, double? Always present or only protracting while biting?'

*'You guys don't have fangs.'*

'… Or do we, and can we only appear in public at Halloween and gothic parties and renaissance fairs…'

*'I suppose this is all a joke to you.'*

'No, just a hypothesis.'

*'You know what I look like, right?'*

'Yes. Why?'

*'Well, since you do, then you can guess I am no stranger to the gothic scene. And that I don't particularly like your hypothesis.'*

'As long as we keep our mutual agreement you are in no danger.'

*'You think of yourself as being dangerous?'*

'Do we really need to discuss this?'

*'I don't care. After all, danger is only relative. Plus I can take care of myself just fine.'*

'Relative, huh?'

*'Yes, even the most serene places aren't always safe.'*

'What happened to you in that church? It must have been really bad.'

*'Why do you keep pushing the church stuff? I just got sick of it and then left.'*

'Not good enough. I want to know more.'

*'Alright. I saw things that I was not okay with. And I brought up the issues with the church leadership."*

*'And that did not end well...'*

'What kind of issues?'

*'Well, a lot of catchphrases were being thrown around that sounded very spiritual, but in practice very few were actually implemented. In reality people even radically went against them.'*

'Be more specific.'

*'Oh um... for example, they kept saying: "Jesus loves you, and so do I." But you should hear them talk about people who think differently in the meantime! And they were quick to label you a heretic. If you didn't dress like them, if you befriended non-Christians, if you did not stand up with everyone else at the same time and dance ecstatically to the worship songs...'*

'If you asked difficult questions...'

*'Yes! And that was precisely what I was doing. To the pastor, of all people.'*

'Was his response very negative?'

*'Not at first, as he initially assumed a fatherly role and even somewhat agreed with me... But towards the end of the conversation – I had requested to meet with him officially, you see – he picked up a pen and wrote something on a piece of paper. He placed it in an envelope, gave it to me and said that God wanted to tell me this. I was instructed to read it when I was alone.'*

'A Bible verse.'

*'So, if you think you are standing firm, be careful that you don't fall!"*

'Corinthians, if I'm not mistaken...'

*'What? Yes... 1 Corinthians 10:12. How on earth do you know that??'*

'If you have a few centuries to spare, there is a lot to read.'

*'I had never taken you for a Christian...'*

'It's not just Christians who are familiar with the Bible, Rhona.'

*'But...'*

'We were talking about you. What happened next?'

*'What do you think happened?'*

'You kept attending for as long as you could, but were only reaffirmed in the things that you had a problem with. The number of instances of misconduct that you witnessed grew steadily, other church members made more and more comments at and about you, and week by week you felt less and less comfortable. Your negative expectations became a self-fulfilling prophecy, in their eyes their tactless meddling was just 'loving concern'. And after you realized that you had reached the point at which you felt extremely unsafe in that environment, you left. Things were left unspoken and bitterness planted its roots.'

*'But I tried to discuss so many things!'*

'I'm sure you did.'

*'And I was never looking for trouble...'*

'I know.'

'It's okay to cry...'

*'I'm not crying.'*

*'I feel so embarrassed...'*

'No one can see you. You are alone in your room. Just be yourself and let it all out.'

*'It's just that I feel so stupid... were my expectations really that high? Aren't they just human like everyone else? Isn't a church nothing more than a group of people participating in a common activity?'*

'Strictly speaking it is. Similarly there are also soccer clubs, bridge clubs, theater companies... however, there is one major difference. Christians are each other's family.'

*'Yeah, duh...'*

'You don't believe that anymore?'

*'No, I think it's meant to be symbolical, at most.'*

'Regardless, the manner in which it has affected you was very concrete.'

*'To me it is nothing more than an expression. Just like that nonsense about being 'ambassadors for Christ on this earth'.'*

'An honorary title for those of faith, I presume.'

*'It is, if you really live it. But that's the part that's lacking in most people!'*

'... And your foundation of expectations is cut off from under you, like the legs of a table.'

*'Exactly! But even so, is it that wrong to think that a church should be a safe haven??'*

'That's up to you to decide.'

*'I thought that the people there could be trusted...'*

'But people are not gods.'

*'And that's something that they really should recognize a little more.'*

'Therefore, let him who thinks he stands, take heed that he does not fall."

*'Oh you are such a hard-ass!'*

'But you are right, I'm afraid.'

*'Something completely different: if you're of mixed ethnicity and grew up in France, how come your Dutch is so good?'*

'I'm often in the Netherlands.'

*'Wowww, you answered just like that... it's unbelievable!'*

'Oh. Sorry. You did not deserve that. I don't know why I said that...'

'I'll survive.'

*'No, that was really mean of me. You've been so patient and sympathetic towards me... while I've subjected you to nothing but cross examinations, I feel. And that is not okay.'*

'I do understand.'

*'It's just that I don't know what to do with you... Our conversations are so*

*precious to me. Yet I find it hard to take you seriously as a person. But then I still find myself getting caught up in this game you're playing and I forget that there are no such things as vampires and then I end up asking you serious questions about it and... do you get what I'm trying to say?'*

'Do you enjoy our conversations?'

*'What kind of question is that?'*

'I would like to know.'

*'You're confusing me. Didn't you hear what I just was telling you? But to be honest, I do. It's strange but true: I really do enjoy talking to you...'*

'Let's talk about the Netherlands then. As I mentioned before, I travel a lot and often visit your country.'

*'For business?'*

'That's the main reason. But for a vampire the Netherlands is a pleasant place to visit.'

*'But not to live in?'*

'No, I don't believe so. The country is too small and too crowded for that, I think.'

'The mentality of the Low Lands is not one that leaves much room for spirituality. Which is good for us, because should anything happen, people do not immediately associate it with 'vampires'. Five decades ago, or so, I went through a rebellious phase. I literally played with fire at that time: telling any and everyone to their face that one is undead goes against all rules, against all common sense. But it gave me such an incredible thrill to see those people's reactions. I was simply ridiculed. Or they responded with dry remarks such as: 'you know, the carnival doesn't start until one month from now...'

*'Only in the Netherlands, hey?'*

'You definitely shouldn't try this in Eastern Europe, or in places like Mauritius.'

*'Because they're more superstitious there, I bet.'*

'Superstitious or realistic. Take your pick.'

*'But why don't you move to the Netherlands anyway?'*

'I can't survive in rural areas. The towns are situated too close to one another and people talk amongst themselves too much.'

*'Then why not live in the metropolitan district?'*

'That would be a possibility. At least, it was doable in the olden days. But not anymore. Now there are television programs like Hart van Nederland.'

*'Now that you mention it... you've got a point there! Yes, cause all the local tidbits get some screen time in that program. And then a vampire can't afford to stand out at all!'*

'Exactly. 'The small-town wheeling and dealing of the common people, coming daily to your living room.' That's why I can never stay in one place for too long over there.'

*'And so you limit yourself to short stay visits: fly in and out again.'*

If you suddenly realize something frightening it can trigger an ominous sensation rushing through your body. I knew that. Like when I was still a child and I was told that I had to go for a checkup with the dentist. But I had also experienced that bodily sensation when falling freely on a roller coaster. Or during downward turbulence on an airplane. For instance during that flight from Iceland to the Netherlands. Filled with passengers traveling for shorter or longer trips...

How *could* I have been so stupid? How could I have accepted the fact that this man, with whom I had been chatting for days now, would always remain nameless and faceless, if it were up to him? Why didn't I think this through further? Because of course, of course he was not a secret admirer from the Dungeon. And he was not one of the models I had worked with either. Not to even mention a total stranger I had failed to noticed among the hustle and bustle of the shopping crowd in my city.

The truth was much closer than that – to be precise: it could be traced back to a week and a half ago, at the airport in Keflavík and on the return flight from Iceland!

Aeolus was the man who had caught my fall on the travelator at Schiphol Airport... the mysterious figure with red-brown hair who had captivated me with his gaze and immediately pushed me away with his standoffishness. And this was followed by the sudden appearance of a little note in my pocket...

7

SCORPION


By impulse I moved the cursor on the screen to the Rhona-icon and changed
my status to 'offline'. Must think. Don't do anything stupid. Shit, this
changed everything. I had a face. I had a reference. I could even find a name
via a passenger list. Or no, those lists are most likely classified. And I didn't
have any connections within that airline. Perhaps a private detective?

I had to get back online. Fast. And act like nothing's wrong.

Aeolus says:
'Are you there?'
*Rhona says:*
*'Yeah, little problem with my connection. But I'm back. Where were we?'*
Aeolus says:
'Hart van Nederland.'

No, there was no way to track him down. He would disappear immediately.
He had made that more than clear.

*Rhona says:*
*'Yes, Hart van Nederland.'*

I looked out my window. It had already been dark for hours and in the
distance the geese of Noordsingel Boulevard sounded alarmed... I felt uneasy
and closed the curtains.

Aeolus says:
'*The* reason that there aren't any vampires living in the Netherlands.'
*Rhona says:*
*'Hahaha...'*
'Have you lost your tongue?'
*'It's getting late.'*
'Hmmm, you're right. You must be tired.'
*'But you don't want to call it a night yet?'*
'I do have to admit that I am happy with our talk today.'
*'Okay, but just a little longer.'*

... And there I was, balancing between fear, power, excitement, curiosity...

The interactive story that I had found myself caught up in had changed into a real connection with a physical person. Somebody I had actually met. And he wanted to talk to *me*.

*Rhona says:*
*'What else would you like to tell me?'*
Aeolus says:
'What else would you like to hear?'
*'Is your hearing better than ours?'*
'Many times. As is our sense of perception.'
*'Is everything louder then, the things you hear? Or...?'*
'If I choose it to be. My ears are better at focusing than yours. In a crowd of hundreds of people I can understand a single person...'
*'And your eyes?'*
'They are more sensitive to light. Someone observant would be able to tell by looking at my pupils.'
*'Don't all those famous authors talk about that? And have you seen those ugly white contacts in the gothic scene?'*
'The stories that have been written in the last two centuries have all been based on legends. Local folklore. Its core, however truncated has stood the test of time, but that's the only thing that can be said about that.'
*'Still those authors obtained more influence than they realized when they worked on their books.'*
'Not just in the genre of "vampire novels".'
*'That's right. Now of course this is a fairly innocent subject. But when you find out how impressionable people can be... The flow of information is so complicated! News that everyone writes off as nonsense still affect people and are passed on all over the place. And combine that with the fact that the majority of people never do any additional research...'*
'Which brings us back to my question of who should be believed. The person who came with the information first? The one who has built the strongest reputation? Or even the one that happens to be from your own circle of acquaintances and "thus will probably be trustworthy"?'
*'Don't get me started, Aeolus! What do you think about all those books written in Christian circles that are overflowing with prejudice? I'm not saying that every Christian book is like that, but some of them... the false facts just jump off the pages. Imagine being the target of that prejudice. You have no idea how damaging that can be!'*
'Yes I do, I know it all too well.'
*'And the kids. What kind of adults will they become when they are raised with so much xenophobia? Shall I tell you something that I heard about a Dutch woman who had married a Turkish man? It's not a perfect example for what we're talking about, but in some way it totally is. She once went to get some fries and snacks and while she was waiting she recognized a boy from*

*the elementary school that her children go to. He looked at her with that cheeky head of his and said out of the blue: "Hey, Turkish whore!" Now this woman isn't the type that just rolls over so she immediately asked: "Who told you that, that my name is Turkish whore?!" And then the kid goes: "Daddy always calls you that when he sees you walking down our street."'*

'You are intelligent and your heart is in the right place, Rhona. Your concerns are not without merit... not so long ago a bunch of teenagers beat a twenty year-old girl to death in England, solely because they didn't like her 'looks'. She was gothic.'

*'Yeah, Sophie Lancaster... I know the story. It still breaks my heart when I think about it.'*

*'Do you believe that there are people who are pure evil?'*

'I would like to believe there are. But that immediately reminds me of a Chilean dissident, who I once saw on TV. She talked about her time in prison. She was tortured there horribly and her prison guard was a man who to her was evil incarnate. Until she accidentally overheard a conversation he was having with his colleague. In it he spoke with endearment of a little puppy he had just bought for his daughter... That added a completely unexpected dimension to her feelings towards her tormentor. So, are there people who only consist of evil? It sure would simplify our judgment of people, but...'

*'Have you heard of the fable of the frog and the scorpion?'*

'Do tell...'

*'There once was a scorpion standing on a river's bank. He wanted to go across, but couldn't swim. Then he saw a frog pass by and he shouted: "Hey, come over here. Can you help me cross the river?"*

*The frog sneered: "How do you suppose we do that?"*

*The scorpion explained that he could sit on the frog's back while he swam, but immediately the frog protested: "Do you take me for a fool? You could bite me and that would mean certain death!"*

*"No" the scorpion replied, "of course I won't do that. I want to get to the other side and don't I need you to get there?"*

*Hesitatingly the frog gave in. He let the creature hop on and he began to swim. In the middle of the river, however, the frog suddenly felt a sharp sting in his neck. While they lay side by side in the water thrashing about he asked the scorpion bewilderedly: "Why did you sting me after all? Now we will both drown..."*

*The scorpion said: "I can't help it. It's in my nature..."'*

A knock on my door and before I could answer Claire was standing in the middle of the room. She had brought a pot of tea and two mugs with her that she planted on top of my desk in a matter somewhere between 'resolute' and 'audacious'. She then stood beside me and glanced at my laptop. My first instinct was to quickly move the cursor on the screen to 'minimalize', but I changed my mind. After all, I had nothing to hide. Right?

With her eyes fixed on the text Claire asked: "Are you talking to that so-called vampire again, or should I say still?"

I looked at her, intently, and said: "Well aren't you Miss Strategy?"

But she ignored me and as she was reading her grin grew wider. No choice but to surrender. I sighed and asked: "… May I have a minute of privacy, please?"

My flat mate did a little victory dance all the way to the couch. She kicked off her shoes and installed herself into a lotus position.

In the meantime I read the text that had appeared on my screen:

Aeolus says:

'Your fable really hits the mark following the example I presented to you… and that perfectly completes the circle, you see?'

*Rhona says:*

*'Yes, definitely.'*

'Not that it gets us any further. Ultimately the Bible does say: "Those who think they know something do not yet know as they ought to know".'

*'What verse is that?'*

'1 Corinthians 8:2.'

*'Wow, I can't believe you just said that off the top of your head… But something came up: my flat mate just entered my room and demands my attention.'*

'Aha, so you would like to leave it at this for now.'

*'No, I really don't want to. Don't get me wrong.'*

'We'll talk soon. I hope.'

*'Yes, talk to you soon, okay? And thank you…'*

'Talk to you soon.'

I poured the tea, handed a mug to Claire and sat down beside her.

"Your timing couldn't be worse, you know that, don't you?"

"Yes dear, love you too…" she mumbled, upon which I reluctantly said: "We were just in the middle of a somewhat heavy conversation."

"Something heavy? Okay…" And then there was silence. Until I began to explain.

At the end of my clarification Claire could barely contain her amazement: "You, discussing matters of religion with someone. And you did not even object?"

"Yeah, hello, of course I did! Especially in the beginning. In that respect he is the worst conversation partner I could have in front of me – seldom have I talked to someone who was so confrontational…"

"Doesn't sound very friendly."

"Oh no, he *is* friendly. But he just has life experience, you know? That means he has enough perspective to shed light on things from every angle and continually holds that mirror up to me without being afraid of how I might react, however emotional the reaction that comes out may be... and this combined with that IQ of his... can you imagine what that's like?"

"What, imagine it?"

"Well, just how bizarre our chat conversations can be! For example, I constantly have trouble keeping up with Aeolus because he types so fast. So like a fool I keep trying to come up with good answers and formulate proper sentences, which then takes an eternity before I can hit the 'send'-button. While he just sits and waits for me patiently..."

Claire made a frown.

"... He uses complicated words, he's polite. At least, most of the time, cause he knows exactly what he does and does not want... he has superiority, charisma."

"Charisma? I thought you only knew him through the internet?"

"Yeah, but you've seen for yourself what our chat sessions look like. One could barely call that 'chatting', wouldn't you say? They're more like – "

" – You're avoiding something, sweetie. What do you mean with 'charisma'?"

"Simply, how he comes across to others!" I focused on a chip in my nail and Claire waited, pretending to be patient, until I continued talking: "I um... I've seen him once. In real life," I finally dared to admit.

"You *know* him?" She placed her tea on the floor.

"I didn't say that. But I ran into him once. And you were there. At Schiphol, remember, when we got back from Iceland."

"No, doesn't ring a bell."

"Sure it does. Remember how I fell, on the travelator?"

"Yes..."

"Well, some guy helped me get up..."

"Ahaaa... so *he's* the vampire?"

"Yes, please, could you make it sound any more ridiculous?"

"And are you going to meet up now?"

"No spare me, he doesn't even want to!"

"But does he know that you know that uh..."

"No of course not, Claire, use your brain! He doesn't want me to know his real name, he keeps his profession a secret, as well as his country of residence – if I were to show him even a glimpse of what I discovered, he'll make a run for it."

"And I'm sure that's the last thing you want. But, what *do* you want?"

That question hit me like a truck. I could pretend Aeolus was just some friendly stranger, but even if he had never reached out to me through that note, I still would not have been able to easily forget what had happened at the airport. And to make matters worse, now I couldn't separate that man's piercing gaze from our conversation over the internet...

"Are you in love?" Claire asked.

"How can I possibly fall in love with someone who is practically a stranger," I said mockingly.

My friend remained silent. Her face did not give away what she was thinking, but I knew that she saw right through me. And so I felt all the more relieved when she decided to return to the content of our chat conversation: the church. Who would have ever thought that I'd enjoy a lively and heated discussion about that, of all topics?

8

BOREDOM


As soon as Claire had left I pressed the space bar on my computer. The darkened screen was brought back to life – and unbelievably – Aeolus was still online. How long had I actually been talking with my roommate? My watch showed that it was well beyond midnight. The umpteenth time this week?

*Rhona says:*
*'My friend just left'*
Aeolus says:
'But shouldn't you go to bed?'
*'Um... shouldn't you?'*
'You don't know what time zone I'm in.'
*'What about your work?'*
'Don't concern yourself with that. Right now we are having a conversation.'
*'Yes. You can say that again.'*
'Our contact has grown far beyond my expectations, Rhona. It means a lot to me.'
*'But why? This is the second time you mention that.'*
'When the years pass by, not by the ten but by hundredfold, they seem to come to a crawl. This may be difficult for you to imagine, but having an eternity gives you nothing to look forward to. It feels more like an unbearable threat to your 'joy of living'. Death on the other hand, brings variation. In my opinion death makes life worth living.'
*'You're sick of the endless years?'*
'Ooh, I can't even begin to explain how bad it is!'
'If you're a vampire it is inevitable to be faced with boredom at some point or another. Every little thrill is of nothing new to me. Everything has been said before. Everything has been done before. It just keeps repeating itself in one perpetual, monotonous cadence...'
*'And I guess people of your own kind are of little help in that department?'*
'Well, sort of... you can find mutual understanding...'
*'But?'*
'They suffer from the exact same issue in that respect. And thus talking about it can be deadly. You either bring the other down into your own negative spiral or you reaffirm each other's sense of superiority over the transient nature of humanity. From there it just goes from bad to worse.'
*'But it can't be helped, being on the fringe of society...'*

'Yes, survival mechanisms… all ensued from the circumstances, whether you like it or not.'
*'Would you say you've lost your edge?'*
'Eternal life, or should I say, the absence of death feels like sitting in a waiting room that you know you can never escape. You look for ways to pass the time, but you only become more and more indifferent.'
*'That reminds me of a photo I once took in America. Hold on, I'll send it… It's called "The Road To Nowhere".'*

Smiling while I reminisced about that particular day of shooting photos I looked at the duotone image of a couple of trees that had found their way up right through the crack between two crossties of an old railway bridge. A railroad somewhere in the State of Maryland that had been abandoned years ago.

Aeolus says:
'An illustration such as this is exactly why I enjoy talking to you so much. You are mortal, yet you are closer to life than any one of us.'
Rhona says:
*'Well, I had already figured that the reason why you reached out to me was because I'm not a vampire. But why me of all people?'*
'You seemed to be open-minded.'
*'So are lots of people.'*
'I needed some distraction, Rhona. Isn't that obvious by now?'

And that's where I lost him. Emotionally speaking, at least… it was like Schiphol airport all over again, where he held the reigns tightly, while I got nothing.

*Rhona says:*
*'Okay…'*
Aeolus says:
'Don't you ever get bored?'
*'Not very often, no.'*
'Why is that? Are you in that way different from other people?'
*'How should I know…'*
'I am intrigued. I would like to know how that works for you.'
*'But don't you remember what it was like for you back then?'*
'That was a long time ago and those feelings have lost their value.'
*'Then would it be okay if I asked you something that may be a little sensitive? Something I've been wondering about ever since you told me your story about your past?'*
'Ask me.'
*'What happened to your wife and children? Were you able to watch over them*

*and their children over the centuries that followed?'*

'Not for long. By now, you're probably wondering if I have any descendants walking this earth?'

*'No, not specifically. Although that would be a weird thought... But I'm just curious as to what happened with your wife after that vampire had found you. Unless it's difficult for you to talk about...'*

'No, that's alright. But it's been some time ago – let me think. Right, before I begin you must keep in mind that it had been an exceptionally harsh winter when I left for Venice. At first our household did not suffer from a shortage of food just yet as our family belonged to the upper class of society. In this period, however, that brought with it an unexpected complication. You see, the well-to-do in Paris, but also in Lyon for that matter, were forced to open up their homes and kitchens to the poor. Now we did have staff on hand. But I would have preferred to have been there myself. I *should* have been there, because if I had been none of what was about to happen to my wife and children would have happened... It was unbearable for me to think of how she would be forced to hold her own in this precarious situation, with all those strangers in and around our house...

On top of that, the day would come that they would receive the news of my disappearance. The worries, the uncertainty and finally the point at which all search for me would be called off... Lucas, the vampire that had 'turned' me, had a difficult time keeping me under control those first weeks. I was confused by the physical and mental changes inside of me. I did not yet know how to control my bloodthirst, and at this point Lucas felt the responsibility towards me as my *sire* to 'educate' me and he drove me crazy with his endless lecturing and depiction of my future life as an immortal. Whereas I just wanted to return home. Therefore I frequently escaped his supervision to head for the place that was familiar to me, Lyon.

The desire to embrace my wife and comfort her ran deep, but every time I saw her walking somewhere around town I became overwhelmed with instincts that were more animalistic than they were human, which startled me so much that I didn't know how fast to make a run for it. Good grief, the number of hours I had spent in front of the fire for the paupers on the corner of my own street during those dark nights... and the amount of 'nourishment' that I was able to collect off of the men that I did not want near our home... until my sire would find me again and convince me that returning to the city that we had settled in was really the only option.

Several years passed before I could see my wife as a widow. After all, my existence could not exactly be called living. As a vampire you were forced to break off any contact with all your relatives, friends and acquaintances solely for their safety. And believe me, realizing the necessity of this comes to you quickly once you have felt the force behind the uncontrollable thirst for blood rushing through your body...

But I did not reach full closure of my old life until I heard what tragedy had befallen my wife and children in Marseille. I knew they had moved there, as we had family who lived there. And a peaceful life, surrounded by people who cared about them was all I ever could have wanted for them... Who could have ever foreseen that that love for your own family would become your ultimate downfall? My wife had escaped death a number of times because each time Lucas had extracted me from Lyon at the very last moment, but now death had caught up with her regardless via a different route: the ports of Marseille. Her sister's husband was a merchant in textiles and imported the most beautiful fabrics imaginable from the Levant. And along with those fabrics the black plague was introduced...'

*Rhona says:*
*'How horrible. I feel horrible for you, Aeolus.'*
Aeolus says:
'It happened almost three hundred years ago.'
*'Yeah but you tell it like it happened just yesterday.'*
'Three centuries, Rhona. That should be long enough to preoccupy yourself with other things. So getting back to my being bored and having lost my edge. What advice would you give me?'
*'Oh I don't know... maybe develop an eye for details.'*
'Where did that come from?'
*'Oh that was just the first thing that came to me.'*
'How do I implement that in practice?'
*'Oof... gee, um... look at things that others don't notice?'*
'I'm listening.'
*'It's easy, I can recall a book for teens in which an old ex-convict showed a teenager who was at risk of derailing what it was like to be stuck in prison for years.'*
'Interesting.'
*'He squared off a yard in his garden using some tape and made the teenager sit in it for hours, in the middle of his lawn.'*
'Any result?'
*'Yes, guaranteed.'*
'And *what* was that result?'
*'Whoa now, mister Impatient! Let me think.'*
'Well think then.'
*'Why are you being so pushy?'*
'That is beside the point.'
*'Then I won't tell you any more about that book.'*
'What is that supposed to mean?'
*'I'm not going to sit here and be bossed around by some guy who doesn't think anything more of me than just a few written lines on the screen. Goodnight.'*

Trembling in agitation I went offline. This was not like me – this was not how

I dealt with things – but still there was not a bone in my body that thought about undoing the impulsive consequence of this moment of rage. Because this was *his* fault, not mine. He was being an authoritarian, he wanted to be served his every whim and it was time he learned I find that unacceptable. After all, it was bad enough that our one time encounter at Schiphol had not been enough for him...

The next couple of days I avoided my computer with such carefulness bordering on the comical. I filled my hours by visiting friends, abnormally lengthy shopping trips in the City Center and working on my photography as much as possible. But for some reason I did cross that photo shoot for my own book out of my agenda and canceled the models. I was not in the mood for things like that, my mind was not focused. And in the meantime the nagging pain I had begun to feel when breathing increased steadily... a pain in my soul? – Oh please, how far could you go in your analysis? It was simple really: I met a man, we began to communicate online and rules were implemented to make sure we would never meet in real life. As a result our communication was of the cyber kind. Nothing more than some words on my screen.
And yet... they intrigued me, those words. Like 1 Corinthians 8: 'Those who think they know something still have a lot to learn', a verse that is preceded by: 'Knowledge makes people arrogant, but love builds them up'. You could ask yourself: knowledge, arrogant? Did all knowledge do that? And what kind of love were they even talking about?

9

LOVE


*Autumn 1985. Montmartre, Paris.*

"Help! *Help me!*"
The sudden screaming brings an abrupt end to the pleasant atmosphere that
up until that point had surrounded the touristic street. The people who were
closest to the girl stop what they are doing and look at her in shock. And she
– early twenties with lush blond curls, tight leggings and an oversize
sweatshirt – just stands there, next to a stall displaying art replicas and
cheap postcards, too paralyzed to make a move.
Naturally the pickpocket uses that confusion to his advantage. He is
experienced in maneuvering through a crowd, hopping in a crisscross pattern
and has almost disappeared from sight when an extended leg causes him to
crash miserably. Next he is immediately hauled up by his belt and the collar
of his jacket and set up straight. A memorable kick to the behind sends the
thief on his way tripping and limping, without the purse that he had just
stolen...
"Did you lose this?" A young man in a long coat walks over to the crying girl.
She looks at the shiny, black object that he holds out in front of her and
stammers: "Yes, um... yes..."
"Check if everything's still there."
She opens her purse, checks its contents, nods and starts sobbing again. The
man says: "You're shaking. Come, you need to sit down somewhere." He
motions towards a small café on the corner and takes the girl there.


The young man asks for a glass of water at the bar. A woman with a solar bed
tan and a half-smoked cigarette hanging from the corner of her mouth grants
him his request and together with the girl he takes a seat at a table by the
window.
The walls of the café are covered with old-fashioned Parisian photos and
posters for the theater. There is a piano, left untouched, and the radio plays
David Bowie's latest song: *This is not America.*
"Is that where you're from?" the young man asks.
The girl looks confused. He nods towards the speaker where the music comes
from. Then she says: "yes".
He asks her if she is traveling alone and at first she denies it, but when he
subtly lets her know how obvious her lie is the girl explains that she had
actually traveled to Paris with three of her friends. Yesterday however they

had had a massive argument and now she is passing the remainder of her time here by herself, waiting for her returning flight home that does not leave until a few days from now.

The man has a soft, but unfamiliar accent when he speaks and she asks if he lives in the city. He nods. And they talk. She orders a beer and he a glass of red wine. And after fifteen minutes, while on their second drink, the girl is even able to smile a little.

At the end of the evening he escorts her back to her hotel – with painted-white shutters in front of the windows, of which some have wrought iron balconies.

By then he has already suggested they visit a museum together the next day. An invitation she happily accepts…

In the early afternoon, shortly after 1 p.m., the girl has just finished her lunch as the man enters the corner café. He is wearing the same coat he wore last night with a fashionable, striped shirt underneath. He lifts the large sunglasses that he is wearing as they greet one another. They sit down and the girl stares at him. He raises his eye brow and she explains: "You kind of look like one of those Duran Duran boys…" Immediately her face and neck turn a fiery red. It is obvious that she is painfully aware of this and she quickly recovers and says: "Only those sunglasses are completely outdated. They are *so* 1984…"

"What type would you suggest then?" he asks.

"A pair of Ray Ban's Wayfarers, of course!"

"They already existed in the fifties."

"No man, the Wayfarers are the latest thing. Even Sonny Crockett wears them!"

"Don't know him."

"Oh sure you do. Everyone knows them – Crockett and Tubbs, from Miami Vice!"

The man shakes his head.

"The TV series…?"

"No."

She makes a pitiful face. "Would you mind telling me what planet you live on?" she asks, but his answer is again very simple: "I don't watch a lot of television. Sorry."

At the Louvre the girl does not know where to look. For the first time in her life she sees classical pillars even taller than houses, walks on marble slab flooring laid into artistic patterns and stands so close to the Venus de Milo that she could easily touch her, if she dared. Together with the man she spends time in the hall that has the Mona Lisa in it and he tells her things, explains and philosophizes. And she just stares at him… They also go shopping. In large department stores. He buys himself some sunglasses of the

Wayfarer type, because that makes her happy, and for her an expensive bottle of perfume. When they finish their purchase the girl tries to thank the cashier in her best French. *"Mercy..."* she says, but it is not until the French woman looks away condescendingly without answering that she realizes how thick her American accent really is. She blushes, once more, and apologetically mumbles, "Small town U.S.A...."

The man smiles endearingly.

In the evening they go to a bistro on the Champs-Elysées. In the dimness of the setting sun following their dinner it is easy for two hands to accidentally meet on the table and an hour later, on top of the Arc de Triomphe, he lays his arm over her shoulder while she is enchanted by the view over the city with all its lights...

When they arrive at the hotel it is she herself that asks him to come up with her. Which he does.

At first they just lie side by side, naked – he caressing her neck, and she smiling somewhat awkwardly – and he is gentle, careful even when he finally bends over and starts kissing her, but then he suddenly enters her and has sex with her. Hard, long and desperate, passionate sex...

The following day, towards the end of the afternoon, the girl waits again in the café on the corner. She adjusts her shoulder pads. Pulls up her leg warmers a couple of times. She stares and smiles, at the old man behind the piano. As he plays old fashioned chansons he is apparently capable of reading a newspaper that he has spread out in front of him just above the keys, a spectacle that the girl watches with fascination. But every now and then she checks her watch. And as the minutes pass by she does so more frequently. Eventually, after having waited for over an hour and a half, she gets up, looking pale and blinking from the tears that fill up her eyes.

Elsewhere in the city, in the living room of a top floor apartment the young man sits comfortably reclined on the couch with an opened notebook in his lap. There are names on its pages, names of women, and he flips the pages... looks... reads... Then at the end of the list he adds a name and closes the book.

Out of the cassette player comes the weathered voice of Edith Piaf. Full of passion she sings: *Non, je ne regrette rien...*

## 10

INSPIRATION

Music. Baroque. Never actually looked into that genre. Probably would not be much. And yet... something about all this intrigued me and one day I decided to search *viola da gamba* on YouTube.

A plethora of names unknown to me unfolded on the screen. Names of musicians and composers, names that kept coming up, such as Marin Marais – I believe we had talked about him before during one of our conversations together. Guess I should take a listen, right...? I clicked on a random video and something that looked like a scene from a movie began to play before my eyes. Yes, this definitely must have come from a movie, because why else would that man be in tears while playing that instrument and was that woman next to him dressed in such a beautiful period dress? *Tous Les Matins Du Monde* the video's description said, and apparently the film was a biopic about the life of the composer Sainte-Colombe. He had a chronically ill wife whose health declined as time went on, and due to an unfortunate twist of fate, just when he felt too preoccupied with his work to return home, she died. The composer passed the remainder of his years deeply mourning his loss, unable to forgive himself.

Wow. That was the worst possible subject to talk about with Aeolus...

Nevertheless, I decided to order the DVD immediately.

It is strange how one evening of watching videos could change your mood, let alone cause you to review your life choices. Or did the music have nothing to do with that? The fact remained that I had begun to wonder why on earth I had canceled that photo shoot for my book. It had not been a first and if I were to get anywhere with this project that I had initially started with such enthusiasm, I should really show more perseverance...

Because what was I actually hoping to achieve with this book? Did I even have a topic beyond just 'photos that have a deeper meaning'? And a target audience, did I have that yet, and a storyline? - Come on, a little bit of brain work has never hurt anyone!

Accordingly, I opened the folder that contained all the photos I had taken so far. Maybe, just maybe, a common theme could be extrapolated from this extremely eclectic collection of images...

Nature, or in another word landscapes were an obvious theme. And deserted places, such as abandoned buildings and industrial areas, were among my favorites. Sometimes these two subjects were even combined in a single photo, I just noticed: that broken television, for example, that had been dumped in a moss-covered lava field. Yes, I had recently shot that image in Iceland on one of my trips when exploring the place by rental car. The name I had come up with on the spot was: *Left To Your Own Devices...*

Hmmm, I was pretty good at coming up with titles. Probably something I had picked up when I was a member of that online photography community, where I had taught myself to purposefully come up with a title for each photo that I presented to my colleagues there. Most photographers did not bother with things like that, but I had figured out that it really made a difference. A static image obtained much more eloquence with a fitting title... sometimes you could even suggest an entire story with it. Such as in this image of that pug wearing that neon-pink sweater on a sidewalk in New York. I had edited out the leash that the animal was attached to and titled the whole thing *Love On A Leash.* Hilarious... Poor thing.

In the meantime a playlist of baroque music played a steady stream of classical tones in the background. For several minutes already two women had been singing. The delicate voices of these sopranos made me stop for a minute what I was doing. How in-cre-di-bly beautiful this was! The way in which they interpreted this music... it instantaneously brought to mind the images of two by-whatever-tragedy-that-may-have-befallen-them lost souls, in some godforsaken street, sitting in embrace on the ground while leaning against the exterior wall of a house late at night. From one moment of desperately clinging on to each other, melting together in their joint elegy, to then be separated by their individual agony and seemingly briefly forgetting about the other's existence. To which the other in turn responded with her own emotions, introspectively, demurely. This felt so serene, so intense...! What was this piece called anyway? *Troisième Leçon De Ténèbre* by François Couperin... I quickly looked up more information. It turned out that this 'Third Lesson Of The Darkness' – creepy title by the way – was composed in light of the suffering of Lent prior to Easter. The words being sung came from the Book of Lamentations, in which the prophet Jeremiah mourns the destruction of Jerusalem by the Babylonians. In the Catholic tradition a symbolic connection was made between the loneliness of Jesus and Judas and His frightened, disloyal followers. Wow... so heavy! Couperin knew exactly how to touch a raw nerve, at least, mine. I quivered and at the same time I felt an aha experience: this music had the power to heal people. I was sure of that. If only I could accomplish *that* with my photos...

The power of a composer such a Couperin clearly lay in the words and melodies. My strength on the other hand lay in speaking through visual art. But – if he was able to bring about images in my mind with his music, would I not be able to teach people to express themselves with the help of my photography? And then even professional therapists could incorporate those photos into their therapies... yes, I just *had* to be able make something of that! I vowed I would totally focus on my book more from this day forward.

And come up with an outline of the chapters... I had to start somewhere, right? At the very least I now had a direction, a goal.

By the end of these four days I finally had the courage to log in to the email account that I had used for my contact for my communication with Aeolus. And – surely – there was a new message from him in my inbox...
With my stomach tied into knots I looked at what he had to say:

"Precious Rhona,

It is not an easy task trying to find a section of grass in the park upon which one can sit still for hours straight without being conspicuous. Thankfully my vision at night is no worse than during the day and since our last conversation I have taken the habit of seeking out the exact same spot each time, somewhat sheltered by the shadow of the plane and chestnut trees, at a time at which people in the city have long retired to bed.

You did not make it easy for me. The first time that I sat in my square yard I was more than once tempted to get up and walk home. I had not given myself a time frame and thus I continually forced myself to stay longer than I had desired to. There was no other drill instructor to rely on other than myself.

Remaining in one spot for long periods does strange things with your concept of time. You try to find ways that could speed it up, which is a lost battle to begin with. Nothing can affect the rate at which time passes. In order to protect yourself against that unforgiving truth, after an initial phase of defiance, your soul ends up shifting into a state of self-sedation. It happens automatically, you do not have to do anything for that. Something inside of you is switched off and the minutes glide by. That state of mind however never lasts long and soon you are back to having to deal with reality. Your eyes scan the surroundings and your ears focus on every detectable sound. But everything that you observe is familiar, you have heard it before, seen it before... A homeless person shuffling by across the path. Blind drunk, a travesty of society. The calling of a long-eared owl, his near-silent dive towards a mouse scurrying away and a muffled jab from the impact shortly after. A brief, shrill squeaking and then the disgusting smacking sounds, the peristalsis of the throat and the crushing of bones. Nothing new under the sun. So much to observe, but even under the moon there is nothing new. What else is there for someone like me? What if everything is so tiring that more than anything you want to lie down and fall asleep forever?
Therefore I think of it as nothing short of a miracle that I have sought out that square yard for three subsequent nights. Will I be able to keep this up until I have unraveled the mystery of waiting? I hope so. The fact that you were the one who came up with this idea gives me the motivation I need to at

least give it a try.

Thank you...

Aeolus."

What? How could that be? Not a single word about our fight?
But *then* what did he want from me? To get back in touch, or was there a
catch? And I, what should I do now, mail back or something? But how, and
what words should I use, because with his kindness he had *completely*
disarmed me. What if however, I needed those weapons again later to hold
my own, to maintain a healthy distance between us? And what if I felt as
though weapons of attack alone were not enough, that other means would be
just as necessary? Such as logic, because as long as I kept thinking logically I
would be able to think of him as that stranger with whom I only chatted no
more than occasionally. Something you did on the train or at a café... You are
nice to someone and the other is courteous towards you. And then you each go
your own way. No big deal...
But Aeolus challenged my logic with that of his and knocked me over with it
each and every time. And he did it with the most charming smile a women
could wish for. In a manner of speaking, that is. But I was not going to fall for
it. A day would come that he would *not* win for once.

11

SANDER

More than three hours after I had set my status to 'online' a sound notification announced that a friend had logged in. Aeolus. I jumped off the couch, turned the television down and opened a chat window.

*Rhona says:*
*'Make sure you wear old clothes. Grass can leave nasty stains.'*
Aeolus says:
'Good evening.'
*'No "thank you" for my well-intended advice?'*
'How have you been?'
*'Now you're hurting my feelings a little.'*
'It is not my intention to hurt you.'
*'No no... I've known you longer than today.'*
'There is no cure for distrust. Can't help you with that, sorry.'
*'Is that so? I'm pretty sure both parties have their share in this matter.'*
'How are you doing? How did you spend your week?'
*'Nowhere near a square yard of grass in the park.'*
'I should think not, no.'
*'Why are you so ridiculously tenacious? Should I be getting ready for the final blow, or... bite?'*
'You in turn are not in the best of moods this evening.'
*'Oh sure I am. I can be very friendly if I want.'*
'To then bring out the claws all of a sudden?'
*'You never know when they're needed.'*
'Are you on a war path or is this just your way of flirting?'
*'That's something for you to know...'*
'Are you sure that you want to go through with this? You are aware of what they say about playing with fire...'
*'And then what – with this protective wall called the internet between us?'*
'When are you going to change your hair color again?'
*'Dang it, way to breach a new subject...'*
'If I were to let it run through my fingers, what would it feel like?'
*'Simple, like hair.'*
'Describe it to me.'
'And if I were to touch your neck, what would happen to the humidity of the air above your skin?'
*'Since I will be traveling abroad to shoot photos very soon, I'm not sure*

*whether I have enough money left to go to the hairdresser.'*

'In a situation such as that is your willpower strong enough to keep your heart rate in check?'

*'If you really think about it, it's strange how easy it is to travel. You hop on a train and between that and your accommodation in the place of destination a couple hundred yard walk away, you have barely breathed any outside air... it only takes a few hours to be in a completely different city, or different country, and even the ocean is not an obstacle anymore.'*

'Ask your hairdresser for a good conditioner. You will need it after dyeing it that frequently.'

*'Hold on a minute. Who says my hair is dried out, or not well taken care of?'*

'Nobody. So it is soft and well-nourished, as the commercials say?'

*'Your words, Aeolus. Your words.'*

'You remain temperamental. Very entertaining.'

*'Oh, son of a bitch.'*

'Cursing is merely an expression of incapacity.'

*'Were do you get your wisdom from?'*

'Just trust me, it is the truth.'

*'Oh, talking about truth, are we? And trust – funny you of all people should use that word, Mr. Untrustworthy? Because what if you were a real vampire? Then I can totally picture it already: you, bathing in sweat while lying in a bed or a coffin... dreaming about my exposed neck with a warm blood-pumping pulse – and other veins. But vampires don't exist. Which means you are lying to me. But somehow you still manage to drag me into a story that is rife with said subject and I pretend like it's the most normal thing on earth. Something that obviously shows how easy it is for you to grab my attention by any means you feel like. I'm beginning to realize that this strange world isn't just your domain anymore, but by now has become mine just as well. And I have to struggle on a daily basis against the craving for our conversations. You wrap me around your finger, Aeolus, and it's killing me. There, I said it.'*

'So you think *I* wrap you around my finger?! You don't think it could be the other way around?'

*'That doesn't concern me. I can only deal with what I am confronted with. That's more than frustrating enough.'*

'I am no stranger to that frustration, Rhona.'

*'Then let me give you some advice. To let off some steam: why don't you go and practice Le Tourbillon by Marais until you can play it perfectly.'*

'How – dare – you.'

*'?'*

'If you can only speak disrespectfully about things you know nothing about, I'd rather you remain silent altogether!'

*'I guess that means that particular piece is out of your league? What a pity.'*

'It's best if we end this chat conversation, before we start saying things that we will regret later. Good night.'

And immediately he went offline.

*Yes!* Vindication! Finally I had managed to knock Aeolus off his high horse.
When I turned off the computer a grin crept onto my face... I was going to
sleep so well tonight!
Not even a wink... The tragedy started out with staring at the ceiling wide
awake for over an hour and endlessly replaying the movie of our exchange of
words in my mind. Next came the tossing and turning with, as a result, a
pain in my neck that was so intense that finally out of sheer madness I did
not know which corner of my pillow to lay my head on anymore. But I *did*
triumph over Aeolus. For the first time and hopefully this was just the
beginning...
Suddenly I was shocked by myself. This was a little too vicious, the way I was
thinking right now. While he had not actually done anything wrong. And for
the most part had been fairly kind. And reasonable, and always willing to
listen and sympathize with my troubles and – if those things annoyed me, did
that not say much more about me and my self-image than it did about him?
On second thought?
I rolled out of my bed, groaning. After pulling a sweater over my pajamas, I
started up my computer and began to write an email.

"Dear Aeolus,

With this email I would like to let you know that I am sorry for having
behaved so strangely last night. It was uncalled for, I did not have the right
to do so, even though I thought I did... Sorry!
I just want us to have a pleasant and good time together. I don't want to
argue. In my opinion we have plenty of positive memories of earlier
conversations up to now to continue in that same spirit. But that's only going
to work if you feel the same way...
Therefore, sorry, again. I'll try to behave from now on ;-)
By the way, I have read your email about sitting in your square yard in the
park. How's that going? Did you continue with it?

Take care,
Rhona."

I had just clicked on 'send' when it occurred to me that I was going to attend
a friend's birthday tomorrow evening and that it would probably be a late
night. What if Aeolus wanted to talk to me and I was not there, right after
sending that make-up email?
Quickly I therefore sent a new message saying:

"P.S.: Totally forgot: if I'm not online tomorrow, it's because I'm with my friend Sander. A birthday party. May get late...

Rhona."

What if there was a definition for friendship, what would it look like? What would be the criteria? Unconditional? Loving? Self-sacrificial? And to what extend would time play a role in it? How many months, for example, had to pass before a good acquaintanceship could be called a friendship? And what if you only had two photo shoots, so no more than two encounters, to measure it by?

Well, things just felt right between us. Sander was Sander and that was more than any human could wish for in a friendship – honestly! He truly was the sweetest man. The way in which he had involved me in everything tonight as soon as he picked up on my being uncomfortable... He had introduced me to all sorts of friends and potential models, and had reeled me back into the party when I had ended up withdrawing myself in a corner. And now he had even come outside with me for a minute, without wearing a jacket.

"Have you ever experienced," I asked, while I was wrestling with my bike lock, "that from one moment to the next the faces of the people around you turn into liquid rubber?"

"Liquid rubber?" asked Sander not understanding.

"Yeah, like in that Evanescence music video, *Going Under...* with all those distorted faces. They then turn into horribly demonic masks, remember?"

"Oh, you mean *pliable* rubber." To visualize this he made a couple of extremely supple moves with his arms and upper body. "Then I got something even creepier for you: *Black Hole Sun* by Soundgarden!"

"That's the grungiest of grunge, man – I'm surprised you know it! Were you even born then?" I asked him with such a provocative tone that I hoped would keep him from noticing how much I cringed on the inside at that very moment. The thought alone about that video – those faces with grimaces that stretched from ear to ear and those psychotic, enlarged eyes... With my shoulders raised I turned my bike into the direction that I was about to go. I wanted to get on, but Sander stopped me. "Hold on. You're making all these jokes, but you're not gonna tell me you have actually seen these kinds of things happening this evening, are you?"

"Don't be ridiculous," I said mockingly, "something like that could never happen, right?" I avoided making eye contact and kicked at something imaginary with my foot.

"Not if you're not a magic mushroom user, no..." he dryly answered, upon which I burst out laughing. But I quickly became serious again. "I'm sorry I was so socially awkward this evening," I said. "I'm just a little distracted. Or maybe a bit too focused, I don't know..."

Sander sighed. "Oh, you should see me when I'm focused on an intense piece of choreography. And what happens when the phone then rings...!"

"What? Screaming bloody murder?"

"Usually something worse," he chuckled. He took a pack of cigarettes out of his back pocket and offered me one. I shook my head.

"Say, that reminds me," he suddenly said. "That photo shoot you canceled the other day, are you ever going to reschedule it, or...?"

"Yes of course, I should think so. We'd better set up a new date as soon as possible, since I'm currently in the 'flow'. It's just that I haven't decided on the location yet."

"Something we can brainstorm about. We're standing out here anyway. What kind of sentimental value should the location have?"

"Oh! Well, um... I think it should be some place deserted, or run-down. Or at the very least something that is alienating."

Sander had lit his cigarette and stared at the smoke that he had blown upwards. He slowly nodded. "Yes, something out of the ordinary... but you also mentioned that you had found a common thread for your book. What will that look like? I was thinking, when you talked about your ideas this evening: she's onto something good, but have you thought about how you're going to present it?"

I smiled a little discouraged. "If I only knew... Anyway, at its bare minimum once finished it should directly engage one's emotions. Something that helps or teaches people to recognize their own feelings or the memories they have – you know what I mean."

"Sounds almost like you should highlight one emotion or theme per chapter, hey?"

"That *would* make it look more organized, yes."

I shivered and looked at my friend. This whole time he had been standing there only wearing that thin fishnet shirt... I was so selfish. I should go, let him go. "My dear, I'm sending you back inside," I said, giving him a kiss on his cheek.

"I'll call you, okay?"

"Yes, we'll call. And you take care of yourself."

## 12

WEAPON

And there I was, riding my bicycle, fighting against a brutal headwind that only got worse after I had left the office buildings of the southern part of the city behind me. Panting to catch my breath I crossed the long bridge heading into downtown, hoping the high-rises there would provide a little more shelter.

The streets were practically deserted, like always in the weekends. Interesting how it could differ so much per city, where some cities were a complete contrast and they somehow never appeared to sleep – a loud bang coming from beneath me woke me from my contemplation. With an agitated sigh I dismounted. Great, a tire blow-out... I looked at my front wheel, saw the shards of a broken beer bottle scattered across the bike path and heard my back tire beginning to lose its air as well. I had no choice but to walk. I briefly looked back and tried to estimate whether returning to Sander's apartment would be shorter than the remaining distance to my own place. The hundreds of yards-long bridge across the river was the deciding factor. I was not going to cross it again. No way.

The city center with its wide boulevard, along which the City Hall was situated, was well-lit. But the railway underpass was a different story and before I entered it I looked around me carefully. No one around, thank goodness. Better make a run for it and after that came the long stretch along the Schiekade and then I would almost be home. Unfortunately not everything in this area was as well-lit, especially not from the sidewalk's point of view... To keep my mind off things I decided to reminisce about how Sander and I had often jokingly told people that we 'only lived two streets apart'. And technically that was accurate, albeit that the street connecting us was almost five miles long and changed its name several times along the way.

Someone right in front of me leaving through the front door of his house made me become aware of my surroundings again. He ignored me, I ignored him. That is how we did things in the big city, especially at night. A young couple in love walking towards me did not receive my attention either, however I did pick up my pace. A little. Strictly speaking, one would welcome such a calm atmosphere, but at this hour I would rather have seen a group of noisy youths here and there, or some other landmarks to maneuver around. Or even situations that I could then avoid... Because the way it was now, was too quiet for my comfort. Things just did not feel right this evening – well, I was not right either, in the head that is. A few years ago I had even told an insecure girl on the bus that when being out and about in the dark during the night she should first and foremost draw courage from all the previous times that nothing scary had happened to her. But the sobriety that I had possessed back then was nowhere to be found at the moment…

I looked around me one last time as inconspicuously as possible. Someone was walking behind me now. Just a coincidence, right? I quickened my pace a little more and then some more, until I was almost running by the time I took a right turn – and of course, as soon as I had entered my street, did the person in question continue on his own way. Or…? In any case, he was nowhere to be seen. Darn it, where could he be? It was a man, not a woman, of that I was certain. Somebody I knew? No, ridiculous, this city is way too big for that. And what were the odds that this particular man… I stuck the key in the front door of my house and after I had hung my bike on the hook in the hallway and properly double locked the door, I sat down on the stairs. I dropped my head and let it rest in my hands…

After a minute or so I crawled up the stairs. Good grief, was I ever tired… then why on earth did I still turn on that bloody computer? And what exactly was my intention here? Go online and then what…?

The speakers of my computer were still set to 'max' and the notification sound of Aeolus sending a message hit me all the more abruptly.

Aeolus says:
'Home this late, and still getting online?'
*Rhona says:*
*'Man, you scared the shit out of me!'*
'How peculiar. May I ask why?'
*'I didn't expect you'd be there… I'm a little on edge. Sorry.'*
'Should I be worried?'
*'Oh no, I was just a little stressed out just now. About nothing really. I was on my way home and got two flat tires and then I had to continue on foot. That's all.'*
'And were you scared?'
*'Yes, although I normally never am.'*
'Why were you this time? Was there a specific reason?'
*'Never mind. It's over now.'*
'Couldn't your boyfriend help you?'
*'I don't have a boyfriend.'*
'And what about Sander?'
*'He had his visitors at home…'*
'Right, it was Sander's birthday… what age did he turn?'
*'23.'*
'Not a little too young for you?'
*'Friendship has no age limit. Something you of all people should know.'*

'What I know is how irresponsible the average Dutch adolescent behaves nowadays. Especially towards women. Please be aware, Rhona, that should anything ever happen to you...'

*'Quit it, Aeolus! He's not my boyfriend. Besides, he's gay.'*

'Oh...'

*'But if possible, could we maybe stop bickering for now? I'd rather talk about your square yard, for example.'*

'Sounds like a wise idea.'

'To start with I want you to know how thankful I am to you. For your sweet email from last night and for your sharp wit.'

*'Uh...?'*

'Your idea, that Spartan exercise of sitting in one spot for hours and hours has started to pay off. I can see more things. My attention has improved. I'm beginning to realize that I had isolated myself from the things that really mattered.'

*'Really?'*

'For instance, do you have any idea how beautiful the grass is? That what we take for granted as simply being tufts of green, are in actuality immensely fascinating little plants that each differ in shape and size? And that in between these thousands, no millions of plants there is a very diverse botanical life... a large variety of mosses, weeds and flowers. With so many shades of green and blue and red and brown. Tomorrow I would like to count how many different species of plants are growing in a square yard like that.'

*'And then the day after tomorrow I bet you're going to compare the density of the grass between different square yards?'*

'Excellent idea. This is... yes, this is interesting!'

*'No, don't do that, you dope. I didn't mean that seriously...'*

'Nevertheless, I don't take this as a joke, but as a very reasonable comment from you instead. I feel like you are missing your own point here.'

*'As long as I don't have to do it myself, because it sounds to-tal-ly boring to me!'*

'That's precisely where you and I differ. I have completely different concerns than you do. I am rediscovering the beauty of the micro cosmos, or rather should I say for the very first time discovering, and its importance is significant. Because I had been in desperate need of something 'different' in my life... You must keep in mind that my senses, the moment that Lucas turned me into a vampire, became incredibly more sensitive. So from one day to the next all the world's sensory stimuli became complete overkill. And it's up to each and every one of us to learn to navigate that. A part of this process is developing, as time goes along, the mechanisms to filter out, or in other words that is to say to channel those stimuli. We learn to use our sense of hearing, of observation and even our sense of smell to our advantage, and everything else we pick up we ignore. However, this combined with the long years of immortality and the inevitable boredom... In any case, that side effect, the dulling of the senses and the arrogance towards all things mundane is something we have talked about before.'

'*So you could say that within that square yard an entirely new world opens up before you...*'

'Exactly. The fauna, the biosphere... scientists that do research on it and their findings... Would you like to hear something? I'm beginning to think that this small area that I am focusing on right now perhaps contains just as much activity as the city around it. For starters, there is everything that can be observed 'above ground', but there is also an 'underground', with ants, for example, in their aisle system at a depth of an inch or ten. At night, the only trace by which you can see that they were ever there, is the waste they leave behind on the surface. And believe me, the amounts are staggering. I intend on returning there during the day for a change, to find an algorithm in their walking patterns... Leather jackets, they are the larvae of crane flies. You can see them inside their eggs scattered about in the dirt... Earthworms that begin to stir when I lightly tap the soil. And from deeper underneath the sand I could hear two moles begin to move in agitation...'

'*You heard them?*'

'Sharp ears, remember?'

'*Ah, on that kind of bicycle...*'

'What bicycle? What do you mean?'

'*Never heard of that expression in Dutch? It means: In that way.*'

'I see. Yes, there are some idioms that have evaded me due to the fact that I don't live in the Netherlands on a full time basis.'

'*How many languages do you know anyway?*'

'A handful. My mother languages, naturally: Czech and Italian. French. Latin, English, Dutch... I can get by reasonably well with my Spanish, Russian and German...'

'*Tell me something you find odd about the Dutch language.*'

'I'm not sure I understand your question.'

'*Well you see, when you, like myself, are interested in languages, at some point you will begin to notice certain things. For example, for some words that are very important in the Dutch language no equivalent words exist in other languages... and the other way around: in Greenlandic, I once read, there are a thousand-and-one terms for snow and ice!*'

'I see what you're saying. Well, since you asked, when I look at your native language I have never fully understood why you use diminutive forms of nouns with no apparent rhyme or reason. Why call the sun 'het zonnetje' instead of 'de zon', for heaven's sake? Don't you have the slightest ounce of respect for the largest celestial body that is visible from earth?'

'*Hahahahahahaha!!!*'

'Sure, you have your laugh. Even so, it is extremely annoying to hear someone say, 'that sure was a delicious brekkie' or 'I'll be back in a minnie', and so on, et cetera.'

'Pfft, I suggest you just stick to that 'handful' of languages you speak. Plenty to choose from, I'd say.'

'Ouch. That hurt.'

'When I'm abroad I often enjoy the names that are used for different places... Like in Belgium: Pole, Yellow, Bell, Mole. It's great fun to translate them literally in more exotic countries. What do you think about : 'Honorable-goat-castle' in Turkey. The tour guide informed us as we passed it on the bus.'

'And in Turkish that is...?'

'Şereflikoçhisar, if I spell it correctly...'

'Good for you.'

'No, the Icelanders are the true champions when it comes to naming places. They take the most sober approach. They just give the geographical description as its names for a town or city: Akureyri means 'acre delta' and Reykjavík 'smoky bay'.'

'I knew about that last one. Wasn't that because the Vikings who first arrived there saw the rising steam of the natural sources?'

'Yes, precisely. That makes a lot more sense than calling a train station 'Saint Pancreas'...'

'It's Saint Pancras, not Pancreas. But I get what you're trying to say.'

'Language can be a powerful weapon...'

'Or a beautiful instrument. You should do something with your square-yard findings. Write articles, a book...'

'How do you suppose I do that?'

'– He said mockingly – afraid to be outed? Isn't that what pseudonyms are for?'

'You're in a provocative mood today. What's up with you?'

'You ask for it, I think. But seriously, why don't you write down everything you discover?'

'I already am, Rhona. Still I would rather choose living anonymously over having a career as a renowned writer, if that's alright with you.'

'Yet things like an identity and passports are not an issue for you, right?'

'What makes you say that?'

'Tell me, how long does a passport in your name last?'

'Until it expires.'

'I don't believe you...'

'*Magnificent, he is pressured into telling things that could endanger himself and her*.'

'No one is forcing you. I'm just intrigued.'

'But what comes next? How much closer will you get? This is not right, mon cœur...'

'Oh come on... please?'

'Okay, alright. You win. At least for now.'

'Because I was in my mid-thirties when Lucas transformed me I enjoyed more liberties than, for example, someone who becomes a vampire at the age of eighteen. After all, at my 'age' your appearance and behavior do not change that easily. For this reason a new identity lasts a relatively long time, provided nothing goes wrong.'

*'My thoughts exactly: if you, say, start out with a passport that lists that you are five years younger than what you are in reality, you'll first look a bit older for your age and then you'll look your exact age...'*

'Until five years beyond that, with some luck. But I'm warning you, I won't tell you how far along I am in my current cycle.'

*'And where do you get this new identity each time?'*

'There are some among us who have chosen a lucrative profession. When needed, we know where to find them. The same goes for diplomas and such.'

*'Are you telling me you can buy diplomas without having done the corresponding coursework? That's called fraud, you know!'*

'Would you stop?'

*'No ;-)'*

'You're such a delight...'

*'As long as you drink responsibly, okay?'*

'That's a very sensible thing to say.'

'I am a dangerous man, Rhona.'

*'But also a funny one!'*

'You're online so very often... Why are you even here, always talking with me?'

*'Because I want to. Because I like it.'*

*'And because I'm dying to know what makes you such a dangerous man ;-)'*

'Without even touching you I am capable of getting you to voluntarily allow me to kill you.'

*'Oo, kinky...!!'*

*'Haha, for a second I honestly thought you were going to tell me that you were some uncivilized womanizer. The stereotypical kind, you know, one who keeps a spreadsheet with names of all their conquests.'*

'Actually, I do.'

*'Hehehe... well, I have to admit, this is something only you could come up with.'*

'Fortunately we have an agreement, you and I.'

*'Yes. We are online friends. Nothing more.'*

'It is more than nothing.'

*'It is. Say, a quick question before we finish: is there an algorithm to your pattern of migration between all those European countries?'*

'Go to sleep, Rhona. Talk to you tomorrow, hopefully...'

How I longed to be near this unknown, yet so very intimate friend right now. To touch him, to read his mind... What could he be doing, as I undressed and laid my tired body onto the bed? What would his place look like and what time was it where he was? Would he be sleeping as well, shortly? And if he weren't, what would he occupy himself with instead?

The more Aeolus and I talked, the more I realized how little I knew and how much more I wanted to learn about him. Also, an uncomfortable kind of desire to openly discuss my personal life had developed – it would be so nice to talk about all the things that came natural with, for example, Sander or Claire… but everything that passed between us was with such a terrible amount of circumspection. A single direct question at Schiphol had been enough to make him disappear and that incident had given me enough of an indication as what to expect a second time.

Aeolus had called our communication 'more than nothing'. That was true. But was it enough?

## 13

## BAROQUE

*Tous Les Matin Du Monde.* So that is what it looked like back then... the simplicity of country living, the grandeur of Versailles... With great fascination I stared at my laptop screen. And that music... I began to enjoy the music that predominated the film more and more by the minute. There was so much emotion emanating from the viola da gamba, oh how that music was able to carry me away through the storyline... Or did the cast and the costumes contribute to that as well? Perhaps my own ability to empathize with the characters...? For how would Aeolus even fit in such a film? Could he ever have worn those curly, long wigs? And those distinct shoes with a buckle on top, was he familiar with them as well? The white blouses embellished with lace underneath three-quarter length, velvet frock coats? Could he have ever visited Versailles – and his wife, what had she looked like? Like the wife of Mr. de Sainte-Colombe, caring, pleasant to the eye, a vision in orange dress with a bell skirt and form-fitting top? At the start of the movie they showed something that I had already read on the internet: Sainte-Colombe's wife passed away at a time when he was preoccupied with work – yes, discussing this movie was most definitely off-limits between Aeolus and I. Despite my firm conviction that he could not have come from that period...

I sighed and got up to go to the kitchen. So tired of myself, and tired from that party and chatting into the wee hours of last night. Luckily it was Sunday and on Sundays doing nothing was allowed. So if I wanted to make myself a deluxe breakfast at two in the afternoon, there was no one there to stop me.

Just as soon as I had turned on the kettle the doorbell rang.

On the sidewalk outside my door stood Sander.

"You look like *hell!*" his voice sounded squeaky.

"And you sound like a strangled cat," I chuckled.

We sat down on the couch in my living room. I was so glad that he had come...

He told me he was worried about me. And that he had an ear to lend, he said, all the more now that he had lost his voice. I thanked him for that and told him that we shall see.

First we recollected our brainstorming session of last night and settled on a date to shoot photos at the docks. Albeit that that would not take place until after I returned from my upcoming trip. It so happened that I was leaving for London this Thursday as I had an assignment from a fashion magazine and planned to make a stop at the city's most beautiful spots...

Sander wanted to know for how long I would be staying. "Seven days, six nights", I said.

"Seven days? But the photo shoot itself doesn't take that long... what are you planning to do with the rest of your time there?" he asked.

That was indeed a good question. It suddenly began to dawn on me how little days I had left to prepare, despite the fact that this trip had been in the making for several months already. I still had to inspect my camera, collect the needed accessories... the chaotic mess that I was – this job was not just randomly firing off some photos, for we were talking seriously big bucks here! And had it not also been my intention to collect images for my photo book? Since it was, what sort of locations did I have in mind for that? Sander helped me think. As he scooted an extra chair towards the desk I minimized the film that was still on pause on the screen and opened my browser. There were a few things that I had already researched. For instance, I knew that the best place to start would be the Nunhead Cemetery. It was a lot less well known than Highgate Cemetery but I had been told that it was a very special place nonetheless, with many worn down and overgrown tombstones. We found a couple of little churches as well, scattered across town, and I was curious to see whether I could get myself close to some abandoned industrial buildings, although that would not be an easy task...

With a little note filled with landmarks and their directions I sat back down on the couch and Sander returned the screen of my computer to its original state.

"What were you watching?" he asked, with his eyes fixed on the still image of the movie's scene.

"Something incredibly beautiful," I sighed. And then the whole story got spilled anyway: the reason for buying the film, discovering baroque music, the viola da gamba and finally the only person known to me who played that instrument... I could not keep my secret to myself and I didn't really care at the moment how hard Sander would laugh at me.

His reaction turned out to be the complete opposite of that. He brushed his hand through his messy curly hair. "It is obvious that you have a problem," he said.

"You could say that, yes..." and again I felt that dull ache while breathing...

Sander did not have a lot of experience with online chatting. Nevertheless his analysis was crystal clear, because how many had not fallen victim to it in this day and age on the internet: meeting a stranger, often brought about by little more than naive curiosity, could in a matter of minutes and under the right circumstances turn into 'not such bad company'. And when given enough stimuli that kept you interested and you felt secure enough in your mutual anonymity it was not difficult to reconvene the next day for a similar kind of conversation. Without ever having to leave the door – in the comfort of your own living room or bedroom. No wonder then that the threshold for entrusting each other with more personal matters faded faster than it would in real life. Neither was it any wonder that conversations of that nature within no time began to feel like an alternative sense of coming home... a welcome variation to the long evenings spent all alone in front of the TV. However, I had an added complication. I had met my online chat partner in real life once, had looked him in the eyes and heard his voice. And when it was already way too late did I realize that out of all people it had been that man that I had been having conversations with for all this time. Pretty intimate conversations in fact. And then the flood gates were opened...

Sander sat down beside me and we evaluated the entire situation one more time. But in the end he could not think of a solution either and was only able to confirm what I had long known: I was madly in love with Aeolus.

"Aww, come here..." he mumbled, and for a while he let me rest my head against his shoulders. What would it be like if it had been that other person whom that shoulder belonged to, if that other person were sitting beside me on the couch right now... would that ever become a reality?

And what would be the consequences of having his acquaintance, in light of the three possibilities that Claire and I had come up with when it came to his true background story? The psychopath, for example. He would most certainly kill me after a moment of romance or at the very least lock me up and during long years filled with all kinds of horror keep me all for himself. And the LARP player, who could be a total let-down in real life, of course... what if Aeolus actually was some unsociable nerd, pretending to be the ideal man online? And finally there was the vampire possibility, which we obviously threw out immediately.

"There is yet another possibility," suggested Sander all of a sudden, "although you're not going to like it..."

"That's alright," I said. "Any new idea could help me move forward."

Carefully my friend then said: "It's possible that Aeolus is stuck in a disastrous marriage to a wife that doesn't understand him..."

I felt a sharp sting in my throat. No. Not him, not Aeolus. Everything inside of me protested against that idea – it just did not make any sense. Because a cheating man constantly twisted the truth, whereas Aeolus' most prominent feature was his consistency. But why then, why on earth make such a big deal out of anonymity – let it go, this was pointless. If I continued like this, I would get tangled up inside my own thoughts. First, take a couple of days' break, away from it all, I was sure that would help. Who knows, maybe afterwards my brain would be cleared up enough to allow me to make a decision. But not right now. At this moment, as always, I could not wait for the evening to come. I must have lost my mind.

*Rhona says:*
*'Why Antoine Forqueray?'*

Aeolus says:

'What do you mean why?'

*'Well, I find his style of music to be completely different from that of Marin Marais. So much so that it would seem that someone who likes Marin Marais could not possibly like Forqueray... but why do you?'*

'Because I recognize a lot of him in myself. Marais and Forqueray were colleagues to one another, but they were also rivals in Louis XIV's court. They were both acknowledged as being *the* viol virtuosos of that time. Marais' compositions and ways of playing were marked by gentleness and kindness. It was impressive how he had found an audience despite the strict musical standards of Versailles. Forqueray, on the other hand, was a horrible man. He abused his wife and children, cheated – he was unpredictable and had a temper... qualities that you could clearly pick up from the way in which he played the viol. For that reason many would compare him to the devil, while Marais was more angelic. The dynamic between those two reminds me of the daily inner conflict that I am dealing with...'

*'I see...'*

'So you immersed yourself in viol music. What do you think about it?'

*'It's hard to put into words... I find it so incredibly beautiful!'*

'Well how about that...'

*'But my opinion is slightly biased.'*

'?'

*'I'm in love with the only viol player I know.'*

'You are what?'

*'You heard me...'*

'Do you think it is realistic to be moved by someone merely through conversations by way of a screen and keyboard?'

*'You know, the cat's out of the bag and that's a big deal to me. So can we let it rest for now? Please?'*

'If that's what you prefer... if we do, I'll leave the ball in your court when it comes to this issue.'

*'Oof... I guess that is no more than fair, I'm afraid.'*

'Rhona?'

*'I'm still here. Give me a minute.'*

'Okay. The thing I like so much about the viola da gamba is that its sound resembles the human voice that closely. That hoarseness, the vague trembling... But what I find even more interesting is that often during a solo this gasping, puffing and groaning sound can be heard. I have no idea why that is. At first I thought it was because of the microphone hanging too closely to the musician, but it seems to come from the instrument itself, as if it were breathing!'

'That's because a spirit lives inside each viol.'

*'As in: it's possessed??'*

'No, of course not, hehehe... The background noises are caused by the bow.

Because it is used in an underhanded fashion the hard part of the bow occasionally hits the strings.'

'Oooh...! I have to keep my guard up with you.'

'You certainly do, and you should know that by now.'

'... And he never breaks character either. Anyhow, back to the music for the time being. You know what piece really gives me goose bumps? Sonnerie de ste. Geneviève de Mont-de-Paris by Marais!'

'Your taste is impeccable. My compliments.'

'By the way, what is your favorite piece by Forqueray?'

'Hold on.'

'Take a listen.'

He sent me a link to a video that was titled *Forqueray – La Couperin / II Giardino Armorico*. While the music played in the background he wrote:

Aeolus says:

'This composition... the way in which Ghielmi and Pianca approach it... it has so much depth. And then to be able to talk to you while this is playing...'

Rhona says:

'One of your moves, I bet.'

'No, I'm being serious.'

'Sure...'

'Pardon me?'

'But you don't want to do anything more than just talk.'

'That ship, I thought, had already sailed.'

'We've discussed it, yeah. Still things could change.'

'You want something more. But that's not going to happen.'

'Give me one good reason as to why that is...'

'The reason, you already know.'

'Is that so? Do you even know what the true driving force behind your reasoning is? How well do you actually truly know yourself?'

'Here we go again with the distrust.'

'Again? That distrust has never left. If you don't get enough information, you automatically start thinking, then your mind fills in the blanks. Like, for example, the two following theories. One: you are unhappily married and cyber-cheat with me but are too much of a coward to admit it. Or two: you have just come out of a relationship but keep bathing in its mud pool of grief and are frozen in place, too scared to take a step towards the future and towards change. Like some sort of Saint-Colombe-character really.'

'I wouldn't act so high and mighty if I were you. Do you honestly think I need to scour the internet for some surrogate girlfriend? I would not need to go such a roundabout way for that, you know.'

'That is such a low thing to say!'

'The truth can hurt sometimes.'

*'You can't be serious...'*
'There are plenty to choose from. Apparently.'
*'Then I don't know what else is there to say...'*
*'Bye.'*

That things could go wrong one day was something I had always known
somewhere in the back of my mind. But this unexpectedly? And in such an
awful way? Was I to blame? Or...?
A paralyzing headache emerged and lingered for days. I vomited, was
sensitive to light and stayed in bed. Claire took care of me and asked me on
several occasions what was wrong. I remained silent – my mind had drawn a
blank, probably as a method of self defence. On Wednesday I finally got out of
bed a little shaky and gathered everything for my trip to London. That
afternoon I found an email in my inbox:

"Rhona,

I'm sorry. Can we talk?

De profundis,
Aeolus."

I wrote back:

"No. Not tonight. Have to get to the station early in the morning. Leaving for
a few days and need sleep. Rhona."

We departed on schedule. At exactly 7:55 a.m. the train carried me along
with hundreds of commuters out of the station heading south. I let the
landscapes, railway stations and cities that I saw outside the window pass
me by like some psychedelic sequence. Hoping for sedation. Hoping to be
shielded from everything, literally everything. I did not want to hear the
people and their pointless chit-chat. I wanted nothing to do with the metallic
noises coming from the mp3-players all around me that were set to too loud a
volume by default. They were not distracting, not predominating enough to
make me forget my thoughts.

It was crowded until we arrived in Brussels but things were quieter on the
Eurostar. The seat next to mine remained vacant and in hopes of something
different I took out my iPod. After mindlessly scrolling past tens of tracks I
lingered on *The Game* by Deine Lakaien. The monotonous, somewhat nasal
bass vocals by Veljanov told a surrealistic tale about a manipulative situation
he had wound up being in with someone and how that person then suddenly
had left him. His response floated somewhere between amazement and

confusion: 'Where have you gone, before morning dew? The game will not end without you...' An unsettling feeling came over me and I quickly looked up a different song.

*Illusion* by VNV Nation was a better choice, probably. I closed my eyes... There was a video on the internet, *Dollface* by Andy Huang. Whoever had come up with the idea to merge that video with this VNV track, I did not know, but it was without a doubt that they deserved a Nobel prize for ingenuity! The way in which the audio and video blended seamlessly: Once upon a time there was a mechanical doll's head.

One fine day that doll's head emerges from a metal box by extending her accordion-like neck. She is mesmerized by a woman's face on the television that hangs in the air a few yards away from her. The longer the doll watches, the more beautiful the woman's face becomes in her eyes, so she begins to apply make-up to herself, exactly like the woman on TV. But every time that she almost resembles that image, the television retracts a little further. The doll lengthens her neck and follows, first determined, then frustrated and finally desperate. Finally, in her obsession to achieve the image in front of her, she extends too far and breaks her mechanical neck.

And the singer sings of 'the world making demands on you' and about 'staying true to yourself'...

It was not because of the music. It was not because of the sentiment behind the lyrics of this song and it wasn't the beauty of the video's imagery either. Nevertheless I curled myself up in my seat and cried.

## 14

## SELF-IMAGE

Oh how a series of fortunate circumstances could make all the difference. The St. Pancras Hostel was located a little shy of one hundred yards from the station, thus even with the exhaustion and the heavy luggage it would be child's play to reach. Then came the rare privilege to recover in a generous amount of warm water with soft, freshly scented foam... the room that I stayed in turned out to have an en suite bathroom. And lastly my roommates perfectly understood the meaning of being considerate to others in a quiet and polite manner during the night.

The next morning I was therefore reasonably able to look outward again and face the change of urban landscape, with its completely different office building than I was used to in my own town – Canary Wharf's.

Despite my renewed optimism I had to admit, however, that this district had something almost a little creepy about it. A claustrophobic pragmatism and lack of character, embodied by concrete and glass and steel, did not just allude to but actually convince you of the fact that working was the only thing that there was to do around here. Work here, but do not live here. Work, but not live. The pinstripe and the two-piece suit dictated fashion here seven days a week – that was guaranteed. But not today, at least not for the full hundred percent, as this particular morning a section of Canada Square would be the set for a photo shoot in order to make colors stand out as a contrast to the futuristic facades of the professional buildings.

When I arrived I checked in with a man wearing a dark-blue jacket with the word 'security' printed on it in bold, white letters. He took me to a small group of people and I introduced myself. A woman studied me from bottom to top, laughed a little as though there was something very funny and turned her head away without greeting me. Another woman gave me a lame, disinterested handshake and told me her name. And then there was a man who introduced himself as Charlie. He turned out to be the art director. They all seemed to try their hardest to out-do one another in terms of creativity and exclusiveness. Feelings of revulsion began to creep up, but I held myself together.

The atmosphere on the set could not be worse. Some props were missing and those who were directly responsible blamed others. Charlie proved to be less resistant to stress as one would expect an art director to be and took it out on the make-up artists while the models were being made up. And those models were still so young... what was there to expect from seventeen and eighteen year-olds when the tension could be cut with a knife. That they would deliver a perfect product like robots? Yes, that was precisely what was expected of them. And when that product was not delivered for even one second, because one of the models did not understand what was being asked of her right from the get-go, all hell broke loose. Charlie threw his arms in the air in a theatric manner and stormed off. Right outside the set, but within plain view where everyone could see him, he paced back and forth while muttering to himself. The model burst out crying, upon which a mildly panicking make-up artist came running while carrying everything that was needed for an emergency touch-up. One of the women of the production team then made sure that the model saw her as she impatiently tapped her watch.

That was the final straw for me. I let my eyes survey the entire circus once more, left my spot from behind the tripod and walked up to the model. I grabbed her hand and made an exaggerated gesture to the people around us to indicate that I needed a ten minute break. With the girl in tow I walked towards the office buildings and found an empty bench by the water. We just sat there for a while.
We did not do much else. Sure, we chatted a bit – initially just me. Then, though first shyly, she did as well. We talked about nothing in particular. Just about general things that interested eighteen year-old girls.
Our break did not last long and after a few minutes we got up again. As we leisurely strolled back to the set I asked: "Your name's Helen, right?"
"Yes."
"Okay, Helen, there's something I've been wondering about. I saw something you did that not all models are capable of: you smoothly change your facial expression with every new pose you strike. How do you do that?"
A little taken aback she answered and I thanked her in a considerate tone of voice.
It worked. Helen had reinvented her confidence and delivered a couple of phenomenal frames. Happy me, happy models, happy everybody.
This made things so much easier for the remainder of that day…

At the end of the afternoon I gathered my things. Helen left happily laughing with some other people before I had a chance to say goodbye and for a second it left a bitter-sweet taste in my mouth as I watched her disappear into the Tube station. A little later when I sat in a squatting position while packing my bag a pair of expensive men's shoes appeared in my field of vision. I quickly got up. A man from today that I only remembered vaguely – we had not even been introduced – looked at me all business-like yet with some interest. He stated his name and told me that he was the magazine's editor in chief. "That means that I'm responsible for what is published in our magazine and what it looks like. Today we had a few hiccups during the shoot, as you have seen for yourself. But I have to say you have greatly contributed to bringing it to a good ending. On top of that I have seen your raw material and they are beyond acceptable. For that reason I would like to ask whether we can book you again in the near future."

Do not come off too eager, negotiate first and then take out my agenda! The next moment I was flipping through the pages of the little book... completely reserved and fairly unaffected, while on the inside as excited as a child.

The Nunhead cemetery turned out to be spectacular. And this sun-drenched Saturday morning proved to have been an excellent choice to visit it. Most Londoners were busy at home or at the supermarket and that gave me the opportunity to shoot photos without any looky-loos and to wander outside the paths when needed to obtain the most beautiful vistas possible.

We Dutchmen were not accustomed to these things: remnants of the old Victorian times were completely foreign to us, let alone any other old features from other historical periods... after all, everything in our overly-organized little country had to be saved from the apparently horrible fate that was called *decay*. Had a tombstone become too weathered? Get rid of it. A factory abandoned? Tear it down and quickly build something new. I knew the reason: the Netherlands was densely populated and thus our small surface area was managed pragmatically. But to even apply that policy to burial grounds...? Perhaps we did not recognize the calming effect that an overgrown tombstone could have on you. Not to mention its symbolic meaning! The deeper meaning one could extrapolate from an antiquated, neglected grave that had been completely overgrown with vines and moss and other plants, or in other words nature... it brought hope, as though there would always be new chances for what had become broken and forgotten in your life. I took a note book out of my bag and wrote down: "Book title: Love & Decay".

Embankment was situated on the northern edge of the Thames and, half an hour after my visit to the cemetery, was well-suited to enjoy a sandwich and a drink. From the Tube station I walked along the waterside for a bit until I found an empty bench to sit on.

Yes, it was beautiful here, and lively as well. To my right trains drove up and down across a bridge towards the south end of the city. A little beyond that, across the river, the London Eye could be seen, and to my left, not that far from where I was sitting, was Cleopatra's Needle, guarded from both sides by life-sized sphinxes resting on their massive pedestals. And further beyond that you could find the Waterloo Bridge. If you looked carefully you could even see the steady flow of slowly moving cars and double-decker buses crawl across it, heading nowhere and – I must keep my mind from brooding! There was absolutely no need to feel depressed just by looking around and doing nothing.

There were joggers each with their own personal choice of music in their ears.

And co-workers – oh wait, it was Saturday – so friends then, who strolled by while engaged in heavy conversation, and naturally there were the tour buses that were busy finding a parking spot by the side of the road to allow larger and smaller groups to get off... hesitant foreigners who waddled with a certain amount of excitement towards the city center one after the other. Curious as to whether the city would meet their high expectations... shit, why was I being so cynical? For once try to stay positive while looking at the things that are around you!

But no matter how hard I tried, what was brewing on the inside began to gain the upper hand over what went on outside...

As such I could not particularly appreciate it when at a certain point a motorcycle parked right behind me and the rider decided to head straight for my bench. While he was getting ready to sit down next me and took off his helmet I discovered to my surprise that he turned out to be a 'she'.

"Is this spot taken?" the woman asked.

"No, go ahead," I said and the woman sat down. She appeared to be around my age. She had long, black hair and within it some bright-blue, skinny braids and her complexion was lightly tanned.

She rummaged through her backpack a little. Took out a plastic container that she opened. Lunch, apparently.

"Enjoy." She nodded towards my sandwich that I was holding, and I replied: "Thank you."

We ate in silence.

"Rough day?" she asked after some time had passed.

I shrugged and stared in the direction of the London Eye. From its cabins that looked like fat larvae a flash could be seen every now and then... not a single clue on proper photography, those tourists with their cameras. "Just had a couple of rough weeks behind me," I finally said, probably as a way to apologize for my somewhat cold first reaction. "But things are a little better now."

"Yeah, depression sucks," she replied. She reached out her hand. "I'm Ashley, but I'm usually called Ash. What's your name?"

I returned her gesture and introduced myself.

"You're not from England, are you?" she noted.

"No, I'm Dutch. I'm here for a week or so," I said.

She took her time to respond, and in some way I thought that was cool.

Ash was a bit of an unusual person to begin with. She had an alternative, slightly tough appearance along with a pair of eyes that looked into the world as though she could not care less about it. But still she had something caring about her, an aura that made you feel at ease...

Ash practiced a wide variety of freelance professions that she made a living with. After having taught a motorcycle class this morning she was now on her way to babysit a couple of pets for some rich people and had decided to have her lunch break here, by the side of the Thames.

After having heard her story I shared mine, I told her what had brought me to London and about yesterday's photo shoot and how well that had gone. Ashley's enthusiasm was reserved, albeit sincere.

"I'm sure that was more than welcome, that little pick-me-up, after going through such a difficult time?"

"Yes..."

"And what now?" she asked.

And now. How should I know. Forget the pain, or ignore it. Or would that be unhealthy, and would things grow crooked on the inside? I spoke these thoughts out loud and before I was completely aware of it I told her about how I had left the church and about my struggle with my faith and the insights I had acquired through my recent conversations with someone.

"Conversations with whom?" Ash asked, but I clamped up and waved my hand dismissively.

Ashley had a gift. She knew when to stop asking questions, and when to take a step back to prevent scaring off the other person. Maybe that was why my initial reaction had not been that of rejection when she told me about *Asylum London.* It appeared that a small group of people got together every Sunday afternoon in the assembly room above a heavy metal pub, to talk about their faith, listen to music and pray... Among them there were bikers, metal-heads, punks, goths, artists and people from the world of BDSM. I asked her what the latter stood for.

"Bondage, Domination and Sado-Masochism," she dryly explained.

"But aren't you Christians?" I asked.

"Yes. Or, at least, most of us are. The thing we have in common is that none of us have found our place within conventional churches. More often than not church members and their leaders haven't a clue how to deal with individuals that look different from themselves. But if you read the Bible carefully, you'll find that Jesus did not discriminate whom he befriended. Be it fishermen, children, widows, rebels, adulterous women or even a bloodsucker like Zacchaeus... and out of all people it was him He wanted to visit for dinner."

Talk about ironic. "So everyone is welcome at the Asylum," I thought out loud.

I could make neither her or myself any promises. But, I said, I would try to stop by tomorrow. If that would be okay, I had asked.

"Why wouldn't it be?" said Ash, "it's on the outskirt of Soho and starts at half past four."

On a piece of paper she wrote down the name of their website, *asylumlondon.com*, the address of the meeting place and her phone number. Then she got up. "I have to go. It's been a pleasure." She smiled and reached out to shake my hand.

I got up as well and we walked to the parking spot behind our bench. "Do you know what they would call this in the Pentecostal church I used to attend? A *divine appointment...*" I said with a slight tone of derision.

Ash shrugged. "I'd rather call it God's sense of humor." She put on her helmet, started her motor and rode away.

As for myself, I left for the hair salon where someone was working whom I had met at the hair and make-up department yesterday. Along with the promised discount she gave me a pitch-black hairdo. With a single streak of purple in the front.

15

ASYLUM


On Sunday the rain came down by buckets full. I stayed inside the hostel.
Read some magazines, made myself a cup of coffee in the communal kitchen
and watched the endlessly repeating news on the television in the lobby. I
was doing pretty well, in my opinion. Even doing nothing did not feel
pointless today. The pain was manageable.
But the one thing that I should not have done, was to check my email. For
when I opened my inbox, the one of the email address that I had specifically
created for Aeolus, it turned out to be empty and that had been more of a
shock to my system than I had expected it to be. From that moment on
everything had felt heavier and by 3:45 p.m. I was glad to get out the door.

At the Tottenham Court Road Underground station I pulled the cords of my
hood as tightly as possible – it was still raining – and looked at the note that
Ashley had given me one more time: 'Walk along Charing Cross Road until
you reach the first left turn, right beside the fountains of a large office
building. That's St. Giles High Street. On number 15, across from the church,
you'll find the Intrepid Fox.'
I rang the bell at the pub's entrance and Ash opened the door. She greeted
me, stoically yet welcoming, and let me in.
I was amazed by the lengths that were gone through just for an hour of
'fellowship'... Four people dressed in black were busy setting up the upstairs
room of The Fox for the meeting. A television set was dragged in and a DVD-
player was connected. Someone laid out a bunch of flyers for non-profit
organizations onto the pool table, and behind another table a guy with a
blond ponytail was doing something on a laptop. When I glanced at the
screen over his shoulder he told me that a couple of people from outside of
London and even from outside the country attended the fellowship through
Skype. He introduced himself to me – it was Sam and I really hoped that I
was going to remember his name.
In the meantime the doorbell rang every so often and others trickled into the
room, each dressed in their own, sometimes extreme, outfit.

What a bizarre assembly this was. The table that we all gathered around was
laden with candy, chips and soda and just as I was secretly wondering whose
money had bought all those things, I saw a rubber skull sitting somewhere,
with a cut-out in the shape of a slot on top... so even the donations box fit the
theme. And I swear, I seriously tried to participate in the conversations and

the snacking, but my eyes kept being drawn to the belly of a guy sporting a mohawk, a fairly chubby guy, and to his T-shirt that read: *Fat people are harder to kidnap...*

Andrew, a typical goth with long, wavy brown hair, recited a sonnet by the Victorian poet Elizabeth Barrett Browning:

*'Earth's crammed with heaven,*
*And every common bush afire with God,*
*But only he who sees takes off his shoes;*
*The rest sit round and pluck blackberries.'*

We held a discussion about the meaning of those words. About the extent to which God reveals Himself through His creation in this day and age. We debated whether only churches had the 'privilege' to experience His loving affection or if His kingdom could perhaps be found in places where people were simply kind towards one another as well. Places where people cared about and looked after each other, where one cared for their fellow human without needing something in return... truly, love could be that simple. When everyone split up into small groups to pray for each other I simply joined in, to my own surprise. And from the tower of St. Giles across the street the first chimes of what was to become a long carillon piece could be heard.

After the meeting had ended we descended into the pub downstairs. I confided in Ashley and told her what Aeolus claimed to be. Her reaction was as levelheaded as always: "My goodness, I haven't been to a meeting of the London Vampire Society in ages... I wonder how they're doing."

In the end a few us went to grab something to eat somewhere in Soho. We got to know each other a little better, I told them about my photo book and out of nowhere a guy and a girl volunteered to model for me and promised to take me to a large, abandoned factory.

No, my visit to London was not pointless in the least. And maybe by the time I returned to the Netherlands I would know what to do with Aeolus...

16

ANGEL

Meanwhile the days rolled into Tuesday. The guy and girl from the Asylum
had kept their word and showed up yesterday at around eleven in the
morning in front of the hostel. In an old beat-up car we had left for an
industrial area that I would never have found on my own. The outfits that
they had brought with them were a total riot, and had even included a
wedding dress. When the guy had then dressed up in a three-piece suit and a
top hat, the party was on. And that was how the idea to capture 'frozen
theatrical scenes' was born.

Up until lunchtime I had spent the day at Camden Lock. Combed through
the market stalls and boutiques that were filled with gothic, metal and
everything-else-alternative for clothing and accessories that were so difficult
to find in my own country. And now, after taking a rest in the afternoon, I did
go out for a bit. It was freezing cold, but there were some things that you just
could not skip out on before embarking on the return trip home: buying
souvenirs for friends, stocking up on those irresistible delicacies that are
unique to England...
Oh man, that cold wind sure felt like a thousand blades hitting my ears. I
should get myself a beanie first before hopping on a random bus – something
I would do at least once during each trip abroad. It was the perfect way to
discover hidden gems throughout the city and, if you remembered what route
number you were on, it was easy to find your way back. I would definitely
recommend it to any tourist that worries about getting lost.
As luck would have it the bus passed through Islington, which meant I got off
after only a couple of stops. This neighborhood had become increasingly
popular with the Young Urban Professionals within the last decades, but had
remained a well-kept secret from the trendy shopper.
An hour turned out to be my shopping limit. My energy was depleted and the
train was going to leave pretty early tomorrow morning. So I thought I had
better grab something quick to eat, catch the Tube and go to bed.

At the Angel Underground Station it was crowded, but I should have seen
that coming. Rush hour in London always lasted longer than those sixty
minutes between five and six and I had no choice but to endure the pushing
and shoving... although that actually came in handy on the descending
escalator: this was without a doubt the longest escalator I had ever seen, and
if the people around me had not been standing so close to me I was sure that

I would have experienced vertigo!

My beanie had become obsolete by now. Clumsily, hoping I would not bump into others, but also keeping an eye out for pickpockets, I tried to put the thing away in my already stuffed bag.

"Aaah, just when you think you're standing firm..." This came so unexpectedly and from so close behind me that I became startled and lost my balance and nearly missed the handrail. "Be careful you don't fall!" the same voice said, now coming from my left. In a flash I saw a head with red-brown hair among the commuters on the escalator rushing down. Déjà vu. A jolt of adrenaline. Was this for real? As soon as I saw an opportunity I moved to the same side of the escalator and joined the descending line of people who walked in front of me, trying hard to not lose sight of what I thought that I had seen. I thought, yes, but... why now? Why here in London? Because of the shock and confusion I almost tripped over my own feet when I reached the solid ground. A corridor, a left-hand bend, another escalator. At the bottom the crowd split up into the northbound and the southbound direction of the Underground. Just in time I saw that the man I was looking for followed the sign that indicated *southbound.*

I cut the line, took some offensive comments in my stride, but managed to gain on the man a little bit. Once we got to the platform I ran out of luck. The train had just arrived and because it was so crowded I was forced to enter a different wagon than the one he did. With a lot of trouble I pushed my way to the little window that separated the two units, but no matter how hard I tried I could not see him anywhere, and to make things worse, at the next stop I hesitated too long to get to the doors before they closed again. At Moorgate Station, however, I was one of the first passengers to get off. Briefly thoughts flashed through my mind like "isn't he long gone by now", and "what if he's still there but gets off at this station?" I made a choice regardless and got onto the other wagon. Here it was cramped as well and I was pushed towards the center of the aisle. I had to watch out for legs and the bags of those who had managed to find a seat, and also watch my own things... With one hand I held on to a pole while my eyes feverishly scanned down the wagon. Had I made a mistake? Had he stayed behind on Moorgate and was I on my way to... who knows where? I turned around and suddenly looked right into the eyes of the person that I had been looking for so desperately. He stood no more than two yards from me – I literally thought that I would have a heart attack!

He, on the other hand, showed no sign of recognition. The train slowed down to stop at Bank Station. People prepared to get off. For a second it appeared as though we would stay on, but at the last moment he headed for the exit anyway.

So the pursuit continued, through the maze of underground corridors, among an auditory and visual cacophony of commuters and tourists. He was a little

taller than me, but not significantly so and that made it difficult to keep track of him. Again his pace was fast and I began to hyperventilate. I never did well being in large crowds... The man appeared to head in the direction of the Central Line, towards the *westbound* platform. There he found a seat on a bench. I hovered around, a little off to the side, a little hidden between the people, but slowly and as stealthily as possible I made sure to shorten the distance between us. A train arrived. People picked up their bags from the floor, got up from their seats along the wall and I braced myself. Now I was going to give it my all to get onto the same carriage as him!
Everyone got on, except Aeolus. And myself.

He had begun to read a newspaper – *Le Figaro,* from what I could see – and ignored his surroundings completely. I sat down at the other end of the bench. Pretended to be a random stranger, pretended to casually look around, let him travel through my field of vision... he was wearing a pair of jeans of which the hems carelessly touched the ground. His shoes were made of black suede. His woolen, gray coat of three-quarter length was open and underneath I spotted a black turtle-neck. And – he wore glasses. With a trendy black frame to complete the ensemble... I chuckled a little on the inside, cynically, but also out of confusion.
We did not speak. And the platform filled with people. Trains filled the tube with their rumbling and came to their screeching stops... At times the two seats between us were occupied and the next moment people got up to disappear again on their way to unknown destinations. This repeated itself and, if nothing specific happened, would probably continue to repeat itself into eternity, until all that you could see was one gray blur of a movie that was played back in fast-forward.
What was I supposed to do? We had talked for evenings on end, over the internet, had managed to touch each other's soul with our words... However, in this moment the only thing I could feel was that distance between us, that same distance as when I had tried but failed to strike up a conversation with him at Schiphol Airport. Without being aware of it I ran my hand over the dragon relief of the tiles on the wall right next to me...
Out of the blue I stated in Dutch: "I know it's you."
Just as any stranger would do, the man looked up from his newspaper and politely asked: "Excuse me?"
"I want some answers. I think I deserve them."
No response. At least, at first. Then suddenly he spoke, cold and business-like and again in English: "Bank is an interchange station of five Underground lines. So there are ten directions to choose from. You'll never be able to figure out where I'm heading."
"We'll see about that," I said. "Of course there is the option to stay put. In that case I will do the same. Until Security shows up and demands an explanation from us as to what we are doing. The other option is to continue

your journey. But you should know that I will follow."

His reaction came surprisingly quickly. He folded his paper in an impatient manner and got up. "We will go for coffee," he said.

In the corporate district of London, a couple of streets away from Bank Station, we found a fast food restaurant. Trembling on the inside I stood beside Aeolus at the counter and watched as he ordered two coffees that came in paper cups. He placed lids on them and grabbed sugar, milk and stir bars. In a quiet corner we sat down at a table across from one another.

I asked: "How did you know it was me on the escalator? My hair is completely different..."

"Because of your scent."

I looked at him in disbelief and the man sighed. "You've put us in a difficult position," he said.

"*I* have? It was you who felt the urge to say something to me just earlier, wasn't it? You even came all the way to England to follow me..."

"I live here, Rhona, in London!" he seethed. He leaned in a little. "You placed the bait in my own territory. Where do you get off thinking that I would not take it?"

I felt my blood rush out from me. "How the heck could I have known that?"

"No. You could not have known. But now we have a huge problem on our plate." He sat and leaned against the backrest of his chair again. "I should have taken a completely different approach from the start," he said quietly. "If I had offered you this cup of coffee at Schiphol immediately, things would have been fine... we would have sat down somewhere, would have talked coyly about little nothings and then I would have taken you to some hotel or another."

"To then leave me with a fake phone number afterwards, I bet, and then disappear for good?"

He looked straight at me. The denial never came.

"And you really believe that?" I asked.

"I've done it before."

"Right, and what am I supposed to do with that?"

"It's not about what I believe, but about what you *do* with it. Child, you are so naive!"

"Naive? Perhaps I am. But I'm not a fool, Aeolus. Our communication may have been a little bumpy so far, but at the same time something has developed between us. And I'm not exactly sure why you said what you just said, but there is no way on earth you really meant it."

Aeolus took off his glasses and rubbed his eyes with his thumb and index finger.

"Having trouble seeing things clearly?" I mocked.

"Transition lenses that darken in sunlight. It's easier than constantly having to put on and take off sunglasses," was his response, at which I cynically looked away.

"No matter what I tell you… it is completely lost on you, huh…" he said, and that startled me. I apologized quickly and to keep the conversation going I challenged him to test my trusting his words.

"Alright," he said as he folded his arms, "let's hear your questions."

"Okay. Um… your written Dutch, it is incredibly good. But we are talking exclusively in English. Why is that?"

Aeolus made a face that made it look like he was thinking about something disgusting. He explained that he did not think his accent sounded Dutch enough. I requested of him to give me a demonstration. He refused, but I insisted and eventually he gave in.

His accent was gentle. And completely indefinable. It had traces of French, and some English, yet not quite either one… and that peculiar emphasis of the letter 'a' at the beginning of the words that he pronounced which I had never heard from anyone… I thought it was beautiful. His manner of speaking created a certain feeling of excitement in me…

"Here, wanna see what I did yesterday?" I said while I brought out my digital camera. Using the preview display I looked for an image that I had shot of my new Asylum friends. I showed him a randomly taken comical photo of the couple.

Aeolus looked at it and smiled. Finally, a smile… "So that's where you three had disappeared off to. I was wondering that morning…"

"What do you mean?"

"If you are in a car I'm not able to track you, so I was wondering where you could have gone to."

"That's impossible. You're bluffing!"

The man looked at me with a deadpan stare.

"Shit. It's true, isn't it? Otherwise you could never have known about the car," I concluded.

He moved the cup of coffee to his mouth. Humans drank coffee. Vampires did not. But the fact remained that he had been watching me closely the entire week, apparently. And I was not sure how I felt about that…

"I take it you know where I'm staying?"

"Yes."

"And what I've been doing?"

"And what you've been talking about with the people around you."

"That last bit is highly unlikely. But tell me – " My cell phone alerted me of an incoming text message. I excused myself and opened it. It was from Claire: "Hi hello, long time no message. Everything alright? Tomorrow when back home again?"

I typed a response that sounded as cheerful as possible: "Sorry. Busy, busy, busy. All is well here. Doing coffee with a friend now. Arrive around noon. Is the weather OK there?"

"… But tell me…, you said," Aeolus continued as soon as I had put my phone in my bag again.

"Eh, right. How did you end up locating me?"

He wiped some sugar off the table and explained that my dropping hints about traveling abroad by train and joking about the name *St. Pancras* had been enough to draw some conclusions. After that he had gone through the Eurostar schedule and had waited at the station in an inconspicuous spot. The second train that arrived around twelve thirty turned out to be the right one, and then the only thing that had remained was watching me drag my suitcase to the hostel.

Another text message came in. Claire had written something funny. I grinned and Aeolus gave me a look. Then he said: "Rhona, you're right. I could sit here and proclaim that I have no interest in you as a person and bend over backwards in my persistence, but – "

" – That has long lost its credibility."

"No... There's just something about you. Something that draws me to you with an enormous force. But whether that means I know what to do with you...?"

"You weren't particularly shy about the latter during our long hours chatting online."

"Yes, but *there* we were somewhat able to protect ourselves against acting recklessly."

"Oh, is that what this is, in your eyes? Then may I ask you why you still pursued this outcome of us sitting here right now at this table."

Aeolus shrugged and without him seeing it, I clenched my fists.

"Listen," I said. "I'm beginning to get sick and tired of your little game of pushing and pulling. *You* were the one who initiated our making contact, so it is up to *you* to provide more clarification. That should be the least of the consequences that you should accept. Don't you think?"

"But I really could not be clearer than I am right now, Rhona!"

And with that the mystery that was Aeolus only deepened further – if I knew what was good for me I should have gotten up and walked out right there and then. Without saying goodbye, without deeming him worthy of one last look. But in that moment I was certain that he knew that that action would be physically impossible for me to do and even if I had managed to get up, he would have stoically followed me out.

I said: "We're going to have to make some sort of decision, Aeolus, because this can't go on any longer."

The next couple of minutes we spent staring. At the few other patrons in the restaurant, at our hands and every so often into each other's eyes – "Come, let's get out of here," he suddenly suggested.

We stood up. I wanted to pick up the empty cups to throw them out, but he beat me to it and as we passed the garbage receptacle and he emptied the tray I noticed that one of our cups had been completely full... with a heavy thud it fell on top of the other waste.

Once outside the restaurant door we stood there a little dazed. Then he said: "I want to show you something."

A wave of relief passed through me. No goodbye then... or not yet, at least.

"But to get there we need to get back on the Underground..."

I indicated that that would be alright and inquired where we were going.

"To the Shad Thames Area."

"Isn't that the neighborhood where the Design Museum is located?"

Aeolus smiled for the second time this evening. We walked towards the Northern Line.

Waiting on the platform consisted of several silent, awkward minutes and on the train heading to London Bridge his eyes were continuously fixed on me, seemingly filled with the determination to figure me out, yet also at the same time so frightfully unreachable. Whereas I needed all my concentration to hide my nervousness...

It was merely the evening air that kept us apart when we left the station and headed east, as Aeolus made sure to maintain a courteous distance. The masculine hand at my back that allowed me to go first, while giving directions, did not even touch the fabric of my coat.

On Tooley Street, after several hundreds of yards, my bag that was full of souvenirs began to feel heavy. I switched shoulders. He offered to carry it for me, but I teasingly said: "How hopelessly old-fashioned..."

His reaction was agitated: "Just give it to me!"

It had long gone dark. After having crossed the Tower Bridge Road we turned left. The streets became narrower and looked more and more deserted after each turn. Right when I thought that I would never be able to find the way back to the station by myself, Aeolus stopped in front of a door of what appeared to be a warehouse that had been converted into apartments. To unlock the door he entered a code – was this where he lived? – and ushered me in. We arrived at an apartment on one of the top floors and he handed me back my bag. He said: "This is my home. Welcome."

He took off his coat and helped me with mine. Turned on some mood lighting. Curiously I looked around the space. It looked organized, except for the coffee table. On it was a pile of carelessly stacked books. There were more books in several cases. Books with old bindings, books with new bindings. The furniture covers of the seating were dark-brown and made of leather and by the window there was an adjustable drawing table with blue and white sheets of paper lying on top, covered with lines and numbers... "I was completely convinced that you were a history teacher..." I said, "but this suspiciously looks a lot more like architecture."

Aeolus had followed me and stood behind me. Not far from my left ear he asked, "So your question is what do I do for a living?"

"Yes," I answered, while I turned to face him. He ignored my body language and walked to the seating area. He sat down and said: "I'm sorry for not showing you the bedrooms. In my opinion it is not appropriate to confront a lady with that on her first visit."

I held my ground. "We were talking about your work," I therefore said in a neutral tone, as I sat down on the couch across from him.

Aeolus elaborated: "Among the things that I do is advise architectural firms."

"Seems a bit dishonest to then turn to me and say that you 'do something with computers'," I quietly noted.

He chuckled and briefly looked into a corner of the living room that I had not yet noticed. In it was a computer screen of at least 21 inches. "... with architectural design software and internet", he claimed. Of course.

I thought out loud: "And what would be the name of your profession in English... architectural adviser, or something?"

With a straight face he answered: "Architectural consultant. You can google it, if you want. But I work as a freelancer and with only that bit of information to go by even a junior detective such as yourself will not get far."

I gave him an exaggerated sigh and knelt down by the coffee table to browse through the large number of books that laid spread out on top of it. In the meantime Aeolus got up and offered me something to drink. He said that he did not have anything specific on hand, but that he would not mind quickly going to the neighborhood shop while I waited here... I declined the offer and convinced him that I would be more than happy to receive a glass of water from the tap.

The books on the lowered table were, unsurprisingly, all about gardening, types of grass, insects and biology... I did not open them.

The restlessness that coursed through my body made me get up and look for the kitchen, from where I heard him rummaging. Once there I saw him washing some glasses. My eyes landed on two plastic bottle containers that were standing in a corner on top of the kitchen counter. One was green and the other was red. The labels read: 'Stain remover for grass', 'Stain remover for blood'.


We had returned to the living room. "So somehow we arrived at this point after all," Aeolus mused, "of you sitting across from me, in my own home... how surrealistic."

I asked: "We had already made eye contact at Keflavík Airport, remember?"

"So you know that person was me. How long have you known?"

I shrugged. "But eye contact alone couldn't possibly be the only reason for leaving a note in the pocket of my jacket," I determined.

"That's right. Partially, at least. The other reason was because of the things you talked about with your roommate on the plane..."

And again my skepticism gained the upper hand. A statement like that could go either way. Aeolus changed the subject and said, again in a pensive tone, how fascinated he had been by watching how I had made the decision to allow that insecure model a time-out and offer her encouragement.

"Do you know her?"

"No."

"But you spoke with her, after the event, or something?"

"Neither. I listened in on your conversation."

I shook my head.

"And what sort of thought processes had occupied your mind to make you reach out to the heavens again at The Fox?"

"No. There's no way you could know all this..."

Or was there? Had he attended the Asylum meeting online through Skype...? But even so, we had broken up into scattered small groups for the prayer session and there was no way that a computer's microphone could... I became more and more puzzled.

"Where were you at that moment?" I asked.

"Outside, in the garden of the St. Giles. And no, church bells do not interfere with my listening ability."

"This is insane. There *must* be an explanation for this, because otherwise – "

He stood up. "And that explanation, I'm doing my best to give it to you," he said. He made an impatient, or rather helpless gesture. "The thing is that I don't know how to do that without giving you too big of a shock... oh, whatever... I'll just..." and he left the room.

He had returned almost immediately, carrying with him a viola da gamba and a bow. He pulled the desk chair away from the computer, sat down and said emphatically: "This... is the reason why I brought you here, what I wanted to show you," and that was the first time in my life that I heard the 'live' tones of the so complicated composition of Le Tourbillon.

Aeolus played them with such speed, aggression and beauty that captured my bewildered ears. The musical translation of the whirlwind that I provoked him with the other day in such a sneering manner...

He kept his eyes closed, but I felt that I could see straight into his soul nonetheless. And the tension that arose, made up of frustration and passion, combined with his musical virtuosity, created an almost tangible electric charge in the air that surrounded us. The piece was repeated. And repeated again. His playing became sloppier and, not knowing what to do, I just sat there, captivated by my fascination for him – suddenly he lifted his eyes. There was something sweltering in his gaze when he looked at me.

However, I had not anticipated the nod with which the man tilted his head slightly to the side, as you only see in predators, and in that moment his voice sounded through the music with a ferocious undertone: "Rhona, get your bag *right now* and get out of here! I don't know for how much longer I can control myself..."

With a suppressed shriek I jumped up. Coat and bag under my arm, don't look back, get out of this house. I hit the light switch in the stairwell and began to run down the stairs. I had been such an idiot! The truth had been presented to me, in every which way – I just had done fuck all with that information!

I did not make it further down than two flights of stairs. The music had stopped. It was followed by the noise of an instrument being thrown to the floor and within an instant Aeolus was there, standing in a slightly hunched forward attack stance to block my path. An uncanny smirk slid onto his face as he wrapped his arm around my waist and escorted me back to his apartment. He purred: "Where were you going, precious? The night is still so very young…"

The door was locked. I was propped up against the wall in the hallway. He placed his hands to the left and right beside my shoulders onto the spotless white wallpaper and with his cold breath he whispered into my ear: "Did you forget to look up what my name means? Aeolus, it's Greek for 'keeper of the wind – the swiftly moving, the temperamental…' I must say I expected more from you." Briefly his lips brushed mine. I turned my face away and all I could gasp was: "I don't get you. There are so many others – why *me* of all people?"

His voice was nearly inaudible: "Your fear, chérie, I smelled your fear!"

Then came the hand that stroked my hair, moved it to the side and finally the bite.

The pain in my neck only lasted for a few seconds. At first his teeth felt as cold as ice and then a draining, pulsating warmth went through my body. By now I felt I was weakening and asked: "Why? Tell me, why," but the oncoming loss of consciousness carried me away into a dreamlike void, in which perceptive notions became more and more unobtainable. In the distance the last thing I heard him say was: "… can't help it. It's in my nature…"


END OF PART I

# PART II

*THE ONE DUTY WE OWE TO HISTORY*
*IS TO REWRITE IT*

Oscar Wilde

## 17

DREAM

The borderland between sleeping and awakening was a vast and disturbing no man's land uninhabitable to man. I had no business being here either. But every attempt to escape it felt like running through a plain that was filled to the chest with water. My will power drove me to keep going forwards, but my body was held back, surrounded and imprisoned by invisible forces... and to be in such a state right now could not have been more inopportune.

There was a dream that I wanted to return to, that I needed to find again. There was something important hidden inside, a mystery that I had to solve. Not a mystery as portrayed in British detective series on TV, nor was it anything like, for example, secret initiation knowledge to some sort of witch coven – no, this problem appeared to have everything to do with myself... But how was it possible for me to be able to contemplate on this so consciously? Did this mean that I was not asleep anymore? That I was awake? Oh no, please, no – I had to retrieve that feeling again, that sense of the presence of that person... a person without a face. Or had it been a face with no name?

I tried to lie as still as possible, knowing that if I were to turn around right now, everything would have been for nothing. Ultimately any movement in bed could result in completely new landscapes invading your inner world and so I gave it my all to focus on myself and the other person...

I could have sworn that we were acquainted. Yet at the same time we were not. And I saw a computer screen. Words. Conversations. What kind of conversations? My curiosity increased and seamlessly transitioned into the mutual interest that encompassed those online conversations. A desire emerged to get to know the other person, down to the essence of his being, even. But who was he? How did we start communicating? Why was there such a feeling of intimacy during our conversations through the screen, and why did such an impenetrable cocoon of timelessness unravel around us the more we shared with one another? Hours, days and weeks lost their meaning during our chat sessions and the outside world turned into a hindrance that for reasons yet unknown to me, even felt a little bit like a threat...

Aeolus and Rhona. Rhona and Aeolus. That is what we called each other. And slowly but surely this Aeolus began to accumulate a profile. Auburn hair, gray eyes... I saw a collection of character traits in a devastatingly beautiful face, but with each single trait came a flip side, although I did not understand why.

The scenery changed. The warmth of my living room was traded for the harsh wind on the north bank of the Thames river in London. I was sitting there, in the cold, behind my computer. And on the other side, just to the left of the

Tower Bridge, he sat right in front of a building that was called *Butler's Wharf.* Again, or rather still, we were caught up in an intense conversation online and a certain level of frustration existed between us. Aeolus got up and began to shout things at me. His message was important, apparently, because he put his hands to his mouth and alternated his yelling with performing wild gestures of his arm. But no matter what he did, I could not understand him. The wind scattered his words and in the background another sound could be heard, a sound that resembled a deep growl. Then, what came as a shock, I saw a creature that I had never seen before, but that most definitely possessed the characteristics of a predator, appear behind my friend.

I wanted to warn Aeolus about the oncoming danger, but no sound could escape my throat. I gasped for air as I saw how the monster now approached him with a speed like lightning, threw him to the ground and inflicted several bites... to then completely merge with the man!

The next moment I was standing on the Tower Bridge. It had become evening by now. About fifty yards away from me stood Aeolus. He beckoned me and I began to walk. It was not until I was just in front of him that I discovered the long canines in his mouth... "Why didn't you listen to me?" he asked in a seductive tone. "Don't you know it's too late for warnings now?" And I, I stood there. Paralyzed, will-less. Then he took me in his arms, forcibly turned my upper body to the side and planted his cold teeth in the skin just below my skull.

The bed in which I found myself was enormous. I lay between cold and damp sheets and seemed to have been sleeping, but now I screamed myself awake. My hands instinctively swatted at my neck as though trying to thwart a creeping insect.

Somewhere in the background I heard a voice say: "Time to wake up."

My eyes opened and I realized that the nightmare had not yet ended, because there he was, too close for comfort, hovering above me. The person whom I thought was my friend. However, he turned out to be something completely different: a creature inherent with extreme danger! By reflex I sidled to the right, away from this threat, only to immediately feel a hand on my shoulder and my hip that relentlessly pulled me towards him.

"Come to your senses, Rhona," I heard, "before you hurt yourself!"

Restrained in a militaristic hold I lay with eyes wide open staring into his for a moment. Discombobulated I experienced becoming aware of completely regaining consciousness. Something changed inside my muscles, to which Aeolus' grip instantly reacted. "Would it please be possible for me to let you go now?" he asked in an almost begging tone. I nodded.

Visibly relieved he sat down in a chair that stood close to the bed's headboard. During the silence that followed I became aware of my surroundings little by little. I saw heavy, eggplant-colored curtains, closed shut. In the semi-darkness I could vaguely make out that a single art poster hung on the white walls and across from me there was a dark wooden wardrobe. The linen that I lay between was made of a smooth fabric. Satin? And to the left, approximately by the foot end, there was a door. Where would I wind up if I…

"It seemed as though you were never going to stop dreaming…" the man said softly. Timidly I looked to the side. His chair was upholstered with dark-brown leather. Where had I seen that before…?

"That door leads into the living room."

"What living room?" I asked with a squeaky voice.

"Of my apartment. You're in London. Surely you remember that much?" He leaned forwards and brought his hand to my forehead. The skin of my face made a twitch upon his brief touch. He pursed his lips and turned his head away. The reason for this he did not share.

## 18

ILLUSION


London. That's right, I was going to go there, yes... to do a photo shoot or something. I was going to stay there for a week, I remembered. And he was the person with whom I came into contact through the internet a short time ago.

"How long have we known each other?" I asked, while I did my best to sit up.

"Since the fourteenth of February," he answered, while he helped me prop up the pillow behind me.

"And what day is it today?"

"Wednesday."

It was difficult for me to get my thoughts straight. Wednesday. There was something about this day. It is somewhere around the first or second week of March. But – suddenly I remembered. My week in England had come to an end and I was supposed to catch the train home today! But why was I still here... and what time was it anyway? I checked my watch and was shocked. It was past ten. My train had already left three hours ago! And my luggage was still at the hostel. I jumped out of bed, but that deed was punished with extreme dizziness. It turned black before my eyes, I lost my balance and immediately Aeolus was there to catch me. "That... was too sudden," he said as he helped me sit down on the edge of the bed. Gently, yet quite assertively, he pushed my head downwards, between my legs.

After a while I pushed his hand away and slowly sat up. I looked around me searching. As though having read my mind he noted: "Your shoes are at the foot end of the bed, next to your bag. But before you begin to move about again, I want you to tell me how you feel first."

Miserable, to be honest. And tired. "Hungry," I said.

My friend smiled. "In that case I will need your help, I'm afraid. It's not very often that I have a Dutch beauty for company... let alone that she wants to have breakfast in my home. How about we make a little grocery list? Then I'll go to the corner store in a bit."

"But... I still don't quite understand what I'm doing here."

Aeolus' answer to that began with a rhetorical question. About our online conversations. Whether I recalled how I had given him several cryptic hints as to where I was planning to go this week.

Yes, that I still remembered.

Well, he then told me, due to the bizarre coincidence of his living in this city he had the opportunity to wait for me at the station and find out where I was staying. On the last day of my stay he had finally decided to meet me. And

then we had gone for coffee near Bank Station. After that we had come here
and for no apparent reason I had suddenly fainted. Perhaps I had
overexerted myself during the past few days. Or I had caught a cold…
Sheepishly I looked at the man. Clearly there were some gaps in my memory,
but not in his. I should consider myself lucky to have fallen ill while being at
a friend's house – I had no idea what I would have done if this had happened
somewhere in the middle of the street…

Now, however, I had to take care of a couple of things. Once I had finished
those, I would really feel at ease. Thus I asked him to hand me my bag and
took out my cell phone that had the hostel's number saved in it. I inquired
about my luggage and ended the call with a sigh of relief.
"Do you have Wi-Fi?"
Aeolus gave me a sarcastic look. Yes of course he had access to the internet.
What did I need it for?
"My return trip…" I replied.
Aeolus reached out his hand, which I refused. Carefully I got up. He led me
into the living room and picked up a pen and a note pad. "I want to discuss
your return trip only after you've had something to eat," he said. "Sit down
over here." He gestured towards the lounge area. He himself remained
standing, leaning with his back against the door that led into the hallway.
I did not stay put for very long in the spot that was assigned to me. I got up
and walked back and forth a little, all the while being followed by his eyes. I
was hoping that my body language would make him believe that pacing
around a room helped me to think better.
Some things I recognized from last night. The drawing table by the window.
The cabinets filled with old and new books…
"I have to go pick up my luggage in a bit."
"I'm sure your luggage will be fine," he reassured me. "But first your
breakfast. What do you usually eat in the morning?"
"Ummm… nothing in particular. Some bread, coffee…" I had walked to the
window.
"You're going to have to be more specific. I'm not an expert on this at all."
"Don't you ever have breakfast?" I asked. It was difficult for me to make my
voice sound teasingly; Aeolus seemed to have some sort of force field around
him with which he sometimes attracted and other times repelled things that
were around him. The range of this force field varied significantly, but at the
moment it reached to where I was standing and I had a hard time coming
across as feeling comfortable.
"Why don't we go to the store together?" I suggested. That would be a great
way to get some air and give me the opportunity to see the exact location of
this apartment. I had already figured out that this street ran parallel with
the river. That was because you could look straight into a cross street and at
its end, beyond the converted warehouses and modern, white buildings, a

ship passed by every now and then...

Aeolus' response sounded hesitant. He was not sure whether it would be wise for me to come with him at this moment. It would be easy for him to pop in and out, it would not take more than a minute or five.

"To then come home with whole coffee beans while you don't even own a grinder?" I objected. Oh how sharp witted I thought I was... especially when I saw him shrug. He admitted that he indeed was the stereotypical bachelor who never had anything decent to eat around the house.

"Shall we go then?" I suggested, afraid that he would change his mind.

"After you, young lady," he said, and with one elegant swoop he cleared the path for me.

As soon as I set foot in the hallway, however, it hit me in the face like a swarm of disorientated bats: flashbacks to the nightmare I had earlier! About teeth that looked for my neck... of charm that could kill.

"The toilet, I have to quickly go to the toilet first," I mumbled.

A brief nod pointed me towards the bathroom. Once inside I looked in the mirror and immediately received the next shock: dark circles surrounded my eyes, my mouth was defaced by a bright-red smudge... I had slept without removing my make-up first! And Aeolus had seen all of that. What would he think of me??

Using some warm water and soap I washed my face as carefully as possible and for a split second, even though I felt ridiculous doing it, I inspected my neck.

Of course there was nothing to discover there. There was not even a trace of pain to be found as I gently ran my fingers over my skin.

After a final splash of water to my face and a stroke through my hair I considered myself to be decent enough to go out in public.

The fresh air outside was soothing. It was partly cloudy and Aeolus had put on glasses. They looked good on him. But anything would probably look good on him.

I looked down the cross street that I had just looked out unto from the window and discovered that one of the white buildings further down was the Design Museum. I could hardly contain my amazement.

"Now do you understand how strong the effect is that you have on me?" I heard him say, "Last night I told you what neighborhood I live in and in your innocence you immediately mention a building that I happen to be able to see from my window... somehow you manage to keep doing that."

I lifted my eyebrows.

"What street is this?"

"We're on Gainsford Street. That there in front of us is the street that this neighborhood is named after, the Shad Thames." We made a right turn. "And at the end you can see Tooley Street. If you take another right turn there you'll end up at London Bridge."

"But – last night it felt like it wasn't all that easy to get here." I slowed down my pace. "It feels like we took a detour that time…"

Aeolus stopped walking. "Guilty as charged," he said. He stuck out his hands towards me while holding his wrists close together – the shackled hands of a convict. I knew that I was expected to smile now. And so I did, albeit insincerely. He grinned and asked: "Or didn't you appreciate the scenic route through my environs?"

"I did, but – " That's where our conversation ended. We had arrived at the grocery store and Aeolus held the door open for me.

I stepped inside and had to suppress a shriek of surprise. Because even though I had always found supermarkets in foreign countries to be fascinating, this one was exceptionally wonderful. "What kind of place…" I quietly wondered. Despite the small dimensions of the shop, they carried literally *everything* here. From organic products to ready meals, from magazines and travel plugs to gourmet delicacies…

Aeolus walked up to me from another aisle. He had heard me and asked if everything was okay. I clarified that I had never seen a local shop quite like this, in which both sticky mass-produced bread *and* four types of rye bread could be found.

"Yes, that sounds about right," he said. "The shops in this area have tailored their assortment to the local population quite nicely."

"Really? In what way? What kind of people are they?"

"High-maintenance. Spoiled," was his response. I cracked up laughing. He did not laugh but continued to tell me that most locals were successful professionals. Who earned a huge salary and were always chasing the next step up on the corporate ladder. In addition, there were a lot of expats around here: foreigners who came to work for a couple of months to a few years at most in banking, for example, in The City across the river. I wondered whether Aeolus was part of that group of successful professionals. "To the outside world, absolutely," he dryly said.

"And why did you choose to come here?"

"The neighbors leave you be. Things are wonderfully anonymous here…"

"Or lonely…" I reasoned.

The silence that followed was awkward, but did not last long. "… Anyway, let's not forget what we came here for. Are you almost finished?" Aeolus asked, and for a second he looked completely helpless the way he stood there in the center of that aisle. Could he not even estimate how far along I was in putting together my breakfast by taking a quick glance at the contents of my shopping basket? He was so odd…

We paid at the cash register, walked out the door and, to my annoyance, I noticed that I had trouble keeping up with my friend. When we got back to the apartment I was even considerably out of breath… In spite of that, I suggested, immediately after eating, to head out again and go recover my luggage.

"Very well, go get yourself ready, I'll pull up the car. The door locks behind you automatically."

Aeolus had almost disappeared from the room when I stopped him. "Are you crazy? Drive through the heart of London by car? Why don't we just take the Tube?"

A crooked grin appeared on his face. "I've had a sneaking suspicion for a while now that there was something masochistic about you... okay, if you think you can make it to the Underground station by foot..."

"Never mind," I grumbled.

And at the hostel my dignity took another punch: I was already halfway in the process of retrieving my luggage that was waiting for me behind the front desk, when the words 'not today' stopped me dead in my tracks. Before I could out any form of objection, Aeolus was on his way outside with my suitcase in his hand.

Still, I was happy to be able to slide into Aeolus' generously proportioned bed moments later for a much needed hour of rest. I was simply exhausted. And for me to continue to deny that... he was right, I had probably caught a bug or something... we still had to discuss my return trip to the Netherlands. Must not forget when I wake up...

But first, sleep...

19

PROPOSITION

The ringing of a cell phone suddenly woke me up.

"Hello." Aeolus' voice sounded hushed, but clear. "Speaking. ... No, not at all. ... Oh, that's good. So you had been right all along about that fund. ... Certainly. What matters most is that they agreed to pay. ... We frequently hear that, yes. Some municipalities have quite the reputation, sadly. ... An appointment and a primary survey on site. ... No, I won't be able to accommodate you on such short notice. I'm fully booked this week. ... Certainly. ... Alright, then I will look forward to your call. ... If you give me a window of about ten days, I'll see what I can do. ... Yes, to you as well. Until then."

With a groggy head I got out of bed, upon which I discovered that it was almost 6 p.m. I got dressed and opened the door into the living room, where Aeolus' was sitting on the couch with his feet up.

"Are you busy with work? I hope I'm not interrupting you or anything," I asked.

He told me that I was not and that he himself had slept for a bit. He immediately asked whether I wanted anything to eat. The same way of speaking as during our chat conversations of not even a week and a half prior, when we had still been a world apart.

And now...

Now it was half an hour later and we were sitting in a small restaurant, right beneath the Tower Bridge. He stared at me and I looked out of the window. The underside of the bridge that was diagonally above us was constructed with steel beams that had ridges upon which a couple of pigeons shuffled about. I made a fairly pointless comment about it...

Luckily the waiter came quickly. We ordered, Aeolus a salad, and I a somewhat more elaborate meal.

When we were alone again he said: "I don't fall in love easily."

I wrapped my hands around the cold glass of my drink.

"Quite the opposite even..."

I stared at the lemon wedge that floated in my mineral water.

"But I have feelings for you, Rhona. And it's been a long time since that last happened to me."

I picked up the piece of fruit between my thumb and index finger and began to squeeze it into my drink.

"Do you understand what I'm trying to tell you?"

"I do…" I said, without looking at him.

"But do you believe me?"

"Eh… I think so, yes… but I've only known you for such a short time…" The lemon wedge was completely used up by now. Still I tried to squeeze out a few more drops. "And to talk about this here, so suddenly…" I mumbled.

"Even so, I feel that it is important for us to make certain things discussable," my table partner said, "since you have feelings for me as well. It's obvious by everything that you do. May I ask you what your calendar looks like for the next week?"

Astonished I looked up from my glass. My calendar… that term was much too official-sounding for the little amount of plans I had. At least for the upcoming days being home…

Suddenly I exclaimed: "Shit, *shit*! I completely forgot to call Claire!"

Hurriedly I looked for my phone, but Aeolus made a calming gesture. "Don't panic. Take a few calm breaths first."

I did as he advised. Then he began to instruct me: "Call her now, but keep it short. Say that you have received another photography assignment and that you'll be staying for another week. Say, till Thursday."

I nodded and walked outside. I felt relieved that Claire did not answer her phone — she was probably still at work — and I left the exact message that was dictated to me on her voicemail. When I got back to the table he was looking at something across the water. I waited until our eyes met. Then I slowly asked: "How do you do that?"

"How do I do what?"

"What you just did. You coolly tell me what to do and I actually obey."

"You are free to do what you want."

"So if I get on the train tomorrow morning, you're okay with that?"

"Of course."

"Hmmm…"

"Hmmm, what?"

Silence.

"I take it that you want to go home?"

I looked pensive. "I don't know…", I said, and that was the truth. I really did not know what to think, but Aeolus hardly seemed fazed by my indecision: "Should you decide to stay, there is something you need to know," he said. "You're welcome to stay at my house. One hundred percent. Having said that, I think of it as my responsibility to make sure that you quickly recover. In fact, until that happens I don't think I can let you go."

I needed a second to digest that.

"The added tension between us, however, makes it inappropriate for you to stay at my apartment any longer than is strictly necessary."

Puzzled I looked at him.

"Rhona, I would like for you to be my guest for another week… but stay at a hotel."

I immediately responded: "*That* changes everything!"

"Good. Tomorrow we'll reassess your state of health and then we'll go from there. Only you can't go back to that miserable hostel."

Miserable.... interesting choice of word. I asked what was so wrong about the Youth Hostel Association and his reaction seemed sincerely astonished: "Nobody who makes a moderate living would set foot in there, would they?"

I laughed at him. "We could hold long discussions on that topic, but beware, I would win them, guaranteed."

But he kept a straight face and declared: "Since I will be paying, that won't happen."

Our meals had arrived, a great excuse to quietly prepare for my objection. A few minutes later with both an empty plate in front of us, I informed him that I would not accept any money from him.

"We'll get back to that later," was his brief response. And that was the end of that, apparently.

We got up. In a nonchalant gesture he planted ten pounds on the counter and walked toward the restroom.

Once we got outside I did feel a bit guilty over my attitude. "Shall we go for a little walk?" I asked, in an attempt to set a different tone. To which Aeolus agreed.

Shortly beyond the restaurant's patio, below the block of houses to our left, there was a narrow passage way that led down to the water. I instantly recognized it. In my dream, this is where Aeolus had been sitting. This is where he was attacked by that monstrous creature and had become one with it in a horrific manner... And there, on top of the Tower Bridge, he had been beckoning me... I shivered. After forcing myself to get over that awful memory, I stepped out onto a mooring dock. From a short distance I looked at the facade of an immense building in front of me. "So that's the illustrious Butler's Wharf..." I said.

He had followed me onto the landing and now stood beside me with his hands in his pockets. For a moment he observed the different windows with me, some were back-lit, some were dark. But soon we began to move again upon his initiative and as we strolled along the dock he told me: Butler's Wharf had once been the largest structure of warehouses by the Thames. It had been built in 1873 and for many years functioned as a distribution center for coffee, tea, spices... until it was abandoned and closed around 1971. "And now the crème de la crème of London lives here" concluded Aeolus with mocking emphasis.

"Hang the rich..." I retorted.

"Aaah... *Somewhere Down The Crazy River*... when they still made real music," he chimed in, and spontaneously I touched the sleeve of his coat. In terms of physical contact that was all there was to it that night. Passers-by definitely saw us as colleagues or as two friends at most. But we were in love and I greedily ingested every second that we spent together.

We wandered past the Design Museum and crossed the small street that this neighborhood was named after. Two, three and four levels above ground there were some sort of pedestrian bridges that in some places connected the apartments to the left to the ones on the right. In the olden times used to transport goods from warehouse to warehouse, now functioning as balconies.

"This has all really been converted beautifully... You could have lived here as well, right?"

"Perhaps."

"But you won't."

"I don't necessarily need to be in a front row seat. It is much quieter where I live."

"Despite this being a pedestrian area?"

"That doesn't mean anything. Do you know how many movie scenes and music videos are filmed here each year and how much of a nuisance that is? No, at least I'm able to walk out the door without any trouble..."

"But in reality your motive is completely different... You simply don't want to be associated with the cream of the crop," I said, and in reaction to my teasing, Aeolus made a playful lunge at me. I dodged him while laughing, but suddenly everything was overtaken by a scooter with a broken exhaust pipe that passed by – and a bomb inside my head exploded. My first reaction to the eardrum-piercing ruckus was to curse and curse loudly. At the same time I pressed my hands to my ears. The pain...! No, no pain... or was it, my brain – my head, my *head*! Make that moron go away, please! Make him get lost... no, he was already gone, where did he go? Where am I? That pounding in my head... Bewildered, I stared at the person that stood beside me.

Aeolus, right, Aeolus... we had been talking, but about what, for heaven's sake? With difficulty I began to realize the where, what and how of this moment and became aware of the horrified look that my friend gave me... He must have been shocked... clearly I was nowhere near being my old self yet.

20

TRACEUR

The next morning I felt much better. I had a good night's rest and what
happened in the evening was left for what it was. After taking a hot shower I
had put on my black and mint-green argyle dress and some black tights that
I had bought in Camden. The difference that new clothes and a well-groomed
appearance could make... I almost felt completely fit again.
Apparently Aeolus had noticed this as well. From his chair he followed my
every move, during as well as after I had finished breakfast. Appreciation
and endearment were written all over his face, but I could not manage to feel
flattered. His attention only made me painfully aware of my imperfect self.
"Cheater," my lips mouthed silently while I was blow drying my hair into
shape. One day I would defeat him, reverse the roles and – out of nowhere
Aeolus turned his head towards the window. He sat up straight and his facial
expression changed. "Boy, you sure are on guard!" I joked after I had turned
off the hairdryer, but he was not paying attention to me anymore. Under his
breath he said something in a language that I did not understand and he
looked alarmed when he got up and ordered me to stay in the room. Right
when the man walked into the hallway, the doorbell rang. Whatever took
place there was hidden from me, because he had closed the door behind him,
but I was still able to hear a thing or two. The front door opened and Aeolus'
voice sounded more high-pitched than usual, almost shrill even. He said:
"Père..." Someone else said something in return, in French, and there was
some talking back and forth. Much of it I could not understand, but there was
one thing the other reacted with that I could clearly pick up. He asked:
"Raph, qu'est-ce que tu fait?" The visitor had to have an animal with him,
because I suddenly heard some growling or huffing... of a dog?
My curiosity became satisfied after the door to the hallway opened. A pet was
nowhere to be seen when Aeolus and a blond guy came in, he appeared to be
in his early twenties, maybe twenty three or something near to that.
I was introduced to him. His name was Egare. With outstretched arm he
reached out his hand to me and our eyes briefly met.
Aeolus explained how he knew me as a photographer from the Netherlands
and that I was visiting London for some photography assignments. In the
meantime by using gestures he insisted we sat down as he grabbed the office
chair from behind the desk. With its back rest turned in front of him he sat
down on it.
"Egare... that sounds French. Where are you from?" I asked the boy, putting
the hairdryer on the coffee table.

"Paris. I live in Paris," he answered. I was actually able to distinguish the soft, French accent in his English. And again he barely looked at me while talking. Yet I felt as though he most definitely was curious about me. As I was about him... what kind of person was this? Was he a friend of Aeolus? He could not be a business acquaintance, because he was not dressed for it. The jogging pants, sneakers, the fitted T-shirt and the sports jacket wrapped around his waist gave away that he preoccupied himself with entirely different affairs.

He carried almost nothing with him, only a tiny, flat backpack and around his upper arm a cell phone, attached by Velcro.

"Egare is a *traceur,* Rhona," Aeolus explained, after which he took a moment to wait for my reaction. Because surely he knew that I would then ask what kind of person that was. While I listened to my friend's description I noticed how the boy looked me up and down. He had dark eyes, brown, if I was not mistaken.

"A traceur is someone who practices *parkour,* which is also called *freerunning.* It's a phenomenon that finds its roots in the suburbs of Paris. You've seen those tv commercials with people running and rolling over walls and bike racks, right? They jump from rooftop to rooftop, and such - "

'– *JA, JA, SO BLAU, BLAU, BLAU BLÜHT DER ENZIAN...*' Someone was calling Egare. As Aeolus looked away annoyed Egare grabbed his cell phone and turned it off. And then he simply provided an addition to the information that Aeolus had just given: "Parkour is a movement discipline that was made popular by David Belle. It's a method to get yourself from point A to point B as quickly and efficiently as possible, over, under, past or through architectural elements that others have learned to avoid. Being a traceur means, among other things, to reclaim your natural or unnatural surroundings and to learn to use your body optimally."

With a flat hand Aeolus slapped his thigh: "See, only an expert can explain it so well," he said.

I smiled shyly. It was true that I had never even heard of this sport... at least, not of the name 'parkour'. One thing I could vaguely remember were some shots in a television car show of a race against two running teenagers, cutting right through a major city somewhere in England... I asked: "Is there a way in which a traceur could make money with what he does? By teaching, or something?"

Egare responded, but did not look at me as he did so: "Your friend asks intelligent questions," he said to Aeolus. I did not get the chance to continue talking about this subject, because my friend went out of his way to praise my sharp-wittedness and then immediately began to make small talk.

Perhaps I had missed something. Perhaps my presence was the reason why a real conversation never really took off... it was a possibility. After all, it was never the intention for me to be staying here... Therefore I picked up the hairdryer from the table and said: "Well, I have a bunch of things to do. So do you guys mind if I, uh…?" I pointed towards the bedroom. The boy's mouth widened into a courteous smile and Aeolus remained silent. He looked at me with big puppy eyes. Could he be feeling let down?

Once I was alone I quickly grabbed my mp3-player and turned it on loud enough to not be tempted to listen in on the two of them in the living room. For a moment I was trying to figure out what to do with myself. I decided to empty out my suitcase and re-pack it. Threw out some unnecessary stuff. But that did not take more than fifteen minutes. So I sat down again, at the foot end of the bed. In front of me there was a large poster on the wall. It was a reproduction of a painting… two men, sitting on a marble bench, both naked, with nothing more than a sheet of fabric draped around their hips and shoulders. Between them was a round, stone ornament that functioned as a frame around an idyllic scene. The word *Idylle* was actually marked on the stone bench underneath the men, as well as the identifier *G.K. 1884*. And within the round frame a red-haired woman sat squatting, again half-naked, loosely dressed in a similar sheet of fabric. She was holding up a bowl for two small children… whether they were looking into it or drinking out of it was not quite clear to me. But what intrigued me the most was the difference between the two men. The one on the right seemed to observe you, the spectator, and the white piece of fabric around his shoulder reminded me a little bit of an angel's wing. The figure on the left, on the other hand, had a completely different personality. With folded legs and his chin resting on his hand and arm he was deep in thought staring into space. Or was it nothing more than disinterest? Strange how, despite these differences, when it came to their looks the men seemed to be exactly the same… I was just busy wondering whether I knew this painting from somewhere, when the door was opened and Aeolus stuck his head in. "I'm sorry, but you did not respond to my knocking…" I stood up and followed him into the living room.
"And now, back to business," he said relieved.
Egare had left. "Where do you know that boy from, by the way?" I asked.
"Oh, from France…" was the reply, but with such little information I was not satisfied. So I pried for more: "Those surprise visits are the best, huh?"
"Well, that's typical for Egare. He's in the area and then he stops by unannounced. His first visits never last very long…"
"So he will be in town for a while?"
"For a few days, yes…"
"And what a peculiar ringtone, on his phone."
"It sure is."
"A Frenchman who likes German *schlager* music…"
"Yes, even I was never able to figure that one out, Rhona," Aeolus sighed.
I had walked over to the front of the room and opened the window. With my eyes closed I let the fresh air in as it passed across my face.
"*Père*," I muttered, "doesn't that mean 'father' in French?"

Aeolus stood beside me and closed the window. "You look much better today. We must make sure you don't get sick again," he said. He made a stern face. "And something that sounds like *père*, could also be *frère*. And that means 'brother'. But after all your questions may I inquire about something as well? Do you feel as good as you come across to me at the moment?"

"Um, yes... I do feel a bit better."

"Then I think it's time for us to find you a suitable hotel. Some place where you will feel comfortable. That is, if you would still like to be my guest here In London...?"

I nodded, albeit a bit uncertain.

"I'm happy to hear that," he smiled. "Although there is a slight logistical problem: the internet on my computer stopped working this morning and I'm having trouble getting it operational again. So I'm afraid that you will have to look at some websites somewhere else, in an internet café I presume."

We jumped right into action and found ourselves standing by a bus stop shortly after. He gave me instructions. I was to search for hotels that had at least a three-, but preferably a four-star rating and since it was such a last-minute thing, he advised me to arrange the accommodation by telephone. Oh and furthermore, I was to specifically ask the hotel whether it would be possible to pay in cash, then he would be notified of the amount by me and give me the money. As for him, he was going to tinker with his computer now in hopes of getting back online soon. He would be waiting for me at home and close to the check-in time in the afternoon I could then leave for my new lodging with my luggage.

That sounded perfectly reasonable. Endearing as well, the way in which he helped me think... no, it would be wrong for me to tease him now. Not everyone was as independent as I was and not everyone was as caring as him. It was just too sweet, all the things he tried to arrange for me.

In the distance we saw the bus coming. "I would briefly like to go back to what we discussed yesterday," Aeolus said suddenly. He rubbed his chin. "The thing is... I'm not entirely sure that you understand our situation."

"What do you mean?"

"We are in love with each other. You do realize that, don't you, Rhona?" He looked into my eyes.

"Yes, of course I do..."

"Thank heavens! Yeah, I hope you don't mind me saying, but to me you still come across as being a little bit foggy-brained from time to time and I would hate to see you forget, uh – "

" – To find my way back to your house?" I asked, and this time I really was not able to hide the pity in my smile. I quickly found a pen. Gave it to him and said: "Here. Write down your address on my hand. Then you can be certain that I won't lose it."

The bus had arrived and the doors opened. We parted with only a brief goodbye. I got on. As soon as the doors of the bus closed loudly. However, Aeolus said something else that sounded like: "No matter what happens, Rhona. You and I..."

How peculiar. Why lay so much emphasis on what we feel for each other? It seemed as though he is not certain of himself... Or was he feeling guilty over putting me out by making me stay at a hotel? But there was absolutely no reason for that. Because if there was one thing that I had no trouble with, it was staying somewhere by myself. In fact, I quite enjoyed having my own place with some breathing room...

It should not be some place expensive. For thirty or forty pounds I should definitely be able to find something, even if it could not be a hostel.

And with what I had in mind, I succeeded. At Elephant and Castle in the shopping center I had found the opportunity to go online. Within half an hour I had found a one-star rated hotel located on the outskirts of Clapham Common, one of the many extensive parks in this city. I was actually quite proud of myself: it was situated exactly between two stops on the Northern Line and by the Underground you could be at London Bridge within fifteen minutes. Accessibility was so important... The hotel also had a reception area with a couple of comfortable chairs, in which I could sit for a bit and watch people, if I should feel like it. To boot, within the low price that I had obtained, breakfast would even be included.

Aeolus would be so impressed...

## 21

TRUTH

In a happy mood I returned to the house an hour later. He asked: "Mission accomplished? Want something to drink?" I nodded and with a grin across my face I walked straight to the kitchen, where I turned on the kettle and placed a few spoonful's of instant coffee in two mugs. After we had settled at the dining table, sitting across from each other, Aeolus said: "And now the time has come for you to start working for me."

"Huh?" What was he talking about so suddenly?

"I'm the one taking care of your accommodation for the upcoming week and I should get something in return, I think… so you are going to take some photographs for me. It so happens that I need visual documentation of a couple of projects that I'm working on. You do shoot architecture, correct?" Aeolus looked as though he would crack up laughing at any second.

The bastard! Under the table I kicked in his direction, but he dodged my foot and the next moment I found myself being trapped between his ankles with my right leg. After which he immediately loosened his grip so that I could free myself.

"Sorry, Rhona, I couldn't help myself. You are just such a delightfully easy target…"

"Were you being serious, about my taking pictures for you?"

"Yes I was. You're not mad are you?"

"Not at all." No way was I going to let him get to me…

"So you'll do it?"

I made a reluctant face and answered: "I'm afraid I don't have much of a choice. Or do I? After all, I don't want to end up being homeless… But I have to warn you that you won't get more than half an hour of work out of me per day. You see, I charge seventy pounds by the hour and since my hotel only costs thirty five, breakfast included…"

Aeolus looked at me. "You got me there, young lady, and I'm not at all pleased with that…" he said, "… but hats off to you."

Feeling a wonderful sense of triumph I took a sip from my coffee. I did not feel sorry for him… this was way too much fun!

But after a slightly too lengthy moment of silence I inquired anyway, just to make sure, whether he was not mad. The man sat there with his head tilted downwards, as though he had to think. Then he looked up in my direction and I saw a mischievous twinkle appear in his eyes and I had to think of something to talk about quickly, or I would melt!

"Say, about this morning. Why did Egare call you 'Raph'?"

"What do you mean?"

"Well, my French isn't that great, but one of the things he said, I do remember: 'Raph, qu'est-ce que tu fait?' Doesn't that mean something like: 'What are you doing'?"

"No," he gritted his teeth. He got up, walked away from his chair and returned. And once more. Then he stopped pacing: "I can't do this, Rhona," he said. "This cannot continue. It has gone on far too long already…"

I leaned back in my chair and Aeolus sat down again. He was clearly making an effort to keep his voice under control as he slowly began to speak: "There are a couple of things we desperately need to talk about. I would like to begin by asking you a few questions. Think carefully before you answer and please don't ask me anything in return."

I was silent.

"Do you ever talk in your sleep? Or to be more precise: do you know, about yourself, whether you speak out loud during your sleep, while you're dreaming?"

"No, I mean, yes. I know that I do not talk in my sleep…" I was fairly certain about that. I had tested it once while on vacation with some friends and even at home I had been told that I was a quiet sleeper.

"And you haven't told me anything about your nightmare from the other night. We can both agree on that, can't we?"

No, of course I haven't. What kind of question was that?

"Nevertheless, I am fairly certain that I know what the dream was about, Rhona. Did you see any elongated fangs? Were you being bitten by someone?"

"Uh… yes…" *Shit.*

"Were you, perhaps, bitten by *me*?"

I was shocked. Did I really…? I looked at Aeolus bewilderedly.

"No, you did not talk in your sleep. There is a different reason for my knowing this."

"And that is…?" I asked.

"That bite, it really did happen to you. And I am responsible for it."

If this was part of our little game, I did not find it very funny.

"Do you understand what I am trying to tell you?" Aeolus asked.

"I do, but I'm not really in the mood for this."

"Can't you tell I'm being serious?"

"If you are, I think we're having two entirely different conversations here. What, for Pete's sake, is your point?"

"Alright," he said, "let's go back to a day and a half ago. To Tuesday evening. We ran into each other in the city, you remember that much. We had coffee near Bank's. And afterwards we came here…"

"… Okay, hold on. Let me think for a moment…" I had to concentrate to recall that specific evening. Slowly the layout of his apartment appeared in my mind's eye. It had already turned dark and the lights were on in the living room. Taking in the new surrounding with wonder, yes… and conversations. Also, music…? I opened my eyes.

"There was a viol. Don't you own a viola da gamba?"

Aeolus got up and walked towards the bedroom. He motioned me to follow. The large wardrobe was opened and there was the answer to my question – among the suit jackets, dress pants and shirts stood the object I had inquired about.

He took out the viol, held it in his arms as one would hold an injured child and lay the instrument, or at least what was left of it, on top of the bed. It was an unsettling sight: the body was almost completely ripped in half and the neck had broken off.

With my stomach in knots I said: "That doesn't look too good".

"A total loss."

"Was it very expensive? Were you attached to it?"

"It's just stuff. If I were you, I'd be more worried about myself," he said and left the wooden wreckage behind on the bed without giving it another look. He picked up my suitcase and brought it to the hallway. Next he showed me a couple of times how to lock and unlock the front door. "When you leave shortly, you'll know how it works," he emphasized. I even had to practice doing it once in front of him, but I refused. As I walked back into the living room I asked: "What, Aeolus, is it that you've been trying to tell me for the last ten minutes and why do I feel that, in spite of that, I'm still completely in the dark?"

Aeolus sat down at the table by himself.

"I can tell you many things about that," he said, "but I won't. For a variety of reasons. It is of great importance for you to remember certain things again."

He had a point there, yes. I had to admit that it was taking a surprising amount of effort for me to recall what happened last Tuesday… there were still many things that I did not understand – for one, I could not figure out for the life of me as to why that viol was broken. He answered me with a question of his own.

"Do you remember that I played it that night?"

"I believe so…"

"I played Le Tourbillon for you, that composition by Marin Marais about the whirlwind."

Le Tourbillon… that musical piece that lasted no more than a minute and a half. But the intensity and velocity of it, I would never forget for the rest of my life… a classical piece that, in my opinion, only true virtuosos could convincingly deliver to the audience.

How did Aeolus manage that again? Gradually the image took shape in my mind. Yes, he was sitting in his desk chair, there in the middle of the room. And I was sitting on the couch… on the edge of the couch, completely in awe of him. Man, he could play so well… The ease with which his fingers traveled along the strings, the emotion that he was able to put into the music – his eyes had been closed the whole time, and then… that terrifying look!

Sometimes an experience could only be compared to what you saw on TV in series such as *Lost,* in which you could hear the violins of the accompanying orchestra produce an ascending, eerie sound, at the exact moment that you make a macabre discovery. As in this instance. Suddenly everything, and I mean everything, was crystal clear to me: the nauseating sense of shock after seeing that subtle, animalistic movement of his head – my escape through the hallway into the stairwell – the way in which he, now having become a completely different person, intercepted me and brought me back upstairs – the almost erotic tone in his voice right before he bit me…!

I had to get out of here. My eyes searched the space I was standing in, looking for a way to escape… Impossible, completely impossible. As soon as I were to even make a flinch in that direction, he would slam me to the floor and pull me in, drag me over his immaculately scrubbed hardwood floor in the process…

With my limbs feeling stiff I walked to the table that Aeolus was sitting at. I sat down in my seat across from him again, although I did not entirely understand why.

"At the moment you are not in immediate danger."

I remained silent.

"I have fed myself a little while ago and my mood is different than it was Tuesday evening."

"When. When did you drink last?"

"Tuesday evening." He avoided making eye contact.

"I see…" my voice sounded raspy. I cleared my throat.

"The fact that you still don't know the complete truth, is my fault."

"There is more?"

"Oh, there's more, yes. And I'm going to tell you all of it now."

I stared at the table surface, looking for support in studying the grain of the wood.

"To begin with, after I had pinned you against the wall in the hallway, I have pierced the jugular vein in your neck with my teeth. You remember that. Don't you?"

He did not wait for my answer and continued talking. "I then proceeded to drink your blood to beyond the point of you losing consciousness as a result of hypovolemic shock."

"What…?!" my mouth dropped.

"You lost blood. That takes its toll on your body."

"I am familiar with hypovolemic shock. How much blood?"

"In your case it was almost half a gallon."

I held up my hand in repulsion, hoping that he would stop. He did not.

With a face that one could see on bodyguards of important politicians, cold and lacking emotion, he said: "I was well on my way to take your life. But then the doorbell rang. And something that usually never happens, happened to me: there was someone at my door. While I was squatted on the floor, with you in my arms. In a split second I then decided to bite myself and apply a little bit of my blood onto the wound in your neck, in hopes of it disappearing, which it did. After I had laid you on the bed and closed the bedroom door behind me, you looked like someone who was merely sleeping. The downstairs' neighbor – we're practically strangers – had heard a loud noise and was worried about it. I was able to get him off my back by using some sort of excuse. I returned to you after and watched over you for the rest of the evening and all through the night."

"I believe you," was my immediate reaction. For a moment I was shocked by my own words, but I really could not make anything else out of it: I believed what Aeolus was telling me. There may not have been a single trace of any bite marks to be found on my neck, but I would never forget for all eternity the coldness of his razor sharp teeth. Nor would I ever forget the awareness of my blood being drawn out of all of my limbs, going either with or against its normal circulation, and into one spot, warm and wildly pulsating... My head had lain in an unnatural position, my chin touched his cold cheek, his forceful lips firmly adhered to my skin. The vice grip of his arms around my head and waist compelled me to follow in even the tiniest of his movements. Never before had I ever felt someone this close to me... How could I have assumed for more than a full day that such an intense, physical sensation could have been pulled out of thin air during a dream?

A frown appeared on Aeolus' forehead. "What makes you suddenly believe me now?"

"Some dreams come true..."

"Too true to be good?"

"Sadly, yes," I replied.

He sighed. Not so much out of impatience, but more like someone who is hopelessly fighting against emotions that he has no idea how to deal with. "I'm sorry, Rhona – and I want to show you how sorry I am, from the bottom of my heart. What had possessed me that night, how things had gotten this far out of hand...? It was a feeling, I think, an almost desperate need to become absorbed with someone – I don't know..."

"You wanted sex?"

"*No!* No, it was something entirely different. I am perfectly familiar with how sex between mortals works. It had more to do with the big picture... something territorial, or in that spirit... I honestly don't know what came over me."

"Yeah, you and me both..."

"And aside from that I also took advantage of the nightmare you had."

"In what way?"

"It was fairly easy to predict what you would dream about, after what I'd done to you. And to top it off you even took a swing at something imaginary close to your neck as you were waking up... After that I couldn't resist the temptation to let you believe not only what happened during the night, but also what happened during the evening before, had merely been a fabrication of your mind."

"Why." At this point this was not even a question from me anymore. It sounded more resentful, more like a demand for an explanation, and he said: "To protect you, my dear, I was trying to protect you. That was the least I could do after all this... And I longed to experience an uninhibited friendship with a mortal, even if it was only for a moment – "

After he had reestablished the control over his voice, he said: "However, over the long run this convoluted version of the truth could never have lasted. I could never have looked at myself in the mirror. That's one thing I can't do anymore anyway. A lie is a lie..." – I interrupted him with my finger held high. "From this day forward, never lie to me again. *Ever* again." My voice trembled. And then I broke down. My eyes were stinging... I closed them shut, but it did not help.

"Oh, sweet child..." Aeolus said. He laid his cold hand on top of mine, but I reacted as though being stung by a wasp: "Don't touch me!" It was time for me to leave and not a moment too soon! I loudly pushed my chair back and stood up to look for the shortest route possible to get to my coat and my suitcase. A hand against the front door prevented me from opening it. "Not just yet," it sounded stern, followed by, "We must discuss a couple of things first, for your own safety."

Impatiently I faced him.

"You haven't booked your return trip yet, I presume?"

No, sadly I had not.

"This means that you will spend this upcoming night here in London. And that is fine. You need time to get back to your old self again. But since an emotional connection exists between us – "

" – Could you please talk normally?" I cut him off.

"Okay, as you wish: Because you are attracted to me, you will seek out contact with me in spite of everything that has happened. If not today, it will be tomorrow or the day after. But before you do, you're going to have to take some measures. Firstly, I want you to keep your address of accommodation a secret from me. I mustn't be able to track you down at any cost. That's why you will take a taxi to a station of your choice shortly: London Bridge, Waterloo, Liverpool Street... and once you get there you will transfer to a randomly picked, different taxi. If you don't, there is a risk that I will trace you, ambush you and..." he did not finish his sentence.

The sarcastic look on my face was immediately answered with the words: "I have stalked you for a week and in the end nearly murdered you. Do you want that to happen again?"

He left the hallway and returned with a little box that he handed to me: "This is a prepaid phone. I have programmed my number into it. Only use this to call me, wherever you are."

And that was that. A cab was ordered. I went downstairs, accompanied by

Aeolus, and we waited in silence. When the car pulled up and I got in I did not feel upset anymore, instead I felt sadness. As I looked through the rear window I said goodbye with nothing more than the look in my eyes. He stayed behind on the sidewalk with his hands in the pockets of his pants...

"Cheer up love, it may never happen," the cab driver said to me. What kind of stupid comment was that?

He asked me the reason as to why I looked so sad. I answered: "My boyfriend lied to me..." And again I burst into tears.

22

HOTEL


From a modern luxury apartment to a white-plastered Victorian dwelling
that seemed to be hanging from a thread that was composed of maintenance
that was long overdue – it was a bit of a mental switch. But in any case, I
would be surrounded by normal people and be safe from him here. At least
that is what I hoped...

Therefore I had played it safe in getting to the hotel. Got off twice during the
tube ride getting here, once at Elephant & Castle and once more at
Kennington. At both stations I had left the carriage and gone out into the
street carrying all my belongings. Outside, near a random bus stop, I had
then run the sleeve of my coat over some poles and fences to scatter my scent
a little. Whether it would lead him onto the wrong trail should he decide to
track me down? No clue whatsoever. Just as I had no idea whether I could
trust the staff at this hotel in their ability to uphold a certain level of security
and such...

After a dispassionate girl at the front desk had checked me in I dragged my
suitcase and bag through the fire doors that loudly slammed shut behind me,
over soiled carpet, through narrow hallways, up the stairs and finally into my
single room. It was the size of a shoebox, really no bigger than that. But I did
manage to pay for it using my own money, for the whole week upfront.
Between the foot end of the bed and the window there was just enough space
for a single suitcase with a bag on top – a bag that was knocked down from
said suitcase very easily if you carelessly opened the spring-loaded bathroom
door.

The shower knob would not budge and on the towel that hung over the
shower curtain rod I found a long, black strand of hair... The miniature piece
of soap, on the other hand, that lay next to the sink ready to be used, was still
neatly left untouched.

My room was located to the side of the building. So when looking out of the
window at an angle past the brick wall of the neighboring house I could just
make out the main road out front and the border of Clapham Common. I
closed the curtains. No reason, just making sure. I would take a little rest in
a minute. To get some sleep. And to forget. But first I had to pee. I used my
suitcase to prop the bathroom door open. This coop felt cramped enough as it
was, and the idea of being locked up in an even smaller space and not being
able to hear what went on in my room was something I just didn't feel like
facing – with an unexpected bang the door slammed shut anyway and in my
wildly startled reaction I cursed loudly at the empty space that surrounded

me. Then I cried. Intermittently bawling my head off, with heaving shoulders and all...

For the longest time I lay there staring at the outdated huge monstrosity of a television that sat precariously balanced on a slightly too wobbly side table. Would it work if I were to turn it on later in the evening? I doubted it.

It was sometime in the early evening and I found myself at Blijdorp Rotterdam Zoo. All visitors had already gone home and the gates were closed. It was bad enough that I was locked in, but to make matters worse I was also lost and had no way to call someone for help, since I had lost my cell phone. Thus I had been looking for the exit for quite a while, but it turned out that I kept going in circles, because I kept winding up in the exact same spot. At a complete loss on finding a solution to this problem I wandered past cages and enclosures of different animals. They all became more active the closer it got to sunset – I had read something about that once – but today the twilight lasted unusually long: the sun painted the sky a deep scarlet red and just hovered there, stationary, right above the horizon, as though time had come to a stop. It left me feeling estranged from reality and it seemed to negatively affect the animals as well: some were pacing back and forth restlessly, whereas others remained hidden in a corner. But the one thing that they were all doing was staring in my direction. And slowly but surely the commotion turned into chaos... Birds beat their wings crashing into the fences of their cages as soon as they noticed me, apes widened their eyes and exposed their teeth while screeching loudly. Similarly, every animal reacted to my passing-by in its own frightened manner: the ostriches, the zebras, the kudus... like a psychedelic wave they were overwhelmed with a kind of panic that one only witnessed in nature documentaries. It seemed as though they saw me as an enemy... a completely horrendous enemy!
Meanwhile I had arrived at the main square in front of the closed entrance for the umpteenth time. The flamingos let out wild noises of alarm when I sat down exhausted on a bench at the edge of their pond, but for now I really could not afford to be considerate towards them. I needed to rest. And if everyone could dial it down a notch?? Especially the lions across this square would not let off for even a second. Literally everywhere I had walked the roaring from their enclosure could be heard. Something that when I thought about it, was not even possible, I just realized, as the zoo's grounds were much too vast for that. And then there was that one lion whose call was slightly different from that of its fellow species. His roar was not as prolonged, it sounded even a little truncated, as though he wanted to correct himself each time he let that threatening sound escape from his mouth. Even now, I heard him do it, but for some reason it came from much closer behind me than I thought was normal and – as a strong sense of imminent danger crept over me – I turned around and I was right, there he was, standing

barely seven feet away from me! Apparently he had been following me right from the start: a gigantic, fully grown male lion. With auburn hair and light gray eyes.

Disorientated I sat up straight in my bed staring across the room. This kind of dreaming had to stop right now, if I were to keep all my ducks in a row, psychologically speaking... With the roar of that lion still echoing in my ears I rolled out of bed. But when the noise, contrary to what seemed logical, continued, it dawned on me that what I heard had not originated from my dream. It was actually the dream that had formed around it. But how was it that I could still...? I listened by the door of my room and then by the window for a bit until I finally discovered that the mysterious sound was caused by the hotel guest in the room next to mine. It sounded like he was taking a bath and every time he shifted it caused friction between his limbs and the inside of the tub... I took a breath of relief. Man, the walls in this place sure were thin!

I had not had lunch today. This was probably why I did manage to eat most of my evening meal, despite not being in the mood for food at the time. Luckily there were a few small restaurants next to the hotel and the sidewalk was well-spaced enough to allow me to monitor my surroundings even under dim lighting conditions. As a result while getting here, just now, I could have been fairly certain that if I did not see anyone behind me, there really was no one who had been following me...
It was high time for me to figure out what I was going to do with the rest of the week. Shoot photos for my book, that was for sure. And walk around the city, or hang around this neighborhood and familiarize myself with the area...
Clapham Common. *Common...* I had looked it up in a dictionary once. Apparently it meant 'communal pasture' and at that time I wholeheartedly had to laugh at that crude description, but now, even in the dark, I could appreciate the amount of truth there was in that statement: the surface area with which these fields extended was truly immense. And this was even just the southernmost point of a much larger whole, criss-crossed by walking and cycling paths, surrounded by rows of trees and the adjoining residential areas.
I wondered what kind of activities one would be doing in a typical urban park such as this one on sunny days. Would it be crowded? Probably. And what about at night? Would Aeolus think of this as a good spot for his sitting sessions, for example? Was there a suitable square yard to be found where he could learn to develop his eye for detail? Or had that meditating been a whim that only lasted for a few days?
Do. Not. Think. About. It. No ifs or buts! I had to get back to the hotel and turn on the television! Find some distraction!

After a film and an episode of Top Gear there was nothing on the other channels worth watching anymore, and so I decided to get ready for the night. While looking for some toiletries in my bag, however, I came across the box that I had received from Aeolus earlier that day. It was the original box of a cell phone. I hesitated for a second, but then I fished the thing out from all of my belongings, between my thumb and index finger, as though a creepy bug could crawl out at any moment. And lo and behold, as soon as I opened the package, something did fall out. I uttered a little shriek, but noticed soon after that it was only an envelope. In capital letters it had 'to Rhona' written on it. With a confused frown on my face I tore it open and then, to my astonishment, I was confronted with no less than eight banknotes of one hundred pounds... for a while the only thing I could do was to stare at all that money. Then I took out the phone, skimmed through the user manual and went through the steps that were needed to ready the device. My fingers trembled as I opened the contact list and selected the only name that was saved in it...

His phone rang five times before he finally answered. "Rhona," came from the other end of the line.

Immediately I let him have it. "What kind of nonsense is this?"

"I'm not sure I follow. You're going to have to be more specific," he said.

"All that money! What the heck is that supposed to mean?"

"So you've found it. Good."

"No, it's not good at all. I had already told you that I wouldn't accept anything from you."

"I like to keep promises that I make."

"But I told you that my hotel doesn't cost more than thirty five pounds, so you're going to get five hundred and fifty five back."

"No."

"We'll see about that," I retorted.

"Try me. Just remember that you succumbed to my cunning sleight of hands once before."

I began to bite my lip...

"By the way, I'm going to need you for longer than half an hour a day," he added.

"Ten," I sneered.

"Pardon me?"

"Tomorrow morning, 10 a.m. Where do we meet?"

"8:30. Inquire after No. 1 Poultry at Bank Station. On its lower level you'll find a Starbucks."

"9 a.m. See you then."

"See you then, Rhona," Aeolus said with a little chuckle in his voice.

The bastard. He was actually having fun with this.

## 23

## NO. 1 POULTRY

I came to a halt, at the top of the escalator this time, and to clear some space
for other people to pass by me I took one step to the side. I considered my
options one last time... At this moment it was not too late to turn around. I
still had the chance to go back, pick up my suitcase that I had already packed
just in case, and simply leave. Heathrow was really not that far from my
hotel.

"Excuse me!" Behind me stood a man whose body language seemed to say
'well, how about it,' and before I knew what I was doing, I had given in to the
pressure and there I was, standing on the top step of the escalator, going
down after all. Coincidence? Destiny? Or Murphy's Law in progress? I closed
my eyes shut.

When I walked out onto the semi-covered inner square I saw him sitting at
one of the tables in front of the coffee shop. He wore a long-sleeved T-shirt in
a color that I had always had an issue with: that particular cooler green that
you would come across in more and more clothing this spring. But of course it
looked irresistibly good on him and I knew for a fact of whom I would be
reminded from now on, every time that color would walk by me on the
streets.

"Thanks, Aeolus," I said under my breath.

"Thanks for what?" was the first thing I heard him say when I stopped in
front of his table.

"Never mind," I said. I took a seat.

"You came here of your own volition?" he asked.

I nodded.

"And you experience that as such?"

"At the moment, I do..."

"Good. Also know that in a public place such as this you won't be in any
physical danger."

I nodded again and tried to get up, but he stopped me. He said: "You'd like to
place an order, I presume. What will you have?" Then he stood up and walked
to the counter.

Soon after we were having our coffees and I took a couple of greedy bites out
of the gigantic chocolate muffin that I had ordered.

He watched me in amazement. "Haven't you had breakfast?" he asked.

"I did, but it was nothing to write home about."

"You don't say."

Yeah, he probably *would* be skeptical about my hotel...

So I said: "But other than that it is not too shabby, if you must know."
Aeolus looked at me unconvinced.
"In any case, I feel more comfortable there than I would staying at the
Waldorf, for example."
"You're going to have to elaborate on that..."
"No reason. Once the number of things that are wrong with a hotel reaches a
certain point, it naturally becomes kind of charming. My shower wasn't
working, there wasn't enough toilet paper, my bed is squeaky... and to get
back to that breakfast: the kettle was out of order, there was only one type of
bread available and the tables were hardly cleared."
"And you think that's entertaining."
"Yes, I can find the sense of humor in it. They have absolutely no idea what
they're doing over there, but you should see how hard they try... it could
almost be called endearing," I said. In front of us a steady stream of people
passed by on their way to work. In my mind's eye, however, I saw the girl
behind the front desk at my hotel that had been so disinterested in me when
I arrived yesterday. Since the moment of first meeting her I had made it my
personal challenge to try and win her affection and trust, despite her
negative attitude. Something I achieved right away this very morning: she
had gotten into a huge fight with her female boss and I had witnessed the
whole thing. I had exchanged a couple of sympathetic glances with her after
and apparently that was all she needed to become 'best friends' with me.
Aeolus raised his eyebrows. "I admire your art of living..." he said.
"Oh, everything is relative," I answered, "because at the same time, the level
of noise in that hotel annoys the heck out of me."
He remained silent.
"Is something the matter?" I asked, and he nodded.
Right when the silence between us began to feel a little awkward he said:
"There's something that I need to talk to you about, but I need for you to
watch the volume of your voice when we do. You see, not everything that we
discuss is meant for others to hear." He was hinting at a businessman who
had just sat down at the table next to ours.
Then he said: "I'm worried, Rhona. Something is happening to your ears."
"... Cutting right to the chase, huh..." My ears, whatever made him think
that – just because I mentioned how noisy my hotel was?
"Yes, this may sound a little strange," Aeolus said, "but I think the substance
I used to heal the skin of your neck Tuesday night may have done more than
intended. I have strong reasons to believe that it made your hearing ability
significantly stronger than it used to be."
I let out a snicker. Things should not get any crazier.
"For you to not believe me is understandable. However, by now you must be
aware of... wait. Just take a listen without reacting." Aeolus leaned back
comfortably in his chair. Suddenly he said with a clear voice: "Did you know
that the person at the table to the left of me is having an affair?"

My heart skipped a beat.

"He is sleeping with the wife of his boss and the entire department at the firm knows about it by now…"

A little bit louder Aeolus added: "It's only a matter of time until his boss finds out and when he does, the fraud will probably be revealed as well."

I had the hardest time to keep a straight face, but the person that we were talking about still did not respond…

"He must be deaf," I whispered, "There's no other explanation."

"You think?" my friend asked, and yet a little louder he said: "Excuse me…" Finally the stranger looked in his direction. "Could you tell me what time it is?" The reply came out expressionless and politely. The man appeared to not have the slightest clue as to what had transpired prior to this.

"So… my hearing has improved…?"

"Yes. And in case you need more evidence: what is that woman over there with that white scarf talking about with that other person?"

Aeolus did not wait for my answer and said: "She's talking about her son who plays polo."

" – And she is proud of him because he has won the last couple of matches!" I added. "But… this can't be happening!"

"Apparently it can. It would explain that panic attack you had, after hearing that noise the scooter made Wednesday night. And it's probably also why you overheard something Egare and I would have preferred to have kept private."

My face began to feel warm. "Sorry, but I just heard you talk…"

"While our communication was practically inaudible to mortals."

"Whoa-whoa-whoa, why do you say that – mortals?"

"Egare is like me."

"A vampire?" I would have preferred for him to have brought up that word first.

"Egare's real name is Lucas."

"Who in the world is that?"

"I wrote about him to you one time. He is my *sire*, my maker."

Oh no. "I'm not buying that, Aeolus. The kid is even younger than I am!"

"Make no mistake. It all depends at what point someone is transformed in their life."

"How old is he then?"

"He's from the early twelfth century."

I resolutely shook my head and said: "No way. Egare is not a vampire, 'cause when we were introduced I could feel that his hand was warm." With a look on my face that said 'I dare you to counter that' I looked at Aeolus.

He bent towards me across the table. A smile came over his face.

"Don't be scared, I won't hurt you," he said. Then he took my left hand and gently stroked it. It was still a peculiar sensation feeling something this unnaturally cold on my skin that looked like a perfectly normal male hand…

He let go. Briefly made his hands disappear under the table and then touched me again. My first reaction was to withdraw, purely out of shock, but he prevented that by firmly holding me in his grip. How on earth was it possible for him to be so much warmer than before?!

"Simple physics," he explained, "A tried and true method among vampires for when they are introduced to a mortal: rub your hands together first and they'll become warm."

"But what about his height? If he's from the Middle Ages shouldn't he be much shorter than you and I? So that makes absolutely no sense."

With the utmost patience Aeolus explained that this was a common misconception. As it turned out, during Lucas' time the average height was actually about four inches taller than it was around the 1700s.

"So you were relatively tall...?"

"... And Lucas was averagely built and now we are both of inconspicuous height. Listen, Rhona. Your sense of logic is extraordinary. You use it as a defense mechanism and that is your every right. But given your improved sense of hearing... I know you have all the reasons in the world to not believe me on my word anymore... Once is more than enough, when it comes to lying."

"When was this, according to you, that you lied?"

"You asked me whether something that Lucas had said meant 'what are you doing'. I denied it, I was wrong to do so."

"And then he also called you *Raph*..."

"It's short for Raphaël."

"Raphaël, the architect from the eighteenth century... so that *was* you after all. I narrowed my eyes into thin slivers in hopes of him not noticing that I felt less serene on the inside than I appeared on the outside. That it affected me this much, the fact that he finally revealed his true identity...

Aeolus took a business card out of his wallet and handed it to me. Raphaël Bélusier... wow. "Don't you need an alias here in England," I asked.

"Every now and then you can get away with it for a decade..." he said.

For a while I stared at the card with his personal information. He asked me whether I wanted something else to drink and got up. When he returned I was still trying to come to terms with this 'new' identity. "For a long time I thought that you had studied history," I mused, "I guess I wasn't too far off... Restoration Architect, Consultant and Historian."

He sat down, right beside me this time.

"What am I supposed to call you now?"

"How you will internally process this is up to you. But I would like to advise you to get used to my real name quickly. The people that know me professionally don't know any better than my name being Raphaël. And the undead chiefly use original names within their own circle," he answered.

"So there are more like you, in this area as well?"

"I'm afraid so, Rhona."

"Is that why Egare was so angry with you?"

Aeolus had been blankly staring straight ahead, but now he turned his head toward me. "What makes you say that?"

"That's what he sounded like when he asked what you were doing."

It was as though a dark cloud gathered between the vampire and me. He said: "Your demand towards me was: the truth, the whole truth and nothing but the truth. Alright, my love, from now on you'll get what you want. Sooner or later you'd figure everything out anyway... so when it comes to Lucas: yes, he was less than pleased. The scent of your blood was all over the place, so he knew that I had bitten someone as soon as he entered my apartment."

"But that had already happened a day and half before that, and I must say that your cleaning is meticulous," I quietly objected.

"If any given CSI team can find week-old traces of blood, why shouldn't a vampire? In addition he could hear your pulse and so he knew that you were still alive."

"And that did not go over well."

Aeolus made a reluctant gesture. "Oh, he would not want to kill you immediately. But due to the fact that you're still alive you *are* a threat to our community."

"And you are, in turn, life threatening to me. So that makes us arch nemeses," I observed bluntly.

"No, Rhona, no, never that," he instantly reacted.

"But what are we then?"

"I have completely lost the right to answer that question. So it will be entirely up to you..."

Suddenly I did not want to be here anymore. I had to go, to get moving, perhaps by doing so this macabre conversation would come to an end. Why could we not talk about photography for a bit? Pretend that he was my client and I worked for him?

"Let's go," I suggested, and I got up from my chair. Thankfully Aeolus followed my lead. With his arm in the small of my back he guided me. We entered a pedestrian tunnel that led to the tube station.

"Would it be alright if I showed you a few sites," he asked. "If you're up for it, you might be able to shoot a few photos."

As cheerful as I could, I said: "Of course. That's what you hired me for."

24

WIG


What followed next was a couple of hours of taking a number of underground
rides and looking at the facades of some historic buildings. I captured what I
saw as much as possible and tried to make mental notes of the things that
Aeolus told me about English architecture. He was my client. I, the
photographer. Around us people were busy doing groceries, children were
taken on an outing by the caregivers of some daycare. In offices and stores I
saw staff going about their business. We were a part of it. The working world.
The world kept spinning... but did it, in my case? Was I not greatly fooling
myself? Because it was painfully obvious that my life as I knew it had come
to a full stop and that everything revolved around one single person now.
The phone rang. Claire. Change to 'flat mate mode'. What was I going to say,
what would be the wisest thing? I answered the call and did not even bother
to take a few steps away from Aeolus. "Hey babe..." I said.
"Ah, by the sounds of it," Claire responded, "you've been completely
anglicized. Have you decided to relocate there or will we ever be graced by
your presence again?" She sounded piqued. Be diplomatic, I told myself, and
as carefully as possible I formulated my answer: "Yeah, well... what can I
say? You know me. Leave me in a playground and you won't see me again
until sunset..." My flat mate had a hard time suppressing her laughter and I
quickly told her a few things about what happened during the previous week.
About the photo shoot at Canary Wharf, although it took quite the effort to
dig up the memory of that event out of my brain. Thereby I settled on giving
her a general recap.
Even more summarized was my description of the current photo assignment
and to keep her from grilling me about it, I tried to find a different topic of
conversation... The Asylum! Thank God for the Asylum. This would be such a
comfort for Claire to hear: my attending church. Never mind what *kind* of
church, but still...
After giving her an elaborate account of the gathering of last Sunday it
appeared that I had achieved the result that I had hoped for: for now she felt
sufficiently up to speed. A few difficult last questions I managed to avoid on
the pretext of 'receiving calls while being overseas costs a fortune', I quickly
asked her whether everything was okay on the home front and almost got
ready to end the conversation when she asked me where I was staying. I
cunningly said that I did not have the address handy at the moment and that
I would email it to her later that day when I got a chance. After I had hung
up my head was running a mile-a-minute from all the effort it took.

"You handled that well," Aeolus noted.

We slowly began to walk, away from the building that I had just taken a picture of.

"In the future you will have to carry these kinds of conversations more frequently," he said, "with your friends, with strangers... do you think you'll be up for it?"

"Do I have a choice?"

"No."

"I was afraid you'd say that..."

"And do you realize that out of everyone you know, you'll have to distrust me the most?"

I nodded.

"It's a tricky situation, but if we want to keep seeing each other..."

We entered the tube station for what would be our third trip this morning. At the gates Aeolus briefly slowed down.

"The next thing I want to show you is Eagle House, a stately home dating back to the Stuart period. Do you recall what I told you just now about the characteristics of that time?"

I thought out loud: "Symmetric construction, slanted rooftops, windows with vertical wooden or stone stiles, dormer windows, chimneys on opposite ends of the roof and angular facades..."

He smiled: "Very good. Come, onwards to Tooting Broadway. And this will be our last stop for today."

"Oh? So skimpy with my billable hours?"

Aeolus ignored my teasing and simply said: "It's already been a day or ten that I've maintained a reversed sleep-wake cycle. Not exactly a natural situation for me."

"So you're going to sleep?"

"For a couple of hours, yes."

"And then you'll wake up again in the evening?"

"If you like we can meet up later," he suggested.

"Is it okay if I think about that for a bit?" I asked.

Forty minutes later, on a bus to London Road, Aeolus explained that the interior of the house in question was not open to the public. It served as a school for children with autistic disorders and he did not want to bother either them or the teachers. "But I *am* curious to see your first reaction upon seeing the exterior," he said.

Well, it was one of pure surprise. All the features I had listed on architecture of the Stuart period were represented in this building. It was almost like the image that I had created in my mind was now fully being projected before my eyes: a recently restored estate comprising of two or three levels, with a gable roof, an entrance at the center front, slider windows with those quaint paneled panes...

A couple of dormers, chimneys on both ends, perfectly symmetrical, with at its center the distinct triangular shape of a tympanum. And all of this was crowned with a graceful, white bell tower. Aeolus was watching me and without turning away he said: "... This happens to be the most well-preserved dwelling, built in the so-called *Queen Anne style,* in the entire country. You won't easily find a better example."

I briefly looked around me. "A shame that the surrounding area looks completely different."

At present Eagle House was situated within a working class neighborhood and the section of the street where we were standing could not exactly be called a shining example of good taste or sophisticated architecture. "What would we have seen if we had been able to go inside?"

"A fairly prominent feature is the staircase in the great hall that leads to the upstairs floor. The first and second floor used to be reserved for the owners. Toward the side of the house a smaller staircase connects the lower kitchen to the utility room, domestic offices and the attic, where the servants stayed. Finally, a spiral staircase leads to the central dome and rooftop. A typical feature of properties of the elite of those days is that in most rooms the doors and ceilings and doors were relatively high.

"Why was that? Weren't you all a lot shorter back then?"

The man laughed quietly. "You're forgetting the powdered wigs. Compared to that the teased hair of the eighties' youth was nothing."

I chuckled. "Please don't tell me that you used to wear wigs like that. Like in Tous Les Matins Du Monde..."

"Don't believe everything you see in movies."

"That's not an answer."

But no answer came.

"With that thing on top of your head wouldn't the itching drive you crazy?"

"Lice were quite common, yes."

"And then what?"

"Many shaved their heads as a precaution. And every once in a while one simply boiled the wig." Everything about him gave away that he was trying the hardest to come across as unattached as possible. He was feeling embarrassed and knew that I noticed. A good trump card to keep up my sleeve.

"This house had been restored only recently, hasn't it?" I asked, trying to sound as serious as possible again.

"Yes, during the seventies a significant attempt to that end was made, but they had to seize their work due to financial difficulties. In the nineties English Heritage became actively involved and the house was given a thorough restoration. At that time they had also performed archeological research and added offices at the back matching the eighteenth century style..."

He waited until I was done taking photos. "Finished?" he asked.

"Finished," I answered. "Say, about tonight. Maybe we could do a sightseeing tour with one of those double decker buses."

Aeolus huffed: "There are things less corny a person could undertake in a world city."

"So you feel you're too good for that?"

"No, of course not. But really, Rhona, a bus filled with tourists…?"

"I could just go by myself. No big deal…"

"That won't be necessary. Pick a tour and text me in the afternoon with a time and location."

On Tooting Broadway we parted ways. He took the underground, with me seeing him off on the platform. Another safety measure. Once he had left, I could then choose a direction that was most convenient for me and it would be impossible for him to track me…

I went out of my way to tell him that I thought that that was a little over the top. But whether he believed my words…? I, myself, began to have my doubts about my assertion, as I discovered on the first random bus that I got on, that the palms of my hands felt damp with sweat.

## 25

## HARRODS

A few hours later, after eating a sandwich from the supermarket and spending half an hour at an internet café, I made the short trek at street level from Knightsbridge Underground Station to the entrance of Harrods.

Harrods was a 'must' during each of my visits to London. It was the nostalgic bragging right of my childhood, to have had exhaustingly boring days spent at luxury hotels and mandatory shopping raids with my mother, looking for 'bargains' and 'once-in-a-lifetime opportunities'. Yeah right, looking for bargains. Like hell it was... even back then I already knew my mother's true purpose for visiting this department store. For what other reason was I dragged to the neighbors immediately upon returning to the Netherlands to 'go over for coffee', while insisting I wore those brand new, way too doll-like dresses? Just because they looked so cute on me? As if...
And another thing that I noticed in those instances was that without fail my mother would start dropping fancy words – like 'tailored' – and the names of those women that always made their rounds in her stories, women that allegedly were highly esteemed friends of hers. But the thing was that I had never seen any of those women in our home... Laura Ashley, for example, I could not determine for the life of me who that could be.
Oh, I really could not care less, to be honest. All I wanted to do was climb trees, which was impossible with a stupid dress like that.
No, my father on the other hand, he had it all figured out during those weekends in London: hang out at the pub and slack off all day during – what were they called again – conferences.

For some mysterious reason I had grown to enjoy it more and more as the years passed by: wander around Harrods and elaborately compare pricey, pricier and priciest items. And to then track down the cheapest item in the entire store and buy it. But sometimes I simply did not purchase anything. Then it was satisfactory to look at the endless variety of products and the extravagance of their displays and the fool's gold that was everywhere dripping off everything. There was so much gimcrack showy and grand decoration collected here in just one building that in my eyes it almost became art...
Art. Reminded me of *Idylle 1884,* the piece of which I saw as a poster reproduction hanging on the wall at Aeolus' place. Of course, that would not be for sale here. Incidentally I had discovered on the internet earlier today

that the artist's name was Gustav Klimt. An Austrian...

I always saved the postcards for last. This section, which in my opinion was the absolute highlight of this department store as it carried the most brilliant selection of prints, was ironically located in a remote corner of the basement. You could not find a collection of such comical illustrations and hilarious inscriptions anywhere else and because of this it was the only department at Harrods where I really had to watch my spending. Luckily the little girl's room at our house did not have much more space left on the walls...

Funny... sometimes people seemed to follow the same course through this department store as you were. Take this guy for instance: I had just seen him exit the section with large Chinese vases and area rugs right when I entered it. Next, like me, he had wandered the book section and now I saw his blond head again, this time near the postcards. His back was facing me, three display shelves removed. I tried to observe him as inconspicuously as possible.

The guy had just come from a workout, apparently, as he wore dark gray jogging pants and a sleeveless shirt with his jacket tied around his waist. In his right hand he held a tiny backpack. Yeah, it could not be helped, being at a store where they were scared to death that you would knock over a carefully constructed display with any appendage or protrusion at random. But to then demand someone take off even a teeny-weeny backpack like his... it would hardly even fit a compact camera!

Suddenly an eerie feeling came over me... The kind of feeling of déjà vu that sends shivers up and down one's spine, because I had seen such a miniscule backpack only once before... surely in combination with terry-cloth wristbands used to absorb sweat and most definitely alongside a cell phone that was attached to a well-trained upper arm with Velcro... As I held my breath I retreated behind the postcards and when I looked again extremely carefully I caught a glimpse of the guy deliberately leave the section, heading for the stairwell. His face I had not seen. Yet I knew with a nauseating certainty that I had just almost had a close-encounter with Egare. In other words: with Lucas!

That night I asked as casually as possible: "... So you have stalked me for an entire week?"

We were sitting on the upper deck of a tour bus, along with a few others who, like us, had chosen the brisk outside air over the noise of a group of American tourists downstairs.

"What makes you say that all of a sudden?" Aeolus straightened his back and released his disinterested gaze from the crowded streets south of London Bridge.

"Oh, no reason... isn't shadowing someone incredibly difficult?" I acted like it was a fairly unimportant question.

"To us, it isn't," he answered, cautiously.

"But surely it depends on the terrain, doesn't it?"

"I have put in a year or two. And I possess a few skills that help..."

"Have you ever been detected by someone?"

"No."

"And what about other vampires?"

Aeolus clearly was not pleased with this topic of conversation. "Rhona, you have experienced what it's like yourself. Unless we choose to make ourselves seen, a mortal will never be aware of being stalked by a vampire. Do you have more questions about this or can we talk about something else?"

I gestured that I was okay for now and stared at the Southwark Cathedral that we just passed. I was confused. Pretty sure I had seen Lucas earlier today... but then again, I truly wanted to believe what Aeolus had just told me as well. Perhaps I was mistaken after all.

It was around 7 p.m. and it had just turned dark. Two hours of doing nothing and only enjoying my time. That was the plus side of going on a tour like this. You sat down, shut off your brain and were driven around the touristic highlights of the city. I slumped down further in my seat and pulled up the collar of my coat. "Are you cold?" Aeolus asked.

"Not really," was my reply.

"You did eat something earlier, didn't you?"

"Of course I did. Behind Embankment Station I quickly wolfed down a hamburger. And you?"

"Don't worry about me, my love." And he held my gaze. But from a respectful distance. 'Safety first' he would probably be thinking... I wondered what it would feel like if he were to touch me right now. And how I would respond to that...

The HMS Belfast, Tooley Street and then Tower Bridge, by open-top double-decker bus... full of amazement I underwent the sensation of witnessing the ever-shifting perspectives within my field of vision. Leaned my head back and the first out of the two stone towers passed over me. Chambers, rooms with windows... if only you could live there! As we drove underneath the structures I turned around, watched the whole thing get smaller and smaller, tilted my head back again to let the second tower pass over me... Like a veritable Rainman. I was such a nutcase.

"Are you looking with your eyes or with your mind?" Aeolus asked.

"A little bit of both. And you?"

"I'm looking at how you're looking..."

"No, you are staring at me."

## 26

## CEMETERY

The following day was not any different. I marveled at the sight of all the buildings. I became drunk on his words as he described to me the architectural styles, the history... I took photos and he watched me, constantly, and that had already begun early that morning. At 8:30 a.m. we had agreed to meet in the same spot as yesterday and I was sipping my first Grande Latte. Aeolus' eyes followed my every move as I inspected the lens of my camera for dust. He observed me as I scrolled through yesterday's results one more time on the little display, then put my camera away in my bag and took another sip from the paper cup.

"Rhona, what does coffee taste like?" he suddenly asked.

"What coffee tastes like? Don't you know that yourself?"

"I don't."

"Yet you still drink it."

"If I have to, yes..."

"What does it taste like to you then?"

"That's not very interesting," he said. And he waited.

Thus I tried to explain to him what I thought about something that to me had become so trivial – but at the same time so indispensable for me to drink, and as I spoke my mind jumped from one train of thought to the next, like the conundrum of what was more important in the coffee drinking culture: the actual flavor of the beverage or the surrounding social aspects... and for a moment the look on Aeolus' face with which he observed me resembled that of an alien who had traveled to earth for the first time in his life to study the human race.

With a soft tingling excitement in my body I said: "Your turn. The taste of coffee."

"Have you ever drank blood?"

"I sometimes lick a wound or two..." I answered, quivering with the memory.

"Well, there you go."

No matter how much he managed to tug at my heart strings, something was eating me on the inside and I believed that it had everything to do with the rules of engagement that he had implemented on us. Because the strictness of those limitations, however sensible they may be, made me feel slightly impatient. The result was that I was constantly searching for something and that I genuinely missed him, even if he walked or sat right next to me. But... did I have the right to still feel that way? After all, so many things had already changed. The things I had not even dared to hope for two weeks ago had become a reality as the time passed: we were seeing each other in real time. Daily.

But what if I had not come to London at all? What would our relationship have looked like then? Would our online interaction not have hopelessly come to an explosion by now?

Change the subject... this was completely useless.

"Lucas... what sort of person was he anyway, back then?" I kicked a few pebbles and looked across the river. The light had already begun to dwindle.

"Lucas was an oblate."

"I don't know what that means."

"A juvenile monk."

"Huh? Don't they only exist in Buddhist monasteries?"

"We're talking about the Middle Ages here."

I waited for more to follow, but when that did not come, I asked: "Or is it something you don't want to talk about?"

"You're free to ask questions."

"Alright... he's from France, right? From where exactly?"

"Germany. He's from the border region between France and Germany. His monastery was located somewhere in the Black Forest."

"And how exactly did he end up there?"

"Oh, in the twelfth century it was common practice to bring your children to the monastery. The Swabian aristocrats were trying to keep their territory from splintering and for that reason only the first born child would receive the inheritance. The fate of younger siblings had thus not seldom been sealed from birth..."

"What kind of monastery was it?"

"Of the order of Saint Benedict."

"I see..." I mumbled.

Aeolus turned his head towards me and asked: "What do you mean by that?"

"Well, he has probably been heavily influenced by the teachings in that place. Something like that must shape your character in some way. Especially if you've been there since childhood..."

"Perhaps..." We slowed down to a stroll.

"And then? How did he become a vampire?"

"Umpff... Gee, I don't know, Rhona. He was probably sent out on an errand and then attacked... It would have been a very unfortunate coincidence, if that was the case, because a Benedictine monk almost never ventured out into the *big bad world*..."

We crossed the road, walked onto a minor street off of Tooley and turned left. The traffic noise was muted by the houses here, and the trees that draped their branches over the sidewalk created an intimate atmosphere.

"And what effect did his background have on you?"

"He was not the easiest person to deal with. But then again, neither was I."

"What happened? Did you guys butt heads a lot?"

"We did end up in a fight on occasions," he reluctantly said.

"Ah-ha... so *cat fights* don't only happen between girls after all." It was my attempt to make Aeolus laugh, but it did not work.

He said: "Listen, I'm not really comfortable with this subject. Can't we talk about something other than my world?"

"What world would you suggest then?" I asked, a little annoyed.

"Let's talk about something you've given me and that I'm incredibly grateful for..." Aeolus led me into a walled garden, one you would often see around old churches. However, this one had been converted to a small park and the building that was there appeared to have been repurposed. The bottom two, three yards of the structure consisted of age-old monoliths, but the section above it was much newer.

Aeolus explained that this was the location where he visited his square yard almost on a daily basis. That surprised me, to be honest. He had taken my advice to heart, that I knew. But the fact that he would keep it up for this long... I looked around in silence. A path ran through the park and split in the center to the left and to the right. There was grass that was not maintained properly throughout. And the trees that overshadowed the area at the border were at least a hundred years old...

"The building in front of you is actually built upon the ruins of a parish. St. John Horsleydown was built in the year 1733," he said. "In World War II it was bombed and in the mid-seventies the London City Mission purchased the land from the City of London to build on it. And here..." – he had walked to an inconspicuous corner underneath the chestnut and plane trees – "you can find me nearly every night practicing my patience..." With one smooth motion he squatted down and from his crouched position he looked up at me, waiting for a reaction. I wondered out loud whether he knew this place from way back when. He confirmed that he did. And whether he had lived in this same neighborhood as well. Aeolus got up. "Does *The Leather Market* not mean anything to you?" he asked incredulously.

"No. Yes, only by name, somewhere around here... man, you know I don't live in London, right?"

"You're right. Sorry. But anyway, that street does not carry that name without reason. You see this area was overrun with leatherworkers a few centuries ago and the ingredients that they used in the process were, among other things, urine and excrement of dogs... even a mortal human with their limited sense of smell could barely stand it. And then there was the sharp scent of spices coming from Butler's Wharf that hit you from the other side, not to mention the foul smell of fish that was carried into the city from across the bridge... No, thankfully those days are far behind us. I can open my windows now and revel in the fact that nostalgia is odorless."

I tried to imagine what things must have looked like in those days, and made an attempt to place him in the mental picture that I had created of that time, but quickly returned to the present. I sat down in the grass, with my legs crossed. To see what it was like, or actually, because I did not know what else to do at the moment... Against a wall, in the shadow of the large trees, there were a few graves that I had not noticed up until now.

I thought out loud. "This was once a larger cemetery..."

"That's right. London City Mission had purchased this ground for less than forty thousand pounds, if I remember correctly. A more than reasonable bargain. But the City of London did have a condition: before they began the construction the tombs underneath the ruin had to be cleared."

"Well, good riddance..."

Aeolus had been pacing around, but now stopped right in front of me.

"I beg your pardon?"

"I said: better gone than left to rot. I wouldn't want to work or live on top of a pile of corpses either."

The vampire's appearance, the way in which he stood in front of me in full stature, had something ominous to it. He asked: "Can you come up with even more things that directly have something to do with me?"

"What is that supposed to mean?" I reacted. "The fact that I'm talking about you too much? But what else can I do, since you take no interest in my personal background whatsoever!"

"Then – what –would – you – suggest, given our situation?"

"Well, how should I know?! You're the one making all the rules here, aren't you? So the best we can do is to keep going in the same way that we have, for all eternity, and continue until this conversation is dead and buried."

"The dead – are to be left to rest," he grimly said.

I scrambled to my feet. For a moment we stood there, in silence, with our faces within defiantly close proximity. Then he suddenly walked away, towards the exit of the little park. Without slowing down he looked back at me one last time and growled: "Here's a fun word for you to google: body snatching."

## 27

## GRAVE ROBBERY

What do you do when your boyfriend just stormed off angrily and you are convinced that it is your fault? Then you act like it is simply 'business as usual': you brush the sand and the leaves of grass off of your rear end. You pick up your bag. Check yourself to make sure that you really do not have to cry before you have to face other people in the street and then you go stand by a bus stop. After a little less than forty five minutes you walk into your hotel, ask for the key to your room with a straight face and once you get there you fix your make-up to then go out for a bit to grab some supper... Nope, I think not. At least, that last part turned out differently. I did get to my hotel room, but ended up staying there. Curled up in bed without getting changed and hoped that numbing sleep would come as soon as possible. But it never came, throughout the entire endless night it did not come. And between the horrors of guilt and confusion I counted along the hours and, finally, the minutes and seconds till morning arrived and I was finally, *finally* able to go downstairs for breakfast. There I managed to wash down a miserable slice of white bread with two cups of coffee that was so weak that it could easily pass for tea. I had to find something better than this.

In due course in Soho and satisfied with something pseudo-nutritious in my stomach, I crawled behind the screen of a computer at an internet café. I booked my return flight for the upcoming Thursday and went through some emails. All of that took me less than ten minutes. What to do with the remainder of my thirty minutes?
Perhaps find out more about Lucas' background? Google *Benedictine monastic orders*? Or... *body snatching*?
The bastard – Aeolus could see right through me – he mentioned a single search word and the 'young investigator' in me was immediately triggered! In spite of this, my curiosity trumped my annoyance, and so I began to google.

Body snatching turned out to be a phenomenon that, needless to say, happened frequently in previous centuries and anatomy professors as well as their students played a central role in it. The bodies that were supplied for autopsies in those days were predominantly of those who had received the death sentence. This was the only legal way for schools of medicine in England to obtain material and although the number of cadavers that had been donated to science still ran into the hundreds toward the end of the seventeenth century, it had dropped to no more than fifty five by the year 1800. At that time death by hanging was only reserved for the worst criminals... Nevertheless, teachers still had to fulfill their academic duties and to do so they looked for other resources. And so they took to robbing graves. They either did this themselves or 'specialists', from the ranks of disreputable persons were dispatched to do the needed business.

Because cooling installations for the recently deceased did not yet exist and only fresh cadavers could be used in anatomy classes, time was of the essence for these robbers. At night, immediately after a funeral was the best moment to strike. But for obvious reasons the families of the deceased did not want the grave of their loved ones to be plundered. Therefore they took every possible measure to prevent it from happening. Sometimes wrought iron fences were placed around the grave, the so-called *mort safes.* In addition, guards were specifically hired to make sure nothing happened... unless they in turn were bribed by the body snatchers.

I stretched my back and ordered another cup of coffee. My fifth one of the day. There was something that I did not quite understand. What I had been reading was a part of history that Aeolus must have been involved with himself. And, to be granted, it did fit relatively well into the image that I had compiled in my head as I tried to place him in that period of time. The dark London of Jack the Ripper, for example... didn't this neighborhood, Bermondsey, also belong to that? Or was I mistaken?

But still – why give me this particular search item? What was Aeolus trying to tell me with it?

I decided to pay for another thirty minutes of internet and continued reading. About the techniques that were used for the excavation, about underground tunnels and prying away the head panel of coffins, about the way in which bodies were then dragged up those tunnels and were unearthed through an inconspicuous hole that was only the size of a man... After a while some had apparently adopted a new method to acquire bodies: cold-blooded murder. Anything for big money... Burke and Hare from Edinburgh. And *The London Burkers,* who supplied the enormous amount of 500 to 1000 cadavers to hospitals and universities within a twelve year period... Their punishment was exactly what they had coming: sentenced to death and their bodies donated to science... Finally, one year later in 1832 the Anatomy Act put an end to these practices, because it brought forth many more legal ways for med schools to obtain their bodies.

I glanced over all the information that I had come across one more time. There must be something that I had missed... and suddenly I knew what it was: the reason why the worst criminals not only received death by hanging, but were also handed to anatomy professors afterwards, and the reason why families of the deceased were so desperately afraid of grave robbery, had everything to do with how they believed that the eternal life after death worked! The dead who could not find rest in their grave, a deceased person who was minutely studied by a professor on a table in a medicine program, was thought not to get access to heaven, and its purpose was to totally scare and straighten out those who considered going down the criminal path. Aside from that it must have been an unbearable thought to have something like that happen to your loved one...

All of a sudden the image that was in my mind of Aeolus dressed in historic clothing and wearing a top hat became less remote. It became hauntingly realistic even regarding how I could picture him in the dead of the night at a cemetery, watching over the recently covered grave of those whose life he had single-handedly taken shortly prior to that, from the shadows... ready to attack, as revenge against anyone who threatened to deny his victim access to eternal life!
I had lost all desire to finish my coffee. I closed my session, paid at the cash register and walked to the nearest tube station.

## 28

## OPERA

*Manhattan, New York City, Fall 1878.*

The view of the stage from the first balconies is better than most visitors of the Academy of Music can afford.

They have the four-seater opera box to themselves, the woman dressed in green and her companion, and from this position to the side, right above the orchestra, it almost seems as though they are not part of the audience, but rather of the group of singers and actors that together make up the opera company, and that they are sitting amongst them in the living room of the main character: Violetta, a famous Parisian courtesan. The colossal chandeliers, the curtains draped in front of make-believe windows and the potted plants larger than men, every detail of this production appears so lifelike... The only thing that separates the beautifully clad artists and themselves is the fact that on the stage you are taken back roughly a quarter century in fashion years in time. There the impeccable dress suit has not yet been replaced by the three-piece suit and the women still wear the largest hoop skirts that were ever made in history.

The woman in the private box stares in front of her while her left hand plays with the tulle that is draped over her shoulders. With her thumb and index finger she pinches small, sharp creases into the fabric and then she, seemingly without being aware of it, presses the folds flat again. The man follows the absentminded gaze of the woman to the flickering light of a gas lamp somewhere nearby on the wall, and then returns his eyes back to her. When she notices that she is being watched, however, her attention immediately shifts to La Traviata.

"You're doing it again," he says.

"What am I doing, my love?" the woman asks innocently.

The man ignores her question. "How many times has it actually been for you?"

"This opera? In total?" For a moment the woman acts like she is deep in thought. Then she theatrically opens her fan and looking just over its half-round, black lace rim she seductively bats her big brown eyes. "Hmm, however much could it be? The hundredth time... the *two hundredth* perhaps?" And she throws her head back in laughter.

The man does not bother to hide his irritation any longer. He hisses a precautionary "Siria...!" but Siria is barely impressed. With a whiny tone of voice she says: "Mi amore, I can't help it – I'm just dying of boredom. All that going on and on about the pleasures of life... But most of all, I *cannot* stand her!"

The fan collapses in one vicious motion and points at Violetta, who drunkenly professes her love for Alfredo in song from a practically upside-down position on the sofa.

"Her performance is, in my opinion, not without merit..." the man suggests, but nevertheless she sighs: "Only if you enjoy that insufferable, shrill tone of voice... and totally misplaced vibratos..."

Siria's lover objects again, but eventually has to admit: also for him it is already the ninth time to see La Traviata.

"Then let us leave now, Raphaël," she says hopefully. "Nobody can stop us, right?"

"Alright. Let's go," is the reply. "But may I suggest we do so *after* the first act?"

Needless to say Siria cannot wait that long. The minute the soprano hits the first note of *Sempre Libera* she triumphantly gets up out of her seat while remarking that she can sing this aria better in her dreams and as soon as she links arms with Raphaël in the street she naturally demonstrates this in a theatrical manner, holding an imaginary champagne glass in her free hand that she, at the end of her tune, flips over, pouting her lips in disappointment.

At this hour Irving Place is virtually deserted. Only horses' hooves, coming and going, and the rattling of the wheels of a carriage that passes by resonates against the brown, stone facades of buildings to the left and to the right. The wind, though, is gradually manifesting itself in more intensity. A storm may come tonight...

On their walk they come upon Gramercy Park and as they pass it by Siria looks at trees and bushes behind the wrought-iron fence. Suddenly she pinches the arm of her companion and says: "Raph, I want to play."

He too has glanced at the densely varying shrubbery in passing. Then he looks up, to the houses that surround the relatively small park and to the windows and the lighting that burns behind them. He says: "To be honest, this does not strike me as the place most suitable. Could we perhaps find an alternate location?"

And then she tells him which spot she has in mind – a suggestion that considerably changes the otherwise very distant look on the man's face – and as they proceed towards Broadway a certain spirit of joyful expectation can discernibly be detected in the both of them.

They walk, arm-in-arm, past theaters, restaurants and townhouses, all the way to Columbus Circle. Therein lies the southern entrance to Central Park. Like a small child Siria jumps excitedly...

He has just relighted his cigar and he continues walking while deep in thought, on the sparingly illuminated path, among trees, meadows and rock formations... a man of middle age – a man of the upper class. His stature is easy to read by the flawless black coat that he is wearing and by the height of his silk hat – a hat that he has to grab hold of every now and then to protect it from the sweeping gusts of wind.

Here, in Central Park, no one can see him. Not many people dare to set foot in it after nightfall and that may be the exact reason why he has chosen this location for his evening stroll. Perhaps he prefers to contemplate business or personal affairs in solitude...

A young man and a woman are talking to each other, slightly hesitant, at a point where two paths cross. Most notably, her silhouette stands out against the glare of the street lanterns: her hair neatly done up and a long coat with that unmistakable accent at the back of her hips. The young man disengages from his conversation with the woman and takes a couple of steps towards the man in the hat. He asks him if he perhaps knows where they can find an exit that is close to 6th Avenue. "...for you see, we're not from around here," he explains, "we began to wander while conversing and now we have lost all sense of direction." He goes on to tell him about the hotel that he and his wife are staying at since a few days prior, somewhere south of the park.

The man rubs his beard, looks away from the young man and his wife, who has joined them in the meantime. Then he makes a decision. He removes the cigar from his mouth and mumbles with mild reluctance: "I had better take you there myself."

The two spare no effort in expressing their gratitude. "I must confess that I was beginning to feel a little anxious here in the dark," the young man chuckles.

"What my wife and I believed to have heard, just now – it couldn't have been anything but a wolf. Or at least some other predatory animal... and we'd be damned to wait and find out the appetite of such a monster..."

It appears as though their guide is very knowledgeable on this area, as he immediately declares, with an almost disdainful conviction, their fears to be unfounded. At most "they had heard a dog howl, or possibly an inhabitant of the zoo back there," he says, and he attempts to smile modestly when they ask him whether *he* himself is never scared to be in Central Park, all alone in the dark on a moonless night such as this...

So he shows them the way, across a bridge with elegant wrought-iron balustrades and then past the serene stillness of a pond with some swans in it and he listens to the woman as she begins to talk about La Traviata.

"My good sir, how poor the quality of this performance was, I can't even begin to express in words," she complains. "It truly was an assault to the ears. Out of pity towards the performing artists we have tried to hold out for as long as we could, but eventually we had no choice but to leave the concert hall prematurely…" And while her beloved complements her case by providing examples of musical blunders and abominable acting – one illustration more colorful than the other – the man slides his spectacles a little further up the bridge of his nose.

They enter a poorly lit path that winds its way between the surrounding elevation of small hills and rock formations.

"It's a shame, wouldn't you say, that a lovely lady such as her should become so disappointed with what could have been a pleasant evening about town? It has really knocked her off her senses. Here, I'll show you…" and with a sudden, loud growl the young man presses his face into the neck of the woman, to which she first responds with a high-pitched shriek followed by a girlish giggle. By the body language of the man in the hat it is plain to see how much he is startled as well…

The couple remains in their jolly mood a little longer, but at a certain point it is gone and relieved they suddenly look each other in the eye, as though they experience an 'a-ha' moment at the exact same time. Then the young man places his hand on the arm of his accompanist. "I'm sorry…" he says, "I can't believe it didn't dawn on me sooner: we have completely forgotten to introduce ourselves to you!"

It takes a minute for the other party to adjust to the sudden change of topic, but then he mutters something like: "Oh, it's not that important."

The two now, however, insist on making a formal introduction. "Royston, pleased to meet you," the young man says and he politely tips the rim of his hat.

"Vasbinder, likewise."

"At least, for today that is…"

"Pardon me?"

"For *today* my name is Royston. And what was yours again, my dear?"

"Camelia…! I have always wanted to be a Camelia once!" Delighted the woman claps her gloved hands and her husband praises her name of choice extensively.

Up until now, without giving it too much thought, Mister Vasbinder had probably assumed this couple to be just a tad eccentric, or at most a little inebriated on liquor. However, now his irritation will slowly give way to a mild sensation of uneasiness and the thought will creep into his head that he could be dealing with two lunatics that have escaped from Roosevelt Island. And the wind that howls around chestnut saplings and chases away fallen leaves behind people's feet in sudden gusts, steadily picks up…

"A game! Didn't you say you wanted to play, Camelia?"

"Yesss, a game, I can't wait!" The woman lets go of her lover's arm, hop-skips to the other side going around the backs of the two men and locks arms with Mister Vasbinder. "Will you join us?"

He shakes his head, hastily.

"Don't you enjoy a little game of hide and seek? Or – tag! Maybe you'll enjoy a game of tag!"

They arrive at the east exit of Central Park somewhat sooner than initially anticipated. Mister Vasbinder knows that this is largely due to his own walking pace, as it eventually also enabled him to force the married couple to abandon their 'whims of folly', or 'adventures', or however one might define their behavior. And while the woman looks back one last time, towards the trees and the grass and the finality of the coming night, he lifts his hat and runs his hand through his hair. At least there are people in the street, as well the horse tram runs here – he takes a long draw from his cigar. With new, regained resolution he then says: "I'm not of the game-playing type."

"- You're *not* of the game-playing type?" is the immediate response. "Do you mean to say that we had been right all along? That, like us, you are a true aficionado of the opera...?" Royston purposefully makes eye contact with him. He grins, and then Mister Vasbinder sees something that up to now he has only seen in his dreams, while bathing in cold sweat, or in his mind's eye during his younger years, when he still dared to read the poetry of Lord Byron and the dark novels of Paul Féval. But his eyes could be deceiving him, and with an evasive look to the left he tries to hold on to his rational mind. Camelia looks back at him and exposes her teeth with a big smile. In response to his stupefied facial expression she clasps her hand to her mouth under the guise of a coquettish "whoops!" and when she takes it away everything, including the length of her incisors, has magically turned back to normal.

"What is this?" the man asks. "What do you want from me??"

The woman softly whispers in his ears "*panem et circenses*" and her lover translates: "Bread and games, my friend, that is what the people demand." Pleased, the vampire folds his arms behind his back, while his wife's are still tightly locked with Mister Vasbinder's. In this manner they cross 59th Street, on their way to 6th Avenue.

"We represent the people, you know, Camelia and myself, and you are going to see to our needs. At least, our need for entertainment. You see, we are bored..."

"Bored to death," she chimes in.

They run into people going out and about, pass groups of people that are talking amongst themselves and Mister Vasbinder looks at them, hoping to make contact, looking for an escape. But Royston says: "*Smile*, my friend, you should know that laughter sometimes is the only way by which one can save himself."

Thus he laughs, albeit reluctantly, and he walks the streets with the couple, in which not a soul has even the slightest inkling as to the bleak reality that suffocates him a little further with each step that they take.

The wind howls and roars around the buildings that reach even up to six levels high in this place, and to the left are the steps leading up to the terminal station of the 6th Avenue Elevated – the brand new *El,* that runs to the south of Manhattan on steel pylons, three tracks wide, right overhead of the traffic on the ground. Passengers hurry up the stairs, to the train that sits in wait hissing and blowing off steam, for what could be its final run for the evening to Battery Place.

Royston takes a quick glance behind them, seemingly toward the station, and then brings up the opera and the division of roles in their own, private rendition of La Traviata. He expects, he muses, that his new friend is perfectly suited to play the role of *Giorgio,* the part of Alfredo's ruthless father who, halfway through the story, forbids the promiscuous Violetta to maintain her relations with his son any longer.

"At least you are of an age befitting the part, wouldn't you say?"

But Mister Vasbinder shakes his head. "I am not a singer," he objects, "and I'm really not cut out for acting."

Those excuses are, however, heartily ridiculed. "So precious... that feigned modesty... wouldn't you agree, dearest? He clearly is experienced in playing weak characters."

"And in telling white lies, apparently. Speaking of lies, do you know, Mister Vasbinder, that we don't always tell the complete truth either? For instance, we have told you that we were married, while in reality that is entirely untrue. At most, I am with Royston for, shall we say, companionship."

" – Which, of course, makes *her* perfect for the role of Violetta."

The man in the hat tugs at the tight collar around his neck. The black narrow bow tie loosens a little, but his voice sounds just as pinched as before, when he tells them that a different candidate might be much more suited than he is...

" – For what? To play the role of the bad guy??" it came sharply. "Who else could play that better than you, *Mister Factory Owner?*"

"Huh?" He sputters and then coughs. The cigar tumbles out of his mouth and bounces to a rest on the pavement. "How do you know that I – "

" – Experience, Vasbinder, life experience. If you've been around for as long as I have, it is easy to spot types such as yourself... the disdain with which you look your fellow man in the eye – you of all people should know how deeply it symbolizes the scrupulousness with which you trample others? For money, to misappropriate a certain status or to steal the brilliant ideas of your subjugates... your kind is so painfully transparent."

On 6th Avenue, quite a ways behind them, the steam whistle of the locomotive can be heard... signaling for the train's departure and, seemingly aware of what is about to transpire, Mister Vasbinder starts to plead for his life. "I'm a respected member of society, and supply aide to widows and orphans," he says in an urgent tone of voice, and when the vampires look away in contempt he turns to literal begging: "I have money, tell me how much you want and it's *yours*!"

But his voice seems to fall on deaf ears. In a menacing tone of voice Royston begins to sing *Brindisi,* while Camelia looks back towards the train that now begins to move. "It is time," she says and then she and her lover pull Mister Vasbinder into a narrow, dark alley. There they compel him back to where only the shadows rule and where they are practically invisible to the eyes of passersby.

"Participate, Vasbinder! If we have to do all the work, there's no fun in it. Surely you know the lyrics by heart? 'Let us drink, for wine will bring more passionate kisses...' Go on, and now in Italian: *Libiamo, amore, amore fra ' calici...!'*... Mister Vasbinder, however, has already forgotten his lines since the onset of the 'drinking song'. He can only stare at the distance that is growing between himself and the Land of the Living, the living souls who, without noticing him or his attackers, pass by on the street so unreachably near... And while the huffing and puffing of the steam train grows louder as it gets nearer and the beams of its headlight transform the humid air above 6th Avenue into a white, impenetrable mist, he can only watch as the vampires, here protected by the shadows, sing and dance around him in ever diminishing circles. Then the male vampire suddenly grabs his waist from behind and the woman squats in front of him. She tears the material of his pants from off one leg and sinks her teeth deep into his thigh. Simultaneously he feels a sharp, piercing pressure in his neck. Vasbinder screams for his life, but no one is there to help him.

Meanwhile, the sparks that are flying off the train tracks, along with shards of jet-black cinders, blend with his yelling... and his splattering blood with the hysteric screeching of the steam whistle.

"Whoooo, hahahahaha..."

"Shush...! The neighbors..."

There is some fumbling by the door lock and a few moments later the duo stagger into the living room of the apartment. While he begins to pull off her long, bloodstained gloves, she kicks the door with the heel of her right shoe that slams shut with slightly too loud a bang as a result. He leans into her, kisses her on the lips and then runs his tongue downward, over her chin and down her neck, over the metallic taste of the scarlet on her skin. But she frees herself from his embrace.

"Let me go freshen up first," Siria says, and putting her words into action she walks over to the wash basin. She picks up the water pitcher and begins to pour. Raphaël comes up behind her, takes the pitcher from her hands and puts it back from where it came. "That can wait," he mumbles. He turns her body towards him and while he looks at her desirously, he holds her hand. He begins to walk backwards, but halfway across the walk to the sofa his foot is caught behind the Persian rug and as a reflex his free hand launches for the side table with the Ming dynasty vase on it. Both tip over – the blue and white porcelain smashes to pieces on the hardwood floor. "How unfortunate..." he says – and behind her back his hand feverishly searches for the opening of her skirt – but Siria gasps between a number of heavy kisses: "Who cares... it'll save me some... when packing up for... another relocation." His jacket and waistcoat fall to the floor, are trampled on and shoved aside. Then Raphaël kneels down and directs Siria to lower herself to the floor. While she's sitting opposite him, he removes her skirt and loosens the laces of her shoes making slow movements. He kisses her stockings, takes them off one by one, caresses her ankles, knees and thighs and at the same time he pushes her underskirt upwards, pushing heavily over her skin. When his hands reach her hips, he changes position, straddling her, pushing her down to the floor. Then he places his index and middle fingers at the top of her corset like scissors and he begins to cut, right through lace and satin, straight against the resistance of its metal boning and all predominating rules of decency...

"Sixth Avenue... whatever made you think of that..." She is lying beside him on the floor, half naked, surrounded by ripped off and torn open pieces of clothing.
"Yes, I thought it fairly clever of me as well..." Raphaël folds his hands behind his head.
"Just hilarious, how that fool considered himself to be safe once the park was behind him. And then we sprung that Big Surprise on him... just brilliantly directed, my dear." She looks at him.
"Thank you," he says, and he stares at the milky white crown molding along the ceiling – corner features and rosettes.
Siria sighs satisfied. "Hmmm, making love right after dinner is so immensely delicious... don't you think?"
He turns his head towards her and looks her in the eye: "I do not love you, Siria."
She remains silent.
"I just can't do it."
She shrugs. After a while she says: "You and I are too much alike anyway. I knew this was bound to happen..."
"So you understand...?"
"Of course."
He smiles and strokes her cheek once. Then he gets up and puts on his clothes. He blows her a kiss goodbye. "I'm sure we'll run into each other again some place or another," he says. "Oh, and that vase, I'll compensate you for it."
"And for my corset as well!" she yells as he leaves.
Siria rolls onto her side with her back facing the door that Raphaël has just closed behind him. She curls up into the fetal position and squeezes her eyes shut...

## 29

PIANIST

Aeolus had mentioned before that there was something masochistic about me. And he could be right about that. Why else would this train 'just so happened' to have brought me to London Bridge and for what other reason could I now be heading to the Shad Thames area, completely on autopilot? It was tempting to believe that autopilot part, but I was not stupid. There was no doubt in my mind that I was consciously aware of what I was doing, however dumb it may be. Because what was it that I was trying to accomplish anyway? Visit him, completely out of the blue? Give a break... Oh well, first I had to keep walking. After all, I did not see any reason as to why I should not be allowed to enter this neighborhood. In a trendy area such as this, was it not the most normal thing in the world to enjoy the morning sun in some café or another, with a newspaper and something to drink in front of me? Maybe that would even be therapeutic for me, in any case, it was much better than obsessively associating a neighborhood exclusively with one of its residents and then avoiding it anxiously, filled with misplaced guilt. My walking pace had been steadfast, bordering on zealousness, but became slower when I passed under the pylon on the southern end of Tower Bridge and turned to a crawl when the pronounced shadows of the distinctive balconies came into view on the paving stones of the Shad Thames. Hesitatingly I stopped in front of the Starbucks on the corner. If I really looked inside myself honestly, the fact that I was here at all placed me in a kind of light that did not do my self-image any good – man, I looked like a desperate teenager, or worse, some hysterical, unstable woman...

With an exasperated sigh I decided to forget about Starbucks and made a dash through the gate beneath the houses instead, to the waterfront. I needed to straighten my thoughts. I would walk up and down the boulevard ten times, if that is what it would take. I had to go over my lines one more time, in case I would need them. Because what if I could not resist the temptation and rang his doorbell anyway... Shit, what was I getting all nervous for? What in the world was I so afraid of? Rejection, making a fool out of myself? Or to... I forced myself to stop walking. This was as far as I was going to go anyway: I had arrived at the corner where the Design Museum was situated and everything beyond this point was off limits. With my bad record of luck Aeolus would probably spot me from his place in the distance immediately, if I were to cross the street here...

A bench overlooking the Thames had to do as my base of retreat for now. I was such a stupid cow, with my head in a storm, and all because of one single person! My brain needed a different subject to focus on... But where and how, for heaven's sake, could I find that distraction?

The answer to that question I had already heard briefly in the background, but it did not register until now: the occupant of the corner house right across from the museum had his windows opened wide and was playing the piano most beautifully. I got up and looked for a spot from which I could watch him play. It was unbelievable, how the characters who lived here all seemed to look alike: young, rich and successful. And of course this man reminded me of Aeolus. What would it be like if it had been him sitting there, playing his viol? Would his windows have been fully opened as well?

All of a sudden I was completely sick and tired of myself, the entire situation that I was in and all of my insecurities! I stood up resolutely and after having discharged all the adrenalin out of my lungs I turned into the street that lead straight to his home. My nerves, however, kept creeping up on me, as well as the uncertainty of whether I was being watched as I approached his apartment in such plain view... I tried to ignore it and rang the doorbell before I could change my mind. I was totally convinced that my heartbeat could be heard loud and clear from Aeolus' apartment and I had to fight tooth and nail to not make a run for it anyway. It took so long before the response came through the intercom that I had almost turned myself around. But then a stoic voice emerged that asked who was at the door.

"Rhona", I said, and I cleared my throat.

Amidst loud buzzing the door opened. My legs felt limp and shaky as I climbed the stairs to his apartment. By the time I got upstairs, however, I was a determined woman standing before the man that let me come in.

"What brings you here?" he asked, as he sat down on the couch.

"Oh, I just happened to be in the neighborhood. I'm not interrupting anything, am I?"

His expression did not exude hospitality and he was not forthcoming in his reply.

I had sat down in the reclining chair across from him and did not allow myself to avert my eyes from him. He certainly was insufferable. So gorgeous, in that stylish track suit and with that impenetrable aura of his... but I refused to be swayed by it all. This time things would be different!

"Say, that art poster in your bedroom with that man, woman and children, that's a piece by Klimt, isn't it?" I asked.

He nodded.

"What made you choose that painting in particular? Because you recognize yourself in it?"

His gaze turned dark. He looked me straight in the eye. Silence... But I had given it a shot and now the ball was in his court. When no response came, however, I raised my voice again.

"Did you know there is a man about your age living on the corner across from the museum who plays the piano?" I asked, feigning angelic innocence. "His windows were open, so I stayed and listened for a while. Really brilliant, the things he could do with that instrument..."

Something in Aeolus' eyes burst into flames. He said: "That's strange... in a serenade it's usually the other way around, with the man standing below the balcony."

An explosion of aggression launched me out of my chair. I got to him within two steps and with all the anger that I had inside of me, I hit him on the cheek. A hissing growl was followed by a move quick as lightning that made me fall over and land on the couch. I did not truly realize what had happened until he almost lay on top of me, with a knee pinning down my legs and his hands around my wrists on either side of my head. "I'm not impervious to pain, young lady," he seethed. The subtle, yet clearly visible widening of his nostrils gave a clear indication as to what the man could be feeling...

It took a while for me to regain control over my breathing. Then I lifted up my head as high as I could and my lips zoned in on his.

Aeolus' response came immediately: he pushed me down hard and then his mouth, his tongue and his hands were everywhere. Sucking, licking... finding their way over my hips, kneading my hair, touching the skin of my face and, for a moment, out of sheer madness – even though I had obviously planned for this to happen – I did not know what to do. But then my hands also began to travel and caress, a little uncertain at first and then more and more purposefully, over the curvature of his shoulder blades and along the movements of his spine – he was so agile, so inhumanly agile... and the way in which he raised his upper body and stretched out his arms to my sides and looked at me from above, with that strange look of, of – Aeolus bent his head down. He looked at his lower body, or mine, and planted his knee between my thighs. Slowly his leg pushed his way upwards, towards my crotch... to then move back down again after all... next, he dropped himself with his full weight on top of me. I gasped for air, he buried his face in the pillows beside me and after having stuck his arms through my armpits he clung to me, tightly, very tightly.

For a few moments nothing happened. We just lay there, his breath right next to my ear and his heart, beating wildly, this close to mine... suddenly Aeolus turned his head to the right and his lips made their way to my forehead. There, he painfully slowly left behind traces of cool moisture, thin as silk, as he connected with my temple, across my cheek and onto my jawline. He stopped at my neck. He took in my scent. Carefully, inquisitively. He pressed his face against the side of my throat and inhaled deeply...

"Um, I wish you wouldn't do that," I objected, but he continued and unexpectedly I suddenly found myself wrestling him. How *could* I have been this naive to think that – " – Don't be scared, baby girl," he said, however, and restrained my hands and my legs and like a skilled lover he interrupted my protesting with deeply intense French kisses. And immediately his caresses returned. My shirt popped out of my pants and I could feel his naked skin touch mine and just as I was thinking: "How much further can this go, how much longer…" everything stopped as abruptly as it had begun. Aeolus stood up, helped me up, straightened my clothes and ran both his hands through my hair. He sighed heavily, like one would often hear people do deeply who have just experienced something traumatizing, while feeling suppressed and trembling slightly. Then he grabbed me by my left upper arm and pushed me towards the door, into the stairwell, down the stairs. He flung the front door open. Once we got to the sidewalk he handed me my bag. With his eyes mindlessly fixed on some arbitrary point beyond my shoulder he said: "You have just challenged a vampire. If you have even the slightest notion of reality in your system, you'll never do that again." Then he left me behind as he turned and went back inside.

## 30

INCOGNITO

My new friend at the front desk of the hotel crassly asked: "are you drunk?" when I gave her the wrong room number twice in a row. Yes, I was drunk, or rather, completely hammered. And I desperately needed to sleep it off. And after that, get back to the order of everyday business, which, at the very least, included a visit to the Asylum, later, and if I were to set my alarm to three thirty, I would have just the right amount of time to get dressed, fix myself up a little and take the train ride into Soho. With not a minute to spare to mull things over. Distraction, a different world... The real world. Ashley seemed surprised. And so did Andrew. But they were happy with my unannounced visit and almost instantly I got to talking to a girl that I had not seen here before. She was dressed in a burlesque outfit that, among other things, included a sexy corset and fishnet stockings, and on her head she wore black cat ears made out of plush material. It was not difficult to like her, because she had an infectious, creative mind and a delightful American accent. Still it was quite a challenge for me to keep my attention focused on the conversation with her, as literally everything distracted me. The television set that was being tested compressed all the information floating around in the ether into a wall of sound that was impossible to ignore, and it seemed to be in ferocious competition with the metal-to-metal noise of the set of keys in the hands of the guy who had just come in. All of this was pierced by the deafening siren of an ambulance out in the streets... and *still* I felt the temptation to listen in on the conversation that was happening one level below me between Ash and a guy who had just rung the doorbell and had been let in. Actually that noise was the main culprit here. I should just not try to focus on everything all at once! Something like that would make anyone go crazy – if I did not watch myself I might begin to imagine things, 'hear things', so to speak... I excused myself in front of the American girl, began to wander around and ended up at the pool table, upon which the pamphlets and flyers that I remembered from last time, were neatly stacked. As slowly and carefully as possible I began to lay them out on the table, purely to keep busy, but even that proved to be too difficult for me. I could not keep myself from constantly looking out of the corner of my eyes at the door that lead to the stairwell: Ashley and the person that had just come in had lingered on the lower level and at this moment were talking about how he had heard of The Asylum through a friend. And about the fact that he was passing through, on his way to Prague. And about his work as a musician... this really was not funny anymore. Whatever made me link the voice of this man to that of Aeolus? Why did my obsession get a hold of me even now while I had gone above and beyond to act normal this afternoon, and after what had happened this morning to not let my thoughts get caught in a blizzard? Was it because I did not have enough patience with the speed at which I processed things, that these figments of my imagination would even rear their ugly heads in this place?

No, that was not it. It was because at this very moment Aeolus himself had walked into the upstairs room of The Intrepid Fox...!

I grabbed a hold of the edge of the pool table to keep myself from collapsing. I was fully aware of how wide and shocked my eyes looked as they followed his every move, but I really had no control over it. Why did he just *have* to fit into this setting so perfectly, with those jet black jeans and that weird Rammstein T-shirt? Not to mention that behavior of his, which indivisibly and seamlessly complemented the situation that we found ourselves in: to come across as sympathetic, yet oh so modest – in short, very British – and casually introduce himself to some people left and right while making some small talk like it was nothing... After a minute or so he moved in the direction of where I was standing.

"Hello, my name is Kazimír," he said. He reached out his hand to me. "And you and I are strangers to one another", he then said in Dutch, almost inaudibly. I returned his gesture in kind, but my other hand had tightened around the edge of the billiard table like a vise grip. "You cannot do this! Please go away..." I whispered.

"... You think I come across as too desperate?" he asked.

"No, uh, no..." I stammered, "but my real name..." and I briefly turned my head towards the other people at The Fox.

"Don't worry," he interjected, "I already know that your name is *Lente Sandifer*."

"What the...?" I let slip, much too loudly. I looked around immediately, having startled myself.

"I advise you to mind your facial expression," Aeolus said calmly.

Shit, yes, I had to be careful. Smile. We were strangers and we have just met. I repeated that to myself a couple of times. His name was Kazimír and mine was Lente. But how – how in the world...?

"You're wondering how I discovered your true identity. Did you forget that I have stalked you for a week before we met? I lost track of how many times I have heard you utter your name, but..."

"Yeah yeah, you can stop now," I interrupted... I did not need to hear one more word to feel like the most naive creature to ever walk this godforsaken earth.

Keep it cool. "So that also means you know I live in Rotterdam," I deduced. The man walked to the window and let his gaze wander across the street and towards St. Giles on the other side. "I already knew that during our very first chat session."

"What do you mean?" I had followed him and started to move some bar stools next to where he stood.

The vampire was clearly enjoying the situation. "Never heard of tracing IP-addresses," he asked with feigned surprise. "Anyone with even the slightest internet connection can do that. It is so easy..." and he stretched out lazily, with his arms above his head.

"Sure, you go get comfortable in the reclining chair of your power," I grumbled through my teeth.

"Aaah, the poeticism of a disgruntled woman. How seductive..." he mused.

I wanted to do nothing more than look at him with my most destructive gaze. To which he, with his back towards the others in the room, blew me a hasty, but defiant kiss.


The time had come for the quote-on-quote official part of this afternoon and everyone took a seat on the wooden benches around the table laden with candy and chips. I counted the number of people present; there were twelve of us. Aeolus had sat down on the other end across from me and ignored me just enough to appear to be the stranger that he pretended to be.

Two music videos of a rock band that someone had brought with them on a DVD were played. Then we were given the opportunity to meditate on the material in silence. Next came a silly 'prayer exercise'. The blond guy with the pony tail, whom I remembered from last time, handed out sheets of paper and pens to us. We were all going to fold airplanes, but before we got to that, he asked us to write a prayer on the paper. A prayer that we would then send to heaven symbolically.

Actively participate and come up with something yourself... how, *for Heaven's sake*, was I going to achieve that under these circumstances? "Dear God, please take care of all the lonely people in the world," was the first vague, halfhearted thing that came to my mind and after having scribbled that onto my piece of paper, I began to fold it. Fingers crossed that I would not be asked to share the motivation behind it...

With our paper creations in hand we all walked to a corner of the room and with each plane that was released the corresponding prayer was spoken out loud by its maker. Aeolus participated as well. His prayer was short but intriguing: "When, God?"

It was a fascinating experience to see him move amongst real people. Because – how much effort would it take for him to function normally within a group such as this? Would his years of experience help him with that? Or was he at the mercy of the prevailing situation and how it developed each and every time? His behavior seemed very normal... If someone was talking, he listened carefully. He laughed just like everyone else at the unexpected turns that some airplanes took in their flight... it all seemed to come natural to him. Or was that just an act? After all, he was an experienced actor. But were we not all, did we not all play different roles in our   lives? Then why was it so different in his case? The fact was that this was the first time that I was witnessing his 'game' firsthand. And on top of that, I had literally become a part of that game. What I learned within a mere few minutes was that it was a bloody complicated affair and that with everything you did or said you had to be on your toes. A mistake was probably easily made...

The subject of the group discussion that afternoon evaded me. I picked up bits and pieces of most of the things that were said. Terms like 'being different' made their rounds – for example, a girl talked about her church that took a somewhat questionable stance towards her and her alternative style of clothing... Someone also spoke of God's acceptance, which according to him, went far beyond that of humans. And a comment was made about finding the balance between nonconformity and pragmatically adapting yourself to your surroundings...

Suddenly Aeolus said: "If I were to go to church and completely be myself there, I would immediately be cursed out and excommunicated."

The others nodded sympathetically, I completely froze and Andrew asked: "Excommunication? As in: banishment? Do you mean that you have experienced that at some point?"

Aeolus nodded.

Ash seemed to be the only one in the group who was not impressed. At least, she sounded fairly scornful when she said: "Well, thank goodness that redemption does not depend on the approval of man. Otherwise Jesus, the ultimate expert by experience, would have presented that to us as the gospel back then."

Aeolus ignored her comment. "Anyway," he said, "I'll just keep the 'being myself' restricted to the boundaries of the four walls of my house and to the moments in which I am among those of my own kind." As he said those last words, he made quotation marks with his hands while grinning. For a brief moment the group fell silent. Then a guy sitting somewhere to my right said: "I don't know whether you're a believer, but if you are, I trust that you know in front of whom you can safely take off your mask..."

"Oh, I definitely believe," was Aeolus' response. "In His existence and in His word. However, I'm not sure that the promise embedded in it applies to me as well."

"What do you mean?" asked the same guy. With a keen interest he leaned forward towards his partner in conversation.

"How should I put this," pondered the vampire incognito, "God and I, we have an unspoken agreement. I don't get too close to Him and He leaves me be. And for now, that is for the best, especially since I haven't received an answer yet to my questions about sin, forgiveness and the constant propensity to sin again. Perhaps a moment in time will come in which I will receive more clarity on that..." And all of a sudden I noticed a subtle change in Aeolus' posture, from which I made out that he had reached his limit. He sat up straight on the uncomfortable, wooden bench and placed one elbow on the backrest. With a slightly different tone of voice than previously he asked what we thought about the difference between daily sins and deadly sins and whether such a difference even existed at all. He briefly outlined what the Catholic tradition taught and then retreated to the sideline. With a barely noticeable trace of satisfaction on his lips he observed the emergence of an entirely new group discussion, without the need for him to continue to contribute to it.

"That was a slick move," I softly said to him in passing, while cleaning up. "And that doesn't sound very positive," he reacted during the next chance we had in which we could talk without being overheard. The meeting had ended and everyone was busy collecting, boxing and moving the used materials to a storage room in the back. "I didn't mean it that way. I'm just a bit taken aback. You were so... open," I whispered.

Aeolus only said: "Extroversion is an effective smoke screen, if you want to protect your private life."

## 31

## LENTE

A small group of people went into Soho for a bit to visit the McDonald's.
Aeolus and I had joined them while we continued the game of 'ignoring each
other just enough'. Nevertheless, he managed to end up standing right
behind me in the waiting line in front of the counter... I ordered a burger of
some sort with fries and just when I was about to decide what to drink the
phone rang. My own Dutch cell phone! I had almost forgotten about my
carrying that thing on me... When I saw the name that was listed on the
display, I smiled. "Sander! How's it going?"
"Pretty good... how about you?"
"What do you think? Now that you called *all* my troubles just melt away."
"Good grief, what kind of people do you associate with? You sound more
effeminate by the day!" exclaimed Sander.
"With you," I dryly answered. And we laughed.
"Are you at home? Shall I stop by for a bit?" came from the other end of the
line. I shook my head, while I quickly grabbed the tray that had been slid
towards me. "I'm afraid that's impossible," I said, while I tried my best to not
let everything slip from my hands, "cause I'm still in London..." I walked
further into the premises, looking for a table that would seat five people.
Aeolus, with a cup of cola in his hand, passed me and took the flight of stairs
down just ahead of me, where there were a couple of tables in some remote
corners... and even though I was still talking to Sander, my eyes got caught
by the back of his T-shirt. On it, below the name of Rammstein, it read in
German: *Sex is a battle, love is war.* He sat down and I took a seat across
from him. Sander did not understand why I was not home yet and I explained
to him that I had received another assignment and would not be coming to
the Netherlands until Thursday. In the meantime, I was trying to open a
packet of ketchup with one hand, which was, of course, a hopeless attempt. A
bit impatiently I put it back down again. But it was wonderful to hear
Sander's voice and I told him so. I had missed him...
Aeolus was watching me with his arms crossed with a look on his face that I
could not quite place. I pretended that he did not exist, even when he reached
for my packet of ketchup and painstakingly slowly began to tear it open with
his teeth. While not even for a moment breaking eye contact he licked the
tiny bit of tomato sauce, which was now dripping down his bottom lip, with
his tongue and handed the packet back to me. "Thanks..." I said, upon which
Sander concluded: "There are other people with you, huh? Shall we continue
talking on Friday then?"

"Yes, sounds good, then I'm going to eat my little burger now."
On the stairs the three others appeared: "Ah, there you are! We were afraid we had lost you," said the American girl.

Half an hour later each of us had individually said our goodbyes to the others and as soon as they were out of sight, we had found each other again. We stood a little awkwardly across from each other in the central hall of the Tottenham Court Road Underground station. Just when I was about to tell him that I was sorry about this morning, Aeolus said: "Thank you for introducing this group to me. Seldom have I been able to be myself more in the company of mortals..."
I had to let that sink in for a moment, because it sounded so unreal. Or did it? It must have been pretty special for him to be among people in such a way... The image was still fresh in my mind: him sitting in the upstairs room of the Fox. Simply as one of the Asylum guests. Talking about issues that resonated with others – and the things he had stated were not even lies, save for his fictitious name, that is. When I spoke those thoughts out loud, Aeolus explained: "There are conversational techniques by which you can precisely determine what you are or aren't willing to share, by keeping in charge of the situation." He looked at me inquisitively and continued: "But you... you haven't had it easy this afternoon. I am well aware of that. And given the circumstances, you have done amazingly well. You stand tall, shorty..."
I shrugged and mumbled: "Sorry about this morning."
He grabbed my hands and pulled me towards him. "And I'm sorry about last night."
"No, don't apologize for that! I do understand where you're coming from," I said, "you know, with the body snatchers, and definitely after what you shared at The Asylum this afternoon..."
The rest of what I wanted to say was pointless. Aeolus leaned against me. He kissed me, timidly, carefully. Then he pulled his head away from me and let me go. He took a small step backwards. "Lente... my dear, sweet Lente," he said, "I don't have a pleasant personality at all. I am arrogant and controlling..."
He ran his hand through his hair.
"Don't think of yourself in that way," I objected, but he interrupted me.
" – I want to have a relationship with you, Lente, a serious relationship."
He wanted... a – I could not even pronounce the word in my thoughts – wanted a relationship with me. A being, of which its existence has completely been denied by everyone with even the slightest bit of common sense, but which stood here in front of me nonetheless, visible, audible and irresistibly touchable... Did I have any idea what I was getting myself into? What would be the consequences if I – oh, fuck the consequences – I *wanted* him! Ever since that morning in Iceland I have thought of nothing but him and being able to belong to him exclusively.

"Yes."

"What, yes?"

"I want you too, Raphaël, I want to have a relationship with you."

Time, frozen amidst activity, like a flash and a slow shutter speed combined into a photo. That was what this moment perhaps reminded me of the most. The eye of the camera was open for a relatively long time and collected all the visual information that passed by in about one full second. The result: colors, light and dark, shapes, smudges... the chiming of entry gates, public announcements, the rushed footsteps of passersby, bags that graced us – I was not oblivious to any of it. But it no longer interested me either, because the only thing that still mattered to me was our renewed embrace. Our being together as the center of the universe. The main subject of this photograph, perfectly captured in the light of the flash. There we were, and nobody else... After a while Aeolus asked: "Shall we go?"

We would not let go of each other anymore. Even at the narrow entry gates, where we did have to take turns to go through, his hand held mine in a tight grip and I... I was in seventh heaven. Finally we were a couple. This was *real* and for all to see!

On the eastbound platform of the Central Line we sat down on a bench. As close to one another as possible – caressing, touching, exploring – while we were waiting.

A hissing sound, followed by a cool breeze coming from the tunnel announced the arrival of the train.

"Where are we going, by the way?" I asked, as I released myself from Aeolus' arms and stretched my back.

A tad more sensual than I had expected he sounded close to my ear: "Home, my dearest... where else?"

I got up and wondered whether I completely understood what he had just said. He stood up next to me, inhaled deeply and then said with carefully selected words: "I have to correct myself. We're not going to my place." The train came in sight.

"I'm leaving by myself, Rhona. And I'm not going to wait for the next train, but I'll take this one. Because otherwise..."

Startled and a bit disappointed I nodded. The train stopped, the doors opened and people pushed their way out and onto the platform. If this was what our reality was going to look like for now, so be it. It was already so much more than what it used to be... we would find a way somehow, for sure.

Aeolus told me goodbye by briefly grabbing my hand one last time. Then he got onto the train. "Get out of here," he said with a decisive tone of voice, "head straight to your hotel. Do not linger here for a minute longer."

"I'll call you," I promised, right before the doors closed between us and the melancholy on his face burned onto my retina as the last thing I saw of him... At street level I found a bus with Clapham Common as its destination. I took a seat on the top level, all the way at the front; my favorite spot on English double-deckers. It was nighttime, it was dark and the city was livened up by the light show of headlamps and street lights. My senses were wide open, to all things beautiful and new... or to keep me on my toes. Because, in actuality, I was on the run. From a deadly creature that had tried to kill me once already. A vampire who at the same time was my lover.

## 32

No. 92


And that lover, I was already having coffee with at Bank Underground
Station the next morning at 8:30 sharp. As though it was the most normal
thing in the world... I had been thinking. "Three names," I mused after
taking a careful sip of my hot Latte, "Aeolus, Raphaël and now Kazimír as
well... will there be any more?"
He smiled. "Not for the time being."
"All those identities... Doesn't that really bother you after a while?"
"They're a combination of letters. Nothing more."
I turned my head towards him. "You must be joking. Surely, you know how
important it is to have your own name?"
"Depends on the amount of meaning you derive from it," said Aeolus.
"I don't agree with that," I objected.
The man remained silent.
"No, I'm serious!" I insisted.
Mockingly he looked at me and asked: "What's up with this sudden
zealousness?"
"Because I have seen what not having a name can do to a person,"
I answered curtly and I told him about the story I once heard about a terribly
annoying and aggressive boy in a horribly impoverished orphanage in some
far away country.
When he was brought there as a little orphan they did not name him, but
instead had only given him the designation 'Number 92'. And not just me
now, but even back then and there some people had thought it to be very
unhealthy for the development of his personality. Volunteers from the West
thus decided to name him David and from that moment on the boy completely
blossomed...
The aha experience was clearly readable on Aeolus' face and while I clenched
my fists underneath the table I told him I was going to call him by is original
name from now on, even in my thoughts: Raphaël.
My beloved leaned in towards me, pulled me closer with his hand around my
neck and kissed me on my forehead. "Oh angel," he said. Then he got up on
put on his coat. I followed suit. With excitement I thought about the site that
we were going to visit now and where I was finally going to see him at work:
Westminster Abbey. As little as I knew about the world of restoration
architecture, I had a sneaking suspicion that one did not bring in a contract
of this caliber that easily. To think of the photos I could make there...!
As we walked through the tunnel towards the Tube he glanced sideways at

my feet. He nodded approvingly. "Robust shoes with grip soles. Good thing you had them at your hotel."

I grinned. "You still have a thing or two to learn about youth culture. These are Creepers, and Creepers are a *must have* for anyone wanting to look even the slightest bit gothic."

"So you see me as an uncultured senior citizen."

"Aren't you?" I asked teasingly, and immediately I received a shove which I answered with a giggle and a playful punch against his arm. Against my expectations, however, he did not react to that. He said: "I do worry sometimes, Lente. Because what if you wake up one day and come to the realization that I'm really just a very boring man?"

I puffed and muttered: "... you say that, with that life experience of yours? Compared to you I am practically a spring chicken!"

Raphaël put his arm around me and whispered with his head right next to mine: "Oh, but that issue can easily be overcome. I do love having a young chick from time to time..."

A wave of some sort of hormones came over me and my boyfriend burst out laughing.

## 33

## GRAFFITI

"I'm really curious about the stories of your life," said Raphaël.

We were on the train heading to Westminster Abbey.

As I slightly pinched his hand I said: "Only three days. We only have three more days to do that..."

"... and as far as I'm concerned, followed by many years in which we see each other as often as we want. Lente, Rotterdam is barely an hour's flight from here."

I sighed. "I know that. But this, along with that hassle of using those different names... Like now – now, for example, you call me Lente, but..."

"You have a beautiful name. And I'm happy to use it. Unless I have a good reason to call you Rhona."

"Over the internet, for example?"

"And on the phone."

"And if there are other vampires around?"

"If that were to happen, I'll catch on soon enough. Don't worry, my love. Don't worry, okay?"

At Westminster we got off. At the backside of the Abbey a gate was opened for us and what I saw next was, in every possible way, a new world to me...

The Chapter House, an octagonal building that was attached to the big church, was obscured by scaffolding with green netting wrapped around it. Adjacent there were construction shacks and people were walking back and forth. Noise could be heard of... I did not know, of construction, really.

Raphaël took me with him to one of those shacks that had a couple of men in it. I was introduced to them, promptly forgot their names, but did try to memorize what their functions were. For all they knew I was the professional photographer that shadowed the head architect for today. Some things were discussed and I absorbed everything I saw with eager curiosity. On a coat rack hung jackets. On a shelf were blue hard hats and bright yellow vests and in the corner a small office was set up. My boyfriend answered a few questions from the guy sitting behind the computer and I was just about to study a poster that had some types of rock in different colors, when I heard him say: "Lente, could you come here?"

On the computer screen a couple of head shots of a man were shown, one facing forward and two in profile.

"This is our chief contractor, Patrick. You'll probably see him shortly," Raphaël explained. "Take off your coat and put on one of those yellow things. We're going to climb the scaffolding later. But first I'll show you a thing or

two inside." He picked up a helmet, handed it to me and said: "It should fit snugly in such a way that it won't fall off when you bend your head."
I put on the head gear, tightened the plastic strip on the inside a bit until it fitted properly and then we left. Outside an Indian man wearing a turban addressed us. He turned out to be the head mason and showed Raphaël a couple of male heads that were carved from stone, surrounded by swirly ornaments. At this point they lay on their sides, but when straightened up it was easy to imagine them as hanging decorations, for example, in one of those corners where the wall meets the ceiling. The artworks were critically inspected and as per my boyfriend's directions something was drawn in pencil on one of the faces. Around the mouth, near the nose, in different spots some lines had to be added and when they were done with that Raphaël took me to a semi-covered work site. There he briefly searched among a couple of similar looking ornaments and then he pointed at one of them. Immediately I recognized in the carved head the face of the chief contractor. I let out a shriek in amazement. "Is this some kind of a joke?" I asked.
"Yes and no," was the answer. "These sculptures will be installed outside on those heavily decorated towers, the pinnacles, around the Chapter House. It is my responsibility to approve or reject them. The features of the head that you just saw, for example, were too shallow. The light must be able to cast its shadow on it, so that the object is indeed recognizable as a human head when looking up from the ground level."
"And let me guess: there is no room for errors and you demand perfection."
"Something like that, yes."
"But that still doesn't explain what that Patrick guy is doing there among those heads."
The vampire laughed so softly that someone with normal hearing surely would have missed it. He held a door open for me and we stepped into the big church. "When this complex was built the masons were instructed to create fifty heads that were to be used as decoration around the pinnacles," he explained. "But that was all their job description contained. So it was up to them to find people who were suitable to serve as models for their sculptures. Initially, they thought it logical to use people that had a direct connection to the church. Clergymen, dignitaries and the like. But that didn't get them anywhere near fifty. And then the masons decided to just use each other as models... Hundreds of years have passed and many of those heads have weathered to such an extent that they need to be replaced. We need about thirty new ones."
"... But you have no idea to whose likeness the originals were and have no way of finding that out anymore, because photos did not yet exist back then?"
"Bravo!" He stopped in his tracks, in the middle of the church. "At least, about those photos you are correct," he said. "I have therefore come to the conclusion that copying the method of that time is the most appropriate solution to that problem. In about a year a dozen portraits of our contractors,

ten of the masons and ten of the team of architects will hang on the side of the building at an anonymous level." He raised an eyebrow, but I purposefully did not respond and focused on my surroundings. It was my first time seeing the Westminster Abbey from the inside and, apparently, something important was about to transpire here, because all around us people were occupied with making many busy preparations. We passed television crews and their cameras. We stepped over electricity cables and all sorts of other wires towards a security guard who opened a heavy wooden door for us. Behind it everything was completely different: we stepped into a vaulted abbey corridor that looked out onto a courtyard through windowless openings. The atmosphere here was so much more serene. At least things were quiet here, as it should be in the garden of an abbey... I took a deep breath in, and exhaled.

In the Chapter House the lighting was dim. We were standing in an empty, round space with a mosaic floor and at its center stood a beautifully decorated supporting pillar.

Raphaël explained that there had been a Benedictine monastery at this location as early as the tenth century, but that any trace of it had never been unearthed. Roughly one hundred years after that the abbey, as we now know it, was built. The monastic order had a presence in it until Henry the Eighth put an end to that in 1540.

The Chapter House itself dated back to the year 1250. Though it was mostly known for the British Parliament that convened there for congress over the years and the name of this building was indeed an apt description for its original purpose: this is where, at that time, chapters from the Rule of Saint Benedict were daily recited. In addition, it was the place where the daily announcements were made and where corporal punishment was inflicted on unwilling or unwitting monks.

The Book of Saint Benedict I had read, yesterday morning on the internet. In my opinion I thought it was a bit much, that endless list of rules that constrained clergy into a corset of seclusion and almost inhumane discipline...

Sparse rays of light entered the space through the stained glass windows. They were just enough to illuminate the sober stone benches along the wall. As I sat down and let the things I could see sink in, my imagination took a trip through time: in my mind's eye dark figures emerged, covertly like the cold shivering monks, young and old, in habits that barely shielded them against the piercing draft during harsh winters. A pungent smell that rose from bodies blended with the ambient air – the result of a medieval vision on personal hygiene. Mumbled and devoted chants that were alternated with the viciously smacking sound of wood-meets-skin of relentless flogging...

The monk lay flat on the freezing stones, amidst his praying brethren, with arms stretched out depicting the cross of Christ, face down, eyes forcefully squeezed shut. In a state of total submission to the Almighty he vowed to his abbot that nothing earthly would sway him from his religious determination in the outside world that he would soon brave only on exceptional occasions. A sincere vow, taken by an unsuspecting clergyman. The scene could have played out in this room. In reality, however, my thoughts had drifted to a monastery in the border area between France and Germany. And the evil that was waiting for this monk in the hills of the Black Forest did not care about his pious intentions. It ensured that he never returned to his monastery. It made sure that he was still left wandering the earth, a century and a half longer than the Chapter House was taking root with its foundation in the London soil...

The burnt orange floor with geometric animal and plant patterns was an original feature from the fourteenth century. So was the mural of the Apocalypse and the Final Judgment. Raphaël talked about the secret details that stone masons always used to incorporate into buildings such as these, that hardly anyone knew about. These artists back then were almost without exception deeply religious and therefore saw their work as being in honor of God and not of man... I tried to let that sink in.
"So their sculpture acted as something like a prayer?"
"You could think of it that way, yes."
Later, high up on the scaffolding, I got to see a couple of oddities of the building that you would never be able to notice from ground level: a piece of cardboard was pulled aside and a text, painted in the upper corner of a stained glass window, appeared. I also saw images of a few little airplanes...
"In the fifties, when a renovation took place, the workers have left their names behind. Apparently, they also thought it important to commemorate the Second World War in their own personal way," Raphaël clarified.
My jaw literally dropped. Such wealth, such history... I loved this. "It looks a bit like graffiti," I said. Raphaël placed his hand on my back and laughed. We continued on our tour and came upon the pinnacles where heavily weathered stone faces from past times hung, soon to be replaced by the new sculptures.
"But this..." I softly said, "I find extra special. Someone who constantly has to do his best to remain as anonymous as possible and yet has found a way to immortalize himself."
"... And by doing so he can't help but exclaim a concealed 'remember me' to the heavens."
I stuck my tongue out at him. He said: "Yeah, I figured: I'd better make that comment before you do." The level of defiance with which he looked at me was subtle yet unmistakable. I searched for words, for something witty to say... to no avail. At that moment Patrick the chief contractor approached us, and I again took the role upon myself of the professional photographer, who was here to document the activities of restoration architect Raphaël Bélusier on an average day of work.

## 34

## GARLICK HILL

How an afternoon could seem to last an eternity... The time I was forced to spend by myself – Raphaël had remained on site to continue working and had a scheduled appointment with someone after that – had weighed down on me heavily and I had a hard time hiding my excitement when I heard his voice on the phone at 6 p.m. I was waiting at Bank, as he had requested earlier that afternoon. And I received instructions on where we were going to meet.
"Are you near an Underground plan?" he asked.
"Uh, yeah..." I retrieved my booklet with maps of the city from my bag.
"Good. Are you able to find Bank Station on it?"
I rolled my eyes, replied that I could and tried to hide my impatience in doing so.
"I'm at a pub near Mansion House Underground Station right now. Getting here from Bank is a little tricky, but not unfeasible. You could walk to Monument Station, from there it's only two stops. But the connection between Bank and Monument is somewhat of a hassle due to the current maintenance on the escalators. Therefore I would suggest you go to Liverpool Street first and take the Circle Line from there... Do you think you can manage?"
"Just give me the name of the pub." I was agitatedly shifting my weight between my left leg and my right...
"The pub is called The Hatchet. You'll find it just outside the Garlick Hill exit of the station."
"Okay, I'll see you in a bit then," I said and ended our call. I think he sometimes forgot that I can take care of myself just fine here in London... I really should remind him of that one of these days, before he really started to piss me off and then I would get snarky with him in an unguarded moment. For one thing, he was not always in the right either. The way to Mansion House, for instance. Was it not much shorter to just walk there? On the map I used my finger to measure the length of that one direct street between here and there. Four hundred yards at most... I could do it in a few minutes. Shaking my head I turned into Queen Victoria Street.
I found Raphaël in one of those typical back rooms that you often saw in pubs: with tables and chairs that stood close together and all those authentic features, like a mantelpiece, a white plastered ceiling and vintage pictures on the walls... His surprise was great when he saw me. He got up. I flung my arms around his neck, but it took several seconds before I felt his hands on my back in response to my touch.

"How did you get here this quickly?" he asked.

I looked up at him. "Aren't you happy to see me?"

"Of course I am…"

"… But?"

"I was meeting with someone. With, um… Lucas. And he hasn't left yet," he replied.

"Is that a problem?"

"No, not at all. I just did not want you to be startled by him…"

"Raph, how is that even a concern to you? Even if I was startled, surely I'll get over it. And since there is no reason to worry, then…" I said, sounding as patient as I could. He smiled. We sat down on a bench behind a table, facing each other, with both my hands inside of his. For a few seconds I had his undivided attention, but then his eyes trailed off, leaving the room, to a spot on the left past the bar. I followed his gaze, saw Lucas appear… and immediately all the confident words that I had just spoken lost their meaning. A feeling of nausea came over me, because the outfit that Lucas was wearing was the exact same one as worn by the guy I had seen at Harrods three days ago. I knew it!

"Rhona, hello," he said. And then, turned towards my boyfriend: "You hadn't told me that it was her you were meeting up with now."

Raphaël crossed his legs and said: "Yes… apparently I am less skilled at time management than I thought. Our appointments could have been exactly back-to-back, were it not for Rhona's mysteriously arriving here much earlier than I expected…" He looked at me quizzically, upon which I opened my bag and pulled out my booklet with London maps. I put it down on the table in front of me.

"The A-Z of London…" Lucas sat down in a chair in front of us and carefully observed me. I avoided meeting his eyes and remained silent.

"Well, don't leave us hanging," Raphaël said with a slight chuckle in his voice.

Ha! I bet he thought that I was trying to keep the suspense going intentionally.

"I got here on foot," I then explained and told them that, when in doubt, it was always useful to lay a city plan and Tube map side by side. Because of their geometric layout Tube maps tended to give you a skewed perspective of the location of the stations. Full of interest the two looked at what I meant in the booklet.

Lucas whistled through his teeth. "Intuition *and* IQ… You have met your match, my dear friend," he slowly said.

Did I actually detect a hint of admiration in his voice? Or…? Oooh, this made me so nervous. Here I was sitting between two actual vampires and beneath the surface way too many things were brewing between us. Nothing was as it seemed and the lack of transparency weighed down the air around me…

What had Raphaël and Lucas been talking about before I got here, for instance? And what was Lucas' game, for heaven's sake? The fact was that he said nothing about our near encounter of last Saturday. But he undoubtedly must have had a reason for revealing his presence at Harrods. Otherwise I would never have noticed him standing between the postcard display racks... And now I was sitting here with him, sharing the exact same table. My lover pulled me towards him and laid his arm over my shoulders.

"Time and time again Rhona keeps both my feet on the ground," he said. "And she has no idea how much I need that."

For a moment Lucas' mouth widened. But his eyes did not match that smile. Even so, his facial expression was not unfriendly when he looked at me and asked: "You're a photographer. Tell me something about your work."

I hesitated. Because – what was safe for me to share and what did he know about me already? Should I keep things just as casual as I was during the chat sessions between Aeolus and I? As such I was cautious when I answered: "What uh... would you like to hear? Because the field of photography is very broad..." And quickly, before waiting for a reply, I continued: "Perhaps I could tell you something about my favorite techniques."

After a thorough explanation on 'painting with light' and a couple of other methods I switched to taking an interest in my listener. To my relief Lucas began to talk about his work in response to my questions. He turned out to be a professional parkour athlete. He did demos and taught workshops and traveled from country to country to do so. That's how he made a living. An exciting, but also a lonely life, I imagined. I asked what had prompted him to commit himself to that sport in particular.

Raphaël interrupted me: "Ooh la la, chérie, never call parkour a sport," but Lucas motioned in a hushing manner and said: "A sport always has a competitive element to it. However, that is not what we are focused on. Parkour is a kinesthetic discipline, it's about getting to know yourself, developing yourself. The more you advance in that, the more you will reap its benefits in your everyday life. During a training session you learn to revert to the foundation of your human abilities and to optimally use your physical and mental potential from there. Some even see parkour as a way of life... anyway, come check it out tomorrow. I'm giving a performance at the launch party of a computer game. Seeing us at work might clarify things better than words do."

"Uh, sure, maybe... unless Raphaël has other plans..." Uncertain I looked at my boyfriend. He, in turn, was having trouble hiding his amazement, but managed to sound as neutral as possible when he said: "If Rhona's interested in going, we'll be sure to come watch. Thank you for the invitation."

"Is he gone?" I mouthed, a couple of minutes later. Lucas had given us the address for tomorrow night and had said goodbye to us. And even though he had already disappeared from our sight, I felt anything but comfortable... "He's gone. And he can't understand us. He doesn't speak Dutch," was

Raphaël's answer. "But let's get back to you: is it your dinner time?"
"Yes, I'll just order something," I said. Ten minutes later I was having
Bangers and Mash.

35

VERTIGO

Yesterday morning, when my boyfriend had asked me if I had a fear of
heights, my answer had been an unequivocal *no*. I even thought it was a bit
exaggerated that he had brought it up. But now I changed my mind. I was
halfway up a much too narrow ladder waiting for the person above me to
move out of the way and I continuously told myself that I could do it, hoping
that I would not be tempted to look down. We had come to the Hackney
district to inspect the bell tower of St. John's. And that tower was tall, very
tall. Odd, really, cause I had heard that this one was only eight levels, while
the scaffolding of the Chapter House even had two more... Granted, over
there you were distracted by the people who were working. A handful of trees
obscured the height, and the flying buttresses of the Westminster Abbey gave
a pretty sturdy impression due to their supportive function. Here, however,
the view became wider and the wind stronger with each level we climbed.
There were four of us. Raphaël had brought the chief contractor and a man
who was a specialist in restoring bells, dials and clockworks. The scaffolding,
now that their construction had just been completed, provided access to the
entire tower, including the cross that was situated at the top, and today's
objective was to estimate the costs that this project were going to entail. A
total change from yesterday – when I was able to witness what the input of
an architect entailed as he guided his coworkers amidst the restoration work.
Raphaël had gone over the entire outer shell of the Chapter House on all
levels with Patrick and had inspected every stone and each ornament. At his
instruction the contractor had placed marks with a piece of crayon around
spots that needed to be touched up or replaced.
Man, I had sure felt stupid at certain moments with my remarks and
questions... so for today I decided to just stick to mere listening and
observing.
Raphaël had climbed up to the highest point of the tower with one of the
others to inspect the state of the cross. I had deemed it to be a little too much
of 'exposure to the elements' and therefore I just kept wandering about down
here, right below the clock dials, testing the boards beneath me with my feet
as inconspicuously as possible. I took pictures of the view, ran my fingers
over the stones of which one could clearly discern the maritime origin,
because of the scattered and protruding sea shells. Portland stone, I had
learned yesterday. Most churches in Great Britain have been built using this
type of stone. Westminster Abbey, however, was an exception because it was
built with... what was it called again... Chilmark. " – So, you're shadowing

Mr Bélusier for the day," the contractor interrupted my thoughts. He sat down on a slightly raised ledge of the tower.

"That's right," was my reply. I sat down next to the man. His face had those typical, English, friendly-sympathetic features. He reminded me a little of Lewis, the assistant of Inspector Morse…

Whoa… such a height, what a view! There were not many people who were given such an opportunity, who were allowed to experience this. Except for vampires, that is, in the dark, in the middle of the night. But – how would they get up here?

"How did you say you met him? I mean, it doesn't happen every day that an architect outsources the photography."

"Oh, I'm a professional photographer and I sometimes shoot buildings. That's why… And he thought it would be nice to have a couple of projects documented carefully."

"Okay… I see…"

We both stared at the houses, and at the streets that fanned out from below us to all directions as far as the eye could see. I recognized a couple of famous buildings and, far in the distance and diagonally to the right of us, I was even able to see the London Eye.

"Well, you know," the contractor started again, "I'm just a simple construction worker. Give me an assignment and I'll get it done. But Mr Bélusier, now *he* is different. I can't think of him as anything but an artist. Sometimes I don't have the faintest idea where these restoration architects get their knowledge from. They come up with the most brilliant solutions for problems with buildings, monuments… and landscapes even! I'm telling you: that man, he has a passion for his trade."

I nodded. He was completely in the dark…

"Those large construction sites over there on the left, what's going on there?" I asked, as I pointed to the southeast.

"That's the Olympic village. The entire Lea Valley will be filled with it. Should be finished in 2012. The most beautiful things will be built there."

I looked at him a little questionably and said: "To be honest, that modern stuff isn't really my thing. I prefer old buildings, with all that history and such…"

"Clearly you've been infected by Mr Bélusier's virus then," remarked the contractor. I smiled. If he only knew…

At that moment Raphaël and the clockworks specialist came back down and I returned to playing the professional photographer, who closely followed his pointed finger with the lens of her camera. We did a tour past all four sides of the tower and when we were alone for a few seconds, I teasingly said: "Don't think that I don't know that the only reason you have me do this is to keep me close by." His reaction was stoic and businesslike: "Tomorrow I have taken the entire day off. I want to see a little of your world then."

Once we got back at ground level we said goodbye to the contractor and the three of us walked to a house that overlooked the adjacent park. This was where the lady who took care of the church lived and we were invited to have a seat at the dining table in her kitchen. I had always considered it to be a privilege to be invited into someone's home while in a foreign country. It let you see so much more than what you are normally allowed to see as a tourist... this house, for instance. You could almost call it a cottage, with these features. And located in such a fairylike garden, to boot – you really could not tell that you were in the middle of a big city. On top of that, from the window we had that gorgeous view of the tower of St. John's.

The lady made coffee using an elaborate, old-fashioned method that was so beautiful it caused me to watch in awe and for a moment forgot why we were there. But then Raphaël began to give an account of what he had found up there at the top. He explained about the condition that the cross on top of the tower was in and made an estimate of the costs that its repair would incur. A couple of things were also clarified with photos and drawings... I tried hard to follow what they were discussing, but lost track during their brainstorming on the acquisition of funds... When they finally began to talk about the weather, I knew that our visit here was near its end. The clockworks specialist took a glance outside. He said: "The wind wasn't too bad today, even up there, but still I notice that the years are taking their toll on me. It seems the older I get, the more effort it takes to climb those little ladders. If I didn't know any better, I'd say that I'm starting to develop a fear of heights..." The middle-aged man smiled a little awkwardly and gathered his paperwork.

My boyfriend responded pensively: "Funny how it is the exact opposite for me... When I started doing this work I would sometimes find myself feeling nervous while climbing, but as time has gone by that has only become less and less."

Outwardly he was about twenty years younger than his colleague. But he had three hundred years of experience working in his field as well as in 'appearing normal' among people. He was one of them, one of the members of the renovation team. He was used to all of this.

Would I ever get used to it, though? To everything that makes him 'him'?

## 36

SECURITY FORCES

Take what happened during our Tube ride to Hammersmith, for instance. We had been on our way to see Lucas' performance that evening. We had been sitting close together, I with my head resting on his shoulder, in a half-empty carriage. Somewhere across from us there was this girl of about eighteen years old. She was one of those classic cases of someone who was completely unaware of her own beauty. Unfortunately, some shady figure two seats further away *had* noticed her charming looks and he had begun to talk to her. And it was not in the most pleasant way. His words were rife with sexual innuendo and at times even had a menacing overtone... The girl did her best to ignore him, which I thought was good of her, but sadly it had the opposite effect: His Majesty changed seats and sat down right beside her. Alarmed I sat up. I really could not stand this type of behavior! Why would anyone do something like this? Could he be intoxicated with something? I could feel my anger rising, wanted to do something about it so badly... But the only thing that I could think of, calling the police, was probably not even possible, because you never had any cell phone signal inside an Underground tunnel. So I carefully looked around, quietly hoping that one of the other passengers would make a move and help the girl. My eyes met those of two, three people, but nobody did anything. We were all cowards...

In the meantime, the train began to slow down. We were approaching a station. And out of the blue the voice of Raphaël emerged, calm, yet sharp enough to be heard: "*Sir...*"

The perpetrator looked annoyed in our direction.

"Weren't you supposed to get off at this station?"

What happened next was creepy, to say the least: in a completely different tone of voice than he'd used just before the man said, "right..." as he stared at Raphaël. The emotion with which he did so I found quite difficult to place. It really was not an emotion at all, because it almost seemed like whatever he must have felt earlier, had now slid off his face in an instance, like a person who is falling asleep in a bath tub and is then submerged... Raphaël gestured towards the door and the man briefly shook his head, as though he was trying to shake a feeling of disorientation. Yet, he stood up and when the train had come to a stop, he walked toward the exit. Without even paying the girl any further attention he got off and I would have almost thought that nothing out of the ordinary had just transpired, were it not that the guy, now on the platform, was staring at Raphaël with a dazed look on his face...

When the train accelerated again I was sitting next to my boyfriend with my stomach in knots. I remained silent until we climbed the stairs of Hammersmith Station. There I finally dared to ask: "What, in God's name, just happened?"

No response.

"You just hypnotized that man, didn't you? Oh *shit*..."

There was nothing comforting or reassuring in the way in which Raphaël draped his arm over my shoulder as he said: "This is who I am, Lente. This is all part of the deal."

The building where we were going to meet Lucas was a few blocks away. We were on the guest list and I sure felt grateful for the 'change of scenery' that I found inside... and now I hoped that it would help me get rid of this feeling of unease.

I stood still for a moment to take in the surroundings.

We were in the foyer of an office complex that had been transformed into an, um, whatchamacallit... an urban jungle or something? I saw railings of different floors above one other that converged on the left and the right into two wide staircases. In front of all that a scaffolding-like structure was placed with bars and blocks, which in turn were outfitted with images of apartment buildings, stairs, passages, streets and bicycle racks printed on fabric. But also, around the scaffolds that varied in height and that were placed next to and in front of each other, there were fences, walls and similar obstacles.

They had done a pretty good job. Had probably cost them an arm and a leg.

The audience that was enjoying their drinks and networking while waiting was, of course, interesting to watch. It was composed of business people, paparazzi types, a family or two with kids, a couple of genuine nerds and a bunch of young people that no doubt had been involved with the development of the computer game. And hors d'oeuvres and drinks were served by hostesses in sexy, slightly militaristic-looking, black skirt suits.

I thought all of this was quite entertaining. These kinds of receptions revealed so much about the lifestyle of all those different people...

Raphaël did not follow me, he let me do my own thing and for now that was just fine with me. It did mean, however, that I had to greet Lucas, or should I say, Egare, all by myself. He had been watching me for a while now from among the audience and as soon as I gave away that I saw him, he came straight at me.

"Rhona, welcome," he said. He reached out his hand without having gone through the trouble of heating it up first. "I see you're just looking around."

"Yes... Raph is somewhere down there," and I made a vague gesture in the direction of where I had last seen him. For a moment Lucas examined me carefully, but he excused himself shortly after. He had to get dressed.

Next to me was a guy holding a glass of cola. The fact that he felt out of place was clearly noticeable by everything that he was doing with his free hand.

First he had tried to casually keep it in his pocket. Then he took it out again, briefly held it at his back and finally began to nervously pluck his beard. The guy was wearing a purple and pink Pac-Man T-shirt and on top of that a brown jacket with beige elbow patches – most likely somebody who had something to do with the game. I slightly turned towards him and made eye contact. Asked him how the employees of this office had been able to enter and exit the building during the construction of this circus. The fire department, I asserted, would probably have held their breath during the preparations for this evening. The guy pointed out the elevators and a door that read 'exit' above it. I made an awkward face that said 'Oh of course, how silly of me' and he laughed.

The guy was visibly happy that someone had approached him and we got to talking, among other things, about developing computer games.

After a while he said: "We completely forgot to introduce ourselves. I'm Timothy. Are you one of the clients?"

I said that I was not, introduced myself and told him that I had been invited by someone who was going to perform tonight.

"One of the security forces then?"

Puzzled I looked at the guy.

"There are the security forces and the couriers. What team is your friend on?"

"I don't have the faintest idea," I said. Two other people joined us, colleagues of Timothy, and as I was being introduced to them I saw Raphaël in the corner of my eyes standing with his arms crossed loosely. He looked unapproachable, but not particularly unfriendly and definitely not impatient... for a moment I felt like a child who was trying out a kiddie ride outside a store. The adult was supervising and let the child take her time until she was finished.

And taking my time I did. Had hoped that it would make me feel strong enough for when we were standing next to each other again and it did. His hand, which he lay in my side around my back and used to pull me in closer, was so exhilarating... It was the feeling that I was longing for again and again, and despite everything, literally everything, being close to him was the only thing that I wanted.

"Thank you for speaking up on the Tube when no one else did,"

I whispered, as the lights went down. A smoke machine announced the start of the presentation.

"It was nothing."

"Not to me. You saved a person."

"Helped, Lente, at most helped a little..."

In the lobby the soft rumbling of an impending thunder storm echoed and a couple of flashes of light illuminated the space. In the distance some gunshots could be heard and a heavy, melodious male voice began to narrate.

The setting of the computer game was an apocalyptic urban environment, just a few years away from us. A dictatorship had created a division between the elite and outcasts, between people with all privileges imaginable and a group of people for whom leading a normal life had become nearly impossible. Above the stairs, to the left and right of the scaffolds, were projection screens showing cityscapes from the game. In the beginning the images greatly suffered from atmospheric disturbances and only recovered after about half a minute. I wondered whether that could have been prevented. Or was it part of the script? This thought was confirmed by the stories of censorship and sabotage in present day media that came from the speakers... most of it evaded me, however, because my attention was drawn to the beam of light coming from a spotlight that climbed up a stone pillar right behind the scaffolding. Music began to play. And then I, and many others in the audience with me, could not suppress a shriek of amazement: on top of one of the railings someone had apparently remained hidden behind a pillar for quite a while, upside down, standing on his hands, and now his body slowly began to arch to the left. Hips and legs made half a turn and planted themselves on a horizontal bar and the guy began to crawl to the right on his hands and feet like a leopard. He was dressed in a guerrilla-style outfit in a variety of shades of gray. I picked up something about an underground resistance network and couriers that delivered encrypted information, but was distracted by men in black uniforms, the military that now entered the stage with brute force. They darted towards the railings and the traceur we saw earlier, who was supposed to be a courier, apparently, disappeared. Only to reappear to the far left from there. He leapt down a height of at least three yards, diagonally over the heads of the soldiers. With an almost supernatural precision his feet landed on the ledge of a narrow wall beside them. But before his enemies were able to respond, the courier was already swinging from a horizontal bar further away, dismounted toward us and disappeared into the audience. Light and sound effects interchanged, the music grew louder, faster. A second courier appeared, sliding down the railing of the stairs on the right with his arms stretched out sideways, as though he had found an air pocket to float on. I noticed it immediately: this was Lucas. Right before he reached the point where the diagonal slope of the railing was interrupted by a sharp kink, he pushed himself off and landed on the boards of a scaffold. Security forces turn towards him and gave chase. Gunshots and gnashing commands roared throughout the music and there was running, fast running. Lucas jumped sideways over a large block, supporting himself with one hand. Then he jumped with his entire body stretched out and after that with both his legs through his arms over another obstacle. Next he dove headfirst through the bars of a fence, finishing his move with a roll. The soldiers had to go round. The soldiers lost time because they had to use the stairs. They were forced to slow down in the turns of passages and alleys, while Lucas and his reappeared associate kept their pace in those turns by taking a few steps sideways up the walls. On the projection screens similar action could be seen and in this way it was emphasized that the animation in the computer game was 'of revolutionary level'. In the story, elements such as encryptions, missions that you needed to complete and secret places were shown where information was hidden, that then had to be picked up and delivered by couriers.

The show came to an end and Lucas and his partners executed the final series of maneuvers synchronously: side by side they climbed straight up a wall, past bars and over railings. Finally they were hidden from our sight, as, after an explosive bang, a considerable amount of smoke was blown into the foyer. And when that smoke had lifted, an enormous projection screen was lowered at the center in front of the audience. While the security forces lined up right beneath it the logo of the computer game was displayed. We were given the promise that each of us would get to bring home a copy of the game. All a marketing ploy, of course. But this time I did not mind being a cog in a company's publicity machine. Partly because of what I had just seen, I had found parkour to be more and more interesting.

I told Lucas as much when he joined us as I was having my last drink in the foyer. I asked him how it had been possible for his colleague to have stood upside down on that handrail for that long at the start of the show. Lucas' first reaction was a somewhat surprised look. And even though he did not sound condescending or impatient during his explanation, I still felt, yet again, so foolish in his presence... So I was glad when Raphaël started to get ready to leave about ten minutes later.

"I think it's time for you to hit the hay," my boyfriend said as we walked to the Tube station. "You're so quiet... was it a little too much for you after all?"
"Not at all..."
"But I can tell something's troubling you."
I let go of his arm and dug my hands deep into the pockets of my pants.
"Yeah. Lucas," I answered gruffly.
Raphaël slowed down and asked: "He didn't say anything that made you..."
"– No, of course not. He didn't do anything weird," I cut him short, "but that guy just gets on my nerves. I feel so disgustingly ignorant next to him." Being grouchy to camouflage my fear. I hoped that it worked.
Raphaël scrunched his forehead. After giving it a moment's thought he said: "You are correct in asserting that he exudes knowledge and wisdom. And I can imagine that that would come across as intimidating to you. Lucas is somewhat of a curious figure, but I've got to give him credit for having more respect for mankind than many of the undead that I know. Especially during the last twenty years or so, since he regularly trains with mortals."
What my boyfriend meant with this, I did not completely understand. Was he trying to convince me that Lucas was a relatively harmless vampire? Was the scent of my fear so intense?
Raphaël said, in an obvious attempt to ease my worries: "He might be a little

difficult to figure out, but I have a strong impression that he appreciates you as a person."

"I don't know, though… I don't know."

"Sweetheart, I heard myself what he said to you when you told him goodbye. And believe me, Lucas would never say something he doesn't mean. If there's anybody with a deep seated hatred towards dishonesty, it's him."

I had to admit, that little parting talk between him and I had been pretty amicable. Or innocent, or however you would want to call it…

He had said: "Rhona, you're going home the day after tomorrow, so I wish you a good trip back. Goodbye." Somewhat stammering I had replied: "Yes, uh, perhaps we'll meet again someday."

But in that final moment… had Raphaël really missed something here, or had I simply become paranoid? In any case, it gave me the chills to think back to the cryptic twinkle in Lucas' eyes when he said to me: "Indeed, perhaps we will see each other again sometime. I look forward to it."

37

CANAL

"Tell me something about your parents."
It was our final day together and a quarter to one in the afternoon already…
time flew by much too fast.
We had just left the Camden Town Tube Station and as we walked along the
alternative clothing shops I answered Raphaël's question, albeit reluctantly:
"My dad is a cosmetic dermatologist. And co-owner of a private clinic."
"And your mom?"
"She doesn't do anything."
"Nothing? I find that hard to believe."
"She's a housewife."
"Isn't that a respectable profession?"
I puffed in derision.
"Did I say something wrong," asked Raphaël. He waited until I had finished
browsing through a rack of T-shirts…
"No, you're right," I said as neutral as possible. We continued our stroll.
"Yet I sense a certain bitterness in your voice."
"I'm sure you are…"
"Can you tell me more about that?"
I wavered for a second, but then decided to say what was on my mind.
"You see, there are housewives and then there are trophy wives," I started to
explain. "My mother is one of those types who spends most of her time in
social circles and the thoughts that preoccupy her the most sound something
like: "Will the centerpiece for the party be delivered on time?" and "I'm sure I
had ordered a different type of caviar for that candlelight dinner"… but
things that truly matter in life, she has no clue about. Not a clue."
"And therein lies your heritage."
"Literally and figuratively, yes. I am, sad to say, a purebred sorority bitch."
"… Who will do anything to break free from her environment."
A group of rowdy teenagers blocked a large portion of the sidewalk that we
were walking on. With a cautious swerve we stepped around them and I
somehow felt guilty for their behavior. But Raphaël did not want to hear my
excuses – he stated that he actually found it fascinating to experience this
area in the daytime.

It had been my idea to visit Camden. I had thought that I would be able to
show something about myself this way, about my interests, that is, but now
that we were here I was seriously beginning to feel doubts. Why did I keep

seeking out such banal hustle and bustle? Why put up with these salespeople who either sneered you out of their crammed store when they realized that you had no intention to buy anything, or tried to rip you off when you did decide to purchase some of their merchandise? Was it really just about how much the style of clothing matched my personal taste? Or did it also have something to do with who I was as a person, with a rebellious craving towards freedom, perhaps? The fact remained that I always made the same mistake in Camden by only remembering how much this area really sucked by the time I actually got here.

"Is your dad a hardworking man?" asked Raphaël. Clearly he thought that our conversation about my heritage had not finished yet.

"In the clinic, he is. But at home, not so much," I replied.

"In other words, the fatherly feelings are missing in the moments that he's at home."

"If he's there at all."

"You think he doesn't love you, don't you?"

I pulled an impatient face. "Do I really need to respond to this?"

"Lente, some men are quite emotionally unavailable towards their children…"

"Oh please, spare me to socio-babble!"

But Raphaël shook his head and said: "It's not socio-babble. I used to be one of those distant fathers myself."

I took his arm and linked mine with his. Enough with the black and leather and loud, happy, kiddie colors for today – I wanted to get out of there. "Let's find a quiet spot, I'm done with this place," I said.

At Camden Lock, one of the gates that controlled the water level of the Regent Canal, we crossed the bridge and turned right. Along the water was the head of a combination pedestrian and cycling trail, which was said to run all the way to Islington and even further beyond, and since I had been planning to try out the actual length of it for a while anyway and to see what everything looked like here.

We found a tranquil ambiance; in the heart of London on a weekday afternoon, no less.

There were some bicyclists and joggers and dogs hanging around with their owners, but the lack of motorized traffic undoubtedly contributed to this being a serene place. Naturally, the surroundings here were different than anywhere else in the city: scattered about there stood big trees arched over the walking path and there were quaint backyards, separated from us by walls overgrown with plants, of which, without peeking inside, you could imagine how romantic they must have looked. There were spots where the canal widened and in one area there was even an actual marina… And then there were also a few abandoned factory buildings that directly lined the path where you were walking – something I immediately grabbed my camera for, of course. Raphaël, however, was more interested in the unusual location of a couple of luxury apartment buildings across the water. As he suppressed a yawn he said: "Thank you, my love, for your creative ideas."

"I should thank you," I replied, "because you want to spend time with me, while you can barely keep your eyes open."

"It's not that hard to deal with," he reassured me.

"But you've been switching your day and night rhythm for a bunch of days now..."

"And that is for the greatest cause imaginable," he stated in a determined tone of voice.

Still I felt bad about it. I stopped in front of a bench underneath a big weeping willow. I asked: "Would you be able to sleep here?"

... And it had taken some persuading on my part, but eventually I had gotten him to lay down with his head in my lap. "Just close your eyes. Take as long as you need, I'll be fine," I said, as I lovingly ran my fingers through his hair. Then I took out a book that I had found somewhere in a store that morning and began to read.

My eyes kept drifting off to my boyfriend, though. To his facial expression and to his hands that he kept folded on top of his belly. He looked so peaceful lying there... If you didn't take into account his legs that he had casually crossed, his appearance actually came across a little macabre. It was probably due to his skin being so pale... I smiled. Stared dreamily for a while at the hands that silently rose and fell with the rhythm of his breath, until I could not perceive it very clearly anymore. For a moment I searched for a point of reference near his body in order to pick up the movement again, but when I failed to do that on the first try, I shifted my attention to the clucking of the coots on the water near us and to a couple of those typically British canal boats a little further on... Each one in its own unique color scheme, all just as narrow and elongated and picturesque... I wished this could last forever. Loving each other, taking care of one another... Tomorrow, however, the plane home would take off and that was something that I dreaded beyond belief. It could not be helped, going back was something that needed to happen right now and so I had better savor this moment and commit this to memory as carefully as possible – to remember each square inch of what he looked like to recollect that later at any moment at will. My eyes traveled over the skin of his face one more time. "Flawless, free from blemishes or spots," I could just hear my father say. And his upper body, his hands... so slim, so lean. And motionless. His breathing had now become indiscernible even to the naked eye. I'm sure that was normal for him. But, on second thought... if someone was breathing, his lungs *had* to fill with air and then deflate. Didn't they? And that had to be visible by his abdomen to a certain degree. I had tried it once or twice, 'playing dead', but that was not such an easy feat. How then was it possible that..." Very quietly I brought my fingers up to his nostrils. Air had to be detectable. A long moment I concentrated.

Nothing. I felt absolutely nothing and suddenly panic set in… it seemed as though Raphaël's breathing had stopped! Since for how long? What was going on – was there something that I had to do? Check his pulse, give him mouth-to-mouth perhaps? Come on, think, act! You possess plenty of basic, medical knowledge – an unexpected deep breath made me retract my fingers from his nose accompanied by a little shriek. The eyes of the vampire opened. He said: "I should have told you in advance. When I sleep most systems in my body slip into a seemingly comatose condition."

"Man, you scared the hell out of me!" I panted. "I thought you were dead!"

"There is one thing that you can be sure of, Lente, I cannot die. Unless another vampire separates my head from my body."

A bewildered look on my face was my response. Raphaël reached out his left arm and stroked my cheek. He smiled endearingly. I interpreted that differently than he probably wanted, but I was just so freaked out. So angry. At him? No, at myself really. I turned my face away from him.

My boyfriend sat up straight. "Enough sleeping for today," he said with a decisive voice. "Come here," he instructed and without waiting for an answer he took me tightly in his arms. For a second I resisted, but then I lay my head against his anyway… A normal couple would have been talking about completely different things in this moment. And they would have just been sitting at his or her place, on the couch in the living room…

We were almost normal.

"What are you going to do when you get home tomorrow?" Raphaël whispered in my ear.

"Work. My book," I said lethargically, "Chat with you, hopefully…"

"And count the days until your next visit to this place? Don't you have that fashion shoot in a couple of weeks?"

"On the twelfth of May, yes… that's still a whole two months away!"

"Less than that."

"Hardly less. And I'll only be there for two days…"

Raphaël let go of me and changed his sitting position. "Well, that's how it goes, my love," he said. "Welcome to the professional world. But the Netherlands is really not that far away. And I will not allow for us to be apart for too long."

"You promise?" I asked.

"Look me in the eyes and see how serious I am."

I looked. We kissed. I cried a little…

Around 6 p.m. we left towards Angel Station. I took him to a pub in that area and had supper. Because at a pub, I figured, it would not be too conspicuous if he did not order anything for himself.

## 38

## THE COMMON

Every Underground station in London had its own little quirks. Some were characterized by their endless maze of corridors. At other stations, such as Clapham Common, the air could be stifling on the platforms, and here at Clapham South there was this cold draft every time you used the escalator. If you went down, she lay there lurking, only to attack your head from below halfway along the ride. But if you were going up she would strike you in the face again, blowing from the top. To me, that was an incomprehensible whim of nature. Was I the only person to notice these sorts of things? Or did I simply think too much?

Raphaël had been able to convince me that we would be together real soon and that was comforting, even if just for a little bit. Because I was still feeling sad, even though I was able to see things in perspective now. Our relationship was not a dream, it was a reality. Our reality. Logistic difficulties, like the distance between us, were hard, but we were sure to overcome them. Just like we had been able to always find solutions for our problems up to now.

I stepped off the escalator and took out my Oyster card for what would for now be the final time to hold it up against a checkpoint reader. Tomorrow morning I would call Raphaël early and then he would pick me up at the hotel and take me to London City Airport. My flight was leaving at 9:40 AM... but first I needed to pack my bags and get a good night's sleep.

I joined my fellow Tube passengers at the pedestrian light on the corner. Most of them crossed the road almost immediately, but I lacked the courage for that. Cars tended to drive pretty fast on the Clapham Common South Side and this week I had already witnessed a couple of times how people had barely managed to save themselves life and limb from experiencing a painful interaction with some speeding maniac or other... For that reason I did not follow others and waited patiently for the green light.

Across the street someone who was just as sensible as me, was waiting – a guy wearing a hoodie over his head. After a while the light turned green and then, completely unexpectedly, a couple of things happened at once: as I placed one automatic step forward, the guy across from me took off his hood. Our eyes met and to my greatest horror I recognized Lucas. Immediately I turned around, bumped into some people, heard their irritated reactions, but could think of one thing only: reach the next street corner as quickly as possible. This time I ignored the pedestrian light and took the first chance to cross the street. To the left of me was the southernmost extension of the

Common, to my right the main road and the long row of houses including my hotel further ahead... and if I could only reach it crossing the park in a semicircle..?

With my heart beating out of my chest I walked under the trees, turned a little deeper into the park, along the connecting road that led traffic to the west, passing straight through the Common. Up ahead I would try to get across and then... but what, for heaven's sake, was Lucas' reason for having shown up here this suddenly? Was it a coincidence, or – no, of course not, nothing was ever a coincidence with him. So my instincts had been right when we parted after his performance last night...

Quickly I glanced back, but to my surprise I could not see him anymore. Hesitantly I slowed down a little, scanning the dark surroundings that were sparingly lit by streetlights and headlights of passing cars. Maybe I had been mistaken. Perhaps it hadn't been him at all. In any case, he was gone now. Or... oooh, who was I kidding? Did the exact same thing not happen at Harrods? Only at Harrods it had been much safer than it was here, because here... I had to get away, away from here and get to my hotel as quickly as possible!

First I crossed the road. And then, just to be safe, looped around that group of trees and bushes, clockwise, towards the other section of the field. From there I could then go straight to the road where my hotel was situated, to the urban area. *Don't walk too close to the vegetation, remain visible to passersby... but first things first: get across safely.* A little behind me to the right, in the vicinity of the trees that stood close together, I saw a fox sneaking about with his nose held low to the ground. Were there foxes in London?

"It's already long past sunset, Rhona," I suddenly heard behind me.

He was close by, much closer than I had ever dared to fear. I tried to not show my terror and turned my head into Lucas' direction, but again he was nowhere to be found... shit, shit, what was I supposed to do now??

*Stay near the road. Walk right by the passing cars and if you see a taxi, hail it immediately.*

"Don't you have a chaperone to protect you?"

Without a doubt this sounded menacing. Much too sleek, way too sensual! The guy now stood right in front of me, a yard or ten away. No choice but to go back, in the same direction as the cars were going, until I reached the bushes. Maybe I could hide there, or ask for help from one of those shady types that hung around here at night, in search of forbidden male love...

Turn left now. Oh, why did it have to be so fucking dark near those bushes and trees? Hang a bit more to the right then, cross the field diagonally, make a bolt for the hotel in one straight beeline. With a little bit of luck this was as far as this would go. Perhaps he had only wanted to toy with me and... yeah, right. Was I really that stupid to presume that he had come here just for shits and giggles? It was already disconcerting enough that I had underestimated him by not realizing that he probably long knew where I was staying... and especially now that reaching my hotel was so crucial and being among people could mean my salvation, I had moved *out* of sight of those people and away from the light of the cars!

A cold gust of wind from behind me made me stop dead in my tracks. He had caught up with me and was now walking back and forth at the end of the enormous field near the road. He had cut me off and I began to hyperventilate.

Go to the figure waiting beneath that streetlight then, there, next to the shrub. If I had to choose between two evils anyway... maybe that person would protect me if I explained that I was being harassed by someone.

"I'm not what you're looking for," said Lucas. It had only taken him a couple of seconds, after having crossed the field in a circumferential motion, to appear behind that same man standing beneath the streetlight. For a moment the two faced each other and then I heard Lucas' voice again, cold but entrancing: "You wanted to find love this evening, but now that you see me up close you have lost your desire. Therefore, you turn around, walk home disappointedly and never come back here again."

The man did exactly as the vampire had told him and disappeared. And I was frozen in place with my feet turned to lead. I was still breathing much too rapidly.

He came closer. "Join me," he said. "Three seconds for each breath. One – two – three... one – two – three... *slower.* One more time: one – two – three..."

His compelling eyes did not allow for mine to turn away from him for even a moment. And I had no idea how it was possible, but eventually I really did begin to breathe more calmly.

"The top of the food chain, do you know what that means, Rhona?" he then asked.

I did not answer.

"Well?"

With a tiny voice I asked: "What do you want me to reply with?"

"Being at the top of the food chain means that you don't have any enemies. That nothing in nature hunts you..." Lucas stepped, no, strode around me. He did not lay a finger on me, but I could feel it on the skin of my neck and face when he spoke, that was how near he was. I pinched my eyes shut.

"... It means that you yourself are the hunter... and the animal kingdom has an innate sense for it", he said, as he took a step away from me. "Animals know who their superior is and flee if they have to." He gave me a once-over from head to toe, and continued: "Mankind, on the other hand, is irresponsible and reckless."

This was about me. Oh fuck, he was talking about me!

There was something that drew the vampire's attention. He changed his stance and took a lightning fast jump towards the group of trees and bushes next to us. I heard a strange sort of barking, a cackling noise and the rustling of leaves. After that, Lucas reemerged from the vegetation holding an auburn fox in his arms – most likely the one that I had just seen! The animal was still alive and conscious. Struggling, with his ears flat towards the back of his head, it lay in a relentless stranglehold… As the vampire approached me, my eyes were fixated on those of the animal's that was looking for an escape in sheer terror. Uselessly, of course.

"Have you ever witnessed a murder, Rhona?" he asked.

"What do you mean?"

"What I mean to say is: have you ever seen how one of the undead takes the life of a living creature?" With a nod of his head he ordered me to come with him. In the vicinity of the streetlight he stood still. He turned towards the light so that the critter in his arms as well as his own face became fully visible. "Now pay attention," he said. Then he bent over towards the neck of the animal. He pulled back his upper lip and for the first time in my life I witnessed the canine teeth extend in the mouth of a vampire… The fox cried out a plaintive scream while he underwent the bite of his superior. And that superior drank, with greedy, prolonged gulps. After a while the screaming turned into yelping. The animal's resistance gradually decreased and finally you could only see some jerks in its paws. Then there was silence. Eyes that had stared at mine in absolute fear became lifeless. Eyelids lost their tension and fell half closed… A trauma – this would undoubtedly become a trauma to me, and even though I cursed myself for this immensely, it was impossible for me to take my eyes off all of this… until the animal was flung away with a careless toss, back into the bushes.

"Do you have any idea the kind of rush that drinking blood gives you?"

I shook my head.

Lucas spit out some hairs and wiped the red stain off his mouth with the back of his left hand. Within a few steps he was with me. He let his hand brush right against my mouth and nose. The acidic, metallic scent made me gag.

"Over nine hundred years ago this became a necessity of life for me and even now its attraction hasn't diminished," he said. "This addiction will never pass. The best you can do is learn to control it." Then he made a theatrical gesture and exclaimed in a downright dangerous tone: "Unless it is presented to you on a platter."

## 39

RELATIONSHIP


Oh no, Raphaël! Raphaël and I... So that was Lucas' objective!

"What do you want from me?"

"I'm going to observe you."

"I don't understand."

"Oh, but that will change in due time – tell me, Rhona, are you afraid?"

"I'm afraid of you."

"Is that so?" he asked mockingly.

"I have respect for you..."

"Respect... something that you barely seem to have for my student, on the contrary."

"What's that supposed to mean?" I began to walk into the open field.

"If you had had an adequate regard for Raphaël, you would not be in a relationship with him right now," he said from right behind me.

"Where is this coming from?" I snapped. "We are doing everything we can to be careful. We do take this very seriously!"

"Do I hear you think: why does he distrust me so much? Well, I have a reason to. A very valid reason even..." The way in which Lucas circled around me seemed like a slow form of ballet. The sensual steps of a man who seduces a woman. He whispered: "You are in love and that makes you unreliable. A danger that is not to be taken lightly..."

"How is that any of my fault? I would never betray any of you!"

"Says who? What can guarantee me that you won't change your mind when a bad mood strikes and you decide to blab about what he has done to you? Cause surely you haven't forgotten, Rhona? You were such an easy prey... a quick bite, delivered to his home entirely free of charge..." The vampire produced a slurping, tongue-smacking-teeth sound – the same sound that Hannibal Lecter made after musing over eating a victim's liver with some fava beans and a nice chianti.

What if I were to start screaming really loudly now, would they be able to hear it over there on the side walk or by the bus stop? How many yards were there between here and there? A hundred? Two hundred? Or... run *and* scream, perhaps? I dropped my shoulders. Not a chance in the world. The traffic noises would drown out any sound coming from the Common... I was alone with Lucas and there was nothing that could be done about that...

"Raphaël loves me," I sighed, "He wasn't himself when he bit me, normally he would never do that."

"Are you absolutely sure about that? Have you ever wondered why sex and violence, more often than not, intertwine? Could it be because they are controlled by two adjoining centers in the brain?"

I turned away. I did not want to hear this. I began to walk again with the vampire right beside me. Relentlessly he followed me in every evasive direction that I took.

And he would not give it a rest: "Our brains are not that different than those of humans. Only we have an added bonus. Within us lurks a murdering, bloodthirsty creature. And you, Rhona, have released that predator from his cage inside of Raphaël."

"Stop it. Please."

"Stop? Why? It's just starting to get interesting... Are you familiar with the saying *the way to a man's heart is through his stomach?*"

"Raphaël is perfectly aware of the ever present dangers. He does not take that many precautions for nothing," I defended him, myself, and us...

Suddenly Lucas began to walk slower. "Oh. Right. You do have a point there," he said. "I'm starting to realize that I can't blame you for as much as I had initially believed... you would have spoken differently, I suppose, if you had ever heard the gut wrenching sound coming from his throat during intense emotions..."

Checkmate.

Flashbacks to my slap in Raphaël's face, the reaction of the infuriated predator in him and everything that happened after, shot through my mind. I burst into tears.

The vampire had finally made me cry. But he wasted no time.

"I'd like to get your full name and address now," he coolly said.

A wave of shock. "No, no no no..." I stammered.

He nodded slowly and intently.

I shook my head. "Tell me what to do, but please don't ask me for my address!"

"Then I'm afraid Raphaël..."

" – No, leave him out of this! Here, hold on..." As fast as I could I looked for a pen and paper and started to write.

He accepted the piece of paper, asked for the pen and began to write something beneath my address. Then he tore the note in two and handed me the bottom part. I read, to my great surprise, his own personal information...

"I assume that *Lente Sandifer* is not a false name," he said. Like a customs agent holding a passport he studied what I had written down and after that he sized me up with a suspicious look on his face.

"Not so loudly!" I said in a hushed tone. "You should really only call me Rhona, especially if you're going to mail or call me!"

For a second he was silent. That silence took so long that, after a while, I asked him what he really wanted from me.

"That you break off all contact with Raphaël," was the answer.

"Why?"

"Because he's not being himself. Raphaël is smiling, Raphaël is starting to talk about new hobbies… He has become selective in what he divulges about his activities." As he said that last part his voice turned grimly. He stepped right in front of me. "A day will come when he will make a mistake. And it won't have pleasant consequences. That's why you're going to do yourself, him and our community a big favor. You're going to tell him that you want nothing to do with him."

"No."

"Oh yes, you are. And I will see to it."

"And what if I don't?"

A growl emerged from somewhere deep within his lungs. And then the fangs came out… I let out a shriek in fear and ran away. Immediately tripped over the uneven surface of the turf, fell on top of my bags. Got back to my feet, began to run again, changed direction to get as close to my hotel as possible, noticed him standing underneath the row of trees at the curb of the sidewalk already, swerved to the left… only to corner myself, met by him, at a little hill that was planted with some low shrubbery. "What's the matter, Rhona, can't get to your hotel?" he asked sarcastically. He lightly bent his knees and disappeared, only to appear again on top of the hill. A leap of at least ten yards… I made a run for it, but behind me his voice sounded: "Come on, little girl, don't push yourself too far. Save yourself the trouble."

Panting, I stopped. I hunched forward, leaned with my hands on my knees. My bag and camera hit the ground hard.

"Are you alright?" I heard coming from above me. Slowly I got up. Lucas waited until I was able to listen again. Then he said: "Go home, Rhona. Forget him. You only bring us trouble and our world is not for you."

"Could I please have one more day?" I asked, "he's taking me to the airport tomorrow…"

"That does not seem unreasonable to me. But in the evening you're going to write him an email. Yes?"

With raised eyebrows he demanded a response from me.

"Okay…" I said softly.

"Good. You are intelligent. So I trust that you know how to deal responsibly with the things you share and what you keep to yourself… but be aware that I am always willing to take off a couple days of work and pay the Netherlands a visit for some additional directions."

He pointed to my bags. I picked them up, and he said, "Go to your hotel. Make sure you get some sleep. You will need it."

## 40

CAMERA

Door locked and deadbolted. Unpack. No, first, to the bathroom. Remove make-up... a total scarecrow. Cried way too much these last couple of hours... Splash water on my face, as cold as possible. More water, stay focused. As I buried my face in a towel, I tried to think as pragmatically as possible. What I really wanted to do now was close the curtains and with the lights turned off crawl underneath a big pile of blankets. Hoping for a deep, dreamless slumber that would carry me right through all my troubles... but that was not one of the options. I had to stay awake, otherwise what had happened this morning would repeat itself, that I would oversleep and get woken by a phone call from him... and this time the consequences could not be foreseen. A splitting headache set in. And I already had so much difficulty focusing on what needed to be done. Fear, imagining the worst and a survivor's instinct that bordered on the neurotic were fighting for my attention. The events of the last few hours had resulted in nothing occurring chronologically anymore... not time, not my memories – fragments of then and now alternated with shocks and flashes... I *had* to keep my grip on reality and find something tangible to do. My bag. My suitcase. Unpack them, now. Everything into the closet or to the laundry machine. And get a mirror to install next to the window, so that I could see who was at the door, if the doorbell rang. Where could I find a thing like that? Perhaps in a junk yard. Where was one of those located... near Alexanderpolder. It was beside the train tracks I seemed to recall. Would there be a bus that runs there? Departing from Central Station? But I had to make sure that I would not start crying again for no reason. Because how things went down at the airport, I never wanted to experience again: him, using all possible means to put my mind at ease and I, inconsolable, avoiding each conversation and eye contact. That helpless look on his face, with which he watched me leave as I disappeared beyond security, had literally torn me up on the inside. And then that embarrassment about how I had claimed the attention of my fellow passengers and the air hostesses with my wailing for an entire hour...
But why was I fussing about acquiring that dumb car mirror? I needed my head for other things, I had to find the right words for an email to Raphaël. My final email to him... and again I started to cry. It was a good thing that Claire's bike was gone, that she could not hear me right now... oh Lord, please let her be on a day shift and not come home until six!
Therefore, those lines had to be typed down, and soon. And then I had to make myself representable for when she got home. She with her endless

barrage of questions… Shit, that I had to think through as well. No one must find out anything about last week, about him and I in London and especially about his true identity…

Slowly I opened my laptop. Pressed the power button. While the thing began to start up I plumped down on the couch close to my desk, and immediately got up again and sat down behind the computer. The device that had made it possible for Raph and I to get to know one another…

"Dearest Raphaël,"

Delete. Online his name was Aeolus.

"Dearest Aeolus,"

No, stupid! This was not a love letter.

"Aeolus,

What I am about to write will probably come as a bolt from the blue. I don't love you."

Lying. That was something that I could never keep up.

… Was it even *really* necessary to end things? Could we not just keep it going on the down low or something? But then I would first have to tell Raphaël about last night with Lucas… with the result that I would then have to give it my all to talk him down, because otherwise, guaranteed, he would undertake all sorts of things in blind rage… so, not very practical. But still – what if I were to call Lucas myself? Half a day had passed and I was home in Rotterdam, far away from him and the door was locked. Perhaps with a strong cup of coffee beside me I would be able to come up with an angle. Hesitatingly I rolled my desk chair back… and forward again. Calling him was out of the question. That confrontation, I would never be able to handle it.

Yet, that coffee was a must. Therefore I went to the kitchen, while I forced myself to keep on thinking. What time was it? Past eleven, already. That meant I still had an hour or seven until Claire would come home. At least, I hoped…

Two hours later I still had not found a solution. I had twisted my thoughts in all kinds of knots, but Lucas was waiting for me at each corner, calculating, menacing and with that overwhelming amount of life experience. How could I ever have thought to compete with that? Raphaël thought that his 'father' was a relatively harmless vampire. But the reason on which he based that was, to me, exactly the reason why I was seriously afraid for my life right now. Lucas saw right through me and would always be one step ahead, no matter what I tried. He was probably waiting for a phone call from me at this very moment during which I would beg him to change his mind… he was too familiar with the human mind. Much too well!

"Aeolus,

This message will probably come to you as a thunder bolt from a blue sky…"

My English cell phone rang. In one single leap I reached my bag, held it upside down so that its entire content, along with the phone, fell out. I looked at the screen upon which, of course, the name of my lover was displayed. Without touching the device I ran out of the room, sat on the toilet with my fingers in my ears waiting for the ringing to stop. Then cautiously walked back into the room. A text message arrived with the notification that someone had left me a message on my voicemail. Nervously I bit my lip as I listened to the message: "Darling, I saw that your plane has landed on schedule. I just wanted to make sure you arrived home safely and whether you were feeling any better. Call me soon..."

After having turned off my phone I walked over to my desk. With my third cup of coffee in front of me I began to type:

"Aeolus,

I have received your voice mail. After that I have turned off my phone. I realize that what I'm about to say, may come as quite a shock, but I don't know how else to say it. I'm breaking up with you. I'm ending our relationship, Aeolus. After everything I've seen, I have become too afraid to continue.

Please don't try to call me. Not even on my Dutch phone. I won't pick up and won't answer anonymous calls.

Rhona."

After I had sent the email I closed my laptop. The stand-by light began to blink. And now to unpack my bags.

Near the end of the evening the exhaustion finally hit me. Claire was home by now, we had spoken and I thought that I had fairly managed to come across as normal to her. But the amount of energy it had taken... in any case, the headache had become unmanageable now.

After having downed a couple of pain killers I crawled into my bed shivering. My Dutch phone had gone off twice already and I had not picked up. When it rang a third time I hid my head under my pillow. A message was left. With an exasperated sigh I picked up the device. Looked at the screen. An anonymous number. "Raph, please don't...", I thought, while I went into my messages. It was all hard enough as it was...

When I heard the voice that had left the message, however, my heart skipped a few beats. Because it was not that of my beloved, but of his sire. Lucas. He said: "Rhona, if you give me your number, I expect to be able to reach you on it. Call me back..."

And there it was. I could be in another country and have considered myself to be relatively safe, but the fact that the terror was not yet over... I could have seen coming a mile away... No choice but to obey.

As soon as I heard him pick up I asked: "What do you want?"

"How are you?"

"I had gone to bed already. So…"

"What shape is your camera in?"

"Huh?"

"Your camera is broken. Give it a check. See if you can still get the memory card out."

"How on earth could you know that?"

"You fell on top of your bags last night."

Slowly the fog in my brain cleared. "Hold on," I mumbled.

When I opened the camera bag I was shocked: indeed, the thing was anything but okay… the lens was positioned at an awkward angle to the body and I was barely able to save my SD-card, or should I say, pick it out of its dislodged casing.

"It's broken…" I softly said to Lucas.

"What does your schedule for tomorrow look like?"

"Uh…"

"Go to a professional camera store. Ask them if repair is still possible."

"Alright," I answered phlegmatically.

"I'll call you in the afternoon."

And that was that. He had hung up without saying anything else. Nothing about Raphaël, nothing about my mail to him…

I could forget about reparation. An employee of the photography store had convinced me of that much this morning. The lens had pushed the reflex mirror straight through the CCD.

Lucas called me around three and listened to my report on the damage. He asked some questions about the brand, the model and my motivations for purchasing this camera in particular at the time. I answered and then, yet again, the conversation abruptly came to an end…

And, in a way that was incomprehensible to me, I managed to fill the rest of my day with activities. Until I was stupid enough to check my mail. My boyfriend had responded to my message. My ex-boyfriend.

"Rhona,

You are making a choice that I'm not happy with, but that was to be expected sooner or later.

Better sooner than later.

Aeolus."

That was a tough pill to swallow. I cried, for hours, until the phone rang. Lucas again.

"Do you have a pen and paper handy?" It was not even a question, more like a command. I complied, again, and grabbed something to write on. He said:

"Write down this code and take it to a Western Union tomorrow. They will ask for your ID and for my full name as well. Do not leave that agency before calling me."

Without saying goodbye I hung up. With a mind beaten into submission I entered the night...

Almost an entire day later I called Lucas, this time by my own initiative. I was staring at the brand new upgrade to my broken camera on the desk in front of me and verbalized my thoughts: "I don't get you at all."

"Have you tried out your memory card yet?"

"Yes... but why such a bizarrely big gift?? I don't understand, after what happened the night before yesterday..."

"This photo camera is not a gift. You falling on top of your bags was my fault."

"That may be so, but this does not sit right with me."

"This is not a matter of the heart."

"Not to *you*."

"You are mixing things up. Stop doing that."

"But all that money..."

" – It would have gone to charity at the end of the month anyway."

My mouth fell open with amazement. I wanted to say something, but could not think of anything...

"Rhona, listen. I've got to run some errands shortly and have to go. But I would like to suggest that we keep in touch through a messaging app."

"No, I'd rather not..."

"The signals that you are giving me say otherwise. You feel the need to continue this conversation. Send me a friend request. We will talk later."

41

CHAOS

I had learned from the master: tell the truth in such a way that there was no room for difficult questions. And with Sander there was an added bonus: I felt safe with him. Therefore, I was able to let myself go when he hugged me as soon as he heard that I had not chatted with Aeolus since I had left for London... The tears began to flow when he inquired about the reasons why. Crying, instead of providing a clear explanation.

And then there was the issue of work. I had to keep busy as hard and as continuously as possible. The groceries I did in portions, so that I had reasons to leave to house multiple times a day. I changed my sheets. I went looking for a side mirror of an old car and hung it on my balcony to the best of my ability.

Naturally, the 'Claire' factor played a daily role. And she had, in all honesty, become a problem. Because Claire was sloppy. More often than not she would simply shut the front door behind her and then I would hurriedly run down the stairs after her to put it on the deadbolt. But worse was the fact that she would just leave the door to her room unlocked. As well as the windows... one time, for instance, when she was not home, I had noticed a draft coming from beneath her door, and during my investigation as to its cause I had discovered an open window in her room, just like that! I had then shut it with a loud bang, but immediately after I did that a voice coming from the doorway nearly gave me a heart attack: coincidentally Claire had just come home and asked me in surprise what I was doing. Talking my way out of it had been quite the task, but eventually, thankfully, she had bought my story about the wind and my fear of smashed windows. Still this had not been a great move on my part. I had to be more careful...

And all the while I cleaned. Systematically I went through my entire room, then it was the kitchen's turn and then the whole house. The fact that I neglected to eat my lunches and dinners I took for granted. This was training, after all. Training to get tough, so I'd be able to deal with things – things like this email from my ex-lover:

"Rhona,
I have spent a lot of time this week pondering the dilemma of 'where the boundary between manipulation and sincerely expressing one's emotions' is and I have come to the conclusion that I have the right to tell you that I do not understand you, that I miss you and that the accompanying pain is hard to bear.

What makes things worse is that I know that something is not right, although I can't quite put my finger on it.
De profundis,
Aeolus."


Keep living. Keep going. And a part of that was writing the introduction of my book. What, of course, under these circumstances, despite several frantic attempts, failed miserably. I did manage to finally put my chapters in the right order, albeit with a lot of pain and effort, and I professionally kept my appointment with Sander for that photo shoot in the Botlek industrial area. He clearly showed that he was excited about that shoot. He had to chuckle quite a bit during our car ride, when I explained what our objective was. And once we were on site and when we started setting the scene, he could not even stop laughing…
The concept of the photo that I envisioned was simple: the model, all dressed in white, would stand in front of a backdrop of stacked shipping containers. He would be bound tightly with black rope and over his mouth I would place a piece of silver-gray duct tape. At least, that was the plan. To reinforce the symbolism behind *The Cultural Box* I believed that Sander really had to be bound from tip to toe, so I got myself into spinning around him endlessly, with that unrolling tangled bundle in my hand. Until he, at the exact moment when I had finally finished, deadpan remarked that he felt that things could be a little tighter. So I ended up whirling all those circles back, to then have to start from the beginning again, and by doing so it became more difficult by the second for me to stand up straight. I had not seen the fun in it at all, but Sander only saw the sun, in the cloudless sky of that day, in having a good time by creating a piece of art together and in everything and all things in between. And in the end, ultimately, the infectiousness of his giggling had affected me as well – I burst out laughing when the piece of duct tape over his mouth came loose by one sad corner for the umpteenth time due to a lack of grip on his dark-blond five o'clock shadow.
But to my ears my laughter sounded artificial and the emptiness that I felt inside pierced through it deafeningly.


There were more things that hurt my ears. At home I had started to pick up on Claire's every move. Her radio was regularly turned up louder than I remembered from before. Also tram 4, that never had really bothered me, now made me cringe with its shrill squeaking wheels when it made its turn at Noordsingel Boulevard. One time, when I was downtown, something similar happened. A loudly screeching tram had passed by and I had broken down crying. Transfixed I had stood there, with my hands over my ears… Thanks to an elderly lady, who had helped me to a bench and stayed with me for a while, I had eventually calmed down. But whether my outward appearance represented what I felt on the inside…? In the Koopgoot

Shopping Passage I had then gone to a drugstore of which I knew the owner was an expert on herbs, and I asked him what would help against stress and insomnia. He recommended lavender oil and tea, which was also effective for common colds or neuropathy. I had almost asked him in a cynical tone if it worked for heartache as well, but I had managed to keep my mouth shut in the nick of time.

Lavender... Raphaël had mentioned it before. According to him my eyes were that color...

In my closet I placed two lavender pouches. For my bedding and furniture cushions I bought a spray. It turned out there were web shops that sold all sorts of products which were made with lavender. Lavender water, lavender candies, hand lotion and even traditional Provincial rods of lavender branches, woven together with organic material and strips of fabric. As time went on, my house became drenched in that unmistakable fragrance. And secretly I hoped that it would help me...

However, this illusion was not granted a long life. Another email from him arrived. And from its tone I could tell that this would almost certainly be his last. He sounded bitter and irate and the things he said indicated that he did not appreciate my radio silence. I really wished that he would find someone to talk to... and I kept living my life as best as I could.

## 42

TRAPPED

Meanwhile Lucas has started to send me text messages telling me to meet him online. At first I had tried to give him the cold shoulder. One time I had even outright refused. And surprisingly, he had accepted that.

This game of cat and mouse repeated itself in the weeks that followed with an inescapable regularity. Every third day a request to have contact arrived from him and each time I would fight tooth and nail to get out of it and then…

Until I finally threw in the towel. I should just do myself a favor and admit to myself that nothing had changed since that night in that park in London, that I was still hopelessly trapped by him. And only God knew for how long this would go on…

Our first conversation took place on a rainy weeknight:

Running.gyrovague says:
'Rhona, hello.'
*Rhona says:*
*'What do you want?'*
'I was wondering how you are doing.'
*'How am I supposed to be doing? I'm working. Just like anyone else.'*
'The fact that someone is working, does not say anything about their state of mind.'
*'Why do you call yourself Running Gyrovague?'*
'You refuse to answer my question.'
*'I have the right to keep things private.'*
'Just make sure that you keep your emotions in check. Anger costs you unnecessary energy.'
*'You have no idea how I'm feeling.'*
'How are things going with your book?'
*'Just fine. And how's your work going?'*
'The financial crisis has affected our field of work as well. For the last few months we have been booked less for demos.'
*'Aww, isn't that a shame. I guess you're just going to have to demean yourself and become a dishwasher at a restaurant or work as an overnight security guard, all alone…'*
'For the time being, that is not necessary yet. I can still provide for my daily needs.'

Had he just genuinely missed that sarcasm in my remark? Or was this another one of his strategies? I really had to learn to gauge him better…

That saying, *Keep your friends close, but keep your enemies closer.* Where did that come from again? The film The Godfather, I thought… or had one of those Chinese generals in ancient times said that at some point before? Keep your enemy close, it was an intriguing concept. And perhaps I could use it to my advantage… although, that did mean that I would have to do my best to get to know him better.

The only thing was, what do you do when you dread even the slightest bit of contact with someone like that? Was this really the only way – ask questions, much more than I was already doing – to keep him talking? Oh, fuck…

But as long as there was communication, his IP address *was* traceable. And that was not insignificant, because if I knew what his IP address was, I would also be informed on his whereabouts and on whether or not it was far away enough from Rotterdam. It was the most feasible trick that I could use to protect myself. There had to be some apps that were able to do this through a chat session?

And at the same time I had to find out more about his background. At the moment I did not have much more than the Rule of Saint Benedict. But it was enough. For now.

*Rhona says:*
*'What made you become what you are now?'*
Running.gyrovague says:
'I use to be a monk. As you know.'
*'Where was this?'*
'Sankt Georgen im Schwarzwald.'
*'Never heard of it.'*
'I have been attacked one time outside.'
*'That part I got. But how were you attacked? And why were you outside?'*
'That information is irrelevant.'
*'I don't get you… You, yourself, said that I felt the need to talk.'*
'You're trying to manipulate me. If I were in your shoes, I would probably do the same.'
*'So you don't want to talk about the past?'*
'Its usefulness is debatable.'
*'It's useful to me. I would feel less helpless, if I knew a little more about you…'*
'Even that is manipulation.'
'I was on my way to another monastery. Somewhere halfway along my hike I was attacked.'
*'Which monastery?'*
'Ottobeuren.'

'And who's your sire?'
'I don't know. After the bite and the procedure he disappeared.'
*You've been a vampire for a little over nine hundred years. Does that mean that your abbot's name was Theoger?*
'I see you are doing research…'

It was true. The fact that I was doing my research, I did not keep secret. And I really took my time doing it. While each of his replies popped up as quick as lightning I was coming up with search terms, exploring websites, rummaging through articles… If he wanted to talk to me that badly, he just had to deal with that. After all, I was only human and could not multitask anywhere near as well as his kind… therefore there was often an interval of several minutes between the messages that I sent to Lucas.

*Rhona says:*
*'It must have been horrific, when you were attacked… You probably could not go back to St. George, nor reach your destination anymore. And all that, while you had maybe been looking forward to seeing Abbot Rupert again. Didn't he used to be a prior at your monastery? You've probably seen him as somewhat of a father figure…'*
Running.gyrovague says:
'Rupert, yes… that was that abbot's name…'
*'Weren't you tempted to go and ask for help in Ottobeuren, regardless?'*
'Not at any point during the first decades. When you've just become a vampire the thirst for blood is all-consuming. Other sentiments are overshadowed by it.'
*'If I think about it, you have been orphaned a whopping three times. First you were left all alone as a little boy by your parents at a monastery filled with strange men. In the course of the years those men became the only family you had and then that bloodsucker showed up to forever block your way back to that. He basically made himself your biological father and then, to top things off, he abandoned you immediately after.'*

43

ANGER

How dared I be so rude and mean... it was probably an expression of that feeling in my gut, that sense of being utterly annoyed with his keeping his cool, how truly nothing seemed to affect him... I could *not* deal with it at this moment, not at all, but since I had to keep the conversation going anyway, I continued to come up with things to talk about:

*Rhona says:*
'*... So you've been on quite the rampage in the first twenty-some years, without a sire to keep you in check and to teach you and all... No wonder you think of yourself as a bad monk.*'
Running.gyrovague says:
'You've misunderstood, I think. I'm not a monk anymore.'
*Rhona says:*
'*But still you call yourself a gyrovague.*'

I went over the document on my computer screen one more time. The Rule of Saint Benedict. In the first chapter I had just read that a distinction had to be made between four types of monks: the first group belonged to the strongest kind, the so-called *cenobites*. Those were monks who lived in a monastery and neatly followed the rules and who subjected themselves to the power of the abbot.
The *anchorites* came next; monks who had left the monastery life behind and who, after having gained enough inner strength for the spiritual battle, lived in the desert as hermits.
Thirdly, there were the *sarabites:* inexperienced, 'as soft as lead' and living according to their self-written rules on their own or in small groups. They were considered to be very bad monks who were more loyal to the world than to God.
But the most despised type of monk was the *gyrovague*. He would spend his whole life traversing different regions and spend a day or three or four at a time with other monks, without a place to call home. He was, as the text literally read, a slave to his own pleasures and the snares of gluttony.

Running.gyrovague says:
'You have great empathic ability. But also great imagination. Don't let the latter get the upper hand, Rhona.'
*Rhona says:*

'What do you mean? The fact that guilt and atonement is the glue that's holding you together is clear as day, is it not?'
'You're not referring to that photo camera again, I hope...?'
'Oh no, why would I? That was nothing but pure logic. After all, debts are there to be settled. Aren't they?'
'That's what it boils down to, yes.'
'I bet you're not in London anymore, are you?'
'Since the day before yesterday I've been in Paris.'

The app that I used to trace his IP address did list a location somewhere in the French capital. The bastard, he was speaking the truth, like it was nothing. While I had to bend over backwards to come up with the best way to respond to him, while busting my ass to reach a level of knowledge with which I could, at the very least, keep myself standing somewhat, in the face of the mental violence that he... on second thought, did not even unleash on me, really... no, he was, in fact, not doing anything at all. This was bad! And in the meantime I was losing tons of energy, was just not getting anywhere writing the introduction to my book because of that, began to become forgetful during my daily activities, such as doing the groceries...
The only thing I wanted was to make him feel what I was going through. Why should he not be dragged into the depths of this pain and anger?
For the time being however, everything that I tried worked like one big paradox: the surface of the dark pool that represented my soul had begun to spin in increasingly turbulent circles. And an ominous hissing that was translated into tingling throughout my body, announced that the boiling point of the water had almost been reached...
But I just had to get under his skin.


Rhona says:
'It's a good thing your hairdo is more acceptable than way back when... Did they used to put those ugly flower pots on your head as well when they cut it?'
Running.gyrovague says:
'You are angry with me. Otherwise you wouldn't display such a lack in diplomacy.'
'And that head of yours, was it as bald as a billiard ball up top as well?'
'How far along are you with your book, Rhona?'
'What do you care about the book?'
'Grab a pillow that's big enough.'
'No.'
'Do it. Now.'

In a crazed impulse I yanked the laptop from its place and raised the thing above my head. Just when I was about to fling it right across my room my

phone rang. For a moment I froze and tried to think of what needed to be done first. Place the computer back on the desk. Gently. Pick up my phone. Where was that thing anyway? On the couch. Who was the caller? Shit, Lucas! And why, for heaven's sake, did I answer it without thinking??
As soon as the connection between us was established, however, he hung up again. Cursing I marched back to my desk. He was still online and had written something:

'Grab a pillow. Hit it or clench it against your face and cry your eyes out in it. That is better than doing things you will regret later on.'

I felt like an unbelievable loser when I actually obeyed him. But in spite of that, I gave the cushion an enormous punch with my fist when I got to the couch. He did not need to know about this. And the fact that I envisioned him during my desperate attack on the cushions, he would never hear of. I would flat out lie to his face, if he were to ask me whether I had done what he wanted…
After the aggression came the sorrow. Crying I lowered myself to the floor, with my face against the cushions that I, much like the subject of my anger, had used – only to bounce back to my feet and jump away from the couch again. Lavender! Why now, of all times?! With the penetrating, Provincial scent still lingering deep inside my nose, I typed:

*'Asshole! Motherfucking asshole! Filthy, disgusting piece of shit!!! I HATE you!'*
Running.gyrovague says:
'Go on, there's more where that came from.'
*'Fuck you, asshole, I decide if I continue.'*
*'Why, WHY did you never ask me if I have really sent him that email?'*
'There was no need to. I know that you did it.'

There was only one reason why he could be sure of that. And I was afraid to ask… even though everything inside me craved hearing about the love of my life and how he was doing – no, do not think, do not think! Work. Just keep living.

*London, Westminster.*

For the entire afternoon he has meandered in the vicinity of the Abbey and now he is waiting across the street, in front of the gate to the parliament buildings. The only thing the man wears on top of his business suit is a tightly woven, blue scarf and in his hand he holds a black umbrella, one of those types that is taken out all over the streets of Westminster at the first signs of a rain shower.

That umbrella he has just purchased a fraction of a moment too late, moreover, as his silver-white hair hangs limp and rained-upon on his head and the shoulders of his jacket are stained a bit darker than the rest of his suit.

When Raphaël exits the construction site around a quarter past six the man says: "You're putting in long hours these days."

Raphaël does not react. He walks on the sidewalk on his side of the road along the church buildings, through hordes of tourists and past small groups of peace activists staging their protests at the border of the park-like field. The man with the white hair keeps his eyes on him all the while, joins him in his walk for a short distance and when they both approach the intersection with the traffic lights, for a moment it seems as though Raphaël wants to head into his direction. But then he turns left anyway and he walks into Great George Street, as he picks up his pace. The other has to wait for the green light, then crosses the street and attempts to decrease the distance between him and his subject by making a run for it...

The trees along Birdcage Walk drop thick, wet drops of rain on the rain guards that the men hold above their heads and they walk, one on the left and the other on the right side of the road, with in between them the sound of motor vehicles and rubber wheels against wet asphalt and next to them the southern boundary of St. James' Park.

At the intersection by Buckingham Gate the man with the white hair slows down his pace a little and says: "Come on, enough is enough. Cross the street, we'll take a cab."

"Well well, Fabian... a taxi cab," mocks Raphaël.

Still he obeys, and moments later they sit, again each on their own side, staring out of the windows of a black vehicle driven by a chauffeur. Through rain-dripping gray and reflective puddles they ride back to where they came from, past the Houses of Parliament and into the crowded streets west of the Abbey...

In front of them there is a city bus, and when it stops and the passengers get on and off before their eyes, it can slightly be detected in Raphaël's body language that he is trying to estimate his chances. Fabian, however, turns to him and warns: "That would only delay the inevitable."

Raphaël relaxes, seemingly, and says: "You're afraid that I'll escape?"

"Realistic. Not afraid," is the answer.

They ask one another about their lives in Innsbruck and here in London, and talk a bit about mutual acquaintances. To the outside world it looks like the two vaguely know each other, that they are business associates at most. But when it stops raining and the clouds over the M4 begin to break they take a pair of sunglasses out of their breast pockets with their movements in a level of synchronicity that is strongly reminiscent of identical twins.

After a few minutes of silence Raphaël says: "None of you have been near me.

I am absolutely sure of that. How, for heaven's sake, did you find out regardless?"

"Watching along with Big Brother, that's hacking for beginners. Do you have any idea how many cameras the city has put up in an area such as Bermondsey alone?"

Raphaël exhales sharply and turns his gaze back to the outside.

"You do your work, I do mine," mumbles Fabian.

At a hotel near Heathrow they step out of the car. The lobby, decorated in mint-green with gray and stainless steel, is supposed to appear fresh and innovative, apparently, and the room on the second floor that they enter is of a depressing, dime-a-dozen type of luxury.

Fabian walks to the window. He takes a quick glance outside and closes the curtains. Then he opens a small safe next to the bed, takes out his laptop and places it on the desk.

A video chat program is opened and logged into. Contact is made. Then Fabian gets up to make place for Raphaël. He sits down as casually as possible, at least as much as one can on a desk chair…

The representative of the West-German Territories does not introduce himself. His voice sounds as though he has inhaled helium — some sort of technological trick — and only the webcam on this side of the connection is turned on.

After having exchanged some pleasantries with Raphaël he asks: "I assume that you know why we have decided to invite you for a conversation?"

Raphaël says: "Of course. It's a pity though, that we have to bring our Austrian brother all the way over here for a misunderstanding of this nature. I can imagine that his time is better spent on other things…" and by ways of the mirror on the wall he seeks eye contact with Fabian, who has taken a seat in a chair behind him. Fabian returns his gaze, but does not display any emotion.

The man with the distorted voice asks: "You say: a misunderstanding. In what way?"

"You see the storm. Not the glass of water."

"Yet a recent inspection shows otherwise. Naturally, we could not come near you without your knowing, and surveillance cameras only register images. But the images that we saw spoke for themselves… for a week you have spent quite some time with an infantile, as it seems."

"And in what way is that unacceptable," asks Raphaël.

"You have had coffee with her. On several occasions."

"That was business related. She is a photographer — I needed photographic material. Perhaps you have seen us in Hackney, for example. I am restoring St. John's there — "

" – We witnessed you at an Underground station in the city center. There you were kissing each other in plain sight."

"Ah, that kiss with her... I do remember. A kiss can mean many things. And at the same time, nothing at all..."

"That may be so. But hadn't the regional management of the Danube Monarchy gone through something similar with you before? Roughly fifty years ago, or so – "

"*Fifty six*. And that was something entirely different, that was a friendship."

"And what is the nature of the relationship between you and this girl? How would you characterize your feelings for her?"

"Oh, that probably lies somewhere between toleration and mild sympathy."

"Do you still keep in touch with her?"

"No. She did not mean that much to me."

"Ah. That comes as a relief, because all that hassle with crushes, it's the last thing any of us need right now. Wouldn't you say?"

Raphaël smiles.

"Then I believe the only thing that is left for me is to ask from you her name and address, so that we can take our subsequent measures."

"Measures. That sounds like taking things a bit too far, against the practically negligible danger that she poses..."

"We are aware of that, yes. But you might also understand that we can't take any risks. Before you know it, an infantile like her has drawn the most far-fetched conclusion and since an accident can easily be made – "

And that was how Raphaël's breaking point was reached.

It was so easy to see how it happened: first the skin of his face turned pale, paler than it normally was. Then his eyes traveled to the door and within a fraction of a second Fabian had moved to this only way out of the room. There he took position with his arms crossed.

Raphaël then turned to the webcam on the computer and began to explain, to plead... And finally, he was begging.

44

WRITER


The following day I took two decisions: the lavender products had to go and
the introduction for my book had to be completed *before* sunset.
For the latter I put everything else aside. After my breakfast and the
lavender purge I turned off the phone and made sure that I was not visible
anywhere on the internet.
And I wrote. And erased. Tried different approaches, using imagination,
using associations, and wrote again. Claire, who knocked on my door around
noon, I brushed off.
'This is a wordless book.' Wrong. Again.
'This is a story without words.' No, that was not it either.
'Welcome to my photo book.' Oooh... this was downright pathetic. Focus!
'Dear reader, in front of you lies a book. A book with images, but without
words. Yet this book is filled with stories. They cannot be found as texts, but
they emerge in your head as you look at the photos.' Hmmm, I could be on to
something here, but I was sure I could do much better.
'Dear reader,
Long have I contemplated on the question of whether the photo book that lies
in front of you right now should contain any text.' No, this was *complete*
garbage again! Coffee, I needed coffee.
After a five-minute break – I had been to the kitchen and had impatiently
paced back and forth in my room a couple of times – I sat down behind my
desk again and took one deep breath. It was now or never.


'Prologue.


Abandoned factory grounds, old castles, derelict churchyards... I could spend
hours there. Ever since my childhood these places have had a special appeal
to me. Places that many others would prefer to ignore.
For a long time I didn't know the reason for this. Because why be happy
about something that causes a sense of unease to most of us? Why do I get
excited about just the type of environment that in general is found to be
depressing?
Anyway, the fact was that in the course of time my portfolio was
supplemented more and more with images of these kinds of locations. And
one day I started to notice this uniform style of photos. A good basis for a
book...
But what would be its theme? What is it that is so appealing to me in the

desolation of which is cared for so little that weeds rise up between every joint and crack?

I was in London recently. On my wish list was a photo shoot of Nunhead Cemetery, a graveyard that is much less known than for example Highgate, but at least as impressive, I had been assured. And none of that had been exaggerated: my heart literally opened as soon as I passed the gates of its main entrance and saw the neglected disarray of the jumbled tombstones under the trees. Most of them were half sunk into the ground. The consequences of the ravages of time could be seen on every single one: some were broken, others crumbled or heavily weathered… and all were more or less overgrown with plants and shrubs.

English graveyards are so much more beautiful than those in the Netherlands. Here everything is controlled and neatly taken care of. Neglect doesn't stand a chance, because the old is restored as quickly as possible or needs to make way for the new. And that doesn't only apply to our resting places for the deceased. Lack of space, a small country – they are understandable arguments, but in my opinion this approach does history no good. Everywhere in our country the present is predominant while the past is anxiously hidden or replaced by something better, by objects that apparently matter more.

Since I became aware that this is how I think about this subject I have also realized what it is that I find so beautiful about abandoned and neglected locations: both the past and the present are awarded a place there.

'What was' can still be seen everywhere, breathed in, and if you listen carefully, heard. 'What is', that is you and what you make of it based on your own references. And even the future, 'what will be', announces itself with the promise of nature, which with its new roots, branches and leaves interweaves itself with reality. It always finds a new way, no matter how strong the resistance may be, preferably through the cracks of tombstones, concrete and asphalt. Just pay attention, the prettiest flowers, the greenest ivy and the most delicate beginnings of trees are found – right where in the distant or near past damages in hard material occurred.

I am a symbolic thinker. In a metaphorical sense I see numerous links to my own life when I study the dynamics between those three time frames. Therefore I came up with a suitable main theme: 'Love & Decay'. And that also became the title of the book.

Lente Sandifer.'

'Introduction.

'Love & Decay' is a collection of photos without additional text, a format I chose purposefully. Yet much preceded the moment I made this decision... I had tried everything, had been looking for quotes, considered writing appropriate poems, and for a moment I even thought of an interesting imaginary correspondence with a philosophically literate person.

Nothing worked, however. The process was stuck and I couldn't figure out why. Until one day I learned what was going on. It was because the stories I was searching for had already existed for a long time, even if they had yet to be given words.
Because those words can be found in the mind of the reader. In your mind. As humans we make associations when observing images, we give them an interpretation with our thoughts, consciously or unconsciously. So in response to my photos, with your background and your outlook on life, you can create your own story.
That basically means therefore, that you are the author of this book.
So turn the pages and have a look at the photos. Allow what you see to affect you. Maybe it will trigger something – it doesn't matter what you do: write, write poetry, paint, mourn or celebrate or just look and daydream...

'Love & Decay' contains eleven chapters, each of which represents a theme. Themes that relate to emotions and sentiments, expressed in landscapes, cityscapes and by means of stationary plays, the so-called staged photographs. None of the people who collaborated with this are professional models. Thanks to them however, my photos have acquired a depth and personality and I am very grateful that they have helped convert my feelings into images with such enthusiasm and love.
Each photo in my book has a title, even if it is not indicated on the relevant page. That way you have complete freedom to associate. If you are still curious about the name of any given photograph, then you can make use of the title index at the end of this book. There you can also find a list with the locations where the images were taken.

Dear reader, dear observer, dear writer... Love & Decay is now in your hands. Look into your heart and make it your story.

Lente Sandifer.'

## 45

## PUSHBACK

An introduction *and* a prologue. Unbelievable. Never knew I had it in me...
But I had made it, before my deadline. And now I really had to go outside.
Stretch my legs, get some air, go to a shop or something, to celebrate
breaking free from the burden that I had allowed to be on my shoulders for
such a long time. And tonight, finally consume a decent meal again. From
now on I was going to take better care of myself.

However, Lucas remained a dark factor in my life, that kept swinging me
back into the reality I was struggling so hard to break free from... a reality
that hurt me more than I wanted it to, even now.
Take the way in which he asked me how I was doing this evening. It came
across as being sincere. But it only resulted in more salt being poured into my
wounds. And perhaps that had been his intention all along... although I did
not dare bet my money on it.
The thing was – I wanted to move on, I wanted to move forward, get my
normal life back. And the fact that that happened so painfully slow, was *his*
fault. The frequency with which he intercepted me on just about every path I
took in my search for 'normal' and 'as before' was annoying, nothing but
annoying! At least, as long as I was able to ignore the cold shivers at the
thought of him...
Now, for instance, he wanted to hear how I was feeling after my temper
tantrum from two nights ago. I indicated that I didn't want to talk about
that, to which he asked me what I did want to talk about.
I was on to what he was doing: he was yet again – without my permission –
playing the therapist. But I was going to fight against that humiliation. We
should see what effect it would have on him, if I were to fight his fire with
that of mine... what could be left for him to say then? And, more
interestingly: What would he feel? If he were even capable of feeling at all...

*Rhona says:*
*'So you live in Paris?'*
Running.gyrovague says:
'Yes'
*'In what kind of house?'*
'I'm renting a loft south of the city center.'
*'Okay... and what does it look like?'*
'What do you mean?'

'Simply, what does your loft look like? For example, what is the color scheme of your decor?'

'I never thought about that, when I moved in.'

'A typical apartment of a single man then. And what's in it?'

'A bed. A chair, a table.'

'And a closet?'

'A chest of drawers.'

'TV?'

'I don't own a television.'

'No television, huh… and what about a stereo system?'

'No.'

'But you must have something to entertain yourself with?'

'I have a phone and the internet. For work.'

'I bet you have a notebook. Probably one of those tiny ones with a ten inch screen.'

'How do you know that?'

'A bigger one would be senseless.'

Could he really be as predictable as I thought? And would he really never lie? Hmmm… that would be weird, cause if that was the case I could totally pick his brain.

Rhona says:

'In other words: you own very little and most of what you do have, you give away. Why, for heaven's sake, live a life like that?'

Running.gyrovague says:

'I don't need much.'

'I guess…'

'The value of personal possessions is often grossly overestimated.'

'And that little backpack of yours, it always has a new book in it, right?'

'Now you're just guessing.'

'But it's true, isn't it? Carry a book with you every day, preferably one from the library.'

'Yes.'

'Don't get me wrong – I really do admire you for it. You're probably overflowing with general knowledge. And since an idle mind is the devil's workshop I would definitely keep up with the reading. Can't get caught having nothing to do for even a minute…'

'In the Rule of Benedict it is worded differently: idleness is the enemy of the soul. Chapter 48.'

'So I was right after all. Once a monk…'

'Your fascination with my past has still not diminished. But keep the possibility in mind that you are mistaken. I live more in the present than you might expect.'

'Alright, a current topic then. Tell me something about parkour. Why, for Pete's sake, did you decide to practice that sport, when your natural self can execute those 'moves' infinitely better?'

'It was interesting for me to see mortals move in slow motion in a way that only we are familiar with.'

'And so you thought: let's degrade myself and see if I can do it as well, without standing out among them.'

'It was not that simple. First I observed a handful of traceurs. Then I had to learn to hold back my strength to end up at a level that was beneath theirs. And that took me well over a couple of months.'

'End up beneath them? In other words, act like you suck at it?'

'Yes.'

'Where's the fun in that?'

I quickly glanced at the clock. This conversation was starting to take up more time than I actually wanted.

## 46

## DEPLACEMENT

Running.gyrovague says:
'It's about the challenge, Rhona. Imagine how difficult it is to move about at a pace that is dozens of times slower than what you are used to, releasing a minimal amount of energy. That's not an easy feat, it's something you have to learn.'

*Rhona says:*

*'I don't get that at all.'*

'I'll explain it to you. The movements of a vampire are often so swift and flowing that they are not visible to the naked eye. Even our strength cannot be compared to that of a human. But to clarify my passion for parkour I must first give you a short background story.

The pioneers of this kinesthetic discipline have studied through and through how the human body is built and how it can move. Going forward with that knowledge, they trained to reach a level that seems inhumanly high. You remember the awe-inspired reactions of the audience when we did that demonstration in London... L'art du déplacement looks very impressive, a traceur is a lot like a superhuman, but in actuality, what he does lies perfectly within the normal potential of the human body.'

*'What's l'art du déplacement?'*

'The art of displacement. Nowadays called parkour or freerunning. Anyway, back to my story: modern society has taken a lot of physical labor out of our hands. Especially in the last few decades the technological developments have reached a point at which we have become prisoners to our own tendency towards comfort. Practically everything that we need can be found under the roof of one department store, or even worse, thanks to online stores we do not even need to leave the house to go shopping. And if we do need to go somewhere, buses, metros and cars are at our disposal.

These days a mechanical solution exists for just about anything. While you still had to kneed hard to make dough twenty years ago, a bread making machine does all the work now with one push of a button. Walking to the mailbox on the corner has nearly become obsolete since the rise of the internet. Some don't even have to do the daily commute to their office anymore, because they are now able to work from home.

Farmers keep livestock. Livestock is butchered and meat is processed, divided into portions and packaged, ready to be sold. The same goes for fruit, dairy... everything in stock at the same supermarket.

In the past, however, we had to hunt our food. That meant sneaking,

running, climbing, fighting through rain and storm... If you did not go out to track down bears or elk once every couple of days, you had nothing to eat and would die from hunger.'
*'Sure, but now you're talking about prehistoric times.'*

Somewhat impatiently I stretched my back. With shooting pain a stiff muscle protested my thoughtless motion. I groaned. I had no idea Lucas was such a chatterbox...

Running.gyrovague says:
'Even now tribes still exist, in Africa for example, that live that way.'
*Rhona says:*
*'I know that. I'm not stupid.'*
'In any case, the people from prehistoric times are our ancestors. And take it from me, because of their lifestyle they were stronger, their bodies were more agile and they had more stamina. Tell me something, when you are on your way from point A to B, what do you do when your path is blocked by a bike rack?'
*'Now you probably expect me to answer: walk around it...'*
*'Ooooh, I don't know. Just continue your story, okay?'*
'What I'm trying to say, Rhona, is that we are using our bodies in a different way than what it was built for. There is more potential hidden within us than that we tap in to these days.'
*'Hold on. You keep saying 'we' and 'us'. But you're not one of us. You are not human.'*
'That is entirely correct. And that is where we must head to in this conversation.'
'I was, in fact, different than every traceur around me when I began to train with the Yamakasi in the suburbs of Paris. So I had to watch how I carried myself. But staying away from them was not an option either. They were doing something that fascinated me immensely: they were, either consciously or subconsciously, in search of their roots. And in order to do that, they had to work extremely hard. Now it's obvious to think that vampires can do it much better – you said it yourself – that it is a piece of cake for us to mimic those stiff, inferior 'athletes'. Nothing could be further from the truth, though. To do the exact same thing that they were doing, at their pace, while releasing a similar amount of energy... it was a good thing that I practiced on my own first. Using only a fraction of the strength that you have at your disposal is, as a matter of fact, nearly impossible at first. You immediately lose your flexibility. It all goes in jerks and spasms. A vampire has sharper senses than a human, but now I suddenly had to learn to feel things that I had never paid attention to: the reaction of, for example, one individual muscle to – what is to me – a minimal amount of exertion of an arm or a leg.
And to my great amazement it turned out that those traceurs ran into the

exact same challenges. Albeit, their approach was from the bottom. They worked their way up during the training sessions, whereas it was my goal to reach a level that was far beneath me. That is how we turned out to meet in the middle and I actually became one of them. But the greatest discovery to me was: I began to experience moments in which I came close to my own roots. My human roots.'

'*Sounds complicated. To be honest, I'm having a hard time comprehending everything that you're telling me. Perhaps that's because it's getting late already...*'

'Understood. We'll continue another time. Goodnight.'

And gone he was. Offline within two seconds. Weirdo. Still, I was happy to slide into my bed now. Finally, some rest... cause good grief, could that guy go on and on! I wish I had never brought up that all-encompassing hobby of his. Or passion. Obsession?

Oh well, as long as he was talking about parkour we were not talking about me. And I would give anything for that. Perhaps he would become bored himself from his endless monologue about that one topic.

When I was texted by Lucas a few days later, however, I had looked up the Yamakasi after all. And I had watched Youtube videos of them and similar groups, such as Parkour Generations in London... Even though I declared myself completely mental for doing so.

Running.gyrovague says:

'I've been meaning to thank you for our last conversation.'

Rhona says:

'*I didn't do that much. Just some reading. But if you take such pleasure from talking about this... by all means.*'

'Very well, but first I'd like to know what you felt was unclear about my narrative.'

'*I really can't recall.*'

'You were probably low in energy.'

'*Yes. I was tired.*'

'But today is a new day. And I am open to questions.'

'*I have none.*'

'Then I'll just continue with my story, if you have no objections. We were talking about the reverse engineering that I was applying to myself.'

'*And what is that?*'

'Ah, a question, after all... Reverse engineering is something like 'backwards learning', as you rewind your abilities or the things that have become second nature to you. But that process is only one of the many things that you will face as a traceur. Fear is another thing. For weeks you have jumped back and forth in the street between painted lines. Then those lines became curbs. You have practiced those precision leaps so much you could literally dream them.

So you feel pretty sure about yourself... Until you trade the safety of the level paving stones for the walls of an alleyway. Suddenly you are confronted with the thought of whether you are estimating the distance correctly. You start to imagine what would happen if you were to use too little force for your leap and everything you have learned suddenly seems to disappear like fog – but you prevent that just in time. And you take the leap. Overshoot by an inch perhaps, barely manage to maintain your balance, but you have achieved your first victory.'

*'I'm sorry, but I still think it's a little vague. I'm afraid you're going to have to explain it differently.'*

'What is the matter with you? This cannot be jealousy.'

*'Huh?'*

'People who are envious of others, because they possess more knowledge, may react just as you do. They provoke their conversation partners by continuously making them believe that they don't explain things very well. But with you it's just resentment, isn't it?'

*'What are you talking about??'*

'You are still angry with me.'

*'Well, since you're mentioning it, let's be clear on the fact that our having contact has never been a decision on my part.'*

'For the time being you really don't have much of a choice.'

*'For how much longer?'*

'Until I've made certain of a couple of things. So it would be best for you to get a grip on your emotions.'

*'Where does the fear that you encounter during training come from?'*

'What a peculiar leap of thought.'

*'I'm doing what you want me to do. I'm getting over my emotions. So, what were we talking about? Fear, I believe...'*

'Yes. Fear... it makes you question things that you first thought you were sure of – have I checked that ledge carefully enough for sharp protrusions, for instance? Am I sure the surface isn't too slippery? The distance, is it really two yards or is it a foot shorter? And now that I flex my muscles to jump, what kind of feel corresponds with the right amount of energy release that I need, to get exactly where I have to land?'

*'In other words, you're just afraid to fall.'*

'Is that so strange?'

*'Yes, because you are a vampire and vampires can do anything.'*

'Within this context, that is correct. But how do you think the traceurs around me would react, if I were to save myself from an unfortunate miscalculation in a way that I normally would?'

*'I got it.'*

'That's why even I take a fall sometimes.'

*'And what do you do then, when you get injured?'*

'If others see you bleed, you quickly cover that scrape or cut with a band-aid.

And you leave it on for a couple of days, until it is humanly plausible to remove it. The point is not to show that your wounds heal within a matter of seconds. With internal injuries things are easier.'

*'Yeah, cause then you just put on an act: either you suck it up and wait a minute, or you go home limping and take a few days off.'*

'Exactly. Exactly!'

*'But the fear itself, how do you fight that off then?'*

'Fear is not something you should always want to fight. It is useful to familiarize yourself with it. It is even of crucial importance to take it seriously, but also to brush it off of you in the right moments. You see, it's a mechanism for the sake of self-preservation, that simultaneously can promote self-limitation. So when do you listen to that voice in the back of your head and refrain from a *vault* or *leap*, and when do you know you have to follow through? You will only learn that by practicing extensively. By endlessly repeating. Getting to know your body and your surroundings. Through weightlifting, which gives you the assurance that your arms don't fail on you during a *cat leap,* for example. By improving your endurance. Balance. Precision.'

*'Or like you Germans say: Fingerspitzengefühl?'*

'And self-control.'

*'Does that carry over to your private life?'*

'Oh absolutely.'

*'Do tell.'*

'I am able to go for longer periods without drinking blood.'

*'How much longer?'*

'Normally speaking, a vampire has to drink once every seven to ten days. I can do without for a month now.'

*'But you keep raising that bar, I bet.'*

'A man has to have a goal.'

*'A man, L.?'*

'It's just an expression, Rhona.'

*'Okay okay… But, in reality, by taking such a stand, you don't accept who you are. Do you even enjoy what you do?'*

'Now I must take the liberty to say: I don't understand you.'

*'I suggest you think about it for a bit. You'll figure out what I mean.'*

'Will do. If you promise to reflect on the following question: is there a line that can be crossed where self-control does you more harm than good?'

## 47

CONTROL


And that was a direction that I really did *not* want my mind to go to.

Afraid of my inner cesspool or afraid of Lucas – dangerous and emotionless Lucas – it was a choice between two evils. But if it were up to me, the lid on my soul remained perfectly in its place. And I really could not care less how much I realized that my extreme control on my daily life was only a survival mechanism and nothing more.

Okay, the grief, perhaps I could do something with that. If I decided to submit to it carefully, in tiny doses, that *might...*

That evening I looked up a photo of Raphaël, printed it and hung it above my bed. Waiting for the tears, but the tears did not come. Not that night, at least.


It was Sunday and my craving for a change in mental scenery had brought me back to the people of Asylum London after several weeks had gone by. Following the instructions on their website I had downloaded Skype and I had gotten in touch with them online at around 5:30 p.m. At a certain point, after there had been some back-and-forth chatting between myself and some other callers, Sam joined the conversation as well – the guy with the long, blond hair in that ponytail, I recognized his voice. He explained what they were going to discuss today in the upper meeting room of The Fox and when someone online asked him who all were sitting around the table over there, he listed some names over the chat:

'Ashley, Ron, Michaela, Andrew, Nick, Gizmo, Kazimír, Linda and myself.'

Everyone online wrote back a greeting to the club in London, except me, as I half-stumbled over my own legs to get up from my desk chair and stared frantically at my computer screen, verifying that I had actually seen what I thought I had just read: Kazimír... there could be only one within that community: the Kazimír that I knew, *Raphaël!* He was sitting there, at The Fox, and at this specific moment we were merely *one* keyboard, just *one* microphone away from each other. That was close, much-and-much to close...

I typed: 'Listen, guys. I'm afraid I have to leave you. A minor crisis here at the Lente household... a break in the water pipes.'

I did not wait for Sam's response. I shut down my computer as quickly as possible and turned off my phone.

And now the tears did come, in extravagant, disproportionate amounts... I had never known that a person could express their emotions with such heartbreaking passion. That your grief could rip apart your soul in such a radical way. At the same time, however, there was that voice, the voice of my rational brain that told me coolly and compellingly what to do: "Submit to your grief, let it all out. Take another breath of air. Yell *louder!* Ignore the pain in your throat. There's a lot more buried within. Keep going!" And in the background I could hear the instruction to grab a pillow and press it hard against my face. A pillow that was big enough...

That night I fell asleep on the couch. Exhausted.

On Tuesday something had changed. I did not feel as heavy, somehow. Lucas noticed it too. After having made some small talk he wrote:

Running.gyrovague says:
'Something has been set in motion within you. You seem more relaxed... Does it have something to do with that question I left you with on Saturday?'
*Rhona says:*
*'I'll give you an answer to that, if you first tell me whether you've gone over the issue that I raised.'*
'Agreed. I will tell you. I have thought it over, but to my regret I have to admit that I still don't understand your question.'
*'What's there to not understand about a topic like 'fun'?'*
'I'm familiar with the term. I know the feeling of excitement when I execute a new vault for the first time. It pleases me when a performance, travel and overnight stay smoothly come together thanks to making good preparations...'
*'But that's only about work.'*
'Yes. And what do you mean then?'
*'Do you ever take a break?'*
'I sleep on a daily basis.'
*'And when you don't sleep, do you ever simply do nothing? Do you ever sit and stare at the stars for an hour, for example? Or just enjoy the view from the top of a bell tower?'*
'Why would I sit at the top of a bell tower?'
*'Because you are a vampire, L., because you can! Man, if I were you and could climb like that... there are so many beautiful things to see and to do in this world.'*
'The beauty in this world does not pass me by, trust me.'
*'And yet you don't act on it that much.'*
'I am quite busy.'
*'Yeah, duh.'*
*'Ever wondered why you are so busy? Why you do nothing on a whim and everything out of necessity? Who makes you do that, really?'*
'No one.'
*'Just admit it. You yourself are the one who is constantly chasing you with a whip.'*

'Being diligent has its merit.'

*'But you are never strict enough. We've talked about that before, the bar is raised by the day. Why is that?'*

'That bar, I do raise every now and then... you are right in that way.'

*'You did not answer my question.'*

'And you are trying to analyze me. I will overlook that. For now. After all, your behavior is an understandable response to my attempts to help you.'

*'Help me... only because you feel guilty about the stunt you pulled on me in London.'*

'Help is help. You either do something with it or you set it aside.'

*'Perhaps what I'm doing to you falls under the category of 'helping' as well.'*

'Oh, but I have no doubt about that. Thanks to you I have become convinced that despite my headstrong denials I am still that same old monk. That the Rule still determines practically everything I do. And that I still pay daily penance for the innumerable massacres, for the godforsaken beast inside of me that I can't seem to shake off.'

*'Whoa!! I did not see that one coming! What made you suddenly come around like this?'*

'Does it matter? Isn't the fact that it happened more important?'

*'And how will things change for you from now on?'*

'Old habits die hard.'

*'Why not start with something small?'*

48

THERAPIST

*Rhona says:*
*'Crap.'*
Running.gyrovague says:
'What's crap?'
*'Nothing. Just my back again.'*
'Did you pull a muscle?'
*'Something like that.'*
'I can help you with that. If you like, I can give you some pointers...'
*'Hit me...'*
'Very slowly, while remaining seated, move your back and your hips. Long drawn out movements, as little as possible as you start off.'
*'Okay...'*
'Bend, stretch, sideways, rotating, whichever direction does not matter. Do what feels right.'
'No. Slower. You're moving way too rushed. The movements must be barely visible.'
*'How could you possibly know what I'm doing?'*
'Everyone goes through this at first. Even you.'
'How does that feel?'
*'Difficult. Jerky.'*

For a while I solely concentrated on my sore muscles and, as the minutes went by, something actually seemed to feel different...

Running.gyrovague says:
'If a certain movement does not feel comfortable, let your muscles find a different path. Circumvent the pain, so to speak.'
*Rhona says:*
*'Wait. Give me a minute.'*

I did not expect this to happen. It seemed as though I was able to work more and more minutely... From choppy inches to ever smoother becoming fractions of inches... And the pain slowly decreased.

*Rhona says:*
*'Could it really be this simple?'*
Running.gyrovague says:

'What do you feel?'

*'No more pain, at least. And yet I can feel all the muscles in my back. As though I am truly aware of their existence for the very first time... is that even possible?'*

'It's possible.'

*'Thank you.'*

'You're welcome.'

'You were still going to tell me about the question that I had left you with.'

*'I'm sorry, but I honestly can't remember what it was.'*

'Then I'll just repeat it to you: is there a line that can be crossed where self-control does you more harm than good?'

*'Oh, right. Well, I thought about it and it was useful to me. So, thanks.'*


Oh, come on, what was he thinking? That, all of a sudden, I was going to share all my soul stirrings with him? For Pete's sake, we were not friends! And although I had to admit that a special kind of understanding between us had begun to develop, it most definitely could not be called a real connection. The affection that we displayed towards one another was to him nothing more than a repayment of debt and to me it was revenge, at most. My way of humiliating him. To show him that despite his age and his ridiculous level of knowledge on anything and everything, he should not delude himself into thinking that he could make it on his own forever. Surely a day would come in which he had no choice but to acknowledge his pathetic lonesomeness, and when that happened I would have him where I wanted.

Regardless of that I caught myself saying things that gave away the fact that by now, every once in a while, I had begun to see Lucas in a new light.

Then in unguarded moments, for example, I would say openly and without ulterior motives that I missed Raphael terribly. That the pain still had not gone away and then, once in a blue moon, I asked Lucas whether there was no other way. Whether he could change his mind, whether I really could not get in touch with my ex-lover again... The answer was always the same. He consistently did not divert from the decision that he had made a month and a half ago.

He was cruel and, at the same time, incomprehensible. For why on earth, despite the above, did he also make these kinds of statements:

Running.gyrovague says:

'You are brave, Rhona. For the last fifteen to twenty years I have seen from up close how weak and limited human beings are and I have gained admiration for their creativity and survival instinct. Since the beginning of our acquaintanceship I have witnessed repeatedly how even you, with what little means you possess, have managed to tackle difficult situations. I haven't inquired about it for the last couple of weeks, but I am fairly confident, for instance, that your book is ready to be submitted to a publisher

by now. Am I correct?'
*Rhona says:*
*'You are correct.'*
'Very good. For what it's worth: I'm proud of you.'
*'Sometimes an explosion of anger pushes you into the right direction.*
*Although I did not get everything out of my system. But I'm sure you are*
*aware of that.'*
'Nonetheless, I hope that resentment is not the only thing going on between
us.'
*'Oh well...'*
*'We have our moments. Even positive ones, every now and then.'*
'Anyway, I want you to know that I appreciate our conversations.'
*'Yeah, okay. As for me, I don't just hate you anymore. Even though I know*
*that you'll probably always remain such a humorless old bore...'*
'Is that a cheeky undertone that I hear there?'
*'It sure is. And I'm proud of it, haha!'*
*'Say, about something different. Remember how we talked about the subject*
*of 'fun'?'*
'I remember.'
*'Is there anything in life that you really want? The ultimate wish, as they*
*call it?'*
'Uh... yes. That as many youth as possible learn that they are valuable. Thus
within the extent of my ability I want to impart to the youth that practice
parkour, to take home the acquired skills, the values that they have obtained
during training sessions, so that it may benefit them in their daily lives.'
*'L., again you're talking about work. I meant, for you, yourself! What do you*
*wish for yourself?'*
'I have never thought about it that way.'
*'Yeah yeah, I know that the monk inside of you tells you to be selfless. That's*
*probably all you know. So here's a question to help you out a little: is there*
*something in this world that greatly fascinates you?'*
'Meteorology has always held my interest...'
*'Aha'*
'I find tornadoes intriguing.'
*'Why is that?'*
'It must be an unforgettable experience to see the finger of God touch the
earth right in front of your feet. The ultimate way to learn how to feel
completely insignificant, to be violently put in place.'
*'In the context of: dust you are and to dust you shall return.'*
*'For a sportsman you sure exercise your mind a lot. Will there ever be a day*
*that you can let go of all that thinking?'*
'I don't know. I'm going to have to think on that for a bit.'
*'Ooh, you're sooo dry!! But you should know that I'm completely on to you:*
*you're only using this as a facade, of course, cause secretly you totally have a*

*crush on me.'*

'Rhona, I'm warning you…'

*'And one more thing: do you still have that oompahpah-tune as a ringtone on your phone?'*

'Oompahpah? What's that?'

*'German schlager music, man! Heino and the likes.'*

'I do have a song by Heino on my phone.'

*'Really, L. … you are un-be-lie-va-ble.'*

'In what way?'

*'Oh, you just crack me up! But uh, listen. I think it's slowly nearing my bedtime. I'll see you again sometime soon, okay?'*

'Yes. Good night.'

*Saturday afternoon, 5:30 p.m.*

"Dad, it's me."

"Lente! Good to hear you! What do you need?"

"Oh, I was just thinking: why don't I give you a quick call…"

"I see… and there's nothing you need then?"

"No. Am I supposed to?"

"No, of course not… but if you don't have any news, then uh…"

"You're at your work."

"Yes, why?"

"I got it. I'll call you some other time…"

An awkward sigh. "As a matter of fact, that would work out better, sweetheart. You don't mind, I hope…?"

"I told you I understood."

*Sunday morning, 11:00 a.m.*

"Sandifer speaking, good afternoon."

"Dad? Hi, it's me."

"Hi sweetie!"

"Where are you? Outside somewhere?"

"In the Soester Duinen… walking with the dogs."

"Alright. Fun…"

"Yes, it certainly is."

"How's the weather where you are?"

"Just fine. And with you?"

"Can't complain." And after a couple of seconds: "Well, I thought: yesterday we weren't able to talk, really, so…"

"Yes, right… before we begin, I should tell you that your mother is not here right now."

"What do you mean?"

"Weren't you calling to speak to her?"

"If that were the case, I would have called her on her phone. Wouldn't I?"

"Uh, yes. Of course." He clears his throat a few times and asks: "How's Claudia doing, by the way."

"Claudia? Who's that?"

"That little roommate of yours...?"

"Her name is Claire, dad."

"Oh yeahhh... Claire... I keep mixing her up with that, uh..." Dogs barking in the background. "Tendon! Would you knock it off with that nonsense already?!"

"What's he doing?"

"Oh, that fetish of his, for rabbit holes... a day will come that we'll need the fire department to dig him out."

We laugh. A bit. Then he asks: "Lente, is there something you need? Are you okay?"

"Do I have to not be doing well before I can call you?"

"No, that's not what I'm saying."

"Can't I just want to have a chat with you sometimes?"

"Do you have enough friends around you, at the moment?"

"Yes, what are you thinking."

"But then why are you calling?"

"Oh, never mind, dad. I'll just meet up with my 'friends' again. For some decent conversation."

## 49

INTROSPECTIVE

First there had been the shock. The confusion. And then the fear, the anger and the sorrow. The last couple of weeks I had had freak nightmares about men that ran all over the park by the Euromast tower on their hands and feet wearing monk robes and about foxes dressed in athletic wear that stalked me on their hind legs through the dark streets of London. Yet on other nights I had not slept a wink.
Call it post-traumatic stress, call it depression.
But whichever label you would want to give these symptoms – fact was that they had begun to wane. I didn't know exactly how many days ago this process was set in motion, but things were getting markedly better. What had first clouded my ability to see any escape, any imaginable perspective, had now started to lose its grip on a handful of aspects of my life. Was it possible that I was finally learning to let go?

The chat conversations with Lucas, for instance. I had finally begun to accept them as a necessary evil and I had stopped worrying about for how much longer they were going to continue. The clockwork-like regularity with which he asked me to meet him online every three days, I now laughed at mockingly. To his face, even. And though there would invariably come a salvo of protests and pedantic remarks in response to my impertinence, a certain shift toward relaxation had taken place between us. A much better base from which I could sit out my virtual time with him.
Aside from that, I gained a better overview of time in general. Dates began to have meaning again. The news on TV got more of my attention and I finally felt that I was ready to plan some activities outside of my insanely neurotic work schedule.
For example, last Sunday I had gone into town with Sander to celebrate Queen's Day. And no matter how tacky I thought its celebration in Rotterdam was, with all that noise from parade floats at every corner and the worthless junk that was sold on the street market, it was always a party with Sander. And for next Saturday the sixth I had made plans with Claire. It really had been high time. I had pushed her away, grossly neglected our friendship and that had been bothering her, as well as me, more and more. Last week we had even come to a full-on confrontation about stupid things that had never really mattered in the past... Thank goodness she was not easily offended and later that day she had simply accepted my proposal to go to Hoek van Holland Beach with me.

And that was how we now found ourselves with a coffee and a slice of white chocolate cake sitting in front of us at a posh beach café. Staring at the rain. We had left the house with the sun piercing our faces so sharply that especially Claire had badly needed the visor at the top of the windshield. But during our trip west the sky had clouded in a blink of the eye and as soon as we found a parking spot right by the beach a ship carrying cats and dogs literally hung right over our heads. For a moment we had thought that it would pass us by, with high hopes we had gone through the loose sand to the water's edge. And pass us by, the dark, blue-gray clouds did, albeit not without dumping a heavy downpour on kite runners, dogs and people walking along the beach. Quickly we had thus fled to the nearest beach café.

"When I was in London, I was assaulted by a man."
I had blurted it out, completely out of the blue and naturally its effect was that of a bomb going off. With big eyes Claire stared at me as I turned my gaze to the outside, to the gray, turbulent sea. The silence lasted a while and when it became a little uncomfortable I said: "But I'm alright now. Don't worry about me."
"No, but I do," was my friend's reaction. "Now I understand your behavior of late so much better. Did you report him? What do the police say?"
"I did not file a report." Using the quaintly shaped designer spoon that had been lying on a dish next to my latte I began to cut the cake into smaller pieces.
"Why, for heaven's sake, didn't you?" asked Claire.
"He would never be found anyway and it didn't happen in the Netherlands and so. Just too complicated."
"But why didn't you even tell me?"
As an impatient teenager who was trying to set her boundaries I moved my head forward with raised eyebrows. The result that I was hoping for, however, was not achieved. She continued her questioning, in a tone of voice that lay somewhere between worry and offense. She wanted to know why I had not considered her help or her support, or at the very least her listening ear... Yeah, she must have felt rejected. I could imagine.
"Did you go to the hospital, did you get a check-up?"
"That was not necessary. He didn't touch me."
"But he did threaten you, I presume."
No, it had not been literal threats either. As strange as it was. Lucas had played out his game so cunningly... Absentmindedly I let my gaze travel across the lounge-like restaurant with its chic interior. We were the first patrons, it was not lunchtime yet.
"Did you seek out any help somewhere to help you deal with it," asked my friend. The look in her eyes moved me. As tough as I could be on her sometimes, this was without a doubt her sincere caring, and for a brief moment I had to fight the oncoming tears.

But I sucked it up. Told her that I had found my own way, that I had gotten a lot of it out of my system already, that I had thrown myself into finishing my book and that I was really, honestly, alright.

Claire took another attempt. She informed after my online contact with that Aeolus, cause that was his name, right, 'Aeolus'? Maybe it would help to talk to him? I shrugged reluctantly and let her know that I had stopped chatting with him *long* before my departure to London.

I had become such a calculative bitch... and before more questions could arise I suggested to go outside. It had stopped raining and the sun had come out again.

We strolled toward the pier, right along the incoming waves over the firm, wet sand. A fairly strong southern wind was blowing... It was pretty interesting to see how on some areas of the beach that wind was not visible at all, while a little further away complete sand storms blew just above the ground. At least, that was what it looked like, from afar. A white plain lit up by the sun.

Nothing, however, could prepare me for the sheer beauty of these sand drifts once we had approached them from up close. With one hand by my forehead to protect my eyes I stood still. Carefully I turned to face the wind, noticed that no sharp or painful objects hit my face, removed my hand and for the longest time I just stood there, listening. And staring.

Slithering back and forth like snakes in the desert the golden-white waves came toward me. They brushed past my legs to the left and right of me to then crash themselves into the water of the sea. Or feathers blowing in the wind, filmed and played back in fast forward, that is what this scene reminded me of a little, as well. Or of the wind itself, incarnated into grains of sand, only visible to the eye of the observer who was willing to pay attention to details. I dropped both my hands beside my body, spread my fingers in the hopes of grasping some of it to take home with me. To never forget... no, don't think about your camera, just *experience* something for a change!

I turned around and underwent the entire spectacle, now facing the coastline. Tried to imagine what it would be like to be blown forwards like one of those billion grains of sand, in total freedom... blowing like brisk autumn winds... Yes, that would sure be something, if the elements were able to fly straight through me and polish out everything that had been roughened by trauma and pain. One time I had heard about the tiniest particle in the universe, the Higgs boson, or *the God particle*. Being smaller than molecules, smaller than atoms, protons and neutrons it was able to pass through all matter. Through your jacket, through your sweater, undershirt, bra, your skin, your organs, your soul...!

The song *Old and Wise* by The Alan Parsons Project was stuck in my head now. And if someone were to ask me if I knew *him*, I might even manage to smile, and say that he once was a friend of mine... This moment however was for me. For me alone. Finally enjoying myself a little again, independent of anything or anyone – Raphaël may still have existed and he really did have a loving place in my memory, but this stretch of beach, this morning was exclusively for me.

Right in the moment when I was wiping some tears off my face with my sleeve, Claire called me. As the quiet rustling of the grains of sand behind me could still be vaguely discerned among the screeching of seagulls we stepped onto the pier. And I switched back into friendship-mode.

## 50

STALKER

That same evening we biked to the Irish pub in the city center. Meanwhile, the sky had turned perfectly clear. So no more threat of rain. But there had been another threat. At the Hofplein roundabout some careless moron almost hit us, because he ignored a red light. Still totally offended and highly engrossed in conversation we entered the pub a few minutes later, but the ambiance on site quickly put us in a better mood. Good to be here again. It had been such a long time...

A band was going to play, the stage at the back of the place had already completely been set up. At least, if you could call this a stage... everything here was so cramped and stood so closely together. Oh well, you could stuff an Irish band into a broom closet and still music would come out. I asked if Claire wanted a Guinness as well and walked to the front, to the bar.

"M'lady..." a voice behind me and a hand touching my shoulder made me turn around with a shriek. It was a good thing that the glasses of beer that had just been ordered still stood waiting on the counter of the bar, otherwise they would have succumbed to my enthusiasm, guaranteed. "Adrian!! What are you doing here?" I exclaimed.

The reply was a subtle nod.

Adrian was an acquaintance of mine from the gothic scene. He was one of the few *Dandies* that I knew there. He had always intrigued me, with his pristinely white dress shirts beneath vests embellished with ornate silver-colored patterns and black jackets over black trousers with perfectly pressed creases... sometimes he was even wearing that typical nineteenth century high hat of his, with which he was quite the sight. But that completely did not seem to bother him. Shame did not have a place in his vocabulary. He was what he was: construction worker by day and as soon as the sun went down, the gothic Dandy – aficionado of Oscar Wilde and Edgar Allen Poe, at all times minding his language, holding doors for ladies... but also with somewhere under the surface a bizarre and dark sense of humor. That humor immediately resurfaced when he came and sat with us for a couple of minutes. I introduced him to Claire and we got to talking about different topics, such as the temperamental weather of today... and of course my friend and I then automatically came to the fact that the clear skies tonight had been the deciding factor for us to take out the bikes, but that that decision had been mercilessly punished by that incident at Hofplein. Our indignation resurfaced in full swing again during Claire's detailed explanation of our near-miss by virtue of the reckless driving behavior of the driver in question.

Seemingly unfazed, Adrian listened to her story. Then he dryly remarked:
"Do you know what sometimes helps with people like that? Potassium cyanide."
"Or rat poison," I immediately reacted.
"Yes, but that works much slower."
"Correct, but it makes it all the more fun to watch..."
Shocked the man in the three-piece suit looked at me, as did Claire.
"Lente...! I had never expected that to come out of your mouth," Adrian said, and by saying that he basically expressed my thoughts exactly. I had changed, had become tougher. He experienced that during this isolated incident, Claire on the other hand had witnessed it a couple of times before and I, I felt it in my heart, my soul and in each tensed muscle in my body...

It was half an hour later and the band had begun to play. Adrian had left in the meantime. He was on his way to the Dungeon where some party would take place, but Claire and I loved Irish music and so we had not joined him. Moreover, our table across from the stage proved to be quite the conquest, especially now that the pub was slowly getting more and more crowded. Claire asked if I wanted another drink and headed for the bar. During her absence the singer of the band announced that they were going to play one of his favorite songs. It was called *There Were Roses* and it was written by the Irish folk singer Tommy Sands. It was based on a true story about two boys, Sean and Alan, in the Northern-Ireland of the seventies. As their entire world was torn apart by the civil war they refused to let their different backgrounds – one was Catholic and the other Protestant – be a stumbling block for their special friendship. But one day Alan fell victim to the pervasive hatred between opposing groups. He was murdered. And then his friend Sean, of all people, was intercepted on the street by vengeful representatives of Alan's constituency. The lead singer of the band sang about that act of retaliation.
*An eye for an eye was all that filled their minds. And another eye for another eye till everyone is blind.*

I was still caught up in the mood of the song when Claire returned and sat down beside me "Sorry it took so long," she said, "but a guy kept talking to me." She grinned. "Speaking of characters..."
"Oh, a pub like this attracts all kinds," I mumbled absently.
She nodded slowly and said: "It sure does. At first I hadn't even noticed him, but he happened to be standing next to me at the bar and then he said, not in Dutch but in English: "Let me guess: this is your second Guinness in 45 minutes."
"How could he possible know that? Was he one of the bartenders, or something?"
"No, I asked him the same. But he was just a patron. He said he had entered

the pub around the same time as us and that he had seen you at the bar once since then and later me. That was what he had drawn his conclusion from."

"What a strange way to start a conversation…"

"You could say that again." After a moment of silence she continued talking: "No, he wasn't the least bit shy – you wanna know what he said? That he had only arrived in Rotterdam by train this evening and that he had forgotten how beautiful the Dutch women were!"

Just in time I swallowed the gulp of beer that I had in my mouth. Then I burst out in laughter.

Claire topped it off by repeating in a theatrical way how he had pronounced the word 'beautiful' in English: *beootifool.* We died laughing.

"And you know the weird thing was…" she said, when she got a hold of herself again a little, "I had basically just assumed that he was one of those weed-smoking backpackers, from Belgium or something. But then he suddenly changed his tone and became kind of serious. Turned out he had really been watching us, especially you. He said you had a beautiful personality, but also came across a bit sad… Pretty impressive to be able to notice that, huh, especially for such a little puppy."

"How so? How old was he?"

"Early twenties, or mid-twenties at the most…"

"And what else did he say?" With my thumb I wiped the condensation off my glass of beer, but every time I had gone all around, I could start all over again. I picked up the glass and tested to see how far around my one hand could reach.

"I *knew* you would find this interesting," said Claire. "Now hold on to your beer, cause here it comes: he asked if you were seeing anyone."

My second hand was needed to cover the entire circumference of the glass. Neatly I placed the tips of my thumbs so that they touched one another. On the other side my nails pressed into the flesh of my fingertips.

"And then I just told him that at the moment you're not very interested in a relationship. Aren't you? Now, I have to admit he wouldn't be that bad of a catch. Nice outfit… and he came across as very mature for his age," my friend said. And she rambled on.

I asked what else he looked like.

She answered: "Not quite run of the mill. Blond hair, dark eyes, a little hard to read…"

My shoulders stiffened. As neutral as possible I asked what his reaction to what she had told him about me had been.

"Riiight… what was it again?" Claire stared in front of her and said: "I'll try to repeat it as literally as possible. It was something like: 'Oh well, you can't have everything in life. I'll just take it in stride. But your friend, I won't forget any time soon. She so obviously looks like someone has hurt her once… Tell her that she should watch out whom she makes contact with from now on. I'd rather not see such a fragile girl as her be damaged again'." With a face that said everything she looked at me. Was that a part of her imitation of the guy as well? In any case, she sounded completely naive when she told me how he had finally introduced himself to her. And that his name turned out to be Egare...

My hands almost crushed the glass that I was holding. "Where is he now?" I asked curtly.

"I don't know. He had started to put on his jacket by the end of our talk. Why, do you want to meet him? Shall I..."

"No, stay here!" I sneered, as I pulled her back to her chair by her sleeve. "I do *not* want to meet him, okay? But I *need* to know if he's still here. So if you..." I begged her with my eyes to go and investigate.

Claire clearly did not understand at all what was going on. And who could blame her. But what she thought of me, I really could not care less right now. Our safety was at risk, and for that I felt partly responsible. Therefore I urged her, "If you see him, please don't start talking to him again. He mustn't get the idea that we uh... you know."

"I'll go," my friend sighed. Within a minute she had returned. He had left, she said. I asked whether she was sure. She was absolutely certain, sat down and took a sip from her drink.

When our glasses were empty I told her that I wanted to go home. And that I was going to leave my bike there, call a cab and that she had to come with me.

51

COLORLESS


Because I was afraid. Frantic. All the way back to square one.

The next day I did not go online when Lucas asked me to in a text message. However, it was Sunday evening, not a night at which one would go out. That meant that he could be pretty certain that I was at home, near my computer. So it did not take longer than half an hour for his phone call to arrive. I refused to pick up. Hearing his voice was the last thing... But the phone calls kept coming and finally I texted: "Fine, I'll come online."

*Rhona says:*
*'Tell me why.'*
Running.gyrovague says:
'You were starting to feel too comfortable.'
*'And so you come all the way by Thalys from France to tell me that?'*
'Sometimes something like that is necessary to get the message across.'
*'You could have done that differently. Without involving my friend!'*
'Perhaps.'
*'Keep her out of this, from now on. I beg of you.'*
'I promise, Rhona.'


As unpredictable as he could behave, I had yet to catch Lucas in a lie, even after the two full months that we had known each other now. Therefore, I let go of my concerns for Claire's safety. For now.

However, I, myself needed to become much more alert again. Go back to consistently tracing his IP addresses... He was right: I had been dozing off, had become too lax. Lately, I had been listening to his long-winded stories about travels to, say, St. Petersburg, Tokyo and Stuttgart, but I had stopped wondering whether these travels of his really did take place at the specified times. I should ask him much more specific questions from now on and double-check his answers.

And I also hoped that he would keep up with his 'once in every three days contact' frequency. Because that would then mean that we were going to talk again on Wednesday and, after that, again on Saturday...

That would create the perfect gap for me to leave by plane on Thursday, and to do that photo shoot on Friday. Friday, May twelve... once it had seemed so distant, but the only thing that I wanted now, was for that date to go by as quickly as possible – that I could just be at home again on Saturday. Then in front of Lucas I would act like I had not gone anywhere that weekend. Or, at the very least, that I had never visited London.

In any case, this photo commission just needed to be done, because work came first. So I performed my duty, left the house that Thursday evening around 7 and arrived at 8:30 p.m. local time at the hotel that was booked for me. Getting here I had defiantly wondered why of all places it just had to be London City Airport, the airport at which Raphaël and my parting had ended in such heartbreaking drama. Yet I also understood that logistically speaking this had been the best option. The taxi ride had hardly included more than crossing one single bridge, and from my room I even had a view of the landing strips. Moreover, the following day the set turned out to be located no more than a couple hundred meter away in line distance, by the water at the Royal Victoria Dock. I really should have been thankful to the organizers of this photo shoot for this secluded event, because it helped me to focus. On top of that, a tight day schedule prevented me from getting anything other into my mind than working my socks off. And when I noticed that my eyes were wandering to the right a little too often, in the direction of where the Shad Thames Area had to be situated, I decided to turn my back towards it and use the Millennium Mills as an alternative background for my fashion photos. After all, that abandoned flour factory was a much nicer decor than that so-called trendy new urban development next to it.

And life went on. I lived it with a stubborn determination to make something out of it. Don't be too demanding, just do your thing. I worked, ate, slept, worked. Got groceries. And, oh yeah, I had to figure out a way to get my book published. I was lucky: I had been able to turn my hobby into my profession and alongside of my profession I was able to pursue my hobby. That was a lot more than what most people had. Count your blessings. Next weekend I was going to visit my parents. My dad was going to turn fifty five. A milestone. That was how I had to learn to look at things... Thank goodness I still had both my parents. But there was also not much more to look forward to. Because the harder I tried my best to lie to myself, the more colorless my life began to appear.


END OF PART II

# PART III

*THERE CAN BE NO HOPE WITHOUT FEAR,*
*AND NO FEAR WITHOUT HOPE*

Benedict de Spinoza

## 52

## SCENT TRAIL

It was Wednesday evening. Claire and I had had dinner together and I had stayed and hung out with her until she had to get ready for the night shift. "When you're leaving, don't forget to double lock the front door," I had urged her for the hundredth time this week. As I left the room to go and do the dishes downstairs I caught her muttering: "As if I'd ever forget..."
"No no..." was my cynical reaction. In the ICU, working as a nurse, she may have total control over the situation and she might be a star at what she did, but at home she really was not the same. Especially when the moment for her to leave for work approached. I watched it unfold every single time: about half an hour before she left she became flustered, would walk back and forth between her room and the bathroom multiple times, forget to do all sorts of things and at times you would hear her grumble loudly about it. But once she got down the stairs she had all her ducks in a row and she was completely in her working mode. Well, except for the fact that on occasion she still neglected to properly lock the door.
In the hallway – I had just finished cleaning up in the kitchen – we ran into each other. Claire gave me a fleeting kiss on the cheek and ran down the stairs to her bike. "I'm late," she called by way of goodbye.
Barely a minute later I hurled myself down that same set of stairs and double-locked the door.
When I got to my room I turned on the lights. It was dark out. It had been past 10:30 already, I could tell by the big clock in the middle of the square across from my home. She really was running late today.
For a while I stayed there looking at the cars in front of the red light, at the people that walked by across the street. Things had quieted down.
As I closed the curtains I was looking at a man in the shadow of one of the trees that was in the square. He had probably been standing there for a while, because he glanced at his watch. Then he grabbed a phone out of the pocket of his coat and typed in a number, most likely of the person he was waiting for.
Was it three seconds later? Or four seconds? In any case, at that moment my phone rang and I could not help but make the association between that and the person making a phone call in the square. What a funny coincidence... I picked up the device and answered the call.
"Rhona, it's me."
The ground gave way beneath my feet. I had not looked at the call display, had not been vigilant enough and now I had to face the consequences: from

the speaker of my phone sounded the object of my greatest fear, but also of my deepest desires. *Raphaël!*

The fact that this was bound to happen one day, I have known for weeks already. However, that did not dampen the shock, also because I immediately realized how impossible and extremely dangerous this situation was. And aside from that, I had to keep in mind the factor called Lucas…

"What do you want?" I forced myself to ask him.

"I'm not sure if you recognized me just now, but I am in Rotterdam. I'm across from your house. And I'm going to walk towards you now…"

Within a few seconds I reached the light switch and darkened my room. Then I rushed to the rightmost part of the window, slightly pulled the curtain aside as inconspicuously as possible, scanned the surroundings and looked into the car mirror, that was attached to my balcony, that offered a view of the porch at the front door. He had just crossed the street, he looked up and for one long second our eyes met. I let go of the curtain and began running all over the house in a panic, looking for the spot that I thought was the safest. Finally I ended up in the kitchen. But the sound of his voice penetrated this room as well, even with the closed door.

"I know you can hear me."

Nervously pacing, clenching my fists and then painfully spreading them wide open again I tried to think, but my rational mind hopelessly failed me. Everything was one giant overload of emotions, of fear, confusion and excitement… What was I supposed to do now, *what* was I going to do??

"Lente, if you don't let me in this is going to be a long night. I have all the time in the world."

That was all it took for me to get me to move. As though I was controlled by a remote I got out of my hiding place, walked down the stairs and opened the door. Without greeting him I went back upstairs. He followed.

In my room I opened the curtains. He turned on the light. With frantic strides I got to where he was and undid his action by slamming down the light switch. Then I took my position by the window.

"I had no idea that you could be so vicious," he said.

I was not quite sure what he was getting at with that remark, even though I felt highly offended.

"What game are you trying to play, Lente?"

"I'm not playing a game," I said.

"Oh," he feigned his surprise, "so you're not trying to make a statement with all that lavender?"

Shit, my furniture were still permeated with it, of course! And my clothes probably as well…

With a sound of voice of someone who was trying not to inhale and thus not have to smell anything, he said: "Even with a fraction of the amount of all that crap you would have had enough of a trail of scent to lure me right across the god-whole city to your house."

"That was not my intention at all – " I protested, but he cut me short:

"– Why, Lente? Why resort to these means, after having ended things between us in such a cruel way?"

"What should I care?" I let out. "Do I still have to be considerate towards you even after our separation and to how you keep hiding behind those ridiculous sentiments from your past?"

I turned to face him and saw the eyes with which he was staring at me. If I were to have had any doubts on whether his feelings were hurt or not, they had now been taken away. As best as I could I shifted my focus to a point somewhere to the side of him.

"I needed it, to move on," I whispered.

"You needed something to move on…"

"What are you doing here, anyway?" I asked, in the hopes of changing the topic of the conversation.

"Business."

So it was business. Of course. What was there to say about that?

During the uncomfortable minutes that followed, I could not help but keep my eyes from drifting back to him – to the man that everything in my world still revolved around. Because after all this time Raphaël was still firmly lodged beneath my skin and in my blood and he still unrelentingly held this mysterious power of attraction over me, without having to put in any effort whatsoever… I had to ignore it. Stay rational.

His hairstyle was different than before. It had been cut in layers, was loosely combed back to the left and right of a parting. A single nonchalant lock draped over his forehead.

And his eyes, they seemed more vacant, duller. They made his face seem weary. Battered.

"I had told myself to not burden you with my emotions. I'm sorry things turned out differently," he said.

"Oh well…," I reacted apathetically.

Raphaël had been standing, leaning against the closed door and now moved from his place. He began to walk around a little in my living area. "This does not have to take long," he said, "I'm only hoping to find some answers."

Again we were silent. He looked around, studied my book shelves. Took a quick glance at my messy, packed desk and gave the construction of the house a brief, yet critical inspection by applying pressure to the wooden floor with his feet in different locations. A few times he shifted his weight. "I had noticed it already, looking from the outside: your house has subsided quite a bit," he noticed. "Doesn't that bother you?"

"You get used to it quickly," I said.

I asked him again as to what his reason for his visit to Rotterdam was. Why now? He explained that he was going to help with the restoration of a castle in Lisse soon and that he had come for an inspection and some meetings.

"And I have chosen to stay in a hotel here in town so I could come see you. To hear from you whether you have had enough time by now to think about the sense or nonsense of your decision."

"What decision?"

"About our relationship."

Oh no, do not think. Not about this.

"An answer, Lente."

Do not change your mind. "It is impossible," I said. I barely managed to get it out of me.

"And the reason?"

"Does it matter?"

He sighed. Orange street lighting came through the window and fell softly on his beautiful face and the contours of his body. I searched for something else to look at. The city. Traffic.

"A drag-shack? Here? The city campground is really the other way, you know..." I had to talk about something, right?

"I'm not familiar with that word," I heard behind me. He came and stood beside me at the window. I nodded towards a car hitching a caravan that just pulled up at the green light heading to Hilligersberg.

"Aaah, a caravan, I see." He walked away from me, softly repeating "drag-shack, drag-shack..." to himself and sat down on the couch. Suddenly he made a helpless gesture with his arms. He grinned: "You see how desperately I need you, Lente? Who else can teach me new local expressions such as these?"

For a second I joined his laughter. For only a second. Then I fell silent again. It hurt so much...

"I've truly tried anything this month," he said under his breath. "I have expressed my anger. Cried. Worked like a horse. I have spent hours on end in that square yard."

"Have you talked to someone as well?"

"Not much. Lucas could tell right away when he saw me that night."

"And he said?" I kept my face turned away from him and had to make sure to keep my hands still. When I failed to do so I crossed my arms.

"Lucas didn't say much. At most that I knew how he felt about things like this."

My only reaction was: "Oh..."

Raphaël got up. He was preparing to leave.

I felt so incredibly bad for him... "Sorry," I therefore said. "I am so terribly sorry. If the circumstances hadn't been so complicated, then..." I shook my head.

"Complicated, yes. But *too* complicated?"

"It's impossible, Raphaël, I – "

" – Alright," he said. And then suddenly he was quick to reach the door and opened it in a resolute movement. Once more our eyes met. His gaze had

turned colder, distant. Then he stepped into the hall.
"Raph, don't get me wrong – " I tried to...

53

RESET


"Wait. I'm sorry. Don't leave. Raphaël, please!" But he walked down the
stairs without saying goodbye, opened the front door and closed it behind
him. What was left was a dark and abandoned staircase in front of me, along
with a continuously repeating moment in which I fell to my knees and burst
into tears being more lonesome than ever before. Then I woke up screaming.
How many times has this been already? And how many times have I
bewilderedly wondered how in heaven's name I could have possibly been able
to fall asleep under these circumstances? Although I had not forgotten that
sleep had only set in after more than two hours of sobbing in utter misery...
This time, however, I got out of my bed while sleep-drunk, before I could slip
back into that nightmare again. I turned on the main light and planted
myself on the couch with my feet up and my chin resting on my knees. For a
long time I was deep in thought. Finally, at 4 a.m., I grabbed my phone. I
sent out the following text message:
"This night I've made a choice that I know goes against what you want. But I
have thought about it seriously and it is my own decision. So I would kindly
like to ask you to never argue with me about it again from now on. Please
respect that. Regards, Rhona."
Within a few minutes a reply came:
"Rhona, at the time I have told you that I wanted to get some clarification on
a couple of things. I have that clarification now. Good night. Lucas."
Immediately I turned off my caller ID. I phoned.
"Rhona," said Raphaël when he picked up the phone.
"How did you know it was me?" I asked.
"Nobody else who calls me in the nightly hours has half a mind to do so
anonymously. May I ask why you do?"
"I was afraid that you wouldn't pick up otherwise."
"Evidently that fear was unfounded."
"Yes," I answered in a squeaky voice.
"But tell me, Rhona. What can I do for you?"
"Uh – I want you to hear me out for a minute. Just listen to what I have to
say, without interrupting me. Okay?"
It remained silent on the other end of the line.
"Okay. I would like to begin by saying that I take full responsibility for the
decision that led to our separation. I acted at the time in response to a couple
of events. You could think of it as an excuse when I say that at that moment I
did not see another solution and I can imagine that you are angry about it.

You probably won't believe me when I tell you how terrible I feel for having hurt you so much. Because I really do, and I uh... uh – "

"Take your time. Take a minute to think and then continue."

"You were not going to interrupt me."

"I – "

"– Then don't. Please let me say what's on my mind. The thing is: I recognized a lot in what you said tonight about everything that you had tried to do these last few weeks. And even though it took me a couple of hours, I have now also discovered that I need to do something with that realization. Something that I have learned recently: to take my fears seriously, but also to push them away at the right moment. Because otherwise I will only do damage and isolate myself and – "

"You're getting tied up in your words, Rhona. What is it that you really want to say to me?"

"That nothing works without you. I pretend that I've picked up my normal life again, but in reality I am being torn apart on the inside. It's just so hard, Raphaël. I miss you too much..."

There, I said it. Finally.

I moved the phone to my right hand, while I wiped my left, which had become completely damp, off on my nightgown. Then I switched hands again. But the right felt clammy as well and had left a damp imprint on the black case of the device. And I noticed that I had begun to tremble uncontrollably.

"Was that it?" the voice on the other side of the line asked.

"Yes, that was the gist of it," was my answer.

"Alright. Then I will hang up now."


I went to bed, because I did not know what else to do. Because I had no idea what I could expect. Raphaël's parting words had sounded so stoically neutral that I could not have made anything out of it. Maybe he had simply meant to end our conversation with that remark. But what if it had meant something more than that – what if this really was our final moment of contact? The thought of that possibility was almost unbearable.

But should this be the case, then this was the best place to be right now. Then, if I was lucky, I would fall asleep exhausted by dawn. And if I were to wake up again I was going to reset my life – that *should* be doable. If I tried my hardest. After all, I had managed to do it before.

For now, however, I had to deal with a body that just would not stop shaking. My limbs had begun to hurt allover and no matter what position I tried to lie in, nothing helped against the extreme tension in my muscles. Aside from that, I had no inkling as to whether I was cold or hot, or tired or not... And was I going crazy with my overthinking or was it because of that impending feeling of desolation, that void that like a black hole threatened to suck away and forever make disappear everything that mattered to me?

The doorbell rang, loud and prolonged, and within one leap I had gotten out of my bed. I quickly glanced at the alarm clock. I saw that it was seven past four – only seven past four? – and ran downstairs. I opened the door. We looked at each other. We did not say anything. I walked up the stairs, trying my utmost to appear as collected as possible. He followed me. Right before we reached my room he grabbed my hand and turned me around towards him. With a serious face he looked at me. "Are you absolutely sure you know what you're getting yourself into?" he asked me, but I said: "I have never *not* wanted you."

That was, apparently, all that he needed to hear. With his left hand still wrapped tightly around my upper arm he pushed me backwards. He placed his right hand around the back of my head, just in time before it would hit the wall with a loud bang. A shriek of surprise escaped my throat. He pushed himself up against me and began to kiss me fully and ferociously on the mouth. And I kissed him back. "You have no idea..." he moaned, "I have missed you so incredibly much..." and again his lips latched on to mine. "What do you think I've been doing," I tried to respond, though I doubted my words were intelligible. "Don't speak," he said. His hand restlessly graced the contours of my skull and then explored the skin of my neck. For a moment his fingers paused. Then they slowly began to slide along my muscles stiffened with tension, up and down.

Raphael stopped kissing and for a while, as he massaged my neck, he just stood looking at me, as if he wanted to see how I reacted to his touch.

I felt his breath on my face, even cooler than I remembered... Right beside my hip his left hand and my right hand folded together and the massaging of my neck became more intense, turned into a somewhat uncontrolled kneading, hard and a bit uncomfortable. Suddenly he moved his mouth towards mine again. More intensely than before all kinds of pent-up feelings were released, on his part, but certainly on mine as well. The suppressed longing of all those weeks, the still daily present all-consuming pain of missing him... "All of this has taken much too long," he said between two kisses, and with that he precisely articulated what I had wanted to say. Not that I could have said it myself, because I did not get the chance to talk at this moment. I could not even manage to breathe properly – I violently turned my head to the side so that my mouth could break free. I inhaled a couple of greedy mouthfuls of air. But he did not let me take a longer break. "You've got a nose. Just use that to breathe," was his comment. And then he came again... Yes, breathe through my nose. Must not forget to use my nose! As his hands began to wander all over my body I concentrated on matching his moves. Placed my hands on his back, moved up to his shoulder blades... the shoulder blades of a feline. The sensation of his extreme agility I had never forgotten since that Sunday morning over at his place in London. How could I have lasted this long without him?

Raphaël moved much closer against me, with his head against the side of my head, his chest against my bosom. A shiver passed through him and he heavily sighed. Of excitement, of tension? Suddenly he moved back a little, to then spread my legs with his right leg, so much so that he touched the wall behind me. Slowly his knee slid upward between my thighs and he did not stop when he reached my groin. Slowly but surely I was being lifted off the floor and with a fiery gaze my lover looked at me. I pinched my eyes shut, let some air escape between my lips as quietly as possible. A hand in my lower back pulled me towards him over his upper leg. I wrapped myself around him with all four of my limbs.

"I love you so much," I whispered.

"Did you think I didn't know that?"

In search of the total experience of security, I had laid my head against his shoulder. But no sooner than I did, did he pull me up and kiss me again, for minutes, as his hands moved up and down my exposed thighs, leaving behind tingling traces. I became more and more turned on and noticed the change in his body as well. Then all of a sudden he raised his head. He turned around, with me still in the same position in his arms, and moved into my room. To the left was my bed, but he stepped to the right. He stopped in front of the couch. Slowly, with his muscles trembling, Raphaël bent over and let go of me.

"I need a couple of minutes," he said. He cleared his throat. Paced back and forth around my room a little. Walked to the book shelves and stood there for a while, with his back towards me.

Then he turned around again, came towards me and sat down beside me at the end of the couch. "I'm sorry, but this is as far as we will go today."

"That's okay. Everything went well, didn't it?"

He shrugged.

"Or... did your teeth get longer?" I carefully asked.

"No. But it was a close call, and that's too far."

I stroked his back and in response to my comforting gesture he stretched his back a little and he encouraged himself by saying: "Yes, we'll figure it out. With some patience..."

"How did you get here, anyway? You got here so fast."

"Not fast enough," he grinned. "At first I had trouble finding a spot where I could accelerate without being seen."

"Where are you staying then and by which road did you get here?"

"I'm staying at that new hotel, by the Oceanium side of Blijdorp Zoo. So first I had to neatly go around that and then turn into the street at right angles to the main entrance. And then just straight on."

As I thought I frowned my forehead. "That means you got lucky," I said. "On that route there are no speed cams."

He looked at me over his shoulder with a look of disbelief on his face. Then his glance became a little mischievous. He said: "Even if there were traffic cameras, Lente, it will still be long before you see me running by with a license plate on my back."

"Idiot!" I grinned. I slid down into the cushions and gave Raphaël a couple of playful kicks with my feet. But he grabbed them and pushed them away. He enforced his action with the words: "Not just yet."

A little taken aback I nodded. But I quickly recovered.

"So you came running?" I thought out loud. "And where did you come to a stop without being seen?"

"Over there around the corner, right behind the railway bridge. But tell me something, how have you been lately?" He got up.

Ouch. Now came the hard part – or maybe not. I could simply talk about my work, of course. Thus I extensively divulged in all the assignments that I had received and I mentioned my photo shoot in London.

He had placed his hands at his sides. "That was last weekend, yes," he reflected.

I felt my face and neck turn warm. "Yes, sorry I didn't contact you then, but there just wasn't any time to. That day I did nothing but work and then I had to leave again."

"I had secretly suspected that. And to be honest, I wasn't even home around the twelfth. I was in Prague at that time."

"Oh?"

"I have come here straight from there. But we'll get to that later. First I would like to hear about your book."

Things were going well. We were still talking about work, discussed hobbies, and that was how we did not have to dwell on issues that I could not answer to so easily... I started up my laptop and showed him my photos. He read the prologue and introduction carefully, no faster than a human would. He asked me questions about how I planned to get my book published, we discussed the options and pitfalls of, for example, *Printing On Demand.*

And we forgot about the time. At least, I was hoping that we would. But in between talking and listening I anxiously kept my eyes on the sky that was changing in color. And I knew that Raphaël was doing the same. "It's going to be a clear day," he finally said. I agreed as I looked at the clock. It was almost 5:30 a.m.

"I haven't brought any protection with me. Maybe if I leave now, I could still make it... the sun hasn't come up yet, but I'll have to be quick," he pondered.

A wave of disappointment swept through me, though I tried to hide it from him by immediately joining his thoughts: "If you need sunglasses, you can borrow mine..."

He laughed half-heartedly. "Thank you, but I'm afraid that won't be enough. I need a lotion for my skin as well. And I have it in my hotel room."

"Won't regular sunscreen do the trick?"

He shook his head.

"And what if I would bike to your hotel to get you a couple of things?"

"Lente, I can't ask that of you."

"Then there's only one solution. You spend the day here." I could barely suppress the hopeful tone in my voice.

But again Raphaël shook his head.

I sighed a little impatiently. "Okay, then you'll get a hat, a scarf, sunglasses and gloves from me. Then just pretend that you suffer from porphyria and call a taxi."

It worked. He threw in the towel.

## 54

TRIANGLE


Him and I, together in one house. In my house. And he was going to stay all day. It was not easy to give a name to how this made me feel. The effect of a fleeting touch in passing, of the look in his eyes when they met mine... My mind had difficulty processing all these impulses and automatically accommodated my need to create some distance from time to time.

In those moments it was as though my perspective shifted to that of a camera, mounted high up on the wall in a corner of my room. Then everything that could be seen changed into a soundless black and white registration of short and longer scenes, recorded from the same point of view over and over again. Settings of two random people in a room, one standing, the other sitting in a chair. Or the same people, but this time on the couch, sitting at a modest distance from one another, engaged in a serious conversation. And then a couple of hours in which little movement occurred, with one lying on the couch and the other at the back of the room in her bed...

When my mind reconnected with my body I first spent some time trying to shake this persistent insomnia – to no avail. I got up and went to the bathroom, after which I came back into the room as quietly as I could. For a moment I stood there looking at the couch, where he lay so motionless, so beautiful. Then I walked to my bed.

"Can't sleep?" came from behind me.

"No," I said.

He reached his arm towards me. "Come here."

I sat down next to him, tiredly rubbing my face and my eyes. He looked at me endeared, and said: "This is a little bizarre, isn't it? Yesterday, around this time, you had no idea this would happen."

Yesterday, yeah, what day had that been again? A Wednesday, but what I had been doing at the time...? Not the faintest idea.

"And now..." Raphaël continued softly, "all the safety precautions that we observed as closely as possible, nothing is left of it."

"You sound worried."

"That's because I am."

I caressed his cheek. "Maybe it will comfort you when I say that I have really thought about it well."

"About...?"

"About the unlikely scenario in which you'll bite me. I don't live here on my own, and you know that as well. At this moment my roommate is sleeping right above us. She has just finished her night shift. I only need to scream and she'll hear it immediately with these flimsy wooden floors and – " Within a fraction of a second a hand covered my mouth that resolutely put a stop to the rest of what I wanted to say. His other hand held my neck in an iron grip. "And what would such a scream sound like under these circumstances," the vampire asked grimly.

He let go of me. With big, startled eyes I looked into his. They looked back, gray and sad. Then he turned his head away.

And still, this was the only place that I wanted to be. With him within reach of all my senses. Where I could be with him in my sleep and where, after waking from my dream, I still found him tangibly next to me. And where I could talk to him, hear about his life, get to know yet newer sides of him. For example, he seemed to have taken on a different identity. The Italian passport that he handed to me showed not a single trace of wear. I looked at his photo, flipped through the document... Kazimír La Duca, born in Rome thirty years ago. "Since a few months now I've been renting an apartment in the city center of Prague," he said. He was in the process of establishing a living as an architect and a musician there, while he was wrapping up his life as Raphaël Bélusier in London at the same time. He would be traveling there regularly at least until next Spring, as well as keep his apartment in the Shad Thames Area. But once the restoration of the Chapter House was finishes, his life as a Frenchman in England would also be over. Then he would go on a sabbatical leave for a year, supposedly to travel around the world and then he would stay away for a reason that would make sure that his British contacts would never go and look for him.

"And what should I call you here in the Netherlands?" I asked him.

"I'm Kazimír. To your friends, your family, to the people that I work with here. And also to the hotel that I'm staying at."

I nodded. I had a pretty good idea of what job lay ahead of me by now. I repeated the name a few times in my head and was able to put what I had learned into practice that same afternoon. Claire had just gotten out of bed and we ran into each other in the kitchen. I said I had company. She asked who it was. My counterquestion was whether she still remembered that guy that I had chatted with online a while ago. Stupid question, of course she still remembered. Aeolus. Well, I had told her in one breath, his real name was Kazimír. He was in the Netherlands for business and he had called me out of the blue last night. So now he was here. And we were talking a number of things over and that went well and it was actually kind of fun and... Claire had then quietly closed the kitchen door. In a hushed voice, so that my guest wouldn't hear anything, she asked what the deal was with his claim of being a vampire. I had smiled a little awkwardly. LARP. Live Action Role Playing, the explanation that she, herself, had come up with at that time. "But don't you dare making fun of him about it," I said in a threatening tone. "He talks

about it as little as possible with others and I would like it to stay that way."
Defensively she raised her hands. She was going to stay as silent as the
grave.
Then I introduced her to my boyfriend. And to my relief, she behaved herself.

LARP... it was not even that far from the truth. Because after all, Raphaël
was acting on a daily basis. Only to him it was a reverse role play: it was in
his spare time that he could be himself. And I, every time when we were in
contact with the outside world while in each other's company, I would
diligently play along with him. And I seemed to have a knack for it, if I could
say so myself. It even gave me a little kick, walking into the living room with
two plates of food that evening and see Raphaël's surprised reaction,
especially when I explained my intention with it. On each plate I had served
about half of what I normally ate. At the table, sitting across from him, I
would then switch our plates as soon as I had finished the first one. This way,
unexpected visitors would not get suspicious.

Of course, this was not possible for us to do at Hotel Rotterdam-Blijdorp,
where Raphaël was staying. He had invited me the following evening to dine
there. For me that meant an extensive three-course menu with carpachio,
turbot and fruit in a chocolate fondue as dessert. He stuck to a modest bowl of
tomato soup. Food that he ingested with a smile and of which I knew that he
had to get rid of again in the toilet within a few hours. I felt guilty, but he
assured me that he was quite used to this almost daily gruel. A daily gruel,
what a play on words... We both laughed.
"Now that we're talking about language – last night you used an expression
of which I am not sure whether it is correct," I mused.
"Oh? Do tell."
"Well, you said something like 'right across the god-whole city', but there's no
such thing as 'the god-whole city' in Dutch."
"Then what would you advise me to say instead?" He grabbed my right hand
and affectionately moved his thumb and index finger back and forth over my
fingers. I tried to remain focused and said: "You could say it this way: 'right
across this *godforsaken* city'."
"No, that's not correct either," replied Raphaël, after which I looked at him
confused.
"You live here. So it is hard for me to believe that God has forsaken this city."
"Your accent has become more Rotterdam-ish," I remarked, hoping that my
blushing would dissipate quickly. He nodded. And stared at me. I pretended
that my gaze followed my thoughts, wandering from exhaustion, past his
right shoulder to random things that could be seen around us... An enormous
close-up photo of a field of sunflowers that covered an entire section of a wall.
Pretty ingenious, I thought. The interior design of this restaurant was, now
that I was paying attention to it, overall a little peculiar. The at first glance

business-like environment, with clean lines and lots of black, white and gray, had something homely at the same time, probably due to the big plants and the creative use of accessories. Peculiar, another strange word. Where did I get that from again? Oh yeah, from Raphaël... it was the description that he had used for Lucas' personality – and abruptly my breathing stopped. Lucas! Again, even tonight the smallest imaginable occasion seemed to be enough for him to effortlessly invade my thoughts. In my mind's eye I could see him, right in front of me. With raised eyebrows and crossed arms he stood there, exactly between me and all the beautiful things that had happened to me during the last twenty four hours. As for now he was silent, but he could open his mouth at any moment to let me know that it was time to come online and have a chat again. After all, it was Friday evening, three days after Tuesday... and whatever he wanted, had to happen. Air, I needed to breathe!

"What is up with you?" My boyfriend leaned back in his chair a little.

"I think I'm getting my period." A weak excuse, but better than nothing.

"Weren't you yesterday already?"

Much too weak of an excuse. I should have known, because my menstrual blood was obviously ruffling everywhere... I made an apologetic gesture, muttering: "Stomach cramps. Gotta go quick to the restroom." Quickly I grabbed my bag and without looking him in the eye I left for the toilets. Once I got there I immediately turned my phone to silent mode, locked myself in and sat down, waiting for the relief to come.

I had been just in time. Nothing bad had happened. Yet, when I returned to our table in the restaurant, the tension in my body was unbearable and impossible to get rid of. Quietly counting to ten I kept my hands under the table, out of sight, because I could not stop the fidgeting.

I cursed the day that I had met Lucas. Was that long distance mental artillery inherent to the life experience of a vampire? Or...?

55

CASTLE


As far as 'getting what you want' was concerned, Raphaël certainly was no stranger to it either. And especially the little instances in which he pushed his will in such a subtle way that it almost was unnoticeable, were the ones that left the biggest impression.

The previous night for example... it had begun as a simple proposal when we, each from our own end of the couch, had been talking casually. He had suggested in a lighthearted tone: "If you like, you could come to Lisse with me tomorrow morning."

To go with him to an actual castle, of course I was all ears, but after some hesitation I had decided to decline his invitation regardless. The reason was a deadline that I had for some photos that needed editing.

With a plain 'that's too bad' from him that case had evidently been closed and we got to talking about the subject of photo editing. At a certain point I had released my legs out of the lotus position and I had taken him to my computer. There, with the help of some examples, I explained a thing or two about what steps I usually took to adjust an image's color and contrast, and how to remove distracting elements.

Once we had returned to the couch he had listened with great interest to my recounting of the back story of the assignment in question: the clients were friends who lived in a picturesque, old building in Delfshaven. It had been a month already since I had done a photo shoot for my book, with two models in their garden and basement. Raphaël reacted with great admiration when I told him that my friends loved the results of that session so much, that they ordered no less than three enlarged photo prints. Even though I had not initially intended the series of photos for them at all.

... And how much time would I need then, to edit a couple of photos such as those, he had subsequently asked. I had answered: "A few hours at most," and then I began to sense what was coming next. His comment on the feeling of satisfaction that finishing a job of this caliber must bring, was the final push that I had needed. I caved and asked if it was not too late for me to join him, realizing that the choice between an entire day without him and half a day with him really could not be called much of a choice.

The gratified look in his eyes had been so telling... I had walked into his trap, and the sensation of that truly bordered the sexual.

But in spite of the anticipatory excitement with which I sat next to him in his car this morning, I was also uncomfortably aware of the element of my life that I still had no idea what to do with: the spanking new camera lying in my lap, that was given to me by Lucas and that now, unseen but oh so palpably, was scorching a hole in the skin of my thighs... or really I should say, in my conscience. I tried to distract myself by complaining out loud about the traffic on the A4 – cursed at fellow highway users that pushed in front of us or cut us off. Which Raphaël then tried to distract me from, by going ahead and giving me some information on Keukenhof Castle in a calm tone of voice. And I did my best, I really did. I focused hard to absorb the things that he told me about the foundation that had maintained the estate since 2002 and about the endless list of previous owners. And to remember that what was now a castle, had once been built in 1641 as a home for a retired commander of the Dutch East India Company.

The whole thing was kind of sad, really. He was telling these things with a passion that I had not experienced coming from him before and I just could not manage to keep my mind focused.

I had to actively participate in thought. Perhaps that would help. "Why this estate in particular," I therefore asked randomly.

"I've been keeping track of it for about a century and a half," he said.

"And you don't do that with, say, Muiderslot Castle?"

"I do, but the fact that it's at the Keukenhof makes it of special interest to me."

"How is that?"

We had gotten off the highway in the meantime and now made our way on a rural road cutting through the bulb fields that made up the Bollenstreek. As Raphaël slowed down for a red traffic light he explained that he had always generally followed the developments in the architecture of the Netherlands, but that he had unexpectedly run into a name within documents that caught his attention in the mid-19th century: Elie Saraber, an architect in The Hague.

"That name strongly reminded me of the French surname Sarrabère," he said as he made the car accelerate again. "When I was still human, I used to know someone named Noël Nicodème Sarrabère. He was a little younger than I and came from Salies de Béarn in the southwest of the country. For reasons I can't remember exactly, he sometimes visited Lyon."

I took a glance to the left. Two tiny, bright lights, side by side in the cloudy sky, with two more behind them and again two more behind those.

Unmistakably, approaching commercial airplanes. We were driving right beneath a flight path of Schiphol Airport...

"In any event, he got to know my younger sister and those two began a relationship."

Raphaël... a sister? That was such a strange idea. I asked, now suddenly *with* interest: "What was her name?"

"Jeanne."

"And what happened then?"

"Then the trouble started. For you see, the association between Mr. Sarrabère and my sister was anything but appropriate. He was a member of the Huguenots, Protestants in a predominately Catholic France. Certainly during the time of Louis the Fourteenth this was an extremely undesirable, and thus heavily persecuted, minority. And now this man suddenly exposed her to all dangers that came with it…"

"Aha…" I said.

"But as it often goes in love: my sister did not want to listen to our warnings. She got married and left for Béarn with her husband. From that moment on the contact between herself and us was slowly lost. And even though we, as a family, weren't officially on a bad foot with her, we still lost track of one another over the years that followed."

"So you did not know what became of her?"

"Oh, on occasion word reached us in passing of, for example, the birth of their three children…"

"But?"

"I have never seen her again myself."

"Lack of time?"

"That was what I told myself, yes. And when I eventually became a vampire…"

I nodded understandingly. "And that architect…?" I asked.

"Well, this is where things become interesting: Elie Sarabar turned out to be a direct descendant of my sister and her husband. And when I, now in the second half of the nineteenth century, discovered that he had been given the assignment by the Van Pallandt family to construct the towers around the country house, in a spur of the moment I offered myself and my expertise, and I ended up assisting him. Which, naturally, became a unique opportunity to study this person from up close… can you imagine, someone with *my* father as his ancestor!"

I was still lost in thought when we arrived at our destination. Raphaël let the car slow down, waited until the road was clear from oncoming traffic and then took a left turn onto a shaded lot. As soon as he had parked the car he gave me a quick kiss and a pat on the head. We got out of the car and retrieved what we needed from the trunk. We looked like a married couple, together on our way to the same workplace… Hand in hand we walked to the castle that was situated in a cleared area surrounded by trees. Raphaël let go of my hand, however, when we turned onto a gravel path that led to a side entrance of the building.

We entered through the kitchen. Two men were standing there, engaged in a conversation.

"Kazimír La Duca! Speaking of the devil…!" bellowed one of them as soon as he saw us. "We were just talking about you." He amiably shook Raphaël's hand.

My boyfriend returned the greeting of the man by stating half-threateningly, half-jokingly that their 'gossip' hopefully did not jeopardize his reputation too much.

"And then risk the chance of never obtaining an architectural report? No thanks, I also have my own interests to think of," the man said in an overly defensive tone, as he winked at me. With that it seemed like he wanted to communicate something to the effect of: "I know, I'm big and loud and rough around the edges, but trust me, I'm not as bad as I look."

In the meantime the other man clarified that they had just been speculating about the mysterious guest that Kazimír had announced over the phone yesterday afternoon to be bringing along with him. As early as yesterday afternoon. Why was I not surprised?

I let my eyes briefly meet those of the vampire and subtly noted that this 'mystery guest' was *that* mysterious that she did not even realize that it would be her until late last night. Next I reached out my hand and said my name. The boisterous man immediately asked Kazimír: "Your girlfriend...?" To which he replied with an ambiguous "Wellll... that is for *you* to find out." And with that this subject was closed to him.

I was told by the men who they were. One was called Harm-Jan and he was the chairman of the foundation. The second man was a completely different type of person. More restraint, deliberative almost.

He was a board member, and in his capacity as an architect responsible for the restoration. His name was Justus and while he walked over to the coffee machine and began to tinker with cups, sugar and cream, my boyfriend had a chat with the chairman.

Meanwhile I looked around me inquisitively. Granite flooring, antiquated green and mid-brown colors of paint on wooden beams, a workbench with some supplies for cooking... the window was a latticed frame that was subdivided into those small, square panes that you often saw in centuries-old houses. And on the counter in front of that window lay a dead deer in a metal tray, with its skin still attached and everything. I did not catch sight of its head – did not even want to know whether it was still connected. But from what I could see, where once his legs had been were now just bloody, sawn-off stumps. After looking back one more time at the rust-brown haired cadaver, I followed the two architects out of the kitchen. We took the service stairs up.

We sat down in the Master Chamber, a somewhat peculiar room with an eclectic collection of furniture and other objects. It was explained to me that this had served as a reception room for the last occupant, Count Van Lynden, and I could totally picture it. The light coming in through the two windows provided an airy atmosphere – it was undeniable that this room radiated a sense of domestic intimacy. A good starting point for a photo report. After I had finished my coffee I therefore announced that I would get going.

And although I pretended to merely be busy setting up my tripod and my camera, I still kept following the conversation between the two men with fascination and filtered out anything that piqued my interest. That was how I found out that, aside from assembling an architectural report, Raphaël was also working here as a consultant. He helped Justus plan the upcoming restoration of the interior of the castle. They discussed issues that I would normally never think of, but that were so tremendously interesting... Just the considerations you had to take into account when thinking about the restoration of this particular room. How best to return it to its original state... And the ensuing deliberation on whether its original state was even a desirable one to begin with. For if you were to unleash such a rigorous approach on a room such as this, it would mean that a lot of things had to be dismantled, including, for example, the extension with the west-facing window that offered such a panoramic view of the gardens and the surrounding pastures. Not to mention the paintings, book cabinets, the saggy sofa and the godawful cast-iron-and-marble coffee table upon which our coffee cups stood. Throughout the centuries so many people had lived here and left their mark on this building... were you sure that you wanted to erase the traces of all those lives forever?

When Justus had walked out of the room to get something, Raphaël said: "Lente, come and have a look at this." He was standing in front of an impressive mahogany cabinet with wide drawers. They were filled with blueprints and design sketches. He took out a drawing.

"This is a proposal that Elie Saraber has submitted for the renovation at the time," he said. The endeared tone of voice with which he spoke did not evade me. This had to mean a lot to him... and indeed, a document such as this was quite remarkable. With due reverence I examined the drawing that was composed using fine pencil strokes. Yes, this absolutely was something rare. Who else would get to see an almost one and a half century-old document from this close? Carefully I ran my fingers over a corner of the slightly yellowed paper.

"Did you notice the flamboyant characteristics of his designs? That neo-Gothic turret, the lancet shape of the windows..."

I nodded slowly and said: "That thing over there on the right looks almost like the tower of an English church, with those four pinnacles at its corners." Raphaël responded with a little chuckle. "Yes, Elie got his ideas from literally everywhere. If he had had his way we wouldn't be seeing brick walls on the exterior, for example, but instead everything would have been covered by a thick layer of plasterwork. But of course, that could not receive the approval of Baroness Van Pallandt. That's what you get for working under the commission of a Calvinistic family."

"But wasn't Saraber Protestant himself as well?"

"And a Frenchman of origin," he added, although this sounded more like a counter argument. He began to flip through stacks of paper in different drawers, as though he was looking for something else that he wanted to show me. Without success, apparently. After a while he gave up, walked over to his bag, took out some things and opened the door leading to the hallway.

"Did Elie get any offspring? I mean, children, grandchildren…" I asked, as I followed him.

"No, he was never married." A short answer. End of conversation.

During the hours that followed I took photos, many photos. And every once in a while he approached me to ask me politely, almost coyly, to register certain details for him. Something that I found a little strange, as such an attitude did not fit him at all. Nevertheless, I did it with love. After all, despite all my expectations, the miracle had happened: everything that I saw in this place now held my undivided attention. Those rooms with that intense dark-blue, that wine-red, the gold finishing and those grandiose works of art. All those centuries, all those occupants, their priceless culture… The displayed hunting rifles and other objects of use… the bits and pieces of history that I picked up in passing. Exciting, entertaining and sad stories that partly came, as bizarre as reality could be, from the proverbial horse's mouth.

But what fascinated me the most was that Saraber family, so in a moment when Justus was not around, I brought up that subject again. I asked Raphaël whether progeny of his sister could not have arisen by ways of a different lineage. And surprisingly uninhibited he then answered: "Oh of course. Countless descendants have come from Elie's brother Pieter alone. They live all over the world – in Australia, France, Japan. They can even be found in the Netherlands to this day."

Could this be one of those typical instances in which he used openness as a smoke screen? I could not help but getting the impression that he was holding back on something. Cautiously I therefore asked him one more question: "Have you ever met any of those people?"

"No." And then silence.

As casually as possible I then concluded: "Oh well, following history through such a castle is much safer, anyway. Stones are silent after all – they don't ask awkward questions."

Raphaël cleared his throat, took a step away from me and flipped a sheet of his notepad. For a moment he stood there reading, with his hand rubbing his chin, then he walked to Justus and began a long conversation on historical hues and color gradients.

## 56

## NEIGHBORS

Classical conditioning. I believe that I first heard about it in high school. At
the time our social studies teacher had claimed that it did not take much for
a human to be transformed into a near slave-like, programmed Pavlovian
dog... To illustrate that, he had told us an anecdote about someone who was
having issues with his upstairs neighbor. The man in question had been
dealing with noise disturbance that penetrated his home through the ceiling.
And every late night, after hours of racket, all of his annoyance came to a
peak when his upstairs neighbor would get undressed to go to bed. He would
never quietly put down the shoes that he was taking off, like a normal
person, but instead he would let them loudly fall to the floor, one by one.
At a certain point the protagonist of this story had been completely done with
the situation. He had rung the noise maker's doorbell to have a serious talk
about it. Who in turn, seemingly in all sincerity, had promised to do better.
That same night however, as he was getting ready to go to sleep, he simply
dropped his shoe to the floor with a bang again. But this time that sound
reminded him immediately of what he had agreed to. A little embarrassed he
therefore laid his other shoe down as quietly as possible. Shortly after, he
slipped into his bed. But he did not get a chance to fall asleep. Not even a
moment had passed when a tormented voice from beneath him sounded,
shouting: "Are you going to drop that second one yet, or what?"

I was just as hopelessly conditioned as that downstairs neighbor. I as well
had been waiting, but my metaphorical shoe should have dropped yesterday
already and now it was Saturday afternoon and I still had not heard
anything. No text message from Lucas, no phone call, nothing.
I counted myself lucky that I was able to hide behind stressing about tonight.
Behind my nervousness about my mother's stress that she would probably be
having, as with every organized get-together due to my father's pathological
lack of stress. That was what she called his stoic – according to her even
zealous – composure.
And if that did not work I could always pretend to be worried about how my
parents would fall like a log for Raphaël. I could see it coming already,
without any effort whatsoever he would seamlessly cater to their desires
concerning the ideal son in law: a young man who was doing well
professionally and financially. Someone with an impeccable sense of style,
who on top of that had long outgrown the need for an audience. His Volvo S80
was the perfect symbol of his image: on the inside, extremely comfortable

with walnut, beige leather and the latest technological gadgets. And on the outside, royal blue and brand new, yet not extravagant in any way. An unlikely combination of loathing and pride came over me, although it could have been worse. Cause had this vehicle been a Porsche, I would have made sure to take the train instead.

"Here, turn left to stay on the Taveernelaan," I said, just in time. From the moment that we had exited the main road between Zeist and Den Dolder and had entered the forest I had been absentminded. Stupid, of course, since I had insisted on being the navigator.

"Sorry, I guess I'm more nervous than I thought," I mumbled. My boyfriend squeezed my hand and asked: "Would it help you if I said that I don't feel completely relaxed either?"

I smiled, was about to come up with a sweet reply, but got distracted by something that I saw further ahead on the right side of the road, in front of my family home. Filled with shame I buried my face into my hands. "Valet parking..." I verbalized, "I should have *known*."

Raphaël took a gander at the small group of uniformly dressed young men that was patiently waiting in front of our gate. His comment was level-headed: "Well, it *is* a practical solution, if you don't want to cause parking issues with your neighbors."

I sighed. Yes, anything for keeping the peace with the neighbors.

We stopped, got out and grabbed our presents.

After he had handed over his car keys we walked home, side by side along the driveway. My white, soulless, parental home.

But we would manage, Raph and I. I estimated the percentage of 'neatness' that I exuded today at about 75, with my slightly mischievous, gray schoolgirl pinafore, white blouse and equally white 40-denier tights. Beneath that my Victorian lace-up heeled shoes, one shade of gray darker than my dress. Exactly as it should be. Pity that I did not have any cobalt blue lipstick to match my dyed lock of hair and my nail polish... then it would be completely perfect. But anyhow, I could not complain. The fact alone that the velvet accessory around my neck was known as a *choker* in the underground scene, stirred up more sarcastic feelings than I felt that I was entitled to.

And for the conforming counterbalance I had brought my partner, because he was guaranteed to fit the picture this evening, with his dark-red Kashmir V-neck on top of a shirt without a necktie, over neat jeans and suede loafers – my parents were going to eat out of his hand!

The front door opened and my mother came out with a woman dressed in a two-piece suit, who was in her thirties. She was so busy talking with her that at first she did not see us coming. She pointed at a truck of a catering company that stood in front of the garage and gave the woman instructions in an urgent tone, upon which said woman disappeared back into the house with a firm stride. She then noticed me and Raphaël and waved at us.

"Kazimír La Duca," Raphaël whispered in my ear. Almost at the same time I felt his cold kiss on my face.

"Oh shit, that's right... thanks!" I whispered back.

And then came a light touch of both upper arms and three kisses in the air. My mom and I. Our greeting.

I said: "Marga, this is my boyfriend, Kazimír."

"Hello Kazimír, my name is Marga Sandifer."

Kazimír shook my mother's hand and congratulated her with her husband's birthday and gave her a blue and lilac bouquet of flowers. She was flattered, but as expected, her attention to him lasted briefly. She led us inside and said half to herself, half to me: "I really need to go and get dressed up... what time is it?"

"A quarter to five," I answered, and then a little annoyed: "I thought you had a candlelight supper planned."

"Oh child, hadn't I emailed it to you? Surely, you knew I've always wanted to do a *walking dinner*? And especially now that your father is turning fifty five..."

" – Where is he anyway?" I interrupted her.

"I have no idea, I think he's in the garage. Getting the chefs to spill their gastronomic secrets or something..." Muttering to herself my mother walked away. Chasing after yet another detail.

"A Domaine de Trévallon... you *bet* that's to my taste!" The underside of the bottle lay in my father's left palm and he supported the neck with his other hand, as though he was holding a newborn baby. That was how my father inspected the wine that he had just been given by my boyfriend, full of surprised amazement. Then he said: "We will save it for a special occasion. Kazimír, you have my sincerest gratitude."

I had succeeded. The three, no, the four of us were sitting in the sunroom with a view of the backyard. This was probably going to be our only real family moment this evening.

Just before I had indeed found my father in the garage, where he had animatedly been discussing something culinary with one of the people of the catering company. The space that was normally reserved for our cars, had been temporarily transformed into a fully decked out kitchen, populated by three cooks and a host of diligent yet restrained serving and other staff walking back and forth. Quite the spectacle for one singular evening... My mother, I had been able to intercept somewhere between the study and the stairs that led to the first floor.

The gift that I had for my dad, a large macro picture of a skin colored rose with on it the silver, handwritten words: *SKIN by Lente*, was received with just as much enthusiasm as the bottle of red wine from my boyfriend. But the curiosity about the strange young man that was by their daughter's side outweighed it and soon the obvious questions arose.

"… So if I understand correctly, you two are an item… How did you actually meet?"

"Well, mister Sandifer – "

" – You can just call me Otto."

"Alright, Otto – it happened on the way from Iceland to the Netherlands. Didn't it, sweetheart?" Raphaël smiled at me.

And then the whole Schiphol story followed, mainly recounted by him and here and there complemented by me. And next came a brief summary on the months that followed: we had emailed and chatted. A lot and often.

"Conversing with Lente, to me, was like stepping into a whole new dimension. That sharp mind and extraordinary creativity of hers… her love for beauty and fragility. But to say that Lente has always been the easiest of conversation partners…?"

"Was I really that difficult?" I asked innocently, and that innocence was not even feigned.

"Well… your trust is not easily won, you have to admit that," said Raphaël. And then, turning to my father, he stated: "I think, at first, Lente thought of me as a somewhat odd character. She did not take anything of what I said for granted. Especially when we first started talking she literally put everything that I said under a microscope and continued her questioning long after others would have felt satisfied…"

My father mumbled: "Oh, is that right?"

My mother nodded thoughtfully. "Sounds like our daughter…"

And I, I was beginning to feel a bit worried about the direction that this conversation was heading into. But clearly, Raphaël was not finished yet: "I think that as time has gone by, she has exposed all my shortcomings," he grinned. "Not a single stone on the internet was left unturned and she has even spoken to my colleagues."

Okay. To here, but no further. "Yeah yeah, enough of that," I muttered. "Why not talk about what kind of work you do? Because I'm sure my parents would love to hear that by now."

"I'm a conservation architect."

"And consultant, *and* a historian…" I added.

My friend, in turn, used this opening to explain that he was currently involved in a project at Keukenhof Castle in Lisse and with this we had come to the present and together we had laid out a beautifully consistent story. The truth and nothing but the truth. And my parents fell for it with their eyes wide open. "Architecture… fascinating! Very interesting. I look forward to hear more about that." After a pat on both his thighs my father got up from his lazy chair. "But if you would excuse me for now… I still have to discuss a thing or two with the chef before the guests arrive," he said.

We let him go and my mother watched him leave with a pitiful stare. She explained to Raphaël: "My husband loves to cook…" Under her breath she added: "… meanwhile, it is up to me to avert all impending catastrophes."

Then she got up as well. "What time is it anyway?" she asked. "Lente, have you seen Fleur anywhere?"

"That flying goalie, you mean?"

"A party planner, dear. That's what her job is called."

"... You have a cat?"

"Two of them. Scully and Mulder."

"From The X-Files? That's uh… different," grinned Raphaël. We were looking at the cat flap in the kitchen door and I explained why we had chosen for those names specifically. I told him about the indecisive behavior that the two Birmans had displayed when they first lived with us. About how they had constantly darted from the inside to the outside and from the outside back in during the first couple of days and how we had spent one evening in a silly mood speculating on why they did that and that one of us then had come up with that tag line of The X-Files: "The truth is out there…"

"Any more creative names in this household?"

"Nervus and Tendon. Our dogs," I answered.

"A family of doctors," I explained when he looked at me in disbelief.

"The fact that you have dogs I thought I had smelled already. What breed?"

"Dobermanns…"

My mother came in, a little more restless than just earlier and immediately she walked out of the kitchen again. She did not seem to have noticed us. I said "hold on" to Raphaël and went after my mom. Told her to get changed and said that I would keep an eye on things in the meantime. With a kiss to my cheek she thanked me and hurriedly disappeared into the hallway.

With a hint of irony in his voice he asked: "… Try to avert a catastrophe?"

I did not react. I left the kitchen, called back "you coming?", located Fleur and deviously managed to get her to make a couple of praising remarks about my mother – flattering comments about her organizational skills, that I, when my mother reappeared a little later all dressed and made up, quoted within earshot to Raphaël several times. I felt like a calculative bitch, but it was for a good cause and the result was immediately noticeable. My mother became nicer towards Fleur and let her do her job uninterruptedly for the rest of the evening. She let go of her bashful nagging towards her husband and at a certain point I even heard her humming a song that she had picked up from Liesbeth List doing the sound check in the backyard.

Time for the dogs. Finally! With Raphaël at my hand I wanted to hop to the farthest right corner of the garden, but he seemed to be in less of a hurry than I was. In fact, he even slowed down a little.

"You're not scared, are you?" I asked mockingly.

"Not me, no…" he replied, and what he meant by that I soon discovered. From the moment that we had appeared within their field of vision Nervus and Tendon had loudly announced that they recognized me, but as soon as we got closer to the pen their behavior changed abruptly. Their barking silenced, they stopped jumping up against the wire fence and lowered themselves to the ground, as flat as they could. Softly whimpering they then began to crawl backwards, until they could not go any further and came to a stop, side by side in a corner of their enclosure.

Raphaël apologized by saying: "Sorry, my place in the food chain…"

I indicated that I understood and cautiously stepped a few meters back with him. I felt mortified for our dogs, but actually I could only with difficulty suppress the urge to laugh.

The vampire made a fatalistic gesture. "And here your parents thought they had dangerous animals on their property…"

That was the final straw. I burst out laughing, upon which he grabbed me from behind and pressed his mouth against my neck while growling playfully. Giggling nervously I wrestled myself out of his embrace and for a moment we stood there facing each other, catching our breath. Then he said, shaking his head: "… They had specifically warned me: never fall in love with your food source."

I reacted without thinking. "See, *that* is humor! And that is why I like you so much – at least you know what it's like to make jokes. Something Lucas can learn a thing or two from… he's always so serious and – "

"But I am being serious as well," replied Raphaël somewhat surprised.

What to make out of that remark, I did not know. But I was very happy that at that moment the first guests arrived in the garden, because I was convinced that I had just made a mistake that I would rather not have to answer to.

## 57

## CHAMELEON

Kazimír, the chameleon. The man of many faces. Kind and modest towards my grandfather and grandmother. Lavishly bragging along in conversations about cars and polo with the scions of successful fellow villagers. In the company of my father's business relations casually delivering stories embellished with technical jargon in response to questions about his work – or when the situation required it, reluctantly chewing the rag during lengthy discussions on politics and the media. Kazimír, the man who got what he wanted, no matter what it was.

The appetizers and beverages that were carried around on fancy platters I could barely finish. Too busy staring. Being proud of him and wanting him... and being incredibly annoyed with him! Cause at a certain point he had brazenly dared to go and talk to my parents about my book. He had shamelessly stated how unique he thought my photos were and how much admiration he had for my perseverance, as that was what a project such as that definitely demanded... With increasing amazement my parents had stood there listening to him, and of course I had then felt morally obligated to provide a little more explanation.

Later on he did apologize to me – he had been under the complete assumption that they had long known about my book, and I had forgiven him, but the damage had already been done: on my way to the bathroom in the hall I had run into my father, and as expected, he had immediately suggested some pal of his who owned a publishing house and who would probably be willing to help me... Crabbily, or to be honest, flat out aggressively I had declined his proposal.

And that was how things always went between us.

Naturally, he had then immediately introduced a different topic: "Say, that Kazimír fellow... he sure is a nice kid..."

To which I had again responded with a snarl: "Are you really calling someone who is thirty a kid?"

"A nice man then."

"Exactly..."

"Anyway, he looks particularly well groomed... haven't seen such flawless skin very often. Although, he is a little pale."

"Ohhh..."

"Has he ever had his Hb checked?"

"Well, why don't you go and ask him, dad!"

"Sorry, dear, force of habit."

We stood there a bit awkwardly, I with my hands tucked deep inside the pockets of my dress. Control yourself, control yourself, I repeated in my mind. Finally I said, though still a bit more curtly than intended: "Everyone can be a little pale sometime. Ever heard of sleep deprivation?"

And that was all the patience that I could muster for today.

About fifteen minutes later I leaned back in relief in the passenger seat of the car. I looked at Raphaël, a little faintly. I answered his quizzical look with the explanation: "Escaped just in time from a family overdose."

With a crooked smile he started the engine. "So that sigh wasn't an expression of exhaustion?"

"No, I'm not tired."

"Ah! A good opportunity then for an added tour of this area," he said.

"An added tour. In the dark?"

"Sightseeing. I haven't been in these regions for such a long time."

"Alright, makes sense. From your perspective, at least…"

He ignored my banter and put the car in gear. He turned left at Restaurant De Hoefslag and drove past Den Dolder. Then he turned right, initially going towards Soest, but soon after that, following the signs that pointed the way to Lage Vuursche. The headlights illuminated the road in front of us and the trees that lined it. I could not see much more than that. He on the contrary did, judging by the determination with which he drove the car. Had he possibly planned a route beforehand? And now that I thought about it, an added tour, what did that actually mean? Maybe I should have asked some more questions first…

My parents, they were probably standing in the backyard among family and business relations listening to the private concert of Liesbeth List. While their daughter, instead of being on her way to Rotterdam, was driving around the extensive forests of the Utrechtse Heuvelrug with her boyfriend. In a brand new, cleaned and polished Volvo, according to many the safest car in the world.

And it was dark outside.

## 58

ROOTLESS


One time during a harsh winter I had driven right through a heavy
snowstorm to Vlaardingen in the beat-up clunker that I had in my possession
at that time. No reason, just to see what it was like. What in the world had
gotten into me...?
The visibility had been worse than abysmal and I had ventured out on the
roads without winter tires or snow chains, while it was so slippery that
several vehicles around me came to a stop against curbs or simply in the
middle of the lane. Anyway, during the peaks of my concentration I had
attempted to reach a hotel restaurant, at which it had been my intention to
wind down from my adventure while enjoying a cup of coffee, and that also
had a view of the wide canal between the North Sea and the Port of
Rotterdam. And at that hotel I had finally arrived, albeit with a speed of
barely fifteen miles per hour. But the rush... the rush that it gave me...! To
prove to yourself whatever it is that you want to prove, against weather
alerts and common sense... Although, to this day it was still not clear to me
what that 'thing' that I wanted to prove had been.
However, I had not been able to enjoy my triumph for long. The Botlek
harbor area across the water had gradually disappeared from view due to the
heavy snowfall and suddenly I had been in rush to finish my coffee and to
slip-and-slide back to my little car, now completely covered by snow.
Eventually I had gotten home without any trouble. Having gained an
experience and a life lesson.

"Isn't Drakensteyn Castle located around here somewhere?"
"We just passed that. I thought you knew."
No reply.
A long, unlit road through a dense piece of forest. Followed by Castle De
Hooge Vuursche in all its bombastic glory. We stopped to have a look. A
single remark on the relatively young age of this building, a compliment on
the recent restoration of its interior and then the car drove off again, only to
turn left after a hundred yards or so. I knew this back road. It was narrow
and led to nowhere. Or I should say, to the Forest Pool and the mini-golf
course. But it was nighttime. So they were closed and here, aside from us, not
a living soul could be found.
"Stop, you can't go straight there," I warned. "You can only turn left here and
then the road loops around the Forest Pool."
So at a snail's pace, the car followed the bumpy trial I had indicated. It really

was nothing more than that – a bumpy trail. Thank goodness that Raphaël had such good eyes...

At the spot right behind the recreational grounds, where we had supposed to follow the road, he suddenly turned onto a dirt parking lot. He swerved around potholes and a puddle or two. We stopped.

Flashbacks of snowstorms and Vlaardingen hotels... he had invited me to go sightseeing by night and I had not said no. Could this be a classic case of tempting fate? Had we really passed the point of 'too late for regrets'?

"Why did we stop?" I asked.

"We have more space here than in Rotterdam."

"To do what?"

"Let's take a walk."

The car door was opened. He got out, but I stayed in my seat. He opened my door.

"Are you coming?" he asked.

"What are we going to do?" He waited. I did not get out. "I first want to know what we're going to do," I insisted.

A beckoning motion. Reluctantly I began to move.

"Questions, questions, Lente. So many questions that I don't have an answer to..." hummed the vampire softly. I hated it when he acted like this.

"There is something, however, that I'd like to hear from *you* first." He was getting ready to start walking and with a little nod of his head he demanded that I joined him. But I preferred to not give up my position near the car...

"This evening you spoke about my father in the present tense. And I would like to know why," he spoke.

The blood drained from my cheeks. Thinking on my feet I came up with excuses about grammar and the use of tenses in the Dutch language.

"The emphasis of what I asked, however... does not lie within linguistic deliberations," it sounded controlled. He now stood still, with his back towards me.

My hand looked for balance on the side of the car.

"Lente, how do you know that Lucas does not have a sense of humor?"

"Well, isn't that obvious? You don't need to be a psychologist to notice that."

"If you solely base your opinion on that singular brief meeting with him in London, it is. Let me rephrase my question: how do you know that Lucas fails to grasp the concept of humor?" He enunciated the words slowly, one by one this time.

"He grew up in a monastery, Raph. A Benedictine monastery!"

"And what does that have to do with not having a sense of humor?"

"Everything... have you never read the Rule of Saint Benedict?" Oh, I was running my mouth into a corner...

My boyfriend turned around. "I have read it, yes. And apparently, so have you."

I let go of the car. Felt it was time to leave. There was a bike path somewhere around here…

"Are you watching your step?" he said.

I did not react and continued walking. I twisted my ankles a few times on the uneven terrain.

"It's pitch-dark in this place. You can't even see your hand in front of your face."

I pretended not to hear him – and then ended up straight in his arms – within a flash he had appeared before me.

"Didn't you see that barbed wire?" He guided my hand to the metal barrier behind him to let me feel what I had almost walked into. I pulled myself away from him and looked for another way.

"Lente, this is not time nor the place for playing games."

"I'm not playing at all. I am *afraid*," I snarled back over my shoulder. "You're acting scary, you're not telling me what you're getting at and I don't know what you're planning to do with me!"

Immediately after that I tripped and felt cold water, or mud, splash up against my shin.

He caught me, just before I hit the ground. With his face very close to mine he asked, "And you're blaming *me* for these things?"

I remained silent and pretended to be busy wiping down my stockings and shoes. A ridiculous act when you cannot see what you are doing.

"You still don't get it," I heard him say.

The frantic speed at which I was scrubbing slowed down a little.

"You really don't have the slightest notion of the amount of fear that you're causing *me* right now, do you, Lente?"

Now he *really* had my attention. I let out a noise that was supposed to sound like an expression of sarcasm. But it more closely resembled violently coughing up a lump of tough slime. "*You*, afraid of *me*?" I exclaimed.

"Stop doing that, sweetheart. Why can't you take me seriously?" He sounded almost pleading… "Your lack in communicating with me… I have lost you once already because of it…" he said.

"I couldn't help that," I snapped. "I – " startled I stopped talking.

"Go on."

"No."

"Why not?"

"Stop asking."

"No, we keep going until everything is on the table."

"And what if I can't?"

"Then you proceed to explain *why* you can't."

"And what if I'm too afraid of the consequences?"

"Then you tell me what consequences you're afraid of."

"Accidents. I don't know… disaster…"

"And that threat of disaster, where do you think that that will come from? Do I play a part in it?"

"Among others."

"And who else?"

"Don't push me."

"Who else, Lente?"

"Lucas." My shoulders crept upwards.

"Lucas. And what, may I ask, would be his role in this ever growing mystery?"

"He has spoken with me in London."

We had been walking, upon his initiative, arm in arm. But now we stopped. Again, upon his initiative.

I tightly closed my eyes as I said: "Lucas has threatened me. Because of him I broke up with you."

With great emphasis he spoke four words: "His – head – will – roll."

What I had anticipated to happen now, did not: blind panic, screaming, passing out. Instead of that, something within me shifted into a mode that bypassed my emotions and only allowed me to observe.

He stepped a few meters away from me. His silhouette exposed the posture of a man in despair: with one hand at his side, and the back of the other pressed against his mouth. Then I could tell by his head and shoulders that he was straining himself doing something. I could hear him groan and there was cracking, snapping and something that sounded like tough and sticky material being torn apart. He had bitten himself. Multiple times, most likely. An automatic response within me made me walk up to him. "Come, let me have a look," I said, and: "do you have a first aid kit in the car?" At the same time I reached out to carefully hold him by the wrist, but he slid my hand forward and did not stop until it lay on top of the exposed tissue – cold, sticky moisture, a deep laceration where normally the carpal bones would be located... a massacre of broken and crushed metacarpal bones. An entire section of skin was missing and his index and middle finger were pointing upward in an unnatural position. In a reflex I recoiled, but he did not let me. He forced me to keep touching the wound. And then something began to move underneath the palm of my hand. Protruding sharp parts pivoted downward and met in a seemingly natural alignment. Skin that tightly bridged hollow spaces was filled by bone tissue from below, the two fingers popped back in place with a horrendous, clicking noise – again I withdrew my hand – unsuccessfully. His grip was relentless. Finally, something slid over his bones that at first felt bumpy and coarse in its structure, but then transformed into a smooth and supple tissue.

At this point Raphael let go of me. He tried out his restored hand by opening and closing it one or two times. Then he licked off the traces of blood and said, "Watch your clothes. Your hand is dirty." Then he disappeared from sight.

I waited by the car, waited until he was done blowing off steam. Until his roar and the thunderclaps of snapping branches and the screeching of birds flying up in alarm would grow silent...

During an undefined number of minutes, his anger and the effects of his anger came from literally everywhere: from nearby, from further away, from behind me, in front of me and even above me. I underwent the violence with my head tucked between my shoulders and occasionally with my hands covering my ears.

Over time, however, his movements slowed down and his breathing became more regular. He stopped screaming. On and off I could now make out his running figure between the trees and that was followed, in a somewhat hunched-over posture, by him walking. Ultimately, the vampire climbed up a small hill with slow steps, to then descend down the slope behind it.

There was mumbling, unintelligible but menacing. Air that was forcibly in- and exhaled a couple of times. And then a release of force that was catalyzed by an explosive combination of bottomless frustration, pain and hate.

The counter reaction: the screaming moan of wood that attempted to resist at first, but eventually came to surrender with a deafening crash. The disorientating rustle of branches breaking, the protest of vegetation being scraped during the downfall and, once more, alarmed animal noises. Followed by the thundering thud of a tree that hit the ground. The marking of the end of an episode.

A vampire had climbed over the natural elevation in the forest and had disappeared from sight. Now, at the top of the hill however, the man appeared with whom I was so desperately in love. My boyfriend. Completely calm again in appearance he came towards me.

Once he reached me, he said: "Come, let's get into the car."

We sat down beside each other. He turned on the cabin light. I looked at my hands, took out some paper tissues from my purse and began to wipe. I noticed some clotted blood on his chin. Offered him a tissue. He opened the glove box underneath the dashboard and pulled out a bottle of disinfecting gel. We shared a couple of drops of it.

Then he said: "I think I am fairly capable to continue this conversation as a grown-up person now."

"Alright," I replied. "So about Lucas and I..."

A little nod as confirmation.

And I began to tell. About our near run-in at Harrods. Of Lucas' concealed signals in Hammersmith. I described in detail what had happened at Clapham Common. How he had drained that fox right before my eyes, the way in which he had cornered me and had toyed with me. I tried to repeat all the words that I remembered from that particular evening, as literally as possible...

And I did not end it with London. I continued, telling about the trouble with my broken camera. I reconstructed the way in which our three-daily communication via telephone and the internet had come to be, under his strict direction. And finally, albeit summarized, I mentioned the strange bond that unavoidably had developed between us.

"Does he know that we're back together?" asked Raphaël, upon which I looked up my most recent text message to Lucas and showed it to him. Including Lucas' answer. He asked if I had heard anything from him since Wednesday night.

I shook my head.

"And now you're afraid."

"Of course," I admitted, "wouldn't you be?" I put my phone back in my bag. "But still..." I said, "as crazy as it may sound: fear is not the only thing I feel towards him. Somehow he has something caring about him – at least, he had that towards me. Almost like some sort of father, or a good friend..."

Raphaël kept the steering wheel of his car at an arm's length. With his head turned downwards he uttered: "Lente, my dear child. How *could* you confuse such a classic case of Stockholm syndrome with friendship?" He hardly managed to get the word 'friendship' out.

"In Stockholm syndrome they're talking about hostage situations," I mumbled grumpily.

"And what exactly do you think your situation is?"

"Well, not a hostage one, if anything. I can go anywhere I please and so can he – "

" – And with that you precisely indicate what could become our biggest problem. Darling, there is no one as nomadic as him... I mean, all the undead have some trace of it running through their veins, but Lucas... he literally knows everyone in our community!"

"... Cause he never stays at hotels," I suddenly realized. Lucas, the eternal gyrovague, staying in the cells of other monks during his travels... in other words, people like him!

"Still," I insisted, "I don't believe that Lucas will spill the beans. He's has too much integrity to do that."

"Yes, he *has* integrity. So much so, that if he believes that it is the right thing to do, he will give us away regardless."

In firm denial I shook my head. "No, that's not like Lucas."

"Until proven otherwise," it sounded crassly. "In this way you have probably also stubbornly told yourself for weeks that he would never drop in on you in Rotterdam...?"

I glared at Raphaël. Then I said: "Alright. Say, he does go and tell on us. The other vampires know about our relationship – "

"– Part of our community has already been informed," he interrupted me. "For instance, they know about our week in London."

"And you're only telling me this now??"

"Yes. Or are you saying that you could have handled this news two month ago?"

I shook my head, disheartened…

"Listen, Lente. Saving you this misery has always been my number one priority and I still have the hope to resolve it on my own. But, because of the increasing complexity of the situation… I'm afraid there are a couple of things that I need to let you know after all."

"If you think that that is necessary…"

"Yes, I do." And Raphaël began to explain how love relationships between the undead and mortals were regarded. That they were strictly forbidden for as long as he could remember and that what we were doing, would certainly not be tolerated. And now our relationship had even been exposed, as there was someone who had spotted us together in London.

I stared at the inside of my folded hands. "How did you find out?" I asked.

"When I was suddenly summoned by some representatives of the West-German Territories recently."

"The West-German Territories?"

"The community of vampires has been divided into different regions around the world," he clarified.

"So now we have a problem…"

Raphaël looked at me helplessly. "I wish I could paint reality more beautiful than it is, Lente. That I knew what I – what *we* can do…" He softly sighed.

"At least it does not inconvenience anyone that I'm just in the process of wrapping up my life in Great-Britain. And although they'd rather see me leave today than tomorrow, they have permitted me the time to complete my restoration projects."

"Cause that would be less suspicious with your human colleagues."

He nodded. "But the category that we fall under has something to do with it as well. However real our threat may be, at the moment it is not yet critical. However, there will come a time when they will ask us to justify ourselves. And the region in which the Czech Republic is situated, will then play an important role in that process."

I understood. "Because they're the ones that will have to deal with us in the near future," I said. The stone that had been weighing on my stomach for a while now became heavier and suddenly I began to feel some anxiety. "But that means that our lives are in danger! That we could be attacked, kidnapped or killed at any given moment… What if we broke up, Raph? Yes, what if we broke up anyway, wouldn't that influence their decision – there must be *something* that we can do?"

Raphaël shook his head. He placed his hand on my cheek and said: "If I could express how incredibly sorry I am for all this, I would do it. Day in day out I ask myself the question of why, for heaven's sake, I couldn't have been more sensible. Why I so stupidly gave you that email address…"

Somehow I managed to recompose myself during the silence that now fell.

I asked: "Did we even have a chance, at all?"

"What do you mean?"

I took the hand that caressed my face. "Has there ever been a point at which we had a chance to say 'no' to our being in touch, to our relationship?"

Raphaël did not answer. I said: "For me it was already a done deal at Schiphol. And when I later found out during our chat sessions that it was you of all people…"

The vampire looked outside, at the trees and bushes of the forest and to its inhabitants. I stared out of the car window, at the dark, into the void.

Only after some time he began to speak again. "Lente, listen. The fear of being found out or being betrayed is significant to us. You know that the undead have very little faith in humanity. So something will need to be done about you and me. Although, what that's going to look like in practice, is impossible for me to tell. Only a select few in our community have access to that knowledge. And trust me, I have tried everything I could to keep the heat off of you. I have pleaded for you and our relationship, I've literally talked the hind legs off a donkey… But the only thing that they have honored this far, is my request concerning the way in which the verdict will be passed. Thankfully it will, when the time is ready, only be announced to us at a moment when we're together, and not to each of us separately."

"Even so, we don't stand a chance. Purely because I'm aware of your existence."

"There is a small chance," he corrected me.

"Then nothing really matters that much for now, anyway. Then we might as well continue our relationship. Right? I mean, to sit there and wait for whatever Lucas is going to do is pointless as well… so why not, while we still can…?"

"Darling, you are so brave…"

"Fatalistic is a better word to describe it." I half-heartedly smiled.

Raphaël gave me a hug and started the car.

We turned around, and across the uneven dirt we drove towards the exit of the parking lot. Suddenly I was overwhelmed by a severe bout of nausea.

"Stop!" I exclaimed. He hit the brakes. I opened the door, in the nick of time. Gagging, I held my head out of the car, and everything that I had eaten at my father's party that evening came out at once.

Shaking I sat up again, looked for a tissue and wiped my mouth.

"Sorry. Of course, that was bound to happen."

My boyfriend looked at me concerned, but I reassured him: "I'm alright."

"I'll try to drive as carefully as possible," he said.

"Thank you, but honestly the feeling has passed." Again, a quiver went through me. This time, however, from being cold.

"I think you could use something warm to drink," was his observation.

"What time is it? Perhaps the bar at your hotel's still open."

"It is twenty to eleven."

"Still that early?"

What seemed to have lasted for hours and hours, turned out to have taken place in barely fifteen minutes. Dramatic events, compressed to the extreme. I thought that something like that could only happen in dreams...

## 59

DISCLOSURE

"...So you've taken down an entire tree?" I placed my empty tea cup on the coffee table in front of us and nestled back against Raphaël.
"Yup," he replied, and wrapped his arm around me.
"Really, one of those big ones?"
"Uh huh..."
I stared at the trendy lampshades, which were at least a yard and a half across, that hung above us inside the hotel lobby and tried to imagine how big an average Dutch tree would feel like when you wrapped your arms around it. "But you have, I hope, made sure that it didn't fall onto the tracks? A railway track runs somewhere behind there..."
A sarcastic look was his response. "Don't worry, Lente. Tomorrow morning a park ranger will probably face an inexplicable conundrum, but the consequences of my action won't reach much further than that."
We laughed like a couple of children that had just played a naughty prank. It felt good to laugh... A middle-aged married couple that was sitting a little further away looked at us with tender amusement.
I nestled a little bit closer against my lover. "You know what I've always been wondering?" I asked dreamily. "What you were doing in Iceland last February."
"I mentioned that already at your parents' this afternoon: I was there for a weekend of winter sports."
"But you hate the snow."
"Well, I didn't snowboard or ski. I was kitesurfing at Álftanes."
"Huh?"
"A peninsula just south of Reykjavík."
"Yeah yeah, I know the place. That's where the president or something lives. But water sports, in the middle of winter?"
"By night. With a couple of friends."
"What's so funny?" he asked.
"Yeah, I'm sorry, but kite surfing vampires...!"
"What would you rather see me do? Korfball?"
"Something like that," I grinned.
"No, but seriously. Look at it from my perspective. Rock climbing: boring. You're at the top in no time. Team sports, played together with mortals: more depressing than stimulating. And then a bunch of us have tried fencing once, at some point..."
"And?"

"It was a useless effort. Too much speed, too much violence. The material costs soon began to grow gigantically out of proportion."

"But what makes kite surfing so special then?"

"The primal force, Lente! The primal force that drives wind and water... It's just you in a state of play with the elements. If you are somewhat skilled at it, you don't only make great speed, but spectacular leaps as well. Not to mention, that view as you're floating through the air, the color of the kite that's in bright contrast to the moonlight, or this time, the Aurora Borealis even – "

"– Hey, that's the exact reason why I was at Seltjarnarnes, photographing at night, that weekend! That's right across from that peninsula of yours. That means we've seen the same Northern Lights... Whoa!"

"Yeah, I saw you busy doing that," he said calmly, "weren't you that person somewhere to the left of that lighthouse, wrestling with her tripod and the strong wind?"

"You're bluffing," was my incredulous reaction.

But he remained stoic. "And you just kept going at it," he reminisced. "You were barely able to hold that camera steady, but by any means, you *had* to take photos of those polar lights."

"Yeah right, in that manner you could construct all kinds of nonsense! Especially now that you've known me for some time. But I'm not buying it. You're bluffing and that's all there is to it."

"Or it's the true story behind the beginning of a romance."

I rolled my eyes and punched him in the side. Upon which he grabbed me by the chin, turned me towards him and kissed me straight on the mouth. Under the prying eyes of the married couple a few tables over...

My boyfriend sighed with satisfaction. Then he said: "But to get back to practicing sports: the real reason why I kite surf is because it's good for me. As it doesn't matter how well-trained you are – sooner or later you will make an error of judgment. And alive or undead, believe me when I say that you will feel the pain when you crash into the waves going fifty miles per hour. A useful reality check for us megalomaniac vampires."

Pityingly I shook my head. "What is it with you guys and the elements? Lucas was talking about tornadoes and feeling humbled as well, the other day..."

Raphaël's demeanor changed immediately. I felt it, I saw it. And I could hear it by the way he forced himself to stay silent. The threat of inwardly directed wrath.

"You're really very angry, huh?"

"I have made a decision regarding this... person. And I will not reconsider it."

"So, that means that every time we talk I will have to bite my tongue and not mention his name from now on? Well, I'm sorry, but I'm not sure if I'm okay with that."

He remained silent and squeezed my hand. "Weren't we talking about being open with one another this evening? These issues are a part of it as well, Raph. If we're going to have to be this careful already when we're around unfamiliar and even familiar people..."

"Then you will want to feel free around me. You're right. I'll keep that in mind."

I moved the back of his hand to my mouth and kissed it.

"As long as you realize that freedom and total openness are just illusions. No one shares everything. With nobody."

I cleared my throat, shifted my weight as well as the subject: "Tell me something about you I completely don't know yet."

Seemingly without thinking he answered: "I used to be a painting artist."

"Before you became an architect?"

"Yes."

"What made you switch careers?"

"I can't remember the reason why, exactly. I wanted to broaden my horizon, I think."

Him, an artist. It did not surprise me at all, and at the same time, the idea of it was very strange. Raphaël being Michelangelo...

"And do you still paint sometimes?"

"Not lately. But now to you."

"What?"

"Tell me something about you that I don't know."

I hated the topic that I was about to raise now. But it had to be breached at some point, and it was better done here and tonight than under less safe-feeling conditions. So I said, with a slightly elevated pulse: "I was only a year short of becoming a Doctor of Medicine."

Raphaël sat up straight and positioned himself on the edge of the sofa, semi-facing me. "What was that you just said?"

"I studied Medicine for five years and, just like you, I made a career switch. So we can shake hands," I said a bit too cheerfully.

"Someone who's gotten that far into a program doesn't take such a decision easily. Why did you?"

"Some things happened..."

"Like what?"

"I wasn't thinking clearly when I started it. I had always felt more affinity towards the arts. Kind of like what happened with you, but then the other way around. Surely, you know the feeling?"

"No. I did not hate painting and I still don't. So what else was going on?"

"Oh, I don't know. It had probably mostly to do with personal development. Like I said, I wasn't really thinking when I picked my studies. At home we were always talking about my father's practice. My mother had a background in the medical community as well, so you can imagine... Anyway, you're admitted, begin your studies and immerse yourself in that lifestyle. With the hazing, the sorority and all..."

"So you were a member of a social club then?"

"What do you think? That was a given. I was just as much a sorority chick as all the others. And I participated just as hard: partying, drinking, rowing…"
In the pronunciation of the words 'sorority chick' I had placed an empathic amount of self-ridicule.

"And before you knew it, *that* had become your entire world. Studying and being a student."

"Precisely. There was no more room for other things. Including creativity. And at a certain point that shoe began to pinch after all. Don't get me wrong. The profession, doctor, I didn't mind. But the fact that your whole life revolves around it and how that only gets worse after graduating… I needed space, for my brain."

My boyfriend nodded pensively. Without a hint of judgment, or even criticism in his voice he said: "To eventually reach a decision of such proportion, something that defines a moment usually needs to happen. Something that has a shocking effect… What caused you to turn around completely?"

"A classmate, Mathilde. In my eyes, she was the best in our graduating class. Had finished her bachelor's with honors and had great passion for what she did. But because she was from a working class family she had no money to make ends meet, aside from her study allowance. So she always was working side jobs. She has been in catering, distributed meals in nursing homes, she really took up any employment she could get. But one day Mathilde got wind of a job opening that's in extremely high demand with med students: removing organs for transplantation from recently deceased people for an organization in Leiden. She applied the same day, but was coldly rejected. The following weekend I just happened to be visiting my parents, and what took me by surprise, or rather, astonishment? My father told me that if I wanted, I could get a part-time job in Leiden."

"That same position."

"Exactly. An opportunity that lay completely out of reach for someone who was far more deserving than me, was simply handed to me on a platter. I can still picture my father standing there, with his thumbs in his pants pockets. Totally triumphant, because he had managed to pull some strings for his daughter… I thought I'd completely die."

"And then?"

"I didn't flinch. Thanked him kindly, but firmly declined the offer. Returned to Rotterdam a day earlier than I had planned. That same Monday I called the School of Photography to obtain some information. I registered for the application procedure. And when I was accepted I quit medicine. The rest is history."

"That was probably a huge shock to your parents…"

"Oh yes, *especially* when I just broke the news. You should have seen it: my father yelling, my mom crying. And I was doing both and even slammed doors. I was called reckless and completely deranged for just throwing away such a promising future."

"Still, it looks like they've forgiven you in the meantime."

I shrugged. "Oh sure. They've accepted it now. But what else can they do?" I mumbled cynically.

"You, on the other hand, have not forgiven them yet. Have you, Lente?" asked Raphaël.

I jumped up. At least that was the plan. But everything is different when dealing with a vampire. They detect the slightest movements of your muscles. And in the shortest time possible they anticipate it, always inconspicuous to the outside world.

He held on to my hand and lower arm. And they remained in his grip until I calmed down. When I felt that it had taken long enough, I politely asked smiling: "May I please be excused to the restroom?"

His reaction was a kiss on my cheek. He whispered: "I'm proud of you. Your career switch was a wise decision."

## 60

GOLDEN CITY

Almost two weeks later. And thirteen days older. But that much the wiser? I
did not know. I really did not know... Fact was though, that I was alone with
him again. This time at his new residence, Prague. It could not be helped, his
departure from the Netherlands had come much too soon: two days after my
father's birthday. And not knowing how much time we would still have
together, we did everything we could to make the circumstances suit our
needs.

The decision had come so easily: in a matter of minutes we had picked a date.
That same weekend, together with him behind my computer, I had booked a
flight and made reservations for a bed at a hostel. Just like a couple of spoiled
teenagers.

Of course, Claire had immediately come up with a response along the lines of
"aren't you getting a little too carried away with this?" But how could she
possibly know that my contact with Raphaël went further than those four
days of dating that she had been a witness to – after all, I had already spent
an entire week with him in London...

Actually, I think my parents should have been the ones to raise that
comment of Claire's. Then I might have even taken it into consideration.
Maybe.

But all that I could expect from them was excitement. Their rebellious
daughter had captured the interest of a proper, successful young man! Oh the
joy. I wondered whether a blind horse could see more then they could...

By the way, my mother had been of use regarding one little issue. In the past,
she had worked for an ear nose throat doctor and so I asked for her advice.
Hypothetically, for a friend that suffered from hypersensitivity to sound. She
asked what the cause for the 'hyperacusis' of this friend was. An accident, I
said. And then she had told me that this friend's best bet was to go to an
audiologist to be custom fitted with ear plugs with specialized filters. I had
gone immediately that same day and was injected with a warm paste into my
ears that, once cooled down and hardened, would serve as the molds for two
ingenious solutions to my problem... Just in time before my departure, the
silicone earplugs had been ready for collection. From that moment on I never
left the house without those things within reach in the pocket of my pants, in
case I needed them.

And that was how I came to be wandering this city as a glorified tourist for
almost a week now. It goes without saying that I only did that during the

daytime and I mainly stuck to places where there were plenty of other people to be found. As Raphaël had specifically instructed me to do...

Prague. The city of which so many said you had to see once in your life. Firstly, during the hours that Raphaël slept, I had leisurely taken a couple of trams. Simply to get an overview. Line 11 to the concrete jungle of Spořilov in the south. Line 17 that took me, past former hubs of heavy industry and the houses that were held together by long-overdue maintenance, from Holešovice to Sídliště Ďáblice in the northeast, and number 22, across lavishly built terraces and through tree-lined streets to the sleepy district of Bílá Hora in the far west. And each time, after the tram had performed its compulsory loop that the tracks made at each destination, I got on again after a brief stop, to let myself be driven back to the center of the city.

Prague. The word associations piled themselves up. Gothic, baroque, cubism, Jugendstil. Art, classical music, culture and more art.
I explored Jozefov, the Jewish district with all its antique book stores, the synagogues, cemeteries and hordes of tourists. I wandered through Staré Město, the Old Town: a maze of winding cobblestone streets with the oh so characteristic, old-fashioned lanterns on walls of houses plastered in different colors. Staré Město, with its surprising courtyards and its dead-end or connecting alleyways. And the many churches, cafés and souvenir shops, and again the hordes of tourists...
I had adapted my biorhythm to Raphaël's as much as possible from day one and that turned out to be good for my work as well. Walking across the Charles Bridge with your camera at the crack of dawn, for example, had the advantage of actually getting to see the bridge, instead of just a crowd of people driven by commerce. In this way I also managed to capture the Wenceslas Square without getting trampled by drunk Scandinavians. And to be among the first to enter the St. Vitus Cathedral on the Prague Castle grounds, without having to wait in long queues...

In this city, around every corner, behind each gate, a new European deja vu lay waiting. That German '70s *Derrick* vibe you got when you passed through one of those arching doorways in a small restaurant, for example. Artistic or intentionally kitschy murals on the side of some houses that brought back memories of Austria. Colossal historical buildings in the center, with a grandeur that was reminiscent of Paris... Prague was spectacular. Prague was beautiful. But the wow factor was missing and that feeling of displacement that had been gnawing at me, ever since the first moment that I wandered the streets here by myself, kept rearing its ugly head. And the locals certainly did not help me get rid of it. For example, I once memorized a question by heart with great effort, using a Czech travel dictionary, in order to use it at some booth or another. But once I stood there, uttering those

Czech words at the height of my concentration, my efforts were mercilessly chastised with a post-communistic lack of interest and service that you had read about at some point, but never really believed existed. And had you barely gotten over that shock, then you were immediately met by the alienating experience of the entire staff of a touristic attraction suddenly deciding that they could not speak a word about the border, even though you had been as polite as possible in talking with them...

But right when I had convinced myself that the Prague residents were not very friendly, that girl suddenly came walking towards me at the corner of the Karlova, full of sympathetic enthusiasm. She had recognized me from the day before, when I had struck up a conversation with her about the classical matinee concert for which she was handing out flyers. Just for her I had sat down in a richly decorated church in that street the next day around noon, to listen to evergreens from the baroque and romantic era. Friendships had started in stranger situations, had they not? And should her smile unexpectedly turn out to merely be evidence of her extraordinary marketing talent after all... she still had deserved to... anyway, whatever, she seemed nice.

And this was how Prague kept throwing me a curveball.

So did Raphaël, come to think of it. You should be able to expect to know where you stood with him by now, that you would have a picture of what he was all about. But each time, just when you thought you were beginning to understand him, something unexpected happened and you were sidetracked, emotions and all.

The first evening, for example, he had come to the airport to pick me up. That experience of 'finally', when we leapt into each other's arms had been indescribable, and the city that we drove into had seemed so enchanting from the inside of the car, with all those lights in the dark... And the following morning, when he had brought me from the hostel to his place, each lane, every boulevard had literally vibrated with exciting anticipation. And the lead-gray paving stones of Náprstkova Street looked so nostalgic and those ochre-yellow and white plastered houses so authentic and not to mention that Jugendstil building that Raphaël lived in... much more stately than what I could tell from the internet! And then that stucco with those green-cream-golden floral murals at the entrance, that old-fashioned elevator in that cage construction at the center of the stairwell and – I really needed to pace myself with taking in all these new impressions, otherwise I was going to be completely useless for the rest of the day!

At the layout of his apartment I did have to chuckle a little bit. Those dark-brown, wine-red and eggplant accents and those, still a little bare, white walls gave me flashbacks of his London home. But my euphoric mood came to a definitive end when I stepped into the bedroom during my exploratory tour. Because on the wall on the right side of his bed hung an art poster, large and impossible to ignore. Of the same artist as the poster that was in his bedroom in London. What was it with Raphaël's obsession with that Klimt fellow? And why did it just have to be *The Kiss*? It was not like I needed to have that thing within my field of vision on a daily basis to know what it looked like. Everyone knew that image of that man, strong and overpowering, right behind that woman on her knees, with his flamboyant robe draped entirely around her... and did not everyone have an issue with the impossible position in which the head of the woman was forced by his mouth on her jaw or her neck, or who knows where? Or was I the only person whom it made feel uncomfortable? And why did my boyfriend take this particular moment to come and stand so close behind me? He placed his arms around me, folded his hands together on my belly and slowly pulled me towards him. He tried to kiss me, but I turned away from his lips. I got out of his embrace, walked to the window and leaned my behind against the radiator.

With a grumpy head motion I nodded towards the opposite end of the room. "May I ask you why you have hung that poster there?"

"But of course, my love," he replied, and what followed was an elaborate story, first in the form of a series of generalities with which he expressed his appreciation for Gustav Klimt. The successes that he already had acquired at a young age were mentioned, the fluid line play in his work, his frequent use of pure gold for the coloring of his paintings. And not to forget, the mark that this artist had made on the worldwide Jugendstil movement... There was something about Raphaël. His speech had gradually begun to speed up and every last word in the sentences that he spoke, was articulated with a pronounced delay. The things that came out of his mouth progressively took on the characteristics of a carefully recited monologue and in that light he began to make use of the bedroom as well: as though it was a theater, the stage of a theater... With thoughtful steps the man moved through the room. Past the foot end of the bed and back, passing right in front of me, sometimes provocatively close. After a while he stood still and stirred the air that was right in front of his face with a gracious, upward motion, as though he was trying to capture the bouquet of a glass of fine wine. He closed his eyes and said: "Hmmm, the carnal spirit of Klimt, the sensuality of *The Kiss*... Did you know, *chérie,* that his work was dismissed as disgraceful pornography by many at the time?"

I remained silent.

"But, of course, such allegations never arise without the help of a great deal of eisegesis. Wouldn't you say?"

I crossed my arms.

"Thank goodness, the two of us know better, right, Lente? Jumping to conclusions is something we have greatly outgrown."

I shrugged carelessly.

"After all, we know the depth of sentiments that are inextricably linked with the art of painting or music," he said, now looking at me directly. "Or with something like: lavender…"

And then came the thing that I so had not been waiting for: the oration about the sense and nonsense of holding on to the past, delivered with possibly even more fluctuations in volume and pitch than in the previous minutes.

I got up. Stupid radiator, my butt had become completely numb. It was high time to start walking and so I did, into the living room and heading for the hallway. But he followed in my footsteps, whispering closely to my ear about art posters of Klimt in London bedrooms, about idyllic scenes of families gone by… and I, I had even tried to reach the apartment door, despite the fact that such an attempt at getting away was obviously doomed to fail.

Leaning expressionlessly against the doorpost was all that he needed to do to stop me. A triumphant amusement shone through his eyes: "What's the matter, Lente? Doesn't the way in which I have come to regard my present meet your approval?"

Again I raised my shoulders.

But suddenly the man did change his stance.

"Sweetheart," he sighed, "if anything, please think of this as self-ridicule. The Kiss… it's my way to take the edge off our situation. And that's exactly why this painting means so much to me."

The sense of relief that came over me…! This was not a vampire talking here anymore. This was my boyfriend, this was Raphaël. He was back! I stepped towards him and fell into his embrace.

"Why would you do that?" I gasped.

For a moment he held me at an arm's length distance and looked at me questioningly.

"Well, it's just that you can be really scary sometimes," I explained, "then it seems as if you are no longer yourself, as if a whole different person comes out who is completely beyond reason, and then I totally clam up and I don't understand where it's coming from, or… how can such a thing be, my dear??"

We sat down.

"That is not so easy to put into words," he said, as he ran his hand through his hair.

"But you do understand what I'm talking about? You're entirely present when it happens?"

"Why wouldn't I be? I don't suffer from dissociative identity disorder or anything," he said with a crooked smile.

No, but that *was* precisely what it looked like.

"Trust me, a couple of minutes ago I was just as much myself as I am now."

"Raph, I'm not too sure… it happened with Lucas sometimes as well. In that park, for example. But he had a very clear objective to behave like that – "

"– Lucas doesn't do anything without an objective," he cut me short. But he moved beyond his annoyance immediately and said: "Darling, listen. What just happened, will most likely occur more often. That hunting instinct of ours simply gets triggered sometimes."

"But how? What causes it, then?"

"It could have been anything. The change in your scent, something in your posture or the tone in which you spoke…"

I stared at the bare, white surface that the wall in front of us formed. "So I am the problem," I concluded.

"Not entirely."

He reached out his hand. I sat down against him.

"Things will always be different between us."

"I know that…" I mumbled.

"You will always have to take into account that there's a dominant, unpredictable beast within me."

I was examining a peeling cuticle on my thumb. I began to pick at it.

"Still, I hope that you will never forget one thing: I adore you. I love you, with all my heart and with all my soul."

"Which one of us is the pilot, then, and which that boy?" I asked cynically.

"Pardon me?"

"Haven't you heard of that joke? The one with the pilot who asks a boy if he likes to fly. The boy says yes, as any kid would. The pilot goes: Alright, then I'll catch some for you later."

"I understand that you're trying to communicate something in a metaphorical sense with this. But what, exactly, is not clear to me," he said.

"Never mind. It's not that important."

For a while we just sat there. Then I broke the silence: "That poster, you know… The Kiss. I think I better get to terms with that. So if you'd like to leave it there, I'm okay with it."

"That's surprising…"

"Yeah, but I have one condition. I want you to buy a painting for this spot before the end of the week." Defiantly I pointed at the wall in front of us, "…and you will let *me* pick that painting."

He got up, walked over to the dining table and created some order in a stack of magazines. Without making eye contact he said: "That doesn't sound unreasonable."

## 61

MIND GAMES

Just when I thought I had caught him by surprise, did he almost make *me* roll off my chair! Because it really had not been more than a spur of the moment, that idea about that painting. Therefore, I had all but expected for him to comply with my demand...

But the following morning we actually did walk into the Parnas Gallery in a little courtyard in the Old Town. I had come across it on my first wandering through Staré Město. It was a gallery in which solely the work of the surrealist Viktor Safonkin was sold. Oh, how I had reveled in that moment of power – be it genuine or fake, that did not matter for now – when I had dragged my feet for as long as possible in choosing between the two works of Safonkin that spoke to me the most. And when Raphaël had shown out the supplier a day later and plopped down on the couch beside me, I had experienced a kick that I had never felt before. Whether he liked it or not – for the time being, the image of *Branding of Sins* that was hanging in front of us right now would invade his mind on a daily basis. Curious as to how it would affect his conscience, whether he would get the same unsettling feeling as I did, when looking at that grotesquely built blue collar worker so prominent in the foreground of the painting. With his bare chest, military-green pants with belt loops from which tools hung and black knee-high rain boots on his feet, the man dominated the entire canvas. His working stance guided you, through a clever use of perspective, from proximal left to right center. In the background you could see the burning oven, with above it fuming clouds of smoke and fluttering birdlike figures, and its function in the painting was pretty obvious, but the screeching, disorderly pile of hideous creatures on the right, and the in both color and detail depicted blind panic that reigned there unequivocally, caught most of your attention. The creatures scrambled to get themselves to safety. Away from the iron poker in the coal shovel-sized hands of the worker. Away from the Cross of Christ at the tip of that poker, that red hot and mercilessly left its searing brand on the skin of every already-doomed creature on top of the giant pile....

Raphaël nodded slowly, as he looked at the painting. With a voice that did not give away any emotion he said: "You have a good eye for art."

"Thank you," I said in an equally neutral tone.

The gold-colored, heavily carved frame around the 40x50 inch-sized canvas matched this interior well, I thought. A little Baroque, a nice contrast against the completely whitewashed walls.

The only thing that was left for us to do was to vacuum and get rid of that cobweb up there on the right, in the corner of the ceiling. When I spoke that thought out loud he stood up right away. "Allow me," he said. He took off his shoes and walked towards the wall. When he got there he stretched out his left arm upward. But being six feet tall was nowhere near enough to reach the ceiling.

"Shall I grab a chair?" I asked. The man answered me with a quick glance over his shoulder. Then he pulled up his right leg – what on earth was he doing now? – to then place his shin against the wall. What happened next had a level of surrealism many times higher than the artist Safonkin could ever put in his paintings. His right arm reached upwards and with his fingers spread he lay his hand onto the vertical surface, a little higher than his other hand. Then his left leg took off from the floor and his entire body moved, without aids of any kind, slowly upwards. The stealthy movements of an animal, of a leopard, no, an iguana!

My throat cramped up and things began to tingle around my mouth...

Within a few seconds the vampire had reached the corner above the TV. He quickly grabbed the cobweb and turned himself around. Upside down he crawled downwards, placed his hands on the floor and after that his feet. As he got up he beat some concrete dust off his fingers that had ended up beneath the painting during the mounting procedure.

"Now we just need to vacuum a little and then we're done," he said.

I did not respond, sat on the couch, petrified, and all I could do was feel how the tightness in my face and throat expanded to my chest and hands and franticly try to figure out how the heck I was going to get rid of that cramp.

Raphaël sat down next to me. "You're hyperventilating. Does that happen more often?" he asked.

With eyes wide open I stared at him.

"You know what you can do about that. Don't you?"

I nodded, but was not able to help myself.

He waited another moment, but then went into action. "Don't be scared," he said and I thought: a little late to offer such a statement, but I did not fight back when he took both my hands and made them cover my mouth and nose. Obediently I breathed my own carbon dioxide in and out, as long as it took for me to calm down.

Still a little shakily I removed my hands from my face and slowly sat back. "Freak," I mumbled.

"Yeah, that's me."

I wanted to pull him in and he did give me a kiss, but a make out session was not going to happen. "A generously sized cup of coffee seems healthier for you than experiencing more emotions," he said. "Come, let's go downstairs."

And a few minutes later we were sitting modestly across from each other at a table in the café that was located on the ground floor of the apartment building.

It had been so true what he had said. Emotionally speaking, I had literally gone through the wringer: first there was that burning desire, then the euphoria, followed by anxiety, fear and intense relief, infatuation, sardonic feelings of triumph and then back to the fear and, finally, those butterflies in my stomach again... was this even normal? So much in such a small amount of time and so all over the place? Or did I just have to officially admit that I was completely messed up in the head?

Thankfully, there was one comfort: every once in a while I caught even Raphaël at being insecure... One morning, for instance, at the hostel and heading for my breakfast, I was approached by a girl. She said that a package was waiting at the reception desk that was addressed to me and when I did not see a sender listed on the bubble envelope that was sealed with care and generous amounts of tape, my question has been who had left it there. But that was something that nobody in the office could tell me anything about. The staff had just started the day shift, and apparently this did not belong to the type of affairs that colleagues discuss with one another during a transfer. Shrugging I had then left for the breakfast room and there I sat down to open the thing. To my surprise there were two earrings inside. In a box lined with black velvet... And they were nice earrings, too: purple smooth-polished crystals, probably gemstones, surrounded by silver in artfully curled filigree patterns. I knew for sure that it was real silver, because you could see the mark on the backside.

Naturally, after the meal I had immediately phoned my boyfriend to thank him for something so sweet and beautiful, but to my astonishment he said that he did not know what I was talking about. And then a bit of a mystery was born...

Perhaps a mistake had been made and someone had thought they had heard my name, when a different name was provided. And even though the people of the hostel had insisted that the package had really been addressed to me, I had tucked the earrings away in a safe place, just in case. Should the rightful recipient show up anyway, I would be able to hand them over to her properly. If only Raphaël had accepted that as well. Then I would have forgotten the incident that same day. But he did not give me any chance to that: the following days he wondered on several occasions who could have gifted me such a present... something he probably would have preferred to have given to me himself, although I never heard him say that last part out loud, of course.

This was not the first time that Raphaël did not know how to deal with a situation. Like when I suggested to him one day to go the Mozart Museum together at Villa Bertramka. Immediately he had asked mockingly: "Mozart, Lente? I didn't know that that held your interest."

"Oh, It doesn't," I had said in a light-hearted tone, "But what I *do* have a thing for is young, anonymous early-eighteenth century architects and their works."

He had then turned his head away with that typical 'I *should* have seen this coming' look on his face. Reluctantly he said: "I see you have managed to make the connection."

I batted my long eyelashes all cutesy.

"My compliments," he said. "But if you're expecting to find what I have built at that time, I'm afraid you'll be sorely disappointed."

"Yeah yeah, a lot has changed since 1700. I'm not stupid. I have read more about Bertramka than you think, you know," I defended myself.

He huffed in derision. "The blessings of the internet..."

But I had won him over. Finally. He was going to go with me to Villa Bertramka. Although I had to throw in quite a bit of my feminine charms to get him to that point.

"I am not responsible for this," said Raphaël explicitly, in response to my disdainful facial expression. We had just walked into the second chamber on our tour through the museum and were standing in the former bedroom of Mozart. Hanging from the ceiling were the original beams – which was pretty special of course – only, practically every square inch of those beams were decorated with painted grape, pear and leaf patterns in such a voluptuous way that I could barely hold my laughter. Naturally, I made him jump through hoops to convince me that the decorations in question had been applied not right after its construction, but only until a few years later. In that same teasing mood I had then made fun of his mistake concerning the height of the door to the adjoining room. You see, it had not been more than five feet eleven or six feet at most, and how was that even possible during a time in which the aristocrats walked around with those towering wigs? And there he had seen his chance. In an even tone he had asked me about the point of wearing wigs in a country house. Because surely I knew that the function of a country home was basically equivalent to what was now called a farm? And that was how he had driven me back into my corner.

Half an hour later we were sitting on a patio in the lee of the building, him in the shade beneath a parasol and I just in the pleasant warmth of the morning sun.

"Is there really that little you recognize from way back when?" I asked. I glanced at the soft yellow and white painted facade. Against it, there were two staircases that came together from the left and the right on the first floor and in that way provided access to a veranda.

He nodded. "Everything has changed here. Even the surrounding area. At the time this was situated far away from the city. And these trees weren't here yet. Only the rolling landscape, I do remember that," said Raphaël. "The way in which it slopes upwards here on the right, behind the villa... and slopes downwards again over there..." With his hand in the air in front of him he traced the path of the cobble stone road towards the gate, from which an old Ford Escort just entered the grounds at quite the speed. The car stopped right in front of the main entrance. There was a young couple in it, probably married. The man got out. Upon first impression I had felt some irritation over his reckless driving style, but my annoyance made way for surprise when, on his way to a side entrance of the building, he suddenly slowed down as he walked past our table. I knew him! And he had recognized me as well.

"Hey, what a coincidence seeing you here," he said excitedly. "Now I wish I had my day planner on me."

"Petr! What are you doing here?" I called out.

"Oh, just picking up a suit," he replied, and he pointed at the door on the ground level of the building. "Got a performance at a hotel this afternoon." He looked quizzically from me to Raphaël and back to me again. "I see you're here with someone...?"

"Yes, this is my boyfriend," I said. But before I could introduce him to the man properly, without taking the trouble to get up or reach out a hand, Raphaël said: "Kazimír La Duca."

"Nice to meet you..." Petr said.

A deep, almost inaudible growl escaped Raphaël's throat. He was probably wondering... a complete stranger, out of nowhere, who seemed to know me... Quickly I therefore explained: "Petr and I have met at that matinee concert in the Saint Clemens Church earlier this week. Didn't I tell you about that?"

"No, you didn't."

"Oh, well, in any case, Petr is a violinist and we ended up talking after his performance and now I'm going to take photos of him for his website soon," I said in one single breath.

"Well, look at that," my boyfriend said. He turned his head to a point somewhere to the side of us and waited silently until we were done chatting and the violinist got ready to do what he had come here to do.

Right before he left, Petr came and stood with us for a little longer. He said: "Say, Lente, I'm performing tonight with a musical theater company at the Dvořák Museum. If the two of you want to come and watch..."

I took a quick glance at Raphaël. But he still kept his eyes fixed on something else.

"Sounds interesting," I then said, while I tried my best to not sound *too* enthusiastic.

## 62

COMPETITION


Villa Amerika, no idea why it was called that way and whether it had always had that name. But it was unmistakable that this townhouse was from the Baroque, it may even have been built around the same time as Villa Bertramka. The dark-pink stucco work on the exterior walls with the brightly clashing contrast of wide, ornamented white paneling, and the heavily decorated stone carvings, shaped like vases, fruit or flower patterns and small heads that were stuck to the front facade, just screamed in your face. Still, there was something about this building. It looked a little like an old-fashioned dollhouse, so square and compact-sized, and with that elegant, soft-red roof on top... *and* it was, in my opinion, beautifully restored to its original state. This observation, however, I did not say out loud for now. Because the chance that a sneering or an all-knowing comment would come as a reaction from my lover was a bit too high this evening... he was in a somewhat strange mood, ever since the end of the morning.

On our way home from Bertramka I had been meaning to discuss whether or not we would accept Petr's invitation, as that concert had seemed interesting to me. And initially Raphaël had not even responded dismissively. But oh, beneath the skin... when, once we got home, he had walked to the window with his hands behind his back and then revisited the subject one more time, contemplating. He said: "The theater project *Wonderful Dvořák*... hmmm, a completely different approach to the work of such a composer, huh. Fun too, with those historical costumes... It's very popular with the tourists, or so I've heard."

He turned around and sat down on the window ledge. "I have heard good things about the musical level. Although, I'm not too sure about the acting skills of the musicians, but oh well..."

"But oh well...?" I repeated as I raised my eyebrows.

With an aloof movement he crossed his legs.

"Well – what are you getting at?" I asked.

"I notice that you find me arrogant."

"You do sound a tad bit pretentious, yes."

"In that case, I apologize, as that was not my intention. I'm just trying to keep you from getting disappointed. Such a combination of artistic disciplines... it happens sometimes that one overreaches with that. With the result of *either* the singing *or* the acting suffering."

"But aren't I capable of judging something like that for myself?"

He put his hands in his pockets.

"Look, if you're not interested in going, there's nothing I can do about that," I continued. "Then I'll just go by myself. I have no problem entertaining myself and, on top of that, that museum is in the same street as my hostel. So I can easily get there…"

With an appeasing "just wait a minute, sweetheart" Raphaël then came towards me. He looked at me endeared, stroked my cheek and said that this time I had really misinterpreted him. Because, how *could* I even think that he was not interested in spending an evening with me? No, he was going to join me, he *wanted* to come with. Happily, even…

After this little tiff it should have come as no surprise to me that our visit to Villa Amerika turned out to be somewhat of a special experience.

As I feasted my eyes on all the novelty and splendor that this museum displayed, my partner seemed to not be able to keep his eyes off me. Not that anyone noticed. Well, except for me… Because everywhere I went, there he was within my field of vision, or should I say, I within his. In the garden, beautifully styled in baroque, he was kicking at some rocks on the pebble terrace, while I inquisitively walked up to a statue and moved among the flaunting crowd thereafter. When I walked back into the entrance hall of the museum a few minutes later, he joined me instinctively and at a certain point it even looked as though his eyes followed my gaze across the people that trickled in and smilingly accepted the drinks that were offered to them by the staff… But the way in which he watched as I shifted through the CD bins, in search of an appropriate souvenir for my parents, that really put the icing on the cake. And then, all the time, there was that hand of his, that had consistently held my hand on the way from the hostel, that rested softly on my hips as I met a couple of American Dvořák fanatics and initiated a lively conversation with them. Perhaps he might receive a certain amount of admiration from them because of his independent and interesting personality, but he was starting to get on my nerves with him following my every move… So I was relieved to be able to lock myself in the bathroom before the start of the concert.

However, as soon as all of us – how many guests were there anyway, fifty or so? – had found a seat in the music parlor, his arm had lain over my shoulders again and his cold fingers caressed the skin of my neck. I tried to ignore him and stared at the mythological frescoes bordered with gold leaf on the ceiling. But the fingers in my neck caught my attention once more when they froze as the artists entered the stage and Petr threw us a look of recognition with his sympathetic smile.

It was probably pointless to ask, but yet I would love to have known what the issue with him was. Did Raphaël really have that much of a reason to fear this man? Sure, Petr was a gifted musician and he really shone during his violin solos. The standing ovation that he received after *Romance in F minor* was more than well-deserved. But he probably did not have the slightest idea on how to wield the bow of a viola da gamba.

On top of that, he was in a relationship – we had both seen the woman in question in his car – and he even was of the *upside-down egg* type: in every city, I had once discovered, you could discern specific facial features that you regularly saw in random people on the street. Differences could even be found between the crowd in Rotterdam and Amsterdam, but even more so when you crossed the border and were met with, in this case, Bohemian genetic influences. In Prague for example, there were these men, often with light colored hair and blue or green eyes, who had those distinctively shaped heads: wide and as round as a bullet at the top and strikingly narrow tapered towards the chin. Just like an egg that was half tilted backwardly placed on top of a neck. And Petr was one of those men. A somewhat receding hairline also belonged to this type. And to top it off with those studious glasses that he wore… was he really supposed to be competition? I did not see it. Not in any way, shape or form. Petr, with his well-tempered, uncomplicated character and that warm demeanor.

No, take my boyfriend. He was simply being wildly attractive again this Saturday morning, with that mysterious force field of detachment fully operational. How he sat there at that eatery on Wenceslas Square… The way in which he first kept his eyes unperturbedly fixed on the screen of his laptop for a while, subsequently took a sip of coffee and then let a brief, observing glance pass his surroundings, without letting those surroundings in… He was wearing an old pair of jeans and a shirt made of white Indian cotton and that, combined with that nonchalant five o'clock shadow! I could not imagine that there were women out there who would not fall head over heels for him. Quickly I checked my hair and make-up in the reflection of the window and entered the restaurant. Raphaël's facial expression changed as soon as he noticed me. His eyes lit up and he greeted me by getting up from his chair and embracing me.

"What were you doing?" I asked. I sat down beside him.

"Work. I'm gathering some information." He turned his laptop a little toward me. On the screen was a piece of text in Czech with above it the words: *Letohrádek Královny Anny.*

"Right…" I mumbled.

"Have you ever heard of Queen Anne's Summer Palace, or the Belvedere? It's situated in the Royal Gardens."

"No."

"Tram 22 passes right by it, when you go to Bílá Hora. The next stop is in front of the entrance of the Castle."

"Yes, wait, isn't that that rectangular thing? Oddly shaped wavy, green roof, column lined corridors on the ground level…"

"That's right." He googled an image of the structure and showed it to me.

"And you're going to restore it?"

"No," he said decidedly, "I have the privilege of advising on the 'masonry' part of it."

He caught the attention of a waiter and asked me if I had already eaten breakfast. When I nodded 'yes' he ordered what I always drank around this time.

I furrowed my eyebrows. "Are you sincerely happy with this commission, or...?"

"Oh, sure I am. It's just that I wonder whether they have made the right choice with this person."

"This person?"

Raphaël turned off the computer and put it away in his bag. "The position of chief architect. That has been given to, how should I put it... someone who, as we speak, is causing exceptional furor with his work."

"Right... and what's so bad about that?"

He inhaled sharply. "The fact that having a fast-track career doesn't cut it with a project of this caliber, no matter how phenomenal your talent may be."

"Okay... but what other qualities does a chief architect need to have?"

"Natural commanding authority combined with extensive experience. And I seriously question whether this person possesses that to a sufficient degree. The man has only recently entered the scene." He shrugged. "But whether it is my place to say something about that...?"

I took a sip of the coffee that had just been placed in front of me. I gave it some thought and then asked: "What if you are right about this. What could happen then?"

"Then this architect can count on people to take him for a ride. And then it's going to be more like cleaning up messes than building something beautiful for him. It has already happened so many times in this city – historical buildings, ruined by carelessness and a pitiful lack of coordination. And it is the Belvedere that we're talking about here... a jewel of a building that dates from the year 1563. It is the most spectacular example stemming from the Italian Renaissance in this city, or rather Bohemia as a whole. You can find Florentine, Venetian and even Roman elements in it..."

"And I take it that you have a doomsday scenario for this project drawn up already?"

"That, I do."

"Fire away." I tried to suppress a sigh.

"A motley crew that call themselves plasterers will be unleashed on an exterior wall," he mocked. "All local workers, of course, because that is cheaper. And these types then somehow seem to manage to each smear a different version of the same color on the exact same surface. With the result that the final product displays all shades of, let's say, white that are available at a modern-day paint shop. Sea shell-white, winter mood-white, cream-white... each plasterer with his own little blend. So what is going to happen? That you'll see those wonderful, subtle differences in nuances at every five yards, varying in thickness too, if we're lucky. And then you can retrace to the exact inch where one's personal signature ends and where the other's begins."

"I have never noticed something like that," I said.

"That's because you're a layperson – with all due respect – but stucco work is a skilled craft. It's something that you agree upon together, it demands coordination, which includes using the right ingredients in the right proportions... If you want that special yellow color, just to name something, then you make sure that curcuma is flown in from India if necessary," he said grimly.

"Aren't you stressing about this a little *too* much?"

"There has to be someone who cares about this stuff." He looked away and stared out of the window, where more and more people were slowly beginning to appear in the street, running early errands or on their way out for breakfast. For a brief moment he reminded me of a pouting child...

I grabbed his hand to caress it softly; a better idea, I thought, than empathetically shaking my head. "And what other disasters are lurking around the corner with this project?" I asked.

"Poor planning. Some people avoid it like the plague, but time management really is as old as the road to Rome. Without it the railway network would be chaos. Choreographies succeed or fail with it and for restoration projects it is no different. Without planning you end up losing truckloads of money. But here..."Again a derisive gesture.

I objected: "That is not limited to the Czech Republic, you know. When I watch those TV shows on house renovations I constantly see things going wrong."

"Yes, but here things go wrong a little more often than, for example, in England. I wonder whether they have ever even heard of drawing up master plans."

"Perhaps they think other things are more important. Just look at what you were saying about the fifties and sixties a few months ago."

Raphaël looked confused.

"Well. Nowadays people miserably complain about how things were renovated in those years. Now you run into all sorts of sloppily finished details that were done in that period, but at the time they were simply seen as efficient. Functionality was more important than the esthetics in the sixties. Working according to that trend... you have experienced that firsthand. So why can't a lack of organization be the tendency here? Maybe the Czech feel comfortable with that. I think they don't even know any better. Just like those guys in the sixties..."

He pursed his lips and shook his head. "The fact that something is the status quo somewhere does not mean that you have to give in to it. Do you know the kind of damage that can be done with shoddy restoration work? The *singing fountain* that the Belvedere looks out onto used to be a true marvel, because of the resonating plates you could hear the sound of bells instead of splashing water. Now, however, after some moron or another has taken out their ignorance on it, you have to practically lie upside-down to still catch a glimpse of the original sound. A unique piece of history, lost forever."

"Are you watching your blood pressure, dear?"

A second or two, three it was silent. Then a grin appeared across his face and he replied: "I'll keep it in mind, darling." He leaned over to give me a kiss.

"An inexperienced chief architect then…" I pondered. "How old is he, anyway?"

"Somewhere in his early forties."

"Ouch, only ten years older than you… that must sting," I said sarcastically.

"But take heart, babe. In a year or four, five your star will be on the rise again. Then it will be your turn to be praised and the government will throw as many problem cases as you can devour your way."

I evaded a prod by Raphaël's elbow and got up. "Gotta use the restroom," I said.

Arrived at the toilets and therefore alone with my thoughts for a bit, I suddenly realized the truth in what I had just said. This really was his life in a nutshell: move every ten years or so and try to rebuild a career all the way from the bottom. Time and time again enter the workforce as that nameless newcomer – most likely with a made-up or real resume, cause I was sure he would have connections or tricks for that, but still… And then hope that you gain enough recognition within a reasonable number of years for people to entrust you with moderately interesting assignments again. But until that time… It was quite sad, actually. No wonder he reacted that way to his competitor just now.

Once returned to him I asked: "There's one thing I'm still curious about: writing such a report, how long does that take you?"

"Fifteen, twenty minutes."

"Poor computer… your typing speed must take up a great deal of internal memory."

"More like: poor vampire. How many even faster computers I have owned… I've long lost count," he grinned with a hand gesture towards his bag. "But now for something different, Lente. What I've been wondering for a while now is how much you charge when someone buys one single photo off of you?"

I answered without thinking: "Oh, a Dollar or ninety. Unless someone wants to do more with it, like purchase the publishing or copyrights… why?"

"Because I still owe you 450 then. I had asked you to take five photo's at Keukenhof Castle the other day, didn't I? Or were there six?" he asked in a casual tone.

Shit. Here we go again.

"Would you forget about that money," I said under my breath.

What was up with that, him coming up with those *help Lente get through the winter* campaigns all the time? Seemingly reading my mind he remarked: "Don't think of this a favor. This is purely business."

"No, it *is* a favor. But one from me to you."

Raphaël purposefully took this time to think about this. He changed his posture a couple of times and finally sat back with his hands folded across his belly. Then he expressed his thoughts using carefully selected words: "The fact that you gift me no less than five professional photos is no small matter. Thank you for that generous offer. But that creates a somewhat embarrassing situation for me the next time I want to call on you."

I had difficulty not to burst into laughter. As soberly as I could I assured him that it was not necessary to take these kind of favors between friends that seriously, and that I loved to help him out. Whenever possible. At any time.

"Are you sure? Cause I don't want you to, uh..." he said a little hesitantly.

"I am sure."

"Be that as it may, I won't accept any more favors from you when it comes to this. After all, you are a professional," he stated in a decided tone.

"We'll see, okay?"

A satisfied smile danced around his lips.

A few silent minutes passed by, minutes filled with loving gazes and hands holding hands and fingers caressing thighs.

"... Lente?" Raphaël asked after a while.

"Yes, Kazimír..." I answered in the same tone.

"The Belvedere is only partially encased in scaffolding. I'd like to take advantage of that and have some details documented on short notice. Would you be able to play a role in that? Provided we can come to an agreement on a fee that is acceptable to the both of us?"

"Uh, sure, if that helps you..."

- The idiot that I was!

"Shall we do that quickly first thing tomorrow morning then?"

I *should* have seen this coming!

I laid so much patience in my reply that it almost felt painful. "No, that's not possible," I said slowly. "That photo studio of Petr's friend is only available before eleven o'clock tomorrow. And it is the only day Petr has time off."

Surely, he could not have forgotten about this?

Raphaël's reaction sounded a little absentminded. "Petr... Oh yeah, that's right."

I order another cup of coffee. When it was served and the waiter was out of hearing range I asked: "How can I make it clear to you that it is in no way necessary to be jealous of him?"

My boyfriend sat up a little straighter in his chair. "You think I'm jealous?" he asked surprised. And he sounded sincere. But he was a showman.

"Don't tell me that you're trying to deny that."

"I am. If you must know, I am not jealous, I am concerned," he said curtly.

"Aha. Concerned... what for?" I asked.

"Lente, you have to realize that Prague is a completely different city from Rotterdam. You don't know the language, you know nothing about the mentality and customs of this place... sweetheart, I just don't want you to be misled and become, how should I put it, disappointed."

Good grief, what my father was lacking, he clearly had shiploads too much of. And this was not the first time. I had picked up on these sort of vibes on so many occasions before... it was high time to have a serious talk with him about this.

For now, however, I only said: "Listen. You can trust me. I am being careful, you know, especially when I'm in an unfamiliar environment. But I *am* going tomorrow."

"I was afraid you might say that."

In somewhat of a weary tone I then stated: "I am well aware of the fact that nothing is certain for us. Still, there is a chance that I will return to this city at some point, isn't there?"

"I should hope so," he replied with a weak smile.

"Do you see me sitting at home all the time then, with nothing to do?"

He shook his head, cautiously.

"Well then," I said. "Isn't it only logical for me in that case, to get myself into the habit of using my time productively here as well? Dearest, I would go insane if I didn't have that. I need work. Distraction."

"I realize that."

"Then do me a favor and don't be jealous of people whom I merely acquaint for professional purposes, okay?"

Reluctantly he said: "Alright." He got up, walked over to a waiter to pay the bill and then went to the toilets. In the meantime, I was getting myself ready to leave, rummaged through my bag and inspected my camera. After cleaning the lens I checked it again, looked through the viewfinder and aimed it outside, at Wenceslas Square with its people shopping and the cars and...
*Lucas!*

## 63

## GIRL POWER

He was standing on the other side of the one-way traffic that passed by. And the thing that I had been more or less anticipating for days, was happening right now... the vampire that I feared so much began to move and approached our restaurant determinedly.

While crossing the street Lucas preemptively began his greeting: "Lente, good morning," knowing that I could understand him easily right through the window pane, and then he stepped inside. He sat down at a table, at a certain distance from where I was.

From the corner of my eye I saw Raphaël coming. His face was like many days of thunder and fearing that he would go for his sire's throat in plain public I whispered in an urging tone: "Raph, keep walking! Don't go to him, come sit with me."

Thankfully, he followed my instructions and took a seat in the chair in which he had been sitting for the last hour. Under the table my hand searched his, but he did not respond to my touch.

We looked. And Lucas looked back. At me, in particular.

A waiter arrived, he ordered a glass of water. Then he picked up his cell phone. He punched in a number, my number. I answered, the connection was terminated by him and we spoke, supposedly into the phones by our ears.

"So this is how our paths cross once more... how are you?" he asked.

"I'm alright."

"It's been some time since I last visited Prague."

I didn't react.

"Speaking of this city – your lover is right, Lente. If I were you, I'd take his warnings to heart. Don't you remember that the two of us have talked about this once before: that you should be careful with whom you meet? You women get so easily hurt these days..."

That was all that Raphaël needed to hear. He pushed his chair back scraping loudly and stood up. "We don't have to listen to this kind of bullshit," he mumbled, and with a nod of his head he commanded me to follow him. I put away my phone, grabbed my bags and followed my boyfriend toward the exit of the restaurant. But we had to get past Lucas first. He had picked his table strategically and now he exploited that position by opening his mouth again, right when we walked by him. He said: "Lente, do you remember how the author of the Bible book Song of Songs described the neck of the girl that he loved? Wasn't it something like 'the tower of David'?"

I firmly took Raphaël by the arm and did not allow for him to slow his pace.

The moment that we opened the door and stepped outside I heard the voice of our enemy one more time: "I was actually a little curious about how those purple earrings of yours would look against the decor of *your* 'tower of David'... too bad you're not wearing them today."

Once more, halfway across the square, Raphaël was about to turn around, but yet again, I stopped him. "There's nothing you can do to him, this place is packed!" I said, and so we kept walking. Under these circumstances I thought it was safer for me to literally drop him off at the appointment that he had right now, to be a firsthand witness of how he was going to shake the hand of the chairman of the Chamber of Restoration Architecture, because otherwise...

Just before the elevator reached the second floor of the office building my boyfriend rubbed his forehead and said: "I'm well aware of the fact that my father is against our relationship, but what he did just now... I really don't understand, Lente. I cannot make any sense of it."

That evening, at his place, we were probably going to have a lengthy conversation about it. But even now, as I walked back to the big square alone, I could not stop the worrying. As hard as a millstone, it was winding and grinding and pulverizing all possible answers to my questions into a completely useless powder. It was true, I did not understand Lucas for the life of me. Normally he was always dead serious, but earlier... Such a strangely defiant fire had glowed in his eyes, something cheeky almost, although his mood had also not been the same as it was during that episode of horror in that park in London. And then there was that deal with those earrings. Had that really just been bullying or did it serve a specific purpose – could it possibly have even been a diversion? But a diversion from what? Or did his behavior perhaps have anything to do with... was he – no, there was no way that he could be a scout for the Vampire Community. All of this had seemed much too crude for that, much too publicly menacing. In my opinion, at least...

He had brought something up just now, something that him and I had apparently talked about at some point... about being careful and meeting new people – yes, in the Irish pub in Rotterdam! He had indeed told me, through Claire, that I had to watch out for myself... the strange thing was however, that back then it hadn't sounded like mocking at all. What I had taken from that utterance was, above all, his sincere concern. So that meant that something was not quite right, *either* back then, *or* today. Unless...?

No. Out of the question. Lucas could not be in love with me, that was completely impossible. He was a *monk*, for Pete's sake.

Bullying, intimidation, threat – sure, maybe. But infatuation?

Naturally, a brief argument between Raphaël and I had been inevitable. After what had happened he would have preferred to keep me as close to him as possible to keep who-knows-what from happening to me as soon as I would exit that office building. Which I, in turn, wanted to hear none of. Because no matter how dangerous going outside on my own could be, having to look over your shoulder a couple of times was still better than getting locked inside a golden cage, no matter how caring and well-intended that cage may have been. On top of that, I was of the opinion that as long I did not saunter into deserted areas and stayed indoors or close to him at night, the actual threat was mostly in our heads. After all, what could a vampire do in broad daylight, in streets filled with shoppers in a city almost bursting at the seams with tourists? So after our quick reconciliation and a kiss on his cheek, I left a helplessly staring Raphaël at the Chamber of Restoration Architecture and I went to play the tourist. Anything to bring the grinding thoughts to a halt. Do some normal stuff for a bit, because otherwise, I would go insane...

How lucky that even without a trained eye, you could pick out such an enormous wealth of interesting details in this photogenic city. So for starters, I went for a walk towards Staré Město, the Old Town. Onwards to picturesque and exuberant. Absinthe shops! A street with an entire row of those stores. Absinthe, the green fairy... Only legally available in the Netherlands since 2005, but the myths that had floated around it for so long had only intensified the allure of this liquor: supposedly, it would inspire elevated expressions of art, have a hallucinating effect and even incite murder. But to achieve such an effect it should contain a much higher concentration of thujone than it did nowadays, Adrian had once explained to me, because what you were buying these days was at least twenty five times less potent than the original version. Whoa, if there was anyone who should be walking through these streets alongside of me right now, it would be him: Gothic Dandy Adrian from Rotterdam...

Absinthe, green and mysterious. In large bottles, in small flasks, in bottles made of any color and shape under the sun and with for each brand a different, wildly creative label. Absinthe, straight up as a drink in a bottle or with an herb twig or even with an actual scorpion added. Oh, Adrian... And if he had been here now, I already knew what we would have done in the evening: shoot photos in a dark alleyway. Him wearing his creepy, ghostly white contact lenses and I tagging along, carrying a camera, tripod and flashlight. I had once experienced him during the day with those things in his eyes. We had gone to a supermarket together to see what the reactions of the people would be. In one word: hilarious.

You could just see it happening. That inner dialogue of people: "Huh? Those eyes, that *can't* be for real. No, he must be heading to a Halloween party or something. But... Halloween isn't until October, right? And it is nowhere near the evening and he doesn't even walk around in a matching costume – *huh?* What a creep..." Fantastic.

But Adrian was not here. And I felt alone... no, do not think about it! A sporting equipment store. The first one in a week. Or, at least, the first one that I noticed. Probably had to do with Adrian, who practiced downhill cross biking.

Antique shop. Silverware. Jewelry, watches, little spoons. Pretty. Expensive. And after the shopping streets came the Betlémské Náměstí. The square with the famous Bethlehem Chapel. Such a contrast to that busy crowd of just earlier. The silence and colors of this place I simply had to capture with my camera – the lead-gray chapel and the mint-green of that hotel and the ivy on that facade... the house next to it, with that salmon colored stucco work... for a moment I stood still to breathe in and out a couple of times.

Even the Liliová was picturesque, only the sun hadn't come here yet. Here there were even less people than there were in the square and the narrow row of tables, in those two parking spots in front of that eatery over there, was still completely unoccupied. So different from the area that this street turned into: the Karlova had that wide of a sidewalk that entire patios were set up and on the left you could see the exterior wall of the Clementinum complex of which a large portion already lay within reach of the morning sun. I really should go and have a look inside that place, in the library that they had there. Or attend a Mozart concert in the music room that was specifically dedicated to him. Or climb the tower of the observatory, or... man, you could play the tourist for all eternity in this city!

"– Hello, didn't we see each other at the lunch concert this week?" it suddenly sounded behind me.

And there she was. The girl who was handing out flyers for that classical concert last Wednesday. I could not deny it: while taking pictures, I had actually made my way to this place in hopes of running into her. In search for 'a friendly face'...

"What are you doing here?" I asked awkwardly, and immediately I corrected myself: "Stupid question. How are you doing?"

"Fine. And you?"

"Oh, can't complain. Are you working here all summer?"

"Pretty much," the girl answered. She briefly took off her baseball cap and pulled her short, brown ponytail back in shape. Then she put her hat back on. "It's hot out today," she said.

"Yeah, quite."

For a moment we stood beside one another in silence, staring at the hustle and bustle around us... at thirty, forty or so Japanese tourists that, like a herd of sheep, were dawdling after their shepherd with a little flag at the top of a plastic staff.

Right when I was about to say something, the girl asked, "What are you doing right now?"

"Uh... not much," I replied.

"Would you like to take a walk around the block? Or to go for a drink for a bit?"

And again she was faster than me: she commanded me to stay put and hopped, weaving skillfully through the shopping crowd, to the other side of the street. There stood a young man by the entrance of the St. Clement's Cathedral. After a brief chat with him she came back. "I quickly took care of my break. Shall we go?"

"Yes, let's," I smiled. We began to walk, back to where I had just come from. "You beat me to it, I had wanted to ask you the same. Whether you had some free time, I mean."

The girl did not respond to that. She asked "We totally haven't introduced ourselves yet. I'm Małgorzata, but here they usually call me Gosia. It's easier."

"Lente. As in *lentel*, without the *l*."

We laughed.

"So you don't have a Czech name," I noticed.

"No, I'm Polish."

"Interesting... and how long have you been here already?"

Gosia raised her shoulders. "A year or four. Shall we sit down over here?" She pointed at a group of tables at the corner of the Liliová, beneath large, obsolete parasols. All patios that were of any consequence in this street were still completely situated in the shadow of the houses at this moment. "Yes, sure," I said. Not like we would be cold, or anything.

Gosia picked a chair, I sat down across from her. However, she did not remain seated for long. With an ADHD-like unrest, which for some reason seemed to suit her, she sprang back up and said: "Just order a diet cola for me. With lots of ice. I first have to quickly go to the restroom." And gone was Gosia.

After a couple of minutes she returned. A little calmer now. Her cap was in her hand and her hair was draped over her right shoulder in a wet curl. "I just stuck my head under the tap," she grinned. "I recommend it to anyone on hot days like these..."

"No, thank you, I'll pass."

Apparently, Gosia did not notice any of the cynical look in my eyes. She looked at me smiling, with her big, brown eyes. Then she planted her elbows on the table, let her head rest in her hands and asked: "So, what do you think of this place?"

"This place?"

"Yes, Prague!"

"Oh... I see. Well, uh, it's beautiful... very beautiful."

The girl made a skeptical face. The kind of face that made it clear to you that she was far from satisfied with this answer. I joked: "Yeah, I'm sorry, but how can you summarize Prague, of all places, in one sentence?"

"You do have a point there," she said.

"But what about you, what do you think of this city then? What are you doing here, even, cause I presume you don't spend the entire year canvassing for classical concerts..."

"Oh, no, thank goodness, I don't!" she exclaimed, after which she told me that she studied at the university. Sociology and political sciences. With busy hand gestures and a lot of enthusiastic words she told me of how she had come to Prague around the age of eighteen and about how much she loved it here and that this city had such an exciting nightlife, much more fun than where she had been born and raised. Then she elaborately came back to her study programs, using terms and examples that were a bit hard for me to follow. I believe this was inherent to Polish women and girls, there were a couple of them in my circle of acquaintances in the Netherlands. They could *talk*... And simultaneously with that waterfall of words, their speedy, choppy way of moving. So much energy!

I quite liked those Poles. Never a dull moment with them in your company. While Gosia kept babbling I watched the drops of water that fell with a certain regularity, from the wet curl and onto her pink-and-lilac-and-red checkered shirt. Some of those drops rolled downwards, but there was also some moisture that penetrated the fabric of her clothing and that was causing a slowly expanding dark spot.

"Aren't you cold?" I asked, as soon as she briefly took a moment to breathe between two sentences.

Gosia pulled a face. "Nahhh..."

"Just looking at you gives me the shivers."

"I never get a cold, anyway," she said carelessly. "But can't we talk about you instead? You haven't told me anything about yourself yet. Such as, where are you from?"

"The Netherlands."

"Ahaaa, yeah, sorry, I'm not very good at recognizing accents. And you've been here for almost a week now, is that right?"

I nodded.

"Are you in Prague by yourself?"

"Yes. Or actually, no. I'm here because my boyfriend lives here."

"Ha! I thought it would be something like that..." she exclaimed.

"What do you mean?"

"It's easy. We met at the beginning of this week. And now it's Saturday and you're still here. Most tourists leave after a few days. Especially the Americans."

Yes, of course. "And the Japanese," I added. Indeed, if you hung around the center of such a major attraction all day you would pick up on these sort of things.

And to top it off, she was almost a sociologist as well.

"What's the name of your boyfriend, by the way?"

"Kazimír."

"And what does he do?"

"He's a restoration architect. And a musician."

Gosia narrowed her eyes into thin slits and gave it some thought. "What's his last name?"

"La Duca," I said cautiously.

Then she shook her head, quite a bit slower than what you would expect from her, and she said: "No, sorry…"

"He has only moved to Prague just recently. He's half Italian," I explained.

"Wow, an ethnic mix! They're usually super… sexy."

I sighed inaudibly. Yes, he certainly was good-looking. "And you? Do you have a boyfriend?" I asked.

"No, sadly, I don't," she said. She pouted her lower lip and pulled such a pitiful face that I spontaneously burst out laughing. "I'm not as lucky as you. Oh girl, I love romantic stories like these… tell me, how did you meet him, how long have you known each other?"

"Whoa, hold on. It really isn't only romance, such a long-distance relationship," I informed her. She was a *teeny* bit naive, after all…

"How come? Aren't things going okay between you two then?" she asked.

"Yes, of course things are okay," I lied. With a chuckle I added: "Otherwise I wouldn't be here, now would I?" And now I had to watch what I said. Do not bring up Lucas or the Community. Focus on myself and my boyfriend.

But it was to be expected that Gosia saw right through my bad acting. "I guess it's not that simple," she mused. "I can just picture it… at first, you only have eyes for each other. You're still completely in love and you lose sight of things around you. But when the holiday is over, real life begins and then you finally find out who he truly is. With everything that comes with it. Must be difficult. His home, his country, his culture, all totally different. And then his friends, all of whom you have yet to meet…" She paused for a bit to think. "And let's not forget his work. When he's busy doing that, you should be lucky enough to keep yourself busy."

Whow, this girl was a little less naive than I had thought, after all…

"But, oh well," Gosia said casually, "since you, like me, are of the female and therefore stronger sex, I'm sure you have long thought about things like that."

"I'm already trying to establish myself as a photographer here, yes…"

"You see? Good for you, girl! At least that is one less worry for you."

"Indeed…"

"Or not?" For a second she looked as though she did not understand me.

"It is, but you know how it is with men. If they could, they'd protect you from all the problems in the world. Even the non-existing ones." Good thinking!! And now onward, on that same path…

Gosia reacted surprised: "You're not trying to tell me that he is one of those jealous types, I hope?"

"I didn't say that."

"But?"

"Oh, he constantly worries about me and it's getting a little on my nerves. It's not like I'm not being careful, you know."

She nodded. Then she said: "Of course, you could also look at it on the bright side. Cause if a man wants to protect you, it means that he loves you. Right?"

"I wish things were that simple," I sighed. "But anyway, I was already planning to have a talk with him soon..."

"You should. Talking is very important. Imagine having to do without that in a relationship..." Gosia looked at her watch. "Oops, almost eleven thirty. I have to go," she said. She signaled to the waiter. We paid. She ran her hand through her wet hair, shook her head wildly once so that a couple of drops landed on my face. "Hey, quit it!" I giggled. "You're just like one of our dogs."

"You have dogs? How many?"

"Two, at my parents' in the Netherlands. Not here."

"Oh, thank goodness. I'm not a real dog person. Hold on, I gotta quickly go fix my hair."

And again, Gosia disappeared to the toilets, only to return with a neat ponytail and her cap on her head.

We exchanged phone numbers and email addresses. "Call me if you want to go out sometimes. I really know all the good bars here."

"For sure," I promised. We hugged each other and I briefly recoiled – her skin was just a fraction colder than you would expect. But I immediately recovered. "Did you use the champagne cooler this time, instead of the tap?" I joked.

"Hey, I still have an entire afternoon to go..." she explained quasi offended.

Yes, paranoid. I was paranoid. And Gosia, she was simply fun to hang out with.

We left the patio. "Call me," she said. "And don't let that lover of yours run all over you, okay?"

The haste with which she walked in the direction of her side of the Karlova made her almost run into a man and his German shepherd at the corner.

As the dog began to bark wildly and she made a funny leap out of fright, I could hear her grumble: "Stupid dog. I hate those monsters..."

I smiled. Yes, Gosia was fun.

64

ISLAND

Two young adults walk hand in hand along the east bank of the Moldau.
They fit perfectly in the picture of this early, sunny Sunday evening: they are,
like many of the couples walking around here, in love. They hold each other's
hand and are absorbed with each other completely, that can clearly be seen
by their body language and the way they talk to one another.
The weather is exceptionally mild today. The man is dressed in a breezy
dress shirt and light outdoor pants, the woman is wearing a vintage summer
dress and both are wearing sunglasses, his one of a luxury brand... hers is
most likely from the local drug store.
At the traffic lights, at the start of the bridge, the couple makes a run for it
by the man's initiative, and on the other side they stop by the balustrades
and laugh. He wraps his arm around her waist, lays his chin on her shoulder,
and for a while they watch the water and the people and the island to their
right that this bridge runs right over top of. She points to it and asks
something. He answers, her lips attempt to repeat his words, but then she
makes an awkward face and shakes her head. He laughs amused. They
continue walking, now arm in arm and at the wide, stone steps at the
midpoint they walk down onto the elongated, well-vegetated island. She
curiously takes in her surroundings; it looks like it is her first time being
here. They follow the walking trail beneath the stone vault of the bridge, past
children playing, dogs being walked and past tourists, homeless people and
other city dwellers on benches and on the grass. At the north end of the
island the two stand still for a moment, in the shadow of the chestnut trees.
She admires the view, stares at the Charles Bridge in the distance and he
looks at her. He brushes a couple of hairs from her face and wants to kiss her,
but she evades him teasingly. Then she gives in to his caresses anyway.
Along the path on the other side of the grass the man and woman walk back.
They apparently have a reservation at the restaurant at the south end of the
island, as he takes her up the stairs, to the rooftop terrace. Once arrived
there they follow a waiter, who leads them to a table underneath a parasol.
The young man puts his sunglasses away and his girlfriend does the same.
Then they order their dinner.

That is, more or less, what we must have looked like to an outsider. A couple,
madly in love, in a perfect fairytale world. And in fact, it had started out well
too: At first we had chatted a bit about anything and everything and when
Raphaël had finally brought up his question about how things had gone this

morning with the photo shoot with Petr, I had managed to deliver a beautifully diplomatic answer. The kind of answer that had just enough disclosure to come across as being forthcoming and laid-back, but one in which you also did not divulge on *too* many details. And whether it was because of that or because of something else: with his reaction, Raphaël had been gracious above expectation...

Of the mutual goodwill that that had evoked, I had then made good use later that evening: between the soup and the main course I had once again addressed the subject, his excessive concern, and dropped a reassuring remark along the lines of: "you see now, how I really was not born yesterday?"

However, it had not become the opening to the good conversation that I had hoped for. His nod had been agreeing but brief, and his gaze had drifted off diagonally past me to the golden roof of the National Theater and then downwards, to the river with its pedal boating youngsters and romantic couples in rented row boats.

But this evening I felt feminine and therefore powerful. And I was not going to be brushed off with ambiguous reactions. So while we were waiting for the dessert, I gave it one more shot. This time to raise another hot button issue: the Community of Vampires and what was going to be done about us, if anything.

Last week, when he was already in Prague and I was still in the Netherlands, we had not been able to talk about that over the phone or the internet. That much had been understandable for me. Only, despite the fact that we were together now, this topic had still not come up in our conversations. And it was ten days later already.

You could pass it off with excuses, such as 'we had more than enough on our plate with just the two of us' and 'then, to make matters worse, Lucas showed up, with all the chaos that came with it'. But I felt that things were starting to take far too long by now and that I was entitled to some clarification.

So I asked him. Whether he had heard anything yet.

"Why do you ask?" had been his seemingly automatic counter question.

"Just, cause, it's kind of quiet, for a while now... and I was thinking..."

He said: "It's not necessary for you to preoccupy yourself with this."

"Why not?"

When I saw that he kept his mouth tightly shut behind his outward smile I knew I'd better take a different approach.

So to begin with, I shrugged my shoulders... indifferent, but also a little offended. Then I gave a slight but exasperated sigh and for a while, I focused all my attention on the Apple strudel that had been served in the meantime. After a couple of minutes of silence I began to talk about some random generalities, but not before pretending to first have to swallow something on the emotional front. From the small talk I casually worked my way to classical music and then to Irish folk. Asked what he thought about it. Told him about my favorite artists and how some of their songs could literally stir me to tears. As an example I mentioned that cover I heard at the Irish pub in Rotterdam, a month ago, when I had gone there with Claire. *There Were Roses* by Tommy Sands. Between two bites of my dessert I asked Raphaël if he knew that song and softly sang a section of it. Yes, he had heard it somewhere before, he said. Next, I asked him if he knew what it was about. No, he did not know the song that well, had been his response. So I told him. About Sean and Alan during The Troubles in Northern Ireland, who, despite their different backgrounds, had been such great friends. And about the members of their Catholic and Protestant constituency that did not understand their friendship and could only feel hatred and how, because of that hate, the two friends both met their demise during an accumulation of incidents. I said that because of the circumstances that we were currently in, this song had now acquired another dimension for me.

Raphaël listened to me patiently. He had picked up a fork and let it playfully pass through his fingers. Then he took an unexpected bite out of my dessert. After he had lain down his fork again he said: "You're smart. And you have perseverance. But in spite of the number of angles from which you try to get back to the subject mentioned earlier, we are not going to discuss it tonight." I had asked for the reason of his restraint attitude, but I did not get an answer and he had only looked at me, again with that closed smile. The perfect picture of a couple in love that is out for dinner. And as I poked my apple strudel, my teeth took hold of the inside of my lower lip...

We were standing facing each other underneath the vault of the bridge. Once more I had asked him 'but why – I don't understand'. And again he ignored me. Even arguments such as 'if I know more, I can anticipate the situation better' or 'isn't honesty important in a relationship' made no difference.

Finally, I placed my right foot as gracefully as possible against the stone wall behind me and pulled a pouting Princess Diana-face. That really was the last thing that I could think of... With my head semi-turned away I let my lover know from behind my femininely long eyelashes, that I was still waiting for something that would satisfy me. But he stood still, seemingly unaffected, with his hands in front of him, slightly above hip height. His fingertips and thumbs met and formed a downward pointing tower.

In the meantime, my teeth had breached the lining of my lip and continued chewing, compulsively by now. Something warm and acidic made contact with my taste buds and with my tongue I could precisely trace the striped swelling that had formed...

Then, completely unexpectedly, Raphaël changed his posture. A smile came through in his face. He placed one step in my direction, took both my hands in his. Gently he pulled me towards him and moved my hands backwards. He grabbed my wrists between the thumb and fingers of his left hand and his right hand dragged slowly upwards over my back, pulling with it the thin cotton fabric of my dress in wrinkly portions. With his fingers spread he came to a stop behind my skull. Then something sultry slid over his amused gaze and he moved his mouth closer to me. His tongue felt its way attentively across my lips and he kissed me... let go... kissed me once more and subsequently created some distance again, this time only letting go of my lower lip after he had pulled it back a little. Then he came back and he began to suck on the injury that had just been caused by me. First softly, then more forcefully and finally with such intensity, that I pulled myself away from him in a wild impulse and half stumbling distanced myself from him.

As I stood there startled, inspecting my painfully pulsating lip, he said without looking at me: "I have warned you once before, about tempting vampires. In a less crowded location you might have been in serious trouble."

The couple in love that was walking along the bank of the Moldau yesterday, is back again this evening. They have just taken a stroll around the block and are sitting side by side on a bench, staring at the lights of Malá Strana across the water and at the mint-green and orange-yellow of the spotlights that are directed at the castle. Nightfall has almost completely set in.

They do not talk much. The woman looks tired and when a tram behind them comes to a screeching halt, she covers her ears with her hands. She leans forward with her elbows resting on her knees. After a while she sits up again. She takes something out of the pocket of her pants, a small case that she opens and from which she retrieves two small objects. She wants to put them in her ears, but the man asks something and then she shows them to him first. He takes the items from her and looks at them, rolling them back and forth in the palm of his hand. Suddenly he throws them with a wide arch into the river. The woman lets out a shriek of horror and jumps to her feet. In two leaps she reaches the fence that separates the bank from the water. There she stares down for a moment in astonishment. Then she turns around. Asks the man a question. He replies, calmly and appearing emotionless. She reacts sharply. He explains something to her, but the woman clearly does not want to hear it. She begins to yell, fragments of sentences become audible: "... don't have the right ... ear plugs... my mother..." and "... not an act at all... you troglodytic son of a bitch!"

By now, he has gotten up as well. He wants to say something, but with a scornful finger in the air she silences him, upon which he drops his hands again. With a snub she ends this issue. Furiously she walks by him and around the bench, and uses the first opportunity that presents itself to cut through the heavy traffic and reach the other side of the road.

"Go fuck yourself!" I had yelled, I think. But I wasn't sure anymore. Could not care either. It was too little, too late for him anyway. No one could treat me that way, especially not him! Look at him standing there, with those droopy shoulders and his hands in his pockets. Loser.

Do not go straight, do not go into that blasted Náprstkova. Turn left, past the taxis and then towards the city center. And no matter what, do not look back over my shoulder.

I darted into the little street that led to the parking square with the fountain. Wove through the cars. There in that corner was his. Stupid corporate wheels. Take that alley, cut through to the Karlova? No, much too deserted. Keep going straight. Find a metro and head straight to your hostel. To home. A man. There down that street. He did not look like a tourist. Give it a shot? Shit, how did you say 'where is the metro' again?

*"Kde je metro?"* I asked, as my eyes fell on his beer belly with on it, at the center, a black button that had the greatest difficulty holding the front panels of his jacket together. On top of that, the pants that he was wearing were inches too long.

The man said something. Unintelligible, of course. I could have seen that coming.

I made a gesture that was somewhere between 'sorry' and 'I don't understand you'. Wanted to keep walking, but he did not give up yet. He again said something that I did not understand and took a step toward me. Like in a game of chess, in which you make an attempt to pass your opponent and that opponent outsmarts you, he blocked my path. Quite impressive for someone with a body that plump.

Suddenly I realized that he had been drinking. Smelled like vodka. Recognized the sound of slurred speech. Idiot. No choice but to turn back. More roads led to Rome, as it did to the I.P. Pavlova Metro Station. Cause I was *hellbent* on going home.

The drunkard followed me. Was not finished with his story yet. Why didn't he just quit? I was not in the mood to deal with this right now, this was way more than I could handle.

Wove through cars again. Past the fountain… why, for Pete's sake, had they covered that object so unsightly with that chicken wire? I tripped, was barely able to keep my balance. Stupid, uneven pavers. I hated this city! Using the sleeve of my jacket I wiped some tears of mistreatment off my face.

And he kept following me. With his vodka miasma in my neck and his drawled, incomprehensible words he walked beside me, and occasionally behind me while tugging at my arm, and then next to me on the other side. Do not pick up your pace. You are not afraid. You are much too angry for that…

*"Nemluvim česky."* I do not speak Czech. No response. So I repeated it and in the meantime I entered that alleyway, heading towards the Náprstkova. If necessary I'd pop into that café beneath Raph's place. That sorry piece of shit probably wouldn't dare to enter it and even *if* he did, he would get kicked out immediately.

I better cut my losses. Because I hated handsy guys.

A quick glance over the wall, diagonally to my left, told me that the window of the apartment of my boyfriend was not yet lit. Whatever. I did not need him. In twenty seven long years I had developed into the woman that I was, all without his help, and for the whole life that was ahead of me I was still going to – if that wasted jerk did not desist soon…! "You're going to quit your bullshit *right now*, or so help me God…" I snarled in my native tongue.

## 65

THEATER

What exactly happened during the seconds that followed was hard to express in words, but the fact was that my assailant suddenly fell unconscious in front of me. Right before that moment I had felt a breeze and from the air above me I had seen a dark shadow appear. Also, there had been a loud bang or thud.

Big and menacingly Raphaël stood there, looking down on the person that he had just struck down. I needed a minute to make sense of the situation. "And what was the point of that?" I then asked, with my heart still beating in the back of my throat. I knelt beside the victim and checked whether the man was responsive. He was not. Great. Raphaël squatted down next to me. I checked his breathing and as I moved him into a stable position I could feel something sticky in the unwashed hair on the right side of his head. Blood. I searched through my bag, took out a clean handkerchief and pressed it against the wound. To my boyfriend I said: "Nice going. This man here has a concussion, if not worse."

"A small price to pay for what he wanted to do to you, beautiful." His hand disappeared into a pocket and took something out. Milky-white, rubber disposable gloves – what, on earth, did he have those for? He shook them back into shape in an effortless movement and, honestly, I had seen plenty of those gloves before. I had even worn them on countless occasions, but there was something off, something totally different by the way he put them on. And the look on his face, it seemed to transform in the light of the street lantern, because initially, his gaze had only been smoldering with anger. Now, however, as the rubber snapped back against the skin of his hands with crisp smacks, the eyes of the vampire got a little deadness to them. Yet, at the same time, a fire ignited in them, the kind of fanatical fire that you only saw with… with torture specialists – yes, from those horrible movies – and he was preparing himself for whatever he was about to do. If this were a film, then at this point I would change channels or walk out of the cinema, but this was not fiction. I was sitting here, right beside him and he –

"What are you going to do?" I asked in a narrow voice.

Disturbed, the vampire turned his head in my direction. "You don't suppose I can just leave him here, do you?"

"But you're not going to… You will not hurt him, you hear?"

"Oh no, my sweet, I wouldn't harm a single hair on his head. If you don't want me to…" was his taunting response, but all of a sudden the words got stuck in his throat. Simultaneously with me he looked up, in the direction of the parking square. He grumbled something I could not make out and I was overwhelmed by an unpleasantly forceful wave of terror: a man and a woman approached us arm in arm. They were still several tens of meters away, but... blindingly and nauseatingly, flashbacks to one of our past online conversations crossed my mind: suspicious questions, cell phones, police, more distrusting questions and everything what that would lead to... I had to think, and think fast! And take action.

"Listen to me and do exactly as I say," I snarled at Raphaël. "This guy has brain damage. So when he wakes up he will have no idea what happened. Turn away from him now with your back facing those people. *Do* it!"

He obeyed.

"I will stay between you and them. Get rid of your gloves and pretend like all that blood is making you sick. Stay with me until they get here and follow my lead."

The people had reached us. Raphaël began to dry-heave.

"Do you speak English?" I asked.

"Yes, a little," was the answer of the man. The woman nodded in confirmation.

I pointed at the victim. "He is drunk, I think. And I don't speak Czech. Could you call a doctor?"

My boyfriend stood up and took a couple of unsteady steps away from us. I got up, placed a hand on his arm and said in English: "Oh darling, it's too much for you to take, isn't it? Why don't you go on ahead, I'll follow you shortly..."

Raphaël nodded. Made an apologetic gesture to the two strangers and walked away. Right at the corner of the alleyway he stood still for a moment. He bent over and I could hear him make vomiting noises. Then he disappeared, not to the left, towards his home, but to the right...

"He can't handle the sight of blood very well," I explained.

Waiting for the ambulance I told the couple that the drunkard had hit his head, I pressed the handkerchief against his wound again and gave them instructions on what they should tell the emergency medical workers when they got here. In the meantime, I took a few looks in the direction of where my boyfriend had walked to. Eventually, that hint was picked up by the man and the woman and they asked if I would not rather go after him and make sure he was okay.

To my left in front of me, on the third floor, I could see a light come on in the window. Curtains were being closed. I, however, took a right turn. Following in my lover's tracks.

Still out of breath from my loop past the Betlémská I walked into the Náprstkova again, but from the opposite end. In the distance I could hear sirens approaching. "It's me. Let me in." I said in a barely audible tone and almost immediately the exterior door was unlocked.

He was waiting in the hallway of his apartment, with his hands behind his back, leaning against the wall. He said: "Smart thinking back there, with those passersby. My gratitude."

"Nonsense," I said. I stepped into the living room. On the dining table lay a couple of pencils, a pencil sharpener and eraser next to a sheet of paper of at least 20 by 27 inch, on which the beginning of a detailed landscape drawing could be seen. "What's that?" I asked.

"Cinque Terre in Italy. In the vicinity of La Spezia five picturesque villages are lined up along the coast..." he said.

" – I have heard about it, yes," I interrupted him.

He sat down and pulled the chair to his left closer. I took a seat in it. In silence we both stared into space.

"I can tell that you used to be an artist," I said after a while, simply to say anything at all.

"I lack practice." He sounded casually. "Haven't tried my hand at creative drawing in years." A little absentmindedly he picked up the eraser and began to roll it in different directions between his thumb and index finger. Then he said with a flat voice: "This evening you called me a troglodytic son of a bitch. You had every right to, Lente. In a short time I have lost a lot of my credibility with you, and on top of that, I'm not going to give you an explanation for my behavior. Because any explanation would sound like absolving myself and I don't have the right to do that." He let the eraser escape from his hand. It rolled, bouncing, and came to a stop halfway the drawing. "But those earplugs, they're not good for you in any way. They trick your nervous system and only teach you to compensate and then, in time, you'll just hear even more. What you need to do is train yourself to block unwanted auditory information. And I am going to help you with that. You probably won't believe me, but I only have your best interest at heart."

"It's not that I don't believe that." I was fighting an unfair battle against the tears that were forcing their way out... wiped my sleeve over my eyes. Only now noticed how dirty it had become from the make-up. "My face..." I mumbled.

"Well, go freshen up, then."

When I returned from the bathroom and sat down beside him again, he took my chin in his hand. He turned my head towards him and looked at me with striking intensity. With his finger to his mouth he signaled for me to stay quiet, emphasizing his message by letting that finger rest on my lips for a second. Then he shifted his gaze to the drawing. On it, to my astonishment, something was written between the lines of the sketch work: "We are being listened to. So don't say anything until you read the following."

I nodded, a little confused. Again he wrote something: "Lente, you have to pay attention now. We are going to talk about something, but not in the usual way. You see, outside some members of our community are watching this apartment. That's also why I've been closing the curtains as soon as it gets dark this entire week."

With big, startled eyes I stared at my boyfriend. Raphaël handed me one of the pencils, but before I could write anything, he jotted down some more on the paper himself. "Everything we say and do will be overheard and I know that many of our community can speak German. That's too closely related to Dutch, for my liking. Therefore, we will have to resort to a bit of theater. We're going to pretend that I'm drawing and that you're sitting beside me and watch how I do that. Don't forget the setting: we are lovers who have just made up after a fairly heated discussion and who are still recovering from a precarious situation in the streets. Anything that we share with each other out loud should thus be said within that frame of reference."

With a sick feeling in my stomach I wrote beneath his story: *"I can't write nearly as fast as you..."*

"We're not in a rush. Legibility is more important."

*"Okay. What do you have to say?"*

He gave me a kiss on the forehead, upon which I quickly whispered something sweet. Next, I read along with the movements of Raphaël's hand: "To guarantee the privacy and safety of the undead, several strict rules have been laid out. These rules also include a code of silence."

*"A code of silence. Even now, from you to me? Was that why you were being so difficult yesterday?"*

"Yes. And I've been telling myself for a week now that I can stay on top of the game that I'm playing. That I... what's that saying, again?"

*"... save both the grain and the chicken?"*

Raphaël nodded and wrote: "Only, I realize that the evident impossibility of this situation is beginning to drive a wedge between us."

In the meantime, he asked me a question about summer vacations in Italy that was easy to answer. I reacted as naturally as possible and kept my eye glued to our shadow conversation that continued amidst ever expanding black-and-white images that depicted the sea, rocks and picturesque houses of the subtropical Liguria. Because drawing was what the vampire kept doing, simultaneously with and in spite of the writing and the talking. His way of sketching had a whimsical character... sometimes it went at a calm pace, but every now and then superhumanly fast as well, like little emotional outbursts that had nowhere else to find their release, other than by way of the paper.

"The current status quo isn't healthy for our relationship, Lente."

*"Don't need to tell me that,"* I wrote.

"And therefore, I'm going to put an end to it right now. So my answer to your question from yesterday is: yes, I did get word from the Community of the Undead, the regional 'Danube Monarchy' one, to be precise."

*"Danube Monarchy? What does that mean...?"*

"An area that stretches from Austria in the West to Transylvania in the East, and from Bosnia Herzegovina in the South to Bohemia and Galicia in the North. Got something to do with history."

*"And how many vampires are we talking about?"*

Never thought I could be this stoical under these circumstances.

"The exact number, I do not know. A hundred-and-fifty, two-hundred, perhaps."

*"So you've phoned with them or something. And then?"*

Yes, how was I able to keep my cool like this, at all?

"They have decided to subject us to an investigation."

*"What kind of investigation, for heaven's sake?"*

"They see importance in determining what measures best suit our situation. At some point in time a meeting will be held about that."

But my breathing, however calm it may be, could undoubtedly be heard far outside the walls of this house. And my heart rate, I was worried about my heart rate...

*"Raph, do you know yet what kind of things they could decide upon?"*

"I have not been given any information on that."

*"And how rigid should I expect them to be?"*

"Worrying about that is pointless, my dear."

*"Inhumanely strict, I take it..."*

"We are talking about a couple of thousand souls worldwide here. They all need to be protected."

"I completely forgot to ask you whether you would like to have a drink," my boyfriend said out loud.

"Wasn't there something left in that bottle of cola?" I asked. He nodded and disappeared into the kitchen.

After he had placed the glass beside me and sat down, he read what I was writing: *"But how are they going to do that then, with that investigation of us?"*

"It has already been set into motion."

*"When?"*

"On the first day that you arrived here."

*"Oh man..."* my lips spelled soundlessly. Did I really want to continue asking questions, did I really want to know all of this?

"The arrivals hall of the airport was full of the undead."

*"No."*

"Yes."

*"Why? What could possibly have been there to see? We only hugged and then went to the car..."*

"It wasn't enough for them to distribute your photo by email. They also had to get acquainted with your scent."

*"Please don't tell me that they have been stalking me."*

He looked at me, expressionless.

*"Really, this entire week already?"*

"Yes."

So that meant that… in that restaurant yesterday, during our walk today… but also during all those hours that I had wandered around this city by myself, was sitting in the tram and metro and who-knows-where else…!

*"So that's why you were so worried about me."*

"And they have subjected you to tests."

*"What do you mean? To what end?"*

"On discretion, on ingenuity. And on some other things."

*"But how?"*

"They have engaged in contact with you."

*"I don't get it, Raph."*

"Petr, for instance. He's a vampire."

A pencil rolled off the table and bounced to the floor. In the same moment a hand lay over my mouth and that was a good thing too… With his other hand Raphaël took my pencil from me and wrote: "I'm going to have to kiss you in order to make your elevated heart rate plausible." Immediately he tried his most sensual best to get me in as excited a state as possible. Pulled me in closer. I climbed into his lap. Latched onto him and whispered: "What am I doing here, even? I barely understand you, not to mention myself… why us, why you and I?"

"Because you can't resist. What do you think it is like for me?" His hands rubbed along my back, my side and the side of my breasts.

"I wish things weren't this complicated…" I mumbled truthfully. One of his hands pushed its way between us, in search of the button to my jeans…

"– Stop. Not now," I panted. Hurriedly I slid back to my own chair.

"Not a fan of make-up-sex?" he asked with a crooked smile.

He bent down to the floor to pick up the dropped pencil and then wrote: "Sorry, but that just now was necessary."

*"I understand."*

"I will still have to touch you a couple of times as we go. Seeing the nature of our topic of conversation. Will you be able to manage that?"

*"I don't think I have much of a choice. Anyway, back to Petr."*

"Your meeting had been planned."

*"Did you know about it?"*

"No."

*"I'm so sorry about that…"*

"?"

*"That I wrote off your concerns as jealousy, while you…"*

"What else could you do?"

*"Or you."*

"Or I, yes."

The caresses of his fingers over my lower arm were as light as a feather and almost impossible to sense, but all the more tantalizing because of it.

"Lente, Petr probably wasn't the only one."

*"What do you mean?"*

"Who else have actively sought out contact with you during the last week?" Crazy how the human mind can influence the body so directly. How the tears can spontaneously begin to fall within the same split second that you begin to realize the danger that has surrounded you during the last couple of days... Blurred with moisture my eyes, big and scared and questioning, searched for affirmation in his. He nodded slowly. "It is more than likely. If the person in particular initiated the contact, most definitely," he wrote. "Who was it, Lente?"

With trembling hand I jotted the name on the paper: *"Gosia?"*

"Oh sweetheart..." he let out.

*"What?"*

"I had dearly hoped that you would be spared that."

*"What are you talking about?"*

"What did she do to you, Lente?"

*"Nothing."*

Filled with displeasure he turned his head away from me.

*"Nothing, I swear. Nothing in particular, anyway. It even makes me wonder whether we are talking about the same person."*

"Not many of the undead are as shrewd as Małgorzata. When you say that she hasn't done anything to you, that is all the more confirmation for me."

*"But the Gosia that I'm talking about... She wasn't even wearing any sunglasses."*

Raphaël crossed his arms.

Shit. She *was* wearing a baseball cap... But still. Caps were worn by so many people. And... right, indeed, there was that incident with that German shepherd! *"Darling, she's scared of dogs. She did not only tell me so, I witnessed it happen as well. And believe me, that startled reaction was authentic!"* Relieved I looked at him in hopes of making eye contact, but he had shifted his attention to the paper again. He was busy drawing and intermittently he reacted to what I had written: "Are you sure you didn't let yourself be deceived?"

*"No – yes, I'm sure!"*

"So she ran into a dog and was startled."

*"Precisely."*

"Describe the moment."

Obediently I reported on Gosia's near run-in with the man with the dog, her awkward little jump and what she had muttered in fright.

"And you just happened to understand what she was saying."

*"Because she was speaking in English, Raph."*

"Have you also asked yourself why Małgorzata didn't start swearing in her native language, like every other normal person?"

Just as unexpectedly and inevitably as before the tears came.

"I'm so sorry, my dear... can you ever forgive me?" he asked out loud. And on paper: "If I could have prevented this..."

"Will you let that go, already? Just help me instead. Make the pain go away, of all the things I hear and of – "

" – You know I don't have the ability to do that," he said flatly.

"Then train me. So that I can put up more of a resistance against it. So that things will start to feel a little normal again..."

I stood up, went to the toilet and returned to the room holding quite a large section of toilet paper in my hand. Loudly I blew my nose in it. I sighed briefly and shivered, the way it often goes at the end of a good cry. Then I picked up my pencil again.

*"And there I was thinking I had found a new friend..."*

"A friend? What do you base that idea on?"

*"We have exchanged phone numbers."*

"On her initiative?"

I nodded. *"She told me to call her. Twice, in fact. And that she would love to go out with me sometimes."*

"Then you have no choice but to call her soon."

*"I don't think I feel like doing that anymore..."*

"You're going to have to, Lente."

*"And to think, Raph, we had talked about relationships and also about your excessive worrying about me!"*

Against my expectation he did not react concerned. "Talking about men is what most women do when amongst themselves," he wrote. "So you did the right thing, in that respect. In addition, you have given me a tight alibi for my role as an overprotective boyfriend."

*"?"*

"You don't have to dread spending an evening alone with Gosia at some God-knows-what-kind-of dance club. I'll be joining you."

The sigh of relief had escaped me before I knew it.

"A little longer and you're going to succumb to sleep," was Raphaël's immediate reaction. "Let me quickly finish this and then I'll bring you to your hostel."

"But before we wrap things up here," he wrote, "I strongly advise you to not look around for any undead in the streets. We cannot afford to break posture, especially now."

I used my pencil one last time. *"Is Lucas around?"* I wrote in a corner of the sheet of paper, but my friend replied in the negative. Shaking my head I then collected my things and said: "Gonna pee before we go..."

However, Raphaël stopped me with a gentle hand. With a telling look on his face he began to tear the artwork that he had just created to pieces. I instantly understood what he was aiming at, so I exclaimed half shocked, half offended: "Why would you do that??"

He said that he felt that the result was sub-par and handed me the pile of shredded paper. Grumbling about things like 'natural talent' and 'way too perfectionistic' I took it with me to the toilet and in the meantime, he stepped onto the foot pedal of the garbage can.

## 66

LESSONS

"If you would just make a drawing... you'd have something to do and I wouldn't feel so guilty."

"Sitting at the table with you and not doing much doesn't exactly strike me as a chore."

"Yes, okay, but..."

"Lente, from a social point of view dinner is one of the most important moments of the day. My feeling simply tells me that I would like to share that with you."

"And believe me when I say, I really think that's a sweet thought. But – "

" – You can't bear the idea of my studying your beautiful face uninterruptedly for half an hour on a daily basis."

I blushed.

"Well, if one of us thinks of this as a nuisance, maybe your suggestion is not that crazy after all. I have always wanted to draw a portrait of you anyway."

" – Don't you dare!"

Yeah, come on. Him, drawing a portrait of me? Not in a million years! Fortunately, unwelcome attempts at that could easily be sabotaged. So no worries on that front. More importantly, we had reached a doable compromise. My cooking my own meal and him sitting with me. Me happy, him happy.

Not a moment too soon either. A whole week of eating out at restaurants around this city had taught me that Czech cuisine was not exactly my idea of delicious food. Take that vegetable that was labeled as red cabbage, but unexpectedly turned out to be sauerkraut with a red color or, at the very least, red cabbage with a nasty acidic taste. And then there were those vague, sticky things that were all called dumplings but each were made separately from different ingredients. Where, in the world, did that make any sense? They should try that in the Netherlands... bread fries, potato fries, *fruit fries...*

In any event, from now on it was daily cooking and eating at Raphael's place. And apparently, he thought that that was quite a wonderful development in our relationship. The first night he would not leave the kitchen, even if I beat him with a stick. Fascinated he had stood there, observing me during my activities and when he had started to ask me a bunch of questions on what I was making and what kind of things I liked anyway, I had told him that he should join me on a trip to the supermarket some time. He would be amazed by how much he could learn there...

Naturally, upon his insistence, we had gone to the nearest Tesco the very next day for a crash course in 'obtaining foodstuff for Lente'. As a veritable nerd he had followed me through the aisles with a notepad at the ready, and every time I pointed out something that was to my liking, he would write down the name. At the end of our visit to the supermarket he tore out the written sheets of paper from his pad and handed them to me. Turned out that of each product mentioned, aside from the Dutch name and the Czech translation, he had also written down the phonetic version *plus* the brand name. For me. 'In case I liked to know.'

Exploring each other's world in this way had something soothing to it. And that little bit of relaxation was more than welcome, because this week other lessons had begun as well, and they had a much less voluntary nature to them. I had to learn to deal with my sharpened hearing and Raphaël made no delay in keeping his promise to help me with that.

He was a tough teacher. The first time that I was confronted with his methods I had literally been too shocked for tears: We had been walking in the street somewhere and he had been enthusiastically telling me about the new viola da gamba that he would be able to pick up at the restorer in a few days. I was genuinely happy for him and showed that by asking him a couple of engaged questions about the instrument. But then the loud and prolonged honking of a car somewhere near us had put a sudden end to my concentration. I had made an apologetic hand gesture, but the way in which Raphaël had reacted to that... He slowed his step, looked to the side annoyed. Or was it a hurt look that I saw on his face? Anyway, he asked full of disbelief: "Am I really *that* dull, Lente? Is what I'm telling you so uninteresting that the slightest distraction is enough for you to...?" Next, he increased his walking speed and cloaked himself in a moody silence, after which it was up to me to coax him out of his mistreated shell.

This bit of theater apparently belonged to lesson one. But of course I did not catch on until after it happened a couple of times, when he had returned to being his friendly self and explained to me that the foundation of blocking out noises was focus. Right...

Phase two of the training was possibly even *less* enjoyable: every time I was confronted with sudden, loud or shrill noises, he ambushed me with an unrelenting cross-examination. The instant answering of questions like 'where are you', 'what day is it today' and 'what were we talking about just now' were supposed to make sure that a possible blackout had the lowest chance of happening.

I could see the logic in that reasoning. But still... what made him take such a militaristic approach? Had he ever learned it that way himself? From that old monk perhaps?

By the way, that monk would constantly pop up in the strangest locations in the city. Sometimes, for example, he happened to have been following us for large sections, right in plain view for everyone to see, until I would then notice him in the reflection of some shop window or another. Or inside, in a store... like that one time, when he had suddenly been standing there at the Tesco, near the candy and chocolate. In his hands he held a red, heart-shaped box of chocolates and as he released his gaze from the packaging and aimed it toward us, he said: "I have a girlfriend... She is very dear to me and I would like to let her know how I feel. But I just can't seem to choose a fitting gift for her. What do you think, Lente, might this be something?" With a look on his face laden with undefined emotions he had then stared at me, holding up the box of chocolates.

Raphaël and I then realized that ignoring our annoyance with him was the only sensible thing that was in our power. Time and time again. And which of the two of us was strongest at doing so, that differed per incident.


Perhaps my teaching method was just as ruthless as Raphaël's. Because I simply laughed right in his face every time he slipped up. It was his own fault, after all, for asking me to teach him to cook.

One would think, why teach a vampire at all? Give him a cook book and within fifteen minutes he knows how to prepare all your food.

Oh how reality paled in comparison, though: granted, Raphaël did memorize just about every word that I shared with him. That, he did. But when at the end of 'lesson one' it was time for him to check whether the curry soup needed more seasoning, he immediately committed a fatal mistake. I had just been setting the table and had come back into the kitchen to get the plates, when I saw him raise a spoon to his mouth. Carefully he tasted the soup. Added some salt. Stirred, tasted it again and added more salt. Just before he was going to repeat this action for the third time, I stopped him. I took the spoon from him and sipped on a bit of his concoction, only to instantly spit it out in disgust. The soup had become completely inedible. His somewhat helpless explanation had been that he had tried so hard to relate to my perception of taste...

Spices and salt. Choosing the right spices to your taste. That turned out to be an impossible feat for one of the undead. It was as though you were trying to teach a colorblind person the difference between red and green.

Therefore, I decided to make him do it by sight. I showed him dashes of salt in the palm of my hand. Small dashes and a large dash. Next I poured it in his hand. And that method *did* work. In fact, it worked so well that you were almost tempted to suspect him of counting the grains, or at the very least, using his hand to secretly weigh the amounts.

But conversely, in other aspects of cooking, his extreme sensitivity worked to his detriment: one night, after waiting in the living room for twenty minutes, I had sent him back into the kitchen. The potatoes that were on the stove had to be done right about now, I had told him. He had then gone to have a look, stayed away longer than expected and just when I began to wonder what he was doing, I had heard an exasperated scream and smelled a slight burning scent. Guess what. Raphaël was given the instruction by me to prick the potatoes with a fork first, before draining the lot. "If they don't vibrate anymore, they are done," I had explained to him. And he had done exactly as I had told him, but we had both overlooked the fact that where the sense of touch ended for a human, an undead person was still aware of a world of impulses.

Escapism. Another definition for this idiocy did not exist. Because what other reason was there for us to cling to each other and fill our days so much with activities so that, at night, I would almost collapse from exhaustion? If we didn't, the fear would become too strong and the insecurity too overpowering. Of course we knew that the moment, when our being together would come to an end, was drawing nearer by the day. Also, we were well aware of the fact that the thing that loomed over our head had all the properties of the sword of Damocles. Most likely. But when that sword would actually make our heads roll… we were completely in the dark for that matter, like two disorientated blind people. And the only security that there was for us, we found with one another.

And so it was Raphaël and I against the world. Well, in a manner of speaking.

The choice between wandering the streets by yourself while being followed by God-knows-who or experiencing the illusion of safety by constantly being together with your boyfriend, was easily made under these circumstances, of course. For that I was willing to put aside my stubborn need for independence.

And the fact that at night the parting rituals outside the door to the hostel lasted ever longer, including lingering hugs, intense French kisses and one or two teardrops, was a nice bonus. All the better to fit the romantic picture that we were carefully painting of ourselves.

Or could I perhaps be downplaying the situation and had we actually reached a new stage in our relationship? The stage in which I let go more and more of my resistance and finally dared to give in to what I was really feeling, to Love with a capital L?

## 67

HOLEŠOVICE

*Pražská Tržnice,* I didn't know how I was supposed to pronounce it correctly yet. Therefore, for now, I just stuck to the official English name Rivertown or simply the Prague Market.

Man, it sure looked like the Beverwijk Black Market here, but then in Czech style, and just like there, the entire hodgepodge was housed in several buildings. But here, there were over twenty of them and in between stood an even larger number of semi-permanent boutiques, or stalls, or whatever you liked to call those tiny, wooden shacks – all clustered in that vast lot on the left bank of the Moldau.

The Prague Market very much appeared to be the rightful territory of the Asian people, or rather, the Vietnamese. I had honestly never seen that many in one place before and – knowing that the average middle class individual in Czech had to work even harder than their colleagues in the Netherlands – I estimated that the largest part of family life for these people occurred in and around these little shops and stalls. And yes, despite the facade of serious retail businesses, every now and then you could hear a baby cry, tucked away behind a till, or you could see a jet-black haired toddler hastily being pulled by the hand into one of the shops by his just as jet-black haired mother as you were walking by.

I was glad that I had gone. Raphaël was lying in bed and had I stayed at home, I would have climbed up the walls. And then to think of that hot, stuffy weather... No, seriously, Ralph just *could not* object to my daily outside activities. In that respect, it was almost a good thing that we had to pretend to not know of any undead shadows behind me. But it also was nice to know that he trusted that much in the promise made by the Community, that they would not take any action until The Judgment would be announced to the both of us...

There was something about it, all that junk that lay and stood and hung here for sale, because the variety at markets such as these could justifiably be called endless. Clothing was sold: underwear, dress shirts made out of denim, and faux leather coats. In other spots you could find batteries and porn videos, tacky lamps made up of colored Czech crystal and useful reading glasses in any strength that you could desire. There were vegetables, keys, knives and scary electrical self-defense gadgets, that in the Netherlands even in specialty stores were not allowed for sale. And I had discovered that, in one of the larger buildings at the back of the terrain, there was a store that sold

Dutch secondhand furniture.

The layout of Prague Market seemed illogical, but was actually functional. So basically there were these buildings; halls, really, all late nineteenth century, that either housed medium sized establishments or were subdivided into smaller areas to accommodate the shop owners and their merchandise. And then, in the walkways between those halls, there were all sorts of retail stalls.

The theater, that according to a sign was situated on the grounds, I couldn't find anywhere, though...

The presence of curious photographers was not appreciated here. That's what I found out as soon as I took out my camera – my gut immediately told me that it would be better to not approach my subjects too closely. Explicitly standing at overview points was therefore the most obvious solution, and then act like you were taking a general photo, while you secretly zoomed in with your telephoto lens to take interesting close up.

Despite that precaution, an elderly lady with one of those typical, conical rice paddy hats, who was sitting in a strategic spot among her merchandise was on to me immediately. With every angle that I tried to capture her covertly, she skillfully turned away from my lens and our duel for the registration of her characteristic face eventually ended in a victory on her side when, after some time had passed, she simply disappeared into her boutique and stopped showing herself.

A bit less pleasant was that guy a little further down, however. He first rudely forbade me to use my camera and then began to interrogate me to figure out the reason for my photography zeal. So he had followed me for quite a few yards, with that meddlesome, bad-tempered look in his eyes... Fortunately, putting away my camera and escaping into an ice-cream-slash-coffee parlor in the vicinity was enough to make him retreat.

Shaking Lucas, on the other hand, was a lot less easy to do...

I noticed that he was near me the moment that his cellphone gleefully pounded Dennie Christian's *Rosamunde* into the airwaves. And by the fluent French with which he spoke to his caller – of which of course I could make out nothing, at first.

But when he slowly got closer in those narrow, tarp covered dim pathways and finally stood boldly beside me, it was very clear that he wanted something from me. Initially, I had hoped that a nonchalant 'You again?' would take the fun out of this game for him. So I obstinately continued negotiating a way too expensive, albeit really pretty nightgown that I had found. But with his arrival my concentration was gone and the saleswoman was experienced in haggling, and the more the frustration on my face increased, the more triumphantly she stood her ground. So this was entirely pointless...

Then all of a sudden Lucas mentioned an amount, a pretty low amount, and added to that, "Final price". Within a few seconds the deal was sealed, he paid and handed me the nightwear, neatly tucked into a small plastic bag. With a careless gesture I dropped the thing on a stack of displayed sweaters and walked away, leaving behind a saleswoman who, all confused, exclaimed, "Lady, hello, lady…!"

"Your earrings lie on the bottom of the Moldau," I said.
Again he was standing beside me, now at a fruits and vegetables stall.
"Just like those silicone hearing protectors of yours," was his dry reaction.
"Oh – bugger off!"
I'd better head for the exit of the grounds. Maybe he would give up then. This week he had suddenly disappeared from sight on more than one occasion. Only – this had *solely* happened during moments in which Raphaël and I had been together. So I did not quite understand why now… " – Until the year 1983 this was still a live stock market and there used to be a slaughterhouse over there." He motioned to the building that we passed and asked: "Did you know that, Lente?" The way in which he walked close to me and talked to me… the people around us had to think that we were together.
"How should I know?" I muttered.
The vampire ignored my rebuttal and mused: "For almost a century this place was hard for me to resist. But at the same time it always had that unattainability. You know, those enormous amounts of red meat, all that delicious blood that flowed there, but also the mortals. Everywhere you looked those mortals with their prying eyes."
Take a tram, the next one. If you stay near the people, nothing can happen to you… On the right I could see line 5 coming. I made a dash to the stop across the street and got on. As did he. I found myself a seat. He did not.
After riding along the waterfront for a short bit, the tram turned left, into the neighborhood. As we approached the next stop, the person that had stood next to me got off and of course, Lucas took that as an opportunity.
It was difficult for me to object, even though I would love to – but making a scene really was impossible, because Lucas didn't stand out, not by anyone's standards. He wasn't doing anything that would draw attention to him, and so I was stuck, sitting there with him right beside me. We looked just like a couple in love, as in the meantime the vampire had draped his arm over my shoulder and whispered nonsense into my right ear about the sun and the beautiful, nice weather. And to make matters worse, he was also wearing that black and white striped shirt and I that gray-blue thing with that wide collar that constantly exposed my one shoulder, which was so very inconvenient right now. For thanks to that, to the outside world we *did* have the exact same alternative look…
Sure, I could try to rub the sunscreen from the back of his hand. Under the pretense of lovingly caressing, shall we say, or play along with the game and

then, as part of a fake flirtation session, suddenly take off his sunglasses. After all, we were riding to the west right now and the left window was right beside us, and therefore we were in the sun's direct path...

Hopeless. Completely hopeless. And in the meantime, the tram ran its route past the sad dereliction of Holešovice and past the train station and even further. Suddenly, Lucas grabbed my hand and pulled me to my feet. "Let's go for a walk, my dear," he said and we got off. We really did not have a choice, for this was the end of line 5. Next to a strangely proportioned, small building with way too much unsightly pseudo baroque on its facade, we passed the gates of something that just so happened to be on my 'to-do' list for this week: *Výstaviště,* the exhibition grounds. I had seen it a couple of times as we drove by and from the beginning I had been curious about that spacious pedestrian avenue with to the left and to the right those undefined little buildings behind lines of trees and at the end, in front of you that colossal, wide construction, made of steel, glass and pale painted plaster. And on top of it, that bell tower. Such an abnormal design – I was certain, you would not find that anywhere else in the world.
I saw that it was around 1 p.m., that meant it was lunchtime, and the hottest time of the day...

Ice hockey was a popular sport in the Czech Republic, so I could appreciate seeing the Tesla Arena on the right. But what was done with the rest of this alienating terrain...?
This place, aside from that one car that was parked by the skating rink, appeared completely abandoned and had the circumstances been different, I absolutely would have loved that. This obviously was the ultimate location for urban exploring with all the bells and whistles: the weed growing between the paving bricks beneath our feet, the inevitable questions that popped up while looking at your surroundings... Restaurant Pražan with its patio below the chestnut trees, for instance: now somewhat deserted, but when would it be open? This afternoon again? Or three years since the last time?
"Do you even know what we're doing here? I don't think you have any idea," I tried as unexpectedly and boldly as possible.
"I do. I know that very well. I'm here to spend some time with you," was the calm reply.
Do not get agitated. Focus on your surroundings.
That building over there, around the corner. In the window hung a piece of paper with on it the text 'under construction' or something, but were they actually working on that right now or was the project left for what it was half way through? For the fact was, that there was not a construction worker to be seen in the close vicinity and yet it was a regular workday. Remarkable, by the way; this was supposed to be a fairly closed-off area, because we had entered through gates that were open at this time of day, but they would

probably close again at some point. Were that really the only entrance gates? Or was there something else as well, an emergency exit perhaps?

I made another attempt. "Still, I think you should draw up a clearer plan," I stated, "cause otherwise I might as well carry on with my own business."

Lucas let go of me and made a wide gesture with his arms, like a nobleman who gave you a tour of his magisterial estate. "You only think about work, work, work. But you should learn to *enjoy* yourself, Lente!" he said. "Or don't you love this quiet, this space here after the claustrophobic hubbub at that flee market? Is it, in your opinion, not unique to experience this place, so accessible and in the middle of the city, yet so almost otherworldly desolate?"

"Oh, don't get me wrong. I love wandering around aimlessly in these kinds of places."

"But?"

"But not with you."

"I have to say, that surprises me a little. Could you tell me why, perhaps?"

"Because I don't like you so much anymore."

Lucas made a disappointed face. "I find that such a pity," he said. "Here I was, with such high hopes of having a good conversation, for old times' sake, shall we say. But alas, I should probably have known better. The fact that you did not appreciate my gifts was already not a good sign, obviously."

We were now right behind the main exhibition building. It was possibly even quieter here than where we just walked... not a bird making itself heard and all that could be seen around us seemed to be affected by the weather that was getting more oppressive by the minute, like a decades old postcard with photos that had once radiated life well-lived, but of which the colors had now begun to look more and more the same, faded yellow and blurred together.

What a strange location for a fair...

Behind the trees in front of us, out of the blue I could see the top edge of a giant Ferris wheel looming. And then, just like that, a garbage man was walking around all by himself over there, with a trash picker and large plastic bag and everything!

But Lucas immediately read my mind. "Look, there is one of those uneducated workers," he mocked. "One who can't make any conversation. Don't you find that remarkable too, Lente, that even the most highly educated people in this country speak their languages so poorly? How's it going with your Czech, by the way?" He took my hand in both his hands and give it a moist, cold kiss. Meanwhile, we passed the worker and Lucas greeted him with a friendly "*dobrý den...*"

The fair was out of commission. Probably for who-knows-how-long already. I had always wanted to see this in person, had come across photos of abandoned theme parks on the internet every now and then, images that I could easily let my imagination drift away with. The English had a word for the atmosphere that such a place evoked: 'eeriness'. There was something creepy about abandoned fairs. A feeling that was hard to put your finger on. It was the only type of location in the world in which the concept of being alone in a psychological sense also meant to really truly be alone, albeit only *with* reservation. Here, at all times, it was: 'alone, unless'... Because at any given moment you could expect the barking of a dog, between the high-tech entertainment equipment and the Bozo-the-Clown-like houses on wheels, or from that spacious mobile home over there the voice of a child.

But the undead, you would not hear them. They kept a low profile, in the trees behind the soberly painted merry-go-round or somewhere among the props of the haunted house that we passed...

The vampire led me around the fair in a big circle, all the way past the enclosure between here and the forest edge, where Stromovka Park began. We saw the skeletal pipe construction of the roller coaster from up close and the gondolas of the giant Ferris wheel and we walked, without anything happening. Without him doing anything in particular.

"I hope you realize how incredibly annoying I think you are right now," I said. "Annoying?" was Lucas' immediate reaction. "I think it is *you* who makes it difficult for us, with that petulant silence of yours. We could talk about something pleasant, now couldn't we? Or just go and do something fun. Why don't we get away for a while, for example? Somewhere, say, on vacation or something, completely submerge ourselves into oblivion and our being together... yes, Lente, let's go away, you and I – we've been missing each other for so long and life is short, much too short – tell me, where would you like to go? Vienna, Geneva, Florence?" The manic enthusiasm with which he spoke did not sit well with me. It sat anything but well with me.

"I'm enjoying myself just fine in Prague," I therefore said, but now the vampire made an inpatient gesture. "I don't get you *at all*, chérie! What is the reason of why you don't want to go on a trip with me? Why is *everything* always too much for you to deal with? Sometimes it seems like you're not willing to do anything, not even to participate with my acting, to that little bit of theater play..."

" – Only *I* don't see an audience for whom we should be doing that," I bit back, "or wait – maybe one or two *are* waiting in anticipation outside the light of the spotlights – after all, mediocre performers tend to invite family and friends, to fill the seats at least a *little* bit," I said, with my hand still locked in that grip of his.

Lucas remained silent, a purposeful entire minute. Then he said: "That was a hateful statement. I had long believed that our friendship had potential, but now I'm really starting to wonder – "

"*What* are you wondering?"

"Whether all my attempts at winning you over are in vain."

"Oh, don't make me laugh," I taunted, "do you honestly think that I will still fall for that? Are you really that dumb to assume I would believe someone who displays this sort of unhinged behavior?"

345

"What do you mean?"

"I mean that kind of behavior that goes whichever way the wind blows! 'Cause *what* is it that you're trying to communicate, anyway? Threat, intimidation, plain bullying, or perhaps those totally incredulous 'romantic feelings' of yours? As if you could even fall in love with *anyone...*"

Lucas briefly stopped walking. "Maybe it's difficult for you to understand, Lente, but I am most certainly capable of love. And you I love."

And then I too fell silent for a moment. But immediately after, I recovered and bluffed: "Then it *is* true what they say about you. That you're a monk of the most despicable kind. Because, let's be real here, not only do you go against 'sleeping with your brethren and waking with your brethren' for ages already, now you also prove that you really are the proverbial slave who is hopelessly dependent on his own whims."

The vampire only responded by once more proclaiming his declaration of love, and this time, by doing so, he genuinely bowled me over. The only thing I managed to mumble was: "You know that I can't keep this a secret from Raphaël."

"I'm willing to fight for you."

"You're insane."

"So be it."

In silence we strolled across cracked asphalt and sloppily laid paving stones towards the back exit of the exhibition grounds.

Then suddenly, Lucas asked, "Okay, Lente, by now I would like know what it's going to be. Vienna, or Florence after all," and he sounded again like he did before: provocative and dangerous.

– In the distance could be heard the rumble of an approaching thunder storm...

"If it is up to me, we're not going anywhere," I said. "I'm fine with the way things are."

"But *is* it up to you to decide that?"

"Why wouldn't it be up to me?"

"Because I don't think that I'm done with you for today."

Between the trees of the park tram 5 was parked at its starting point. I could see that the driver was getting ready to begin his route again and between the tram and us a policeman was keeping watch. What if I...? From the change in my body posture Lucas could tell that I was calculating my chances.

"What are you up to, my love?" he asked with sarcastic amusement. "Are you going to call in the help of the local authorities?"

"Yes, that is exactly what I'm going to do," I said slowly, "and it would be wise for you to let go of me now without making too much of a fuss." Immediately I raised my hand to draw the attention of the police officer. To my relief I succeeded. As he walked toward us I noticed how Lucas' amazement grew. In my best Czech I asked whether the man understood English and when that turned out not to be the case, I started using hands, feet and keywords. First I pointed to 'my friend' beside me. Then I tapped my watched and said with emphasis: "Leipzig, Leipzig!" Made the movements and the sound of a locomotive train, enunciated as clearly as possible the Czech for 'Holešovice Station' and pointed at my watch again. With an impatiently questioning gaze I looked at the officer and he got my message, he *understood* me, thank God! Immediately he beckoned Lucas to follow him, I gave my so-called boyfriend a quick kiss on the cheek and within a minute I stood there waving him goodbye.

I had never seen a vampire look as flabbergasted as he did from behind the window of the departing line 5.

## 68

SPIDER

It was Thursday, at the end of the day. Lucas had not shown himself since
yesterday and even though I had told him about what I he had done to me
the previous day and Raphaël had practically flown up the walls in helpless
anger, Lucas was still boycotted from further conversations.
And the determination with which we tried to live our normal, as mundanely
as possible little life, grew…

We had just come home. Raphaël placed the travel case of his recently
acquired viola da gamba on the dining table and opened the lid.
"May I?" I asked.
"Go ahead."
With reverence I let my fingertips glide over the centuries-old dark wood, and
between the strings, I touched the black and gold leaf painted ornament on
the body of the instrument. Graceful, yet not too elaborate swirly patterns,
shaped like a wreath with something like a heart at its center – fine, black
lines that seemed to be burned into the surface. Briefly I bent over to look at
the wood-carved pirate's head at the top of the neck. I had been present when
the restorer had shown us the finished result of his labor half an hour ago,
but only now I could really make out the details of this bass viol. Were all
historical musical instruments like that, that they were so artistically built,
or had my boyfriend managed to get his hands on a very rare piece?
"How old was it again?"
"She was built in 1691."
"A *she?*"
"Naturally."
"An old lady then," I mused. "And a French one, that is. How much luck can
someone be bestowed?" Full of irony I looked at him.
As though he did not pick up on my sense of humor Raphaël responded with
the words: "You could very well say that. The chance alone to run into a
colleague who is a gambist as well is – "
" – Miroslav, was it not? Of the uh… Chamber of Restoration Architecture?"
"Yes. And for him to have gotten wind of that widow, exactly last month…"
"Wasn't it difficult for her to part with the thing? Didn't it belong to her
recently deceased husband?"
"No, surprisingly, it was not that bad," said Raphaël. "She seemed to be
genuinely pleased that a buyer had presented himself. Her words of gratitude
were sincere. And had she left it at that, I could have been out the door

quickly as well…"

"But?"

"Oh, she started a whole discourse on keeping the music of her late husband alive." Annoyed he shook his head. "In short, towards the end it sounded more like she was talking about an organ transplantation than about… well, you know."

"A material object."

"Precisely. And then came the tea and the biscuits."

"So she liked you."

He puffed and pretended to focus on the bow that he took from the case. "Anyway, it's a good deal for both of us. I can play again and her measly pension is supplemented."

With his thumb he pressed against the horsehair stretched across the bow. Then he turned the knob on the one end a little. Felt it again. Next he opened a drawer underneath the dining table. A small box appeared. In the box was an orange cube, partially covered in a little piece of fabric. With awful squeaking the tightly strung horsehair was passed over the cube twice. I tried to ignore the noise and asked: "What is that?"

He answered: "Double bass rosin. I prefer it over violin rosin."

As I took the box from him and carefully touched the somewhat sticky cube Raphaël removed the viol from the case. Routinely but attentively, he began to tune the instrument's seven strings. When he had finished, he stood up, beckoned me with a nod of his head and let me take his place on the dining room chair. He held the object in front of me and said: "Never lift it at the location of the frets, otherwise they shift. And now, bend your knees outward and plant your feet flat on the ground. Yes, like that… no, don't rotate those feet that far. They should be positioned in line with your knees, otherwise it will start to bother you after a while."

Cautiously I took over the instrument from my boyfriend and planted it up right in the space between my legs. I had never realized how light of weight a viola da gamba was.

"Let the body simply rest on your calves. And don't clench it with your legs, just let it stand up right. She should be able to fall over easily, as it were."

He taught me the odd underhand grip with which you were supposed to hold the bow. Told me how the basic principles of the viol resembled those of the guitar and then let me strike the C-string. Awkwardly I let the bow bounce back and forth over the strings of the instrument. "You have to apply more force to it. Yes, a little bit harder. Don't be afraid of something breaking or snapping. Yes, that's more like it."

Sighing I dropped my right arm. "I'll never learn that," I complained.

"That's because you have to relax your arm. Hold on." He took over the bow from me. "Now pretend that you want to throw your right hand diagonally forwards away from you in a horizontal movement. Just shake it to the right, with a loosely hanging shoulder."

After this exercise I was handed back the bow and I stroked over the strings again. A warm, full sound came from the instrument. Surprised I looked at him. He smiled satisfied. Then I handed the viol to my boyfriend: "And now you."

Raphaël stood up and walked toward the case in silence. Placed the object inside it.

"Oh, come on. You haven't tuned it for nothing, now have you?"

"I'll play a little bit tonight."

"Why not now?"

"Have you forgotten what happened the last time when I picked up a viol in your presence?"

"No, but..."

"My love, we're not doing it," it sounded firmly.

"But do you want to timorously avoid your hobby every time I'm here?"

Raphaël slowly closed the case. "What needs to be done has to be done."

"No, what we've got to do is break through this. We're so many weeks further, already. You know that I've forgiven you..."

"Lente, no one can guarantee us that nothing will happen *this* time."

"No, that's right," I sighed. "But if we never give it a shot..."

The vampire ran his hand through his hair.

"Raph, what if I just pretend that I'm not listening? Then I'll just go and start supper and you'll play for yourself a little bit. Preferably a song that's as serene as possible."

"Such as?" He stared down at the viol case.

"Gee, I don't know. Something that isn't too emotionally charged for you. Something light, shall we say."

"*Le Badinage...* that means something like 'light conversation' or 'chit-chat'..."

"Oh wait, that's by Marais, isn't it?"

A brief nod. And a moment of wavering. Then Raphaël said, "You should go and start supper."

He stepped into the hallway and opened the door to the stairwell as widely as possible.

Once back to the living room he opened the case.

With a nervous 'yes' and a tap to my thighs I stood up and walked to the kitchen. There I began to ready some pots and pans. I took the vegetables from the fridge, picked up a bell pepper and held it under the cold running water. From the room it could be heard how the instrument was tuned one more time. Next, the first series of tones of Le Badinage reached my ears, after which this was repeated paper thinly and hesitantly. Twice the same series returned, with little variations at the beginning and end: sometimes an elegant tremor, other times a low note. The sounds of a laid-back dialogue it seemed; between friends, or good neighbors, I imagined. I started to cut the pepper, but soon put down the knife on the counter again. Forced myself – in spite of my apprehension – to get plates and cutlery and bring them to the room. As silently as possible I set the table, right behind where he was sitting.

I went back to the kitchen while the basic theme of the piece was alternated with higher sounding musical diversions.

Suddenly the playing stopped. I heard Raphaël clear his throat and subconsciously I stopped cutting the vegetables. "Keep playing, please keep playing," I prayed in silence. And he continued. He picked up the melody where he had left off, for a few seconds still a little reserved, but eventually he rediscovered the spirit of the piece. Thank God!

I slid the pepper pieces into a bowl, laid out an onion and walked back into the living room for no apparent reason. I stopped in front of the window, then figured I could quickly fluff the pillows on the couch and meanwhile keep an eye on my boyfriend. He did not have his eyes closed, but was so focused on his music that I wondered how much he was aware of the fact that I was now standing across from him. I sat down, initially to pick up the newspaper from the floor and neatly fold it, and then to look at him. He was still playing and I did not see any alarming changes in his facial expression. So far, so good...

The aristocratic, straight posture with which Raphaël sat in the front half of his chair reminded me of the appearance of Vittorio Ghielmi. An Italian as well. Could they have met at some point?

I wanted to get up, but something inside of me told me specifically to refrain from doing so, to remain seated where I was and to keep my gaze on his face and the instrument and on his hands. This was therapy, after all. For him and, most certainly, for me as well...

First, for a while, my eyes followed his right arm and how it made the bow move back and forth from different angles, but always horizontally. Then my attention focused on his left hand. The fingers traveled the neck of the viol in a way that, if you stared at it long enough, had a calming effect. Sometimes a group of tones was played from a single position of the four fingers. Fingers that each went their own way again a mere second later – index finger at the top, middle finger stretched out below that, ring finger and pinkie both in a relaxed, arched position close together. Next, the entire hand moved downward, to higher sounding tones and faster riffs. Like a spider in its web. Yes, that was what it truly looked like, those slender fingers constantly changing in position: the agile legs of a spider, the master of his domain, interwoven with threads. Waiting, stationary. Reaching out a leg to a thread to test the tension with a light touch and after that changing in position – at times slow and thoughtful and then again lightning fast in attack. Graceful, but accurately dropping in scales or once more climbing, heading for an imaginary prey.

After having sent the final notes of Le Badinage into the living room Raphaël slowly lowered his arms. Had there ever been composed a piece for viola da gamba that was about spiders?

## 69

EIGHTIES

Text messaging. Thank God for text messaging! The ultimate means to keep superficial acquaintances at an impersonal distance. And the perfect way to postpone a serious conversation with your loved ones just a little longer. Because having to speak to Claire today, for example, and to face her inevitable, critical questions and undergo her relentless digging... or to deal with the naive enthusiasm of my parents about the new, stable factor in my life?

No, I knew myself. If I were to call now, the temptation would be too high to make statements such as: "Sure, dad, things are fantastic here! Kazimír is the most wonderful guy you can imagine. Honest to a fault, open-minded and a hard worker... and we are totally madly in love with each other! If it were up to him, he'd even risk his life for me... Yes, really, Kazimír takes such good care of me, I truly want for nothing. And to top it off, he also loves to surprise me every now and then with – dad, could you *please* come and pick me up...?"

Clearly, to write a cheerful and at the same time informative text message about innocent touristic events was a much better option, even though that cost me half of my energy reserves. And the largest portion of what was left drained like water from a bathtub when, at my boyfriend's insistence and with pain in my stomach, I sent a message to Gosia in which I asked her whether she was doing anything tonight. Within the minute the answer was displayed on my screen: at 10 p.m. I was expected to show up at some club near Wenceslas Square. And my boyfriend was welcome to come too.

With a little squeeze in my hand Raphaël warned me that Gosia was coming and a second or so after that I felt a playful punch against my shoulder blade. I turned around and there she was, grinning broadly.

"Hey girl, ready to show Prague how it's done?" she asked.

"Hi." I tried my best to make my smile seem unrehearsed.

"This is my boyfriend Kazimír," I said.

"Kazimír! That's cool man, that you're here as well," she said and they shook hands, she heartily and he politely. We entered the club.

"You hadn't told me that he was such a hot piece of ass," she whispered into my ear in an unguarded moment. I nodded and Raphaël did not hear a thing. Supposedly.

We scoped out the bar. Checked out the attached pub and returned to the bar. Tonight was an eighties party, as it so happened. A feast of recognition, for some. The ages of the people in the audience therefore varied quite a bit. People in their twenties, thirties and a handful that were even older. How convenient...

Video clips were shown on a large screen. A song by Talk Talk, *Such A Shame* had just begun to play and before I could stop it I had already let out an enthusiastic reaction.

"An eighties freak as well, I see," smiled Gosia, "so I had pegged you right, after all!"

"And you can tell after one song already. You have talent," I said teasingly, or rather sarcastically. Then I let my gaze drift to the singer on the screen, the little man with his awkward, goofy face that looked into the world so endearingly, almost helplessly, but then all of a sudden startled you with a frustrated malevolence that would bite your head clean off, if you didn't pay attention.

Gosia came and stood beside me, wrapped her arm across my shoulders and hung with her full weight against me, the way girls like to do. She rested the side of her head against mine. My boyfriend softly growled, I could hear it clearly and Gosia probably heard it as well, or no, she did *not* hear that, of course. Because she was a stranger to menacing guttural sounds. After all, she was not a vampire.

"Those elephants give me a kick," I said.

"Uh, what?"

"This song, Talk Talk," I snapped, and I wrestled myself away from her.

We ordered our first drink. She paid. We chatted. Her and Raphaël got more acquainted and they did it quite well, together: the perfect performance of that little play about two strangers who meet through a mutual acquaintance and who, through small talk such as *what do you study, how long have you lived here already* and *where exactly do you live*, wind up at the most logical subject that could follow next: the city that they have both made their home. While they gauged each other's opinion on the height of house renting and the mind numbing character of concrete suburbs I was worrying about when this talk would bleed out. So I had to come up with questions, many questions. Do everything possible to make her keep talking, so that I did not have to...

So as soon as all eyes had turned to me again I subjected my new friend, with my boyfriend's protective arm around my waist, to an interrogation for as long as possible. About her family, her village in Poland, the apartment that she lived in and her friends in Prague, and when I briefly ran out of questions I switched to music, music and even more music. Coincidentally, she loved exactly the same as I did. Ridiculous.

It became more crowded. More people and conversations around me that distracted me. More opportunities to use songs that were being played as an excuse to remain silent and to drink. To remain silent and to listen. And when there was something to be said after all, Raphaël was lovingly considerate with me. Clearly articulated, yet not painfully loud he spoke his words, close to my ear. Even Gosia remained clearly intelligible when she spoke, it almost seemed as though she copied how he did it and carefully imitated his speaking volume. Why all that blasted effort? To spare me, or something? Stupid bitch.

The Eurythmics. *The Miracle Of Love...* I turned my head sideways to my beloved and kissed him, intimately and sexually. Out of the corners of my eyes I could see how Gosia was staring at us. Not enviously or maliciously, but with those big, expectant, curious goggles of her. Why for Pete's sake that comedy? Did she think that I could not handle her if she were to be herself? *All* that I wanted, was to have a friend in this city. Or at least someone with whom I could chat casually or do fun stuff with every once in a while. And what did I get? Games. Theater... Hypocrite bitch.

And now she even started talking about my photography. She asked my boyfriend what he thought of my work and photography assignments in Prague, and he just went with it, told her about my meeting a violinist named Petr and about his own plans to perform as a gambist... Well, it was fine by me.

They could jabber whatever they wanted, I was gonna dance.

And of course, they immediately followed my steps.

Van Halen! *Jump*!! Her and my eyes met and at precisely the same moment and with the exact same intensity we let out a cheer that was inextricably linked to the intro of this song. I hated myself for it, for that glance of recognition, for that click between us that made itself felt on the inside with such a deep sense of naturalness. To make myself forget I danced and we jumped, automatically at the command of the singer, simultaneously with the hustling crowd around us and hence, together. I tried to deliberately jump out of sequence, but the music of Van Halen and the party mood in this bar were too overwhelming and compelled to unity with the masses. And with her.

More energizing songs, more dancing, warm sweat and finally, the exhaustion. "Gotta go pee," I panted into Raphaël's ear. And to Gosia I said: "Be right back."

At a trot I left the dance floor.

That she would grab this opportunity, I could have known. I had not made it halfway down the corridor when she appeared by my side and supposedly amicably hooked arms with me. 'Just us girls' would undoubtedly be her excuse and yes, she indeed said something in that spirit.

At the mirrors she came and stood next to me. Like me, she got busy with petty things like washing hands and checking make-up. Then she combed her hair, put it in a braid and secured it to the back of her head with a black clamping thingamabob. She undid the silk scarf around her neck, put it on again, better this time, and tied it with a fashionable knot.

Next she took out a soft, pink-red color for her lips.

"Say what you like, but you do look happy together," she said.

"Oh, definitely…"

"Have you talked with him yet?"

"About what?" With painful precision I fixed my eyeliner.

"Well, wasn't Raphaël so, uh… protective?"

The blood drained from my cheeks. Keep working that eyeliner. "Who is Raphaël?" I asked.

"Oh, sorry, today I ran into someone with that name. But it's Kazimír, of course."

I forced myself to turn towards her and look straight at her. "Could you please never do that again?" I asked urgently. "Or at least not when Kazimír is with us? Things have just started to go a little better between us and I'm not in the mood for misunderstandings right now. You have no idea what a hard time he gave me when I went to take pictures of Petr…"

"Sure," she said while pressing a friendly fist against my upper arm.

Gosia *had* to smell my fear. And ignore it as well, because she was pretending not to notice anything, of course. Or no more than a normal person would, at least. But the fact that she could smell me was undeniable. And she would act on it too. She would place the emotions that I radiated within a context, draw conclusions from it and report on it…

Would different kinds of fears also come with scents that distinguished themselves from one another? Was it possible for her to figure out who I was afraid of: Raphaël or her, and should I maybe take that more into account – oh shit, I had been really lovey-dovey with Raphaël just before! Or was I worrying too much right now… naturally, couples that were going through a rough patch were good at pretending. In these sort of situation in particular one learned to hide their personal life, just look at – oh, quit it with that nonsense! Did you honestly think that you had any chance when the big bomb would drop, did you *really* think that you – "Gonna go get some fresh air," I said. "I'll come find you in a bit, okay?" Briskly I stepped around Gosia to reach the door, leave the toilets, pass the corridor, exit the main door, to go outside!

## 70

## ABDUCTION

Just for a few minutes. It did not have to take more than that. To be alone for just a little bit, without that disjointedness with that indefinable aftertaste around me, only one moment without hidden agendas.

I turned left in hopes of seeing less faces, hearing less voices and cars, away from the Friday-night-outgoing hullabaloo and the main square. And another left turn – the arm of totally drunk soccer jersey at the corner reached out to me. I was barely able to avoid him.

It had rained for the last hour, the streets were wet…

Breathe in and out deeply. In through your nose and out through your mouth. A couple making out against the front of a shop…

Other than that, things were getting less crowded here – relax! You've said nothing wrong. You could not do better than what you have done just now. Breathe in the silence…

After a few hundred meters of only dark houses and a long row of parked cars I stopped in front of a somewhat recessed facade. And immediately Gosia stood there in front of me.

Impatiently I snarled: "Didn't I tell you I would be right back?"

"Yes, but I was worried about you, so I thought…" she tried.

"Worried? Do I look like someone who needs that much care?"

Behind her I saw Raphaël appear… "Oh, and you're here as well then. What is it with you guys, that you stick your nose in literally everything! Is this what it's going to be like from now on, will I never get one second of peace in my life anymore?" I called out in a cracking voice. I wanted to start walking again, but Gosia blocked my path.

Raphaël said something to her, in Czech. She said something back and suddenly she grabbed both my arms, placed them at the back of her neck and commanded: "Hold on." Then she scooped me up behind my knees, the way in which you would catch a woman that is passing out and protect her from a fall just in time.

"Close your eyes, you'll get less dizzy," she said. Then, with a shriek of fright, I experienced the acceleration and the shearing of the wind in my face, ice cold and piercing. From that moment on everything around me became too much for my senses to turn into a logical narrative. Buildings that turned into frighteningly enclosing dark blurs, a nauseating tilt to the left and then immediately back again. Alongside of us a blue line, gone with the fleetingness of a falling star – the back entrance of the Lucerna Passage? Immediately after that another turn, now to the right. A cacophony of strangely distorted sounds. Cars, music, hollering... then a screeching roller coaster sensation in my lungs – we jumped over something. A fence? Vehicles? On the right I could see the contours of the immense National Museum pass by, big and wide and dark with in the middle that little tower, dome or whatever. After that a slight curve and a long straight section, with once or twice brief jerks to the side and lights passing by way too closely, smeared in white and red – what was wrong with those drivers here – and houses, black with vague yellow and orange streaks of lit windows and store signs...

A deafening ringing, quickly increasing in volume and then dropping in pitch further and further and fading away, made me bury my face in Gosia's neck, but my dazed amazement made it so that I also quickly raised my head again to look over her shoulder and to discover that this shrill ringing had been the bell of a tram of which its taillights had almost disappeared from my field of vision already.

I turned my head to face forwards again and just when I wondered what those silver colored, sometimes white shining lines were that ran in a tapered perspective from underneath us to the horizon, the grip of the arms that held me tightened, and we decelerated considerably. A leap over an object, a little wall or something, darkness that seemed to come down from dim spots above us... and then predominantly the silence, with the city noises merely unobtrusively in the background.

I was lowered to my feet, felt dizzy. Gosia kept holding me, but I tore myself away from her. Promptly I lost my balance, but right away Raphaël was there as well to prevent me from falling. I closed my eyes tightly to let them get used to the darkness. Then I opened them and looked at my surroundings. We were standing at a crossroad of paved walking paths amidst a bunch of trees. A park or something?

"Where are we?" I asked.

"This is the Olšanska Cemetery," said Gosia.

"By Flora metro station," Raphaël added.

"You cannot be serious..." I glanced around me and now also began to make out the creeping vegetation and stones, yes, large, upright standing stones. Tombstones... everywhere around me the graves of dead people!

"Yes, I'm sorry Lente, for this unfortunate decision, but we had to act quickly and this was the only suitable location in the area."

"Suitable for what?"

"Here you can do anything that you're inclined to without being disturbed: curse, yell..."

"Why would I want to yell?"

"You have gone through a lot of stress lately..." Gosia said carefully.

I wormed my way out of Raphaël's grip, took a couple of impulsive steps away from them both. However, she approached me with the same number of cautious, almost animalistic strides. With a panicking pointed finger I tried to mark my boundaries and I snarled several times: "Stay over there, stay over *there*," until she stopped.

My boyfriend stood and looked at us from a respectful distance, yet nevertheless involved, watchful and on standby for what was to come…

"You don't have to pretend anymore," Gosia said.

A ray of moonlight fell through the canopy of the trees and onto her face and the way in which she stood there she did not remotely look like that bubbly human girl with whom I had a fun time with on that café's patio by the Karlova a week ago. Now a woman stood before me, weathered, anguished even, and in some way unspeakably old and wise.

She sighed a helpless sigh. "It's not my intention to cause you this much of a fright," she said and it honestly seemed like she meant it!

"That may be so, but I'm really getting sick and tired of your games. Don't you think it's time for you to just tell me what you want from me?"

"I would be angry too, if I were in your shoes… If it helps you, you may hit me."

"Me, hit *you*?" I uttered, "that's a pretty ironic statement under these circumstances, don't you think? I guess it's better for you to just do your thing, since that's what you were planning all along anyway. Then we'll get this misery over and done with," I said smugly, and from one moment to another I felt completely drained.

"You're right," said Gosia, and as Raphaël stepped in a little closer her hands slowly reached for her neck. She undid her scarf – why would she possibly do that? I had the greatest difficulty understanding what I saw… it looked like she was rolling up that scarf or something to that effect… yes, she rolled it up and after that she held it tautly by both ends and brought the thing horizontally to mouth level right in front of her face. The vampire looked at me, with those strange, focused eyes, as though she wanted to assess what my reaction would be when I finally realized what she was planning to do. And now, with a jolt, I realized it indeed: she thought it was time. Time to do *her thing!*

I turned around and began to walk along the dark, tree-shaded, paved path… casually, as though nothing was wrong. Maybe that would make a difference, but soon after, Raphaël came walking next to me and grabbed my elbow. And when I pulled myself free he took hold of me, tighter this time, with both arms around my waist – I had no idea what was going on, because in what way did he think he was helping me by holding me so – "What are you doing, why aren't you helping me," I exclaimed and again I made an attempt at freeing myself.

"Don't put up a fight, baby girl," he said, "you're only making it worse for yourself," and when Gosia came up to me and killed my screaming with her rolled up scarf, he whispered: "I'm sorry things had to be this way, Lente…"

A second scarf was brought out from a pants pocket, and right before my eyes were blackened with it, the last thing I saw was the sad look on his face.

"We'll be there in a few minutes," said Gosia.

"Hmmm…!" I protested from behind the tight mouth cover, but she ignored me and then I understood that she was talking with someone on the phone, because mechanically and from some distance the question sounded, "Where are you now?"

Her reply was brief. "The cemetery," and then she stopped talking.

Raphaël's voice on the other hand, I could hear constantly. On the left and then on the right side of my head, depending on my struggling and kick-punching attempts to release myself from his grip. He said: "You don't have to pretend anymore," and softer, in my ear: "It's really almost over… just a little longer, Lente," and I really wanted to *scream* "shut the fuck up" at him, but he kept comforting me or – as became more and more clear to me – trying to do his penance, and it made me bat-shit crazy!

Then however, without any announcement, two unrelenting arms picked me up, the arms of Gosia… and the running began again, preceded by the jump across the wall, the sharp turn to the right and the accompanying raging adrenaline kick. In the meantime she explained that we were going to a location that absolutely had to remain a secret and that I was wearing a blindfold for that reason only, but that Raphaël was joining us and would not leave my side for one moment. As if that still mattered at this point…

Going through the city at such unholy speed does strange things to your ears. Cars that you pass by and that are oncoming are no more than swift breaths of winds. The sporadically used horns of those cars on the other hand, sound nerve-rackingly loud and nearby, but also turn out to be far behind you within a fraction of a second. And then there are the people in the city center with their fragments of talking and laughter, and the trams, all so different than usual and always first increasing in volume, but immediately decreasing again… the heavier and therefore easier to identify engines of trucks and city buses…

Something opened ahead of us. Or we had started to run faster – in any case, I felt a change in the airflow against my body – it became cooler and also the sounds around us, it seemed like what was first echoed off the houses and buildings was now subject to a certain distortion. Where we found ourselves, here, it was more open…

The honking of a train. But from below. In fact, quite a ways beneath me. Where, in God's name… no, wait, I knew where we were! The Nusle Bridge! No other bridge in Prague was as tall as the Nusle Bridge, and below it was a railway track. As best as I could, I tried to draw a conclusion from that: it meant that we were heading south, to the southern edge of the city. Do not forget! Remember where you are, perhaps that could help me… and if that jackass next to me could just shut that darn mouth of his, I would be able to concentrate as well.

But he did not stop his rambling about my having to hold on 'for just a little longer' and that it was 'really almost over'. We were not completely finished yet, he repeated himself, but we were soon – why, for Pete's sake, that stupid emphasis on that word *almost*?? I had other things on my plate than those empty promises of his, such as not losing that mind of mine, although that was almost an impossible task. Because if I did not go nuts with his bullshit, then surely with everything going on around me and did that going crazy not happen right this instant, it would very shortly... dissociate. Think of other things – Mathilde had once told me that it helps you to keep a sane mind, and she should know as a recently graduated psychiatrist. So I had to distract myself with happy thoughts. Trees... Climbing trees, perhaps? Yesss, the tall trees at home in Bosch en Duin – I would kill to be able to be there right now. The geometric, white house of my parents. Where life was still predictable and safe, because sheltered... where there was a fence on all sides of our domain, as a protection against uninvited guests.

The blindfold pressed firmly, yet not uncomfortably on my eyeballs. It made it so that even the differences between light and dark were barely visible through the slits of my eyes. I bent my head forward, because I had noticed that that helped to make the scarf around my mouth feel less constrictive. It even made it possible for me to move the bottom part of my jaw, but I was not able to free my mouth completely by doing so, not free enough to be able to scream, in any case, or to throw the most obscene curse words imaginable at Raphaël – way too much silk in front of my face, with only an opening by my nose for breathing. And that was enough for now – yes, in a very strange way this was fine the way it was. I even felt kind of safe with it. Swaddled, like an infant. Back into the womb... I pressed my head against Gosia's bosom.

And then the moment was there at which we slowed down and stopped. Bizarre, how time and space could become so distorted... ever since the Nusle Bridge I had honestly been under the assumption that I had a realistic idea of where we were going, but now everything was different after all. It was quiet here. Not just uncrowded, the way it is in a suburb of a big city, but really completely devoid of sound, and the soil that my feet touched, when I was lowered to the ground, was soft... So no pavement then, no street pavers. Actually I kind of should have known. The turns that we had taken had become so much more numerous at a certain point. From that – if I had kept my head a little better – I could have deducted that we had left the highway. And despite the fact that the surrounding sounds had been reflected by residential units in neighborhoods and such from time to time, the cars and the people and the trams had remained absent... That obviously meant that we were out in the country.

Gosia asked: "Are you still dizzy?"

I shook my head. I lied.

"Then I'm going to carry you on my back now. It's more convenient here," she said and she let herself be held by her shoulders by me, knelt and took hold of my legs.

Twigs that snapped beneath her feet. A gust of wind high above us and the scent of pine trees – we were in a forest. It was hilly, fairly steep even at places. We were not running anymore, but walking, climbing from time to time and after a while we entered some place. A house...? At least it sounded like we were in a hallway, because I could detect the seclusion of it as Gosia's steps hit the floor. It smelled different here as well and I heard the dripping of water – no, wait, this was not a house at all. This was a cave! And an extensive cave as well, given the seemingly endless winding of the corridors we were passing through. Also leaps were made, short and long leaps. At such moments Gosia told me ahead of time to hold onto her extra carefully and to not be scared and then we went airborne, large sections forward, and once even diagonally upwards...

Raphaël had gone on ahead of us for all this time. However, now he stopped and said something to Gosia in Czech and subsequently moved something heavy to the side. A rock? A sliding door or something? And the same thing happened again, a couple of seconds later.

"We're almost there," he said to me and suddenly I could hear movement around me, not just of him or her, but of more people. Vampires. Whispering in English and then once more the sliding of something heavy across the floor.

I was lowered to my feet. My blindfold was removed and my mouth freed. It was pitch-black here and that certainly did not help me regain my balance. I had no choice but to seek out support from Raphaël, who was standing right beside me. While I took an attempt at getting rid of the numbness in my upper lip I heard how a match was lit. For a few seconds my eyes were blinded, but then I could distinguish the yellow-orange lit facial features of Gosia. As she lit a number of candles on the ground and in alcoves in walls, our surroundings slowly became visible: we were in some sort of chamber that was not very big. It was made up of rocks and strongly scented dirt above, below and all around us.

In a corner stood two folding chairs. Nothing more. I shivered.

## 71

JUDGMENT

We were left alone, the stone door was pushed into place again and Raphaël said: "You must feel so betrayed…" He took a few steps toward me, but I evaded him.

"Where are we? What kind of place is this," I asked.

"Honey, you know I cannot tell you that," he replied.

"I. Want to know. Where we *are!*"

"*No,*" he growled. I had punched him in the face and blood dripped from his nose. He wiped it away with the sleeve of his shirt and he approached me again.

"Get the fuck away from me!" I snarled, but he wrapped his arms around me.

"Get lost, asshole, I hate you!" Fervently I tried to free myself from him, but escaping from his embrace was sheerly impossible.

"I *hate* you," I yelled, even louder now, but he said: "I love you, Lente," with his voice smothered against the skin of my neck. He kissed me, and that was the irrevocable breaking point. "Oh, me too, Raph," I cried, "I love you too, so incredibly much – darling, what is left for us to do??"

With his caressing fingers across my cheek and a lot of comforting words he tried to calm me down. That was only partially successful and finally he admitted that he was completely in the dark concerning our fate…

We had sat down, Raphaël in a chair and I in his lap. He held his face at a few inches distance from me and made eye contact. He said: "Listen, Lente. I want to try something on you. What I would like to do, is to appeal to your sense of logic. If we succeed, it will bring you some internal rest, but most of all a better grip on the situation. Are you okay with that?"

I nodded, hesitantly, between two sobs.

"Okay. You're a photographer, right? That means you are a visual person. But you have also learned that what the eye catches at first glance, does not contain all the information that can be abstracted from an image."

I nodded again.

"So things are not always what they seem. The same principle goes for our situation. We are trapped here, far away underground in a space that has no view to the outside and inevitably that does something to our brain. Automatically, we let our thinking be restricted by it. Yet, I seriously wonder whether that response is our only option. Is what you see around you here, really all the information that you have obtained this evening?"

"No…"

"What conclusions can you draw, for instance, from the fact that you were blindfolded?"

"What Gosia said: that I wasn't allowed to know where we were going?"

Raphaël brushed a hair from my face. "Agreed," he said. "But have you also wondered why you were still wearing that blindfold when you were brought in here?"

"As we walked through those corridors?"

"No, think deeper."

"When the others joined us?"

"That's what I mean, yes. And therefore..."

"...that blindfold was meant for the others to not see – no – *I* was not meant to see what they looked like."

"Precisely. And given that fact, how do you think they will deal with that shortly?"

"Dunno. As before? Or would they disguise themselves or something?"

"And if you were them, how would you go about disguising yourself? If you were, shall we say, just as scared of being exposed as they currently are?" Think. Come on! I wiped the last bit of teardrops from my eyes. "There's more of them," I said, "So they will try to, uh... look alike as much as possible. Yes, and they will want to hide their faces. And also keep me from hearing their voices."

"...Or recognize them."

"Shit. Yes, of course."

"So prepare yourself for that, honey. You're about to see some things that will come across as unusual, to say the least. But keep in mind that any measure that they take is purely out of fear. And by the way, you should also know that in front of the door here there are a couple of guards. That is partly to prevent my breaking out, but also to pick up on a thing or two of what we are discussing."

I swallowed down something unpleasant. In thought I quickly went over whether there was something that I had said that I should not have, but the reassuring way in which Raphaël looked back at me, convinced me that that was not the case. And then, suddenly, it began to dawn on me... Just for good measure I said to my boyfriend that these guards would most likely be able to understand German, since German was so similar to the Dutch that we were speaking. But meanwhile all my systems were already switching to a mode that had everything to do with vigilance, being alert to my choice of words, because now it thankfully had gone well, but it very much so had to remain that way when – the sound of massive stone being dragged across smoothly polished rock made our gazes go to the exit of the room. A figure entered, clad from top to bottom in bright-yellow rain clothing. He or she was wearing a mask, one of those Venetian masks, but in white and completely plain and undecorated. For a second it felt as though my heart sank down by a couple of inches in my chest. But I managed to keep my calm.

However, I had thought that we would have had more time to be together and to talk, Ralph and I, just to discuss things. We still had so much to talk about, you see, on so many topics – I still had to tell him that I was sorry about giving him that nosebleed and to let him know that I had forgiven him regarding earlier, cause by now I understood that he had run out of options as well and… and I still had so much to ask him and… my eyes welled up with tears.

In spite of that, I stood up, along with my beloved. The figure pointed at me and when, with a small voice, I asked "me?" the figure nodded without saying a word. Raphaël explicitly said: "Lente, this is not the end yet. Realize that. You have to hold on for a little longer and then, very soon, we will see each other again…"

Our embrace was as intense as it was short-lived, because the guard beckoned me to follow him and I followed him obediently, with strange, cramped legs – where had Gosia gone to, by the way?

Once more I looked into the chamber made of rock, where Raphaël was left all by himself and just before the line of eye contact between us was severed he said: "Keep it together, sweetheart," and he looked at me with those incredibly beautiful, serious eyes of his…

I was given a flashlight to find my way in the dark and made sure as best as I could that no one had to grab me or force me back in line while walking through the corridor. Do not be a smartass and especially don't do anything stupid right now… and I had to watch what I said, because vampires were intelligent and anything I said would be interpreted in ways of which a normal human wouldn't think of as quickly, and every question that they would ask would undoubtedly be a trick question and – now I suddenly understood why Raph had constantly tried to get through to me with that *keeping your head together…*! But first, as long as nobody claimed my immediate attention, I had to reason away my anxiety. Downplay the situation…

The space that I was brought into was almost the same as the one in which I had been waiting with Raphaël. Bare rock and dirt. However, things were a little bigger here, and construction lights were set up in three different positions. Together they created an alienating interaction of sharp edge shadows and streaks of unrelentingly harsh light.

It certainly was a practical choice, those construction lights. They probably had a generator for them somewhere, though I was not able to see one here at first glance. Rain suits, they were wearing yellow rain suits. As expected, they were all similar, as were the gloves that they wore. And the white, face-covering masks with the tightly drawn hoods around that… it was a ghostly picture, all of this together. That I had to admit.

But it was plastic, or nylon, and nothing more than that. Purchased at a sport store or a shop for party goods.

They sat next to each other at a table, five figures in a row. It was remarkable how they all seemed to be of the same height. How had they managed to do that? Were the less tall ones sitting on top of a few extra pillows or something?

I myself was seated in a folding chair, the kind that gives you pain in your extremities within a matter of minutes, due to the impractical shape of the backrest. For a moment I sat there, staring at them, while they in turn looked at me. Then the second figure from the left brought a device up to his mouth and began to speak, in English. His voice had a very strange, unnatural sound, as though he had first inhaled from a balloon filled with helium.

"Your name is Lente Sandifer?" he asked.

Voice distorters, they were using voice distorters... nothing to be afraid of then! Keep a level head.

"Uh, yes, that's my name."

"And you live in the Netherlands?"

"Yes."

"In what city?"

"In Rotterdam." I coughed to get rid of the hoarseness.

After having verified my name, place and date of birth the figure looked to the left. The individual sitting in the middle now took over:

"Tonight you are a guest at a meeting of the International Community of Vampires. Among those present are representatives of the Councils of two involved global regions, namely the West-Germanic Territories and the Danube Monarchy. The Inspector General and two staff members of the Supreme Council are present as well." The voice of this person sounded many times lower than that of the other, and the words that were spoken by him, it almost seemed as though they were obstructed by an unseen force, causing them to come out slower than initially intended.

"I don't know what that is," I said.

"What *what* is?"

Shit, shit, what possessed me to ask such an impertinent question?

"Sorry. The Supreme Council."

"That is the highest regulatory organ of the vampiric community. There are Regional Councils and there is the Supreme Council. The Inspector General has the final say in all affairs."

"Thank you. Again, my apologies."

The voice in the middle briefly lowered his head. Then he asked: "For how long have you known of our observing you?"

"Uh... oh..." Think. Do not make mistakes.

"At least, I assume that you had been aware of that?"

"There was someone, yes... Lucas. But Raphaël and I have ignored him as best as we could."

"When I say 'we' I don't mean Lucas, however. He lives in a completely different region," it sounded sharply.

Now appear startled – "But that means that...?"

"...A number of us have tailed you, yes. All twenty four hours of every day that you have been in Prague, up until this day. Do you have any inkling towards why we have done that?"

"To, uh... um... No, I don't know. In order to answer that I would have to be able to read your mind, otherwise it becomes a matter or guessing. Sorry." With an abrupt gesture the person sitting most right turned on his voice distorter. His voice sounded robotic and shrill, when he asked: "Do you have any idea how little use an infant makes of his brain capacity, compared to us, the undead??" Immediately a reaction from next to him followed – loud hissing, like that of a cat. It was unclear from whom that came exactly, but it had its effect, because it silenced the robotic voice. Then the person in the middle started to talk again. "What my brother or sister here next to me is trying to communicate, is the following: we live our lives among mortals. However, you know that we rarely associate with them on a personal level. Still, we have been able to learn a thing or two about them in the course of the years. Things that make us realize that you, by the circumstances that you currently find yourself in, could form a threat to us sooner or later. You have entered our world. And that now forces us to ask the question whether you can be trusted. Tell us a little about that – what, in your opinion, makes you that much more trustworthy than all those other mortals?"

I stared in front of me, and this time the desperate look in my eyes was sincere.

Because... were they being serious? Was this a genuine question, aimed directly at me, or just a rhetoric one and was there more to come?

"Well?"

"Oh, uh, yes..." Think. Take your time. Repeat the question to yourself: what was it, according to you, that made you so much more trustworthy than all the other mortals? "Yeah, you see – I'm afraid that this is again such a question, the kind that is almost impossible for me to answer. It's not that I don't want to answer you, don't get me wrong, but at this time I would not – for the life of me – know what to say. Because if I were to give you a percentage of my being trustworthy or not, that percentage could change tomorrow again, due to all kinds of unforeseen circumstances, they naturally change constantly and, uh, I think time is the only factor... the only factor that can give you the answer that you're looking for."

The person in the middle looked to his left and to his right. The others nodded in silence. Then he said: "Thank you. That is all, for now," and the next second one of the guards that had been posting in front of the door, was by my side. I had to get up and the stone door was pushed from its position by the other guard.

"But – is it over already, then?" I asked, as I let my gaze alternate between the table with the vampires and the pitch-black hole that formed the entrance to the rest of the cave system.

"We have heard enough," was the response of the vampire in the middle. And that's what I had to contend with.

I saw Raphaël only briefly, in the light of the torch that I was holding, while he was escorted out. In passing his eyes looked at me with the most heartbreaking combination of sorrow, concern and encouragement, and he said: "I love you..."

"I love you too," I whispered and before I knew it, he had already disappeared from sight and I was left to my own devices in the waiting room from earlier. "We have heard enough." That announcement had marked the end of my interrogation. But could this even be called an interrogation? It had been over so much sooner than I'd ever been able to anticipate.

Vampires *were*, of course, quick in their thinking. Quick as lightning. Perhaps that was why. But did it also make them faster at coming to conclusions? Because one did, in fact, need information to be able to draw those conclusions. Did they not? In this case for instance, information provided by me. Or could I be mistaken in my thinking? In either case, the fact was that I had barely been granted the opportunity to provide it to them.... and a judgment, passed on the basis of non-information, was a prejudice. Shit, *shit* – this felt so terribly not okay!

To think that I had completely braced myself for all kinds of trick questions – or had they even incorporated those trick questions into that brief conversation? Oh no... yes, they must have... And there I had been, giving them all those vague answers!

In a panic reaction I ran to the door and began to shout and to punch the bare stone surface with my fists, upon which I instantly hurt my hands and had to lower them again, moaning with pain. After that, I tried by explaining, wild and desperately gesturing in the void at whoever outside wanted to hear my words. And subsequently, I was pacing the room in the most illogical patterns...

I confessed that I had made a mistake in what I had communicated to them just before, and said that there was still much more that I had to tell them, otherwise they would not understand my point of view and reasoning and motives, and surely they would have more things to ask me, because wasn't it important for us to know each other well, or at least, a lot better than we were doing now – but the door was closed and no one was listening to me. In tears I finally slumped to the floor chafing my back against the wall.

I had fallen asleep, apparently. How was I even able to sleep under these conditions?

There was something different about the light. I counted the candles on the floor and in the alcoves of the wall. Three out of seven had now died down. What time was it, anyway? Way past two already, good grief... and Raph still had not returned. I tried to move a little, felt stiff and numb despite the blanket that lay on top of me – a blanket? Did that mean that someone had come in here in the meantime? I heard whispering from behind the door and the voice of someone speaking out loud – the voice of Gosia. Where had she come from all of a sudden? The heavy stone was moved aside and the unmistakable slender silhouette of the vampire girl appeared in the doorway. "Are you awake yet?" she asked as she walked towards me. Somewhat skittishly I pushed myself up, until I sat up with my back against the wall. She squatted down right in front of me and it was not until now that I saw that she had brought a couple of items – a bottle, among other things, and she placed it on the uneven rock floor beside her. Then she took out something that looked soft and light in color from a little bag. A wad of cotton balls. She opened the bottle, moistened a few and slowly brought them to my face.

"What are you going to do?" I asked with a tiny voice.

"You have cried. Your mascara has run," she said and carefully she began to wipe below my eyes. After an initial startled reaction, I let her.

"How is Raph?" I asked. "What are they doing to him?"

"You know that I can't tell you anything about that," Gosia answered, and for the umpteenth time this evening I felt helpless tears well up... the salty moisture, mixed with the make-up residue on my skin, caused even more stripes and smears to form, running far beneath my chin. The vampire caught my tears, gently wiping across my neck, jawline and cheeks. She drenched another cotton ball with her cleaning lotion and continued cleaning my face and as she did, she looked at me in a way that I had also seen Raphaël look at me sometimes: in curious amazement, like an alien creature that was given a chance to observe a mere human from this close for the first time in her life...

It was probably going to have something to do with decapitation. After all, that was the only way to forever silence not only me, but Raphaël as well. I tried to picture the scene at hand, with me, lying in wait on the scaffold, my hands tightly bound behind my back and him right beside me. His eyes, staring into mine with that typical vacant look... no, the opposite, filled with *love*! Heart wrenching, devoted love.

When the time came I did not want a bag over my head.

I was tired, had been for a long time... and in a strange way I felt naked. Odd, really, cause I had not needed to take off my clothing – those rain jackets, could they be wearing them because rain jackets are easy to wash clean? Of blood, for example? And what would they do with our bodies, afterwards? Where would a body go that had to disappear without a trace?

And yet... it did not bother me as much anymore, the way in which the five of them sat there at that table with their ghostly masks and bright-yellow costumes.

At this point, Raphaël's touch was infinitely more important: his right arm, which he had wrapped around my back and his other hand that held mine at belly level in front of us, and especially his softly caressing fingers...

Counting the seconds that we were allowed to spend together, that was the only thing that still mattered right now.

Bizarre, though, that I did not see my life pass before my eyes at all.

Normally speaking, did something like that not happen when you were about to die – my beloved made a wild movement, totally unexpectedly, and with a jolt I returned to the here and now. I was being spoken to, apparently the mask in the middle had been talking for quite a while, and now he said: "...and that is why, Lente, the Supreme Council has decided that, as of today, you enjoy the unconditional protection of every vampire that lives within the boundaries of the Danube Monarchy."

Sheepishly I looked at the figures in front of me and then, not quite understanding, to my boyfriend. He hugged me and said: "Darling, it is over! There's not going to be an execution – you and I, we're allowed to continue our relationship!"

It was as though someone turned off a light somewhere, that was how dark it became before my eyes in that moment. I felt my legs give way beneath me. Raphaël, however, held on to me tightly.

## 72

RING

"I can see your house from here," I said while I pointed to the east, over the trees and over the rooftops of Malá Strana to the other side of the river. It was Saturday evening. We were standing on top of the Petřín Observation Tower, also called the Mini Eiffel Tower, and even though it was manifold shorter than the original, the view was just as grand, because it was situated on top of a hill.

Raphaël did not come closer. He stood in front of the window on the west side, with his hand above his sunglasses for added protected, staring at the horizon. He said: "It is almost time..."

Quickly I joined him. I wrapped my arm around his back and together we watched the sun that was now rapidly descending.

"Congratulations," I said.

Before we took the spiral stairs down I did a final round past all the eight corners of the observation deck. There was so much to see from this height: the Strahov Stadium, Saint Vitus Cathedral and the immense domain that belonged to the Castle, Malá Strana with all its orange rooftops of crisscross positioned houses and the baroque, green-copper turrets of Saint Nicholas Church. Aside from that, there was of course the Žižkov Television Tower across the water, the bridges over the Moldau, the forest right below us and in the distance, on all sides around the city, that stifling ring of communistic, concrete bulk architecture.

"Tell me again, about that feast day of yours," I said when we left the wooden building at the bottom of the tower.

"Oh, it's not that big of a deal," he said shrugging. "In the past, life was much simpler, we were easily able to sleep for days and go about our business at night. But now, in this information society with everywhere closed camera circuits and social insurance numbers and the like, we are forced to live as normal a life as possible, with everything that comes with it, including a substantial number of hours of daytime activities."

"Unless you're an overnight security guard."

"That's right."

"Or a rock star, or a night nurse..."

"Better not any medical professions."

I smiled.

"In any case, despite all lotions and expensive brands of sunglasses, it remains a challenge for us to brave the raging light of the sun day in day out. That will never change and has always been a favorite subject to whine about when in the company of fellow undead. At a certain point during a birthday of one of us somewhere in England, someone jokingly expressed his desire for the solstice. That's the day, somewhere in the middle of the sixth month of the year, at which the number of hours of sunlight begin to decrease again. In other words, when the days start to get shorter. And a lot more seriously than he had anticipated, his friends took a shine to that idea. They picked June 17 as the date, a safe number of days removed from unintended pagan or otherwise religious connotations. Next they came up with a ritual that had to mark the celebratory moment and that is how it has become a tradition for practically every vampire on the northern hemisphere, to go outside at sunset on this date, and to look the so dreaded celestial body defiantly in the eyes for a fraction of a second. With or without protection."

"Did you know that June 17 is a national holiday of Iceland?"

"Iceland, huh... the country that keeps haunting us," he said with a chuckle. We passed a gate in the outstretched brick wall, that separated the grounds around the observation tower from the park at the top of the hill.

"A fraction of a second only, then... and how does that feel to you, looking into the sun?"

"It hurts."

"How much?"

"As though something chemical comes into contact with your eyes. Hydrochloric acid, would be my guess."

I briefly squeezed his hand, but he rejected my sympathy with the sneer, "We do it to ourselves, you know."

It was much quieter here in the park. The wall functioned as a surprisingly effective sound barrier and dampened the clamor of cars and other sounds of the city creeping up the incline. What remained was the flamboyant singing of a late blackbird and some scattered conversations between passing couples.

We came across a piece of playground equipment that looked like something between a swing and an undulating ship: the thing was able to go back and forth and had two opposite hanging seats. As we played footsie we sat there for a while, staring at each other and to the trees and the grass and the sky. He had put away his sunglasses, and his sweater slung over his shoulders with the sleeves casually tied together.

I closed my eyes and sighed: "I think it will take a while for me. Getting used to not having a reason to be afraid, not having to look over your shoulder, being able to speak your mind freely again..."

He was silent.

"Unless...?"

"No, they're not surveilling us anymore. Those involved are more than happy to get back to their daily activities."

He got up and helped me get off the swing. "I want to show you something beautiful. Come," he said.

"Are you sure this is a rose garden?" I asked teasingly.

Raphaël did not reply. He led me around a sea of flowers that would not look out of place as a backdrop of a lyrical poem. The ambient light had started to turn bluer, but in spite of the twilight I could see how richly variated the subspecies in this garden were, and the different ways in which they grew: roses in bushes, roses in the form of neatly manicured trees, and roses that had found their way up along white pergola constructions. And as a demarcation to all that beauty, endless numbers of lavender plants were blooming in slightly curved rows... I kid you not, lavishly blooming lavender! Completely redundantly my boyfriend said: "This is one of my favorite spots in this city."

"Do you ever sit in a square yard of grass over there?" I inquired, pointing towards a small green section between flowerbeds that were obviously cared for with a lot of love. He nodded. We sat down on one of the pristinely white painted benches and suddenly I had to watch myself to not break out laughing at the thought that now crossed my mind, for how many loving couples from Prague had proclaimed this garden to be 'their most romantic private spot', counting themselves far away from prying eyes? And how many lovey-dovey marriage proposals would have been made here over the years by the most sentimental souls of this city?

I turned my face away, keeping my mouth straight with difficulty. No, laughing at him would be childish. After all, even he had his frame of reference – all this here probably looked a lot like the gardens of Versailles, in terms of its layout. Or something.

Through the trees, two domes that were opened aside of the Štefánik Observatory could be seen. Strange, unearthly objects, so close to this idyllic setting in the light of the waxing moon.

Raphaël said nothing, and he had not for a while. I said: "A crazy thought, really, that Gosia passes as being related to Petr and his wife..."

He nodded.

"Is that what one would call a *coven*, when vampires live together like that?"

"Yes. Or a *house*."

"And how did they get together, at one point?"

"Petr's wife has turned Gosia into a vampire. She's her sire."

"Ah ha..."

Raphaël lay his arm across my shoulder, his hand played with my hair a little, a minimalistic, simple act that had a maximum effect.

I tried to stay focused by remarking: "Whatever could have been the deciding factor in that verdict about us...?"

"Yes, that's a mystery to me as well," he said. "It has probably been a combination of factors. But even so – I know how ruthless the members of the Supreme Council can be."

"Do you know them personally, then?"

"No. Almost no one knows who is actually in charge among us. Even notifications and decisions are announced to the community in different ways each time."

"And this time Gosia was chartered to do that."

"Indeed."

"Did she have a choice? Would she have been allowed to refuse?"

"Presumably not. They must have figured: she and Lente know each other a little bit by now and so..." Raphaël exhaled sharply.

"But they *can* be trusted, I should hope – I mean, the decision that they've made about us, can we really be completely sure about it now?"

He shook his head. "Darling. What you're doing right now is torturing yourself. Because with or without our reservations – the Supreme Council will always be a mystery to us. You can't do anything about that and neither can I. But there is one thing that I simply can't imagine, and that is them making a decision that they don't support. Let's hold on to that."

I nodded. Wanted to believe him so badly.

"Which does not change the fact that I'm still intrigued. How they have finally come to this judgment and what they have taken into consideration – there *must* have been something, something that has particularly made an impression on them. Such as your quick course of action, with that drunken piece of shit..."

His fingers stopped caressing me. "And the fact that under the disastrous circumstances of that evening, that you still want to be with me after something like that..."

I shrugged.

"... And also after all those other things that you know about me by now – my personality, my past. Sweetheart, I'm not an easy person to deal with at all."

"Oh, even I come with a manual. You know that."

Raphaël got up and stood in front of me, with his hands resting loosely inside his pockets. "Shall we then just say that we are equal?" he asked.

"No, not equal."

"Oh? Then what are we?"

"We keep each other on our toes. And we could really use that I think, now that we have officially been recognized as a couple." I laughed, a little cynically.

"Still, I don't think that acknowledgement is official enough."

"What do you mean? – Ooh!"

My heart skipped a beat.

And before I truly realized what was happening, my boyfriend had pulled a small box out of the right pocket of his pants, had knelt down in front of me and had opened the box. He said: "Lente, I don't possess the talent of giving passionate speeches and I seldom succeed at finding the right words during special occasions. Still, I want to tell you something. Something that you've heard me say before, but what comes from the bottom of my heart each time:

I love you. And I want us to belong together in the eye of mortal humanity as well. That is why I want to ask you: Lente Sandifer, will you marry me?"

Stunned I stared at the incredibly detailed white-golden engagement ring that softly glistened in the light of the waxing moon, against the contrast of the dark velvet. Then I looked at my boyfriend with big eyes. This was totally nothing like I had expected a marriage proposal to look like! This had nothing sugary to it. On the contrary, this felt frighteningly serious!

"What am I to do?" I whispered squeakily.

Too much in shock by the unexpectedness of all of this, too flabbergasted about the beauty of the piece of jewelry and totally overwhelmed by the storm of conflicting emotions that raced through me. "I – I don't know what to do..." I stammered, "I really don't know, my love."

Raphaël stroked my cheek. "That's alright," he said. He stood up, closed the box that had the ring in it and put it back inside his pocket. He sat down beside me and I tried to find the right words to say, a way to explain myself further. "It's not that I don't love you. Or that I don't want to be with you."

"I know."

"It's just that... if I were to say 'yes' now, I mean, right at this instance, there will be things that I haven't thought about at all yet, but that I *do* have to consider. And I'd rather do that thinking before than after the fact, because otherwise it's not fair to you or me or everyone else, really, and – "

" – Calm down, baby," he interrupted. "I can wait. Why don't you take the time to figure out all the things that you need to? When you're ready, you can let me know, alright?" He pulled me in and with the arm that he draped across my shoulder it truly seemed as though he wrapped me in a blanket of tranquility. It had to come from his demeanor. Incredible, how he was able to hold back the disappointment, which he undoubtedly must have felt. He was so sweet!

The amount of minutes that we have sat in each other's arms in this way, I did not know, but all of a sudden Raphaël sat up straight and began to growl. That growling became louder and, in the moment that he jumped up, it turned into a noise that was something to the likes of the furious hissing of a cat. In a flash he shifted a few meters ahead and he began to trot back and forth on the path where our bench stood, from the right, passing in front of me to the left and back again. Suddenly I saw what caused his alarmed behavior: In front of us, at the entrance of the garden a figure in sportswear appeared. Lucas. Murphy's Law... I should have known that there was still more to come, but why *now*, of all times?

## 73

FINALE

The two assessed the situation, circled precociously around each other, with their backs straightened and their heads low between their shoulders, each trying to find their position along the walking paths of the rose garden. Then, seemingly as agreed, they approached one another, stopped at a couple of feet distance and greeted each other with a tilted nod of the head. Lucas came up to me, watched like a hawk by Raphaël.
"Lente, how are you?" he asked.
I replied with a curt 'hey' and refused to shake the hand that was extended by him.
For a couple of seconds the three of us were just standing there.
Then Raphaël said: "Darling, there is a thing or two that we have to settle. So I will take you to the observatory over there. Wait there, until you are picked up." Putting his word into action he began to walk, with me in hand and Lucas at a certain distance beside him.
He gave me his sweater and sunglasses. He hugged me and briefly I felt his body tremble with emotion. The next moment I watched how my boyfriend walked across the paved path with his father toward the park. It looked like they were conversing peacefully when they disappeared from sight...

> Bílá Hora. The White Mountain. Today no more than a humble grassy elevation in the landscape, entirely enclosed by the westernmost residential areas of Prague. In the past, however, this hill was situated well outside the city limits.
> At the highest point of Bílá Hora there is a monument with some text and a year: 1602. Thousands of people died here... The battle in question lasted barely an hour.

I was well aware of what was about to happen, that the things that they had to settle were the grievances that they had with one another and that those grievances had everything to do with me and that the argument that they would have about that, would not end with words. With a knot in my stomach I walked into the museum, trying my utmost best to pretend to be a normal tourist. Here I was, putting on an act again. But did I have another choice? Would it be even possible for me to do what any mortal being would do, with the knowledge that they now possessed? – Right, let's walk up to the man behind the front desk and yell at him in our best English or German: "Sir, you have to call 911 right away! You see, my boyfriend is a vampire and he is terribly dangerous and his sire has come and he's even more dangerous and stronger and they are going to go at each other's throat, so the police really has to pull them apart, otherwise someone will die!"

"Oh, that does sound quite serious, indeed. Where, should I tell them, the fight will take place?"

"Well, considering how they can run faster than the human eye can see, the police will have to comb an area within a mile or hundred radius..."

Instead of setting this hopeless idea in motion I bit my lower lip and began to saunter past the planetary exhibition. I decided to go over each piece of text and description that was listed with the displayed objects, with neurotic precision. Therefore I regularly forced myself to go back two or three times past each word that I hadn't absorbed consciously enough to my liking – if they left out the roaring, they could go at it near this place, in the park even, perhaps. But that *did* depend on Raphaël's ability to control himself and also on the extent to which Lucas considered himself displeased... Lucas. So he had returned to finish what he had started, to drive my lover and me apart. If I had not been this aware of the severity of this matter I laughed the father and son in their faces for their tomfoolery. But the father was not a father figure anymore and his son could not see anything but a sworn enemy in him. How much one could misjudge a person... there was no trace left of Lucas' integrity and even the judgment by the Supreme Council did not seem to be of any value to him. Had Lucas even heard about what had been decided? And – oh no, *no,* he did not live in this territory, of course! Then, did that automatically mean that, despite all new developments, we were outlaws when around him? After all this trouble, still outlawed?

The moment that the two walk out of the forest by the Strahov Monastery, they have long stopped talking to each other. They turn left onto Bělohorská.

If you follow the tram tracks all the way to the west from there, you end up at Bílá Hora, the end of line 22. But the vampires do not stop at that point. They continue running, till they have left the last houses of the city behind them and have passed the major junction of the highways. They do not slow down until they reach the airport, and in a derelict field next to one of the runways they finally come to a stop.

Count planets. Look at photos from space. Because there was no point in running away.

Now I had regrets. Why, for heaven's sake, had I not loudly shouted *yes* in reply to Raphaël's marriage proposal? Maybe it would have made a difference. Perhaps I would then even have been regarded by Lucas as the exclusive possession of my beloved, and that would have afforded me the protection I felt I was so desperately lacking at the moment. And where were the others of the Community? Where was Gosia, for instance, now that I needed her this badly... could I not go outside and yell as loudly as possible that I wanted to marry Raph, anyway?

With drooping shoulders I dragged my feet back inside. Do not do anything that you will regret later. Allow yourself the time to think and, for a minute, pretend as though that crazy monk does not exist.

The man behind the counter motioned that the observatory was about to close. It was running close to eleven. I pulled a disappointed face and pointed to the space in which the telescope was set up. The man smiled and caved. A real, antique Carl Zeiss... that was quite a different story than that teeny-weeny lens in my photo camera. I waited for a man and a teenage boy to finish watching and then took a quick glance through the telescope toward the moon and stars.

A father and son...

The milky white haze that obscures the human eye in some places on the farmland near Ruzyně Airport tonight, was created by a combination of high humidity and absolute calm.

Those circumstances have made it difficult for the cooling air right above the ground, to mix with the residual heat of the past summer's day, and in this matter a veil of ground mist hovers here that reaches to just below chest height. Every few minutes however, this fog is blown apart in circling shreds by approaching commercial airplanes, next to and in line with the nearby runway.

At such moments a glimpse of the vampires is visible, and their hostile movements towards each other. Nevertheless, in the darkness that prevails here, it is almost impossible to distinguish father from son, and the red and white lamps that cast their light in only specific directions for the benefit of air traffic hardly make any difference to that.

Initially, it had begun as that classical exchange of moving past and encircling one another. Filled with smoldering suspicion they searched back and forth for weaknesses and an excuse to attack, just as feline predators do. Now, however, the vampires have come to a stop. They stand a few yards apart and one begins to say a number of things to the other. The other reacts calmly, in control. At least, if you were to judge by his body language, because he does not use truncated gestures, as his opponent does.

Yet, *what* he says, lands completely wrong. In an immediate reaction his opponent accelerates towards him, like a battering ram, and hits him with his head – a full blow to the stomach area. For many feet the vampires fly through the air... the official start of a dizzying spectacle, in which there is beating, kicking and biting, and in which speed, hearing and seeing intertwine in such a way that most of the time only snapshots of this outburst of violence can be registered. Shouting discussions escalate into roaring, and roaring is alternated with the sharp sound of crunching bones. Lightning fast combat moves flash by, illuminated by the blinding headlights of planes that are landing, and evanesce from sight again when one of the rivals, apparently heavily injured, disappears for a handful of seconds beneath the white haze of a cloud of low-lying fog... only to then jump out, completely recovered, and throw himself into the counterattack with even more aggression. And to make the drama complete, those airplanes only keep coming, with the screeching roar of their engines, as though you are hearing a deafening barrage of bullets, or dozens of cannons, fired almost incessantly in succession.

A father and a son... We had never discussed it, but where did we stand, Raphaël and I, concerning that subject – 'having kids'? Not that I was eager for offspring at this very moment, but it *was* one of those things. Was it even possible for him, with his physiology that was so divergent, to bring forth new life?

On top of that, in order to have children, a man and a woman had to have sex and we were not having sex. Barely three months ago my presence with him together in one room had already been too much and he had almost killed me. And although we had moved on way beyond that by now and, for example, having a moment of rest together in the same house had become quite possible, I still wondered if I was really safe if I drifted off to sleep.

Oh well, there was progress. And a wedding was not something that you could organize in a month.

But what if this aspect of our relationship *would* work itself out? Then there was still that one thing, that issue of taboo that was carefully maintained by us, that we constantly tiptoed around with great caution, so as to not have to talk about it: the question of where the modern-day vampire gets his food from.

What did Raphaël have to do to get blood?

Were all methods that you came across in TV series and books realistic, or was the truth just as raw as the fear of that truth? Could I get away with the cheap downplay derived from fantasy media that lulls you into a seemingly peaceful slumber with explanations like: 'vampires are life-threatening, indeed they are. In fact, they are the most bloodthirsty hunters that you can imagine. But the romantic, undead boyfriend of this angelic girl would really never kill any people. No honestly, you can rest assured about that. He solely drinks blood out of ridiculously expensive donor bags from the hospital that he has paid for fair and square, out of his own pocket.'

What if reality did consist of a disillusioning series of bloody facts and that you could assume that the average undead feasted roughly once a week on...

what number of victims would someone of Raphaël's age end up with then, up until now? Oh shit oh shit oh *shit!* No, do not think about it, otherwise you'll go insane. Besides, it was none of my business, it was not for nothing that he kept that part of his life so far away from me. Even he was entitled to his privacy. I had to respect that and not make a big deal out of it. And also: could today's vampire maybe not simply be compared to the megalomaniac, or at least the somewhat self-overestimating man? The man that thinks of himself to be infallible a little too often, because of his so-called life experience and acquisitions, and who perhaps does not feel the need, but does have the absolute necessity to be set straight every once in a while, or to simply hit a wall at full speed? A wall made up of Icelandic seawater perhaps?

> The gunpowder vapor of a battlefield generally needs less time to clear than do low-lying clouds of fog that have developed during the night. Someone's head appears above the white-gray haze. The head of one person. He briefly bends over again, to pat the dirt off himself, probably. In addition, he takes an attempt to tidy his clothing.
> Then he begins to walk, away from the harm he has just caused, back in the direction of the city.

The museum had closed. I was sitting on the edge of a planter next to the entrance, a little hidden behind the statue of an unknown adventurer wearing one of those old-fashioned aviator caps.
I myself no longer felt like the adventurous girl who went to Iceland without a care in the world at the beginning of this year, and tears rolled down my cheeks at the thought that the arms that my beloved had wrapped around me half an hour earlier, was possibly the last contact that I would ever have with him. I buried my face in the purple sweater that he had given me to hold on to and smelled his soap, his aftershave, his scent...
"Lente."
Abruptly I raised my head.
"Across from you, beneath the tree."
I stood up, hesitantly took a few steps toward where the voice had come from.
"Hurry, some people are coming."
In a little dash I crossed the paved walking path. An arm pulled me towards him, into the darkness of the shadows.
"Stand still for a moment and don't say a thing," the voice said.
 As a group of teenagers walked by and disappeared beyond the curve, the excitement in me rose to an unimaginable height. He was alive! My boyfriend was alive and he was standing right here in front of me now!!
I wanted to jump into his arms, but was stopped. He emerged from under the tree and right away I could see the reason for his reserve.
His polo shirt was covered in blood and was torn in several places.

"You're injured…"

"Not anymore. Can you hand me my sweater?"

Arm in arm we walked to the hill top station of the train that was going to bring us down, back into the city.

So he had survived the duel. "And Lucas?" I asked.

"You will never be bothered by him again," was the reply, and for a second it felt really cold next to my boyfriend.

74

TELEPHONE


Sensual steps, placed in a provocative circle around me. The strides of a master of seduction, a ballet dancer. He reached out to me, I lay my hand in his and amidst blindingly bright-colored flowers we danced our slow lovers' dance. Sweet and spicy acidic scents stimulated my olfactory organ, they carried me to a psychedelic parallel world, far beyond the reality that I called home... I cleared my eyes by blinking, but that did not get rid of my slightly intoxicated condition.

Unexpectedly, my beloved knelt down. He pulled out a small, square box. He opened it, held it up to me and as soon as I saw the beauty of the offered ring, I answered his yet unspoken question with a wholehearted 'yes'. In anticipation of the gesture with which he was about to slip the piece of jewelry around my finger, I reached out my hand. To my amazement my fingers then touched something large and spherical that seemed to be shrouded in a piece of fabric, coarse in texture. The edited sensory information now also got through to my eyes: as if a new chapter in a book had just opened without my knowledge, the ring disappeared and the small box gave way to a silver platter, balancing atop the hand of my boyfriend. Carefully I gave the round object on top of it a little push, the thing rolled to the side and the brown cloth slid off. A contorted face was revealed, the face of a head without its body, the head of Lucas! Like in a nightmare that came true, his eyes opened. They looked straight at me and his mouth emitted the wailing, ghostly bark of a cornered fox.

When I finally took my fingers out of my ears and dared to look around, it had become night. I was standing alone on the immense lawn of – unmistakably – a London park... and echoing in my mind, like a maddening mantra I heard the words: "His-head-will-roll, his-head-will-roll, his-head-will-roll..."


It was a problem, waking up startled from this dream every couple of minutes. Against the screaming I could not do anything with the best will in the world. Yet I wondered what I preferred: the nightmares, with the consequence of my disturbing my roommates' sleep with embarrassing regularity, or the first half of the night, when I couldn't get to sleep at all and tossed and turned endlessly in my bed – almost noiselessly, of that I made sure. Because being as considerate as possible towards others, that was easy to learn after sleeping in a youth hostel for three weeks.

From the moment that I had crawled into bed with that eerie feeling, I had been racking my brain about the previous night, or actually, about all days and weeks of the past months. Questions that I had asked myself, while waiting at the observatory, had just kept intruding and challenging me with a sardonic tenacity to seek answers and to continue searching for them, until they were actually found. The question, for example, of whether I really knew the man whom I loved so much, and whether I could tell myself with certainty that I would really get all the information about him that was of significant importance to me...

But was that the only issue? Were all those questions and the answers, whether or not they had been provided to date, the only thing that prevented me from responding positively to Raphael's marriage proposal? Or was there something more? Something that had to happen first?

The ringtone of my telephone did not really worry me, because I was able to lower the volume so much so that others could barely hear it. What time was it, anyway? As I quietly crawled out of my lower bunk and blindly searched through my bag for my phone, I noticed that it had almost turned light outside. Close to six then...

I looked at the screen and the breath that I gasped in shock because of that, produced an unexpectedly loud and screeching noise.

A few people in the room turned over in their sleep muttering disturbedly and as fast as I could I tiptoed barefoot with phone and all out of the room. After I had closed the door behind me, I shakily pressed the answer button. "Hello?" I said.

"Lente, how are you doing?"

"How is this possible? This isn't happening!" I whispered, pacing across a short, enclosed section of the hallway. The fingers of my free hand kneaded uncontrollably through my messy hair.

"I take it that you recognize my voice."

"Yes, of course, but I thought you were deader than a doorknob!"

"No. I'm still here."

"But didn't you have a fight, then? So much has happened and he only got more and more upset with you lately and I really thought that he would rip your head off – "

" – Lente, I'm calling you, because I want to offer you my apologies."

"Huh? Say that again..." I walked over to the internet corner, sat down with my elbows on both sides of the keyboard of the computer table in front of me. Nervously I rubbed my forehead.

"I have confused you," said Lucas, "I have insulted you on multiple occasions and willingly scared you. For that, I would like to ask your forgiveness."

"Is this a joke, or something?"

"No, I am serious."

"Hold on, cause I don't get it. So you suddenly want to be forgiven. Does that mean then, that you have come to realize everything you have put us through? And does that mean that you know *why* you did it?"

"It's over now. That's the main thing. And to give you the peace that you deserve, I'll disappear from sight for the time being."

"And that's supposed to be good enough?" I was startled by my own speaking volume. Whispering again I continued: "First you scare the shit out of us, then you say you're sorry and basically want to skip town, leaving us with loose ends and a lot of questions… Don't you know how quickly you can lose friendships that way?"

"The happiness of two souls has more value than that of one."

"Whoa, stop right there. What do you mean by that?"

"Exactly as I said it."

"That's a pretty nonsensical thing to say."

A roommate shuffled by. As a way to say hi she raised a lazy hand and then disappeared into the bathroom. I got up, looked for a place where I had more privacy, the communal kitchen. "You're really going to have to explain this to me," I said, as I pulled up a chair. "Because what you said, sounded like you *wish* us our happiness."

"I do."

Suddenly I remembered something that Raphaël had said about him once: "Lucas doesn't do anything without a purpose."

"Keep going, I'm listening," I hence insisted.

"There's nothing to say, Lente."

"I beg to differ."

"Then we disagree on that."

"Oh, for fuck's sake, Lucas – do I have to *beat* it out of you, or something? I just want to know, and I think I'm entitled to that too. So again, how is it possible that you first pull out all the stops to drive us apart and that you then suddenly come with statements like 'wishing us our peace and happiness'?"

"I was against your relationship, initially."

"But?"

"It became clear to me that, in spite of everything, the urge to stay together is stronger for you two than life itself. And that got me thinking."

"Then when did you stop, with that 'being against us'?"

"Sometime during that online communication between you and I, when you were in Rotterdam by yourself."

"But still you continued with your terror. Even here in Prague."

No reply.

"And so I remain in the dark about the underlying motive."

Silence.

"It's okay, Lucas, cause I'll find out anyway. I'm not averse to a little puzzling."

"The purpose of that, however, is debatable. Besides, I'm not sure I'm in the mood for all this – "

" – If you hang up, I'll call you back," I quickly warned him. "And if you won't answer, I'll call again. And again. Until I get a hold of you."

Lucas let out a sigh, which I chose to interpret as a sign of capitulation.

"Okay, let me think…" I then said, and acting as though it could be seen from the other end of the line, I lazily leaned back. As I lay my legs on a chair across from me I spoke my thoughts: "So it seems we have a number of ambiguities on our hands. Riddles, so to speak. Such as, for example, the reason why you did what you did. Now, for the last weeks, you have really gotten under our skin and I take it that you thought we had it too easy, for some reason or another. Too easy in what area? That could again be a mystery in itself, but the fact that you think that we weren't being bullied enough is clear as day."

"It's not like that…"

"Aha, so it really is 'bullying' that we're talking about here. I thought so. But then the question naturally arises: what was the purpose of this bullying? Because most of the time something like that is used to provoke someone, wouldn't you say?"

"Rhona, Lente, do we really have to do this," asked Lucas, but I cut him short:

" – Just give me a moment, I'm busy doing an analysis. So, let's say that we are right to assume that it was your intention to provoke us. That comes with a reaction, as a result. Right? And in the eyes of the bully, such a reaction can go two ways: to 'desirable' and 'not so much desirable'. Usually however, the victim will react precisely in the way the average bully wants: hurt, and maybe even aggressively. Only in *our* picture something is wrong, because you were on our side, so why the provoking? The only logical explanation I can think of for this at the moment is that you, by hook or by crook, wanted to see a reaction from us. To get us moving, so to speak, to… oooh shit." A shock went through me.

"Lucas, is it really true?"

"What is?"

"That you provoked us, not so much for yourself, but mainly to show our reactions to others? Others, who were observing us?"

Discretion, inventiveness – criteria that I had heard Raphaël mention…

"…So that they would come to a better judgment?"

He remained silent.

My eyes welled up with tears. "You must have so much faith in me…"

"The ones at the top of our hierarchy are quite conservative."

"And you were worried that they weren't making enough effort to collect evidence?"

"Something to that effect."

"Oh man, oh Lucas…" I cried, and all kinds of things were racing through my mind now; how he had been prepared to lose our favor and even our friendship with him for this and how he risked his own life… "You could have been killed! You must have known that – Ralph was really out for blood! He was ready to rip you to shreds."

"For him to burden his conscience with such an act, I would never have allowed."

I cried, as soundlessly as possible, yet intensely, with heaving upper body and all, with emotion, with sorrow, with... "Lucas, I am so sorry. I have been so mean to you," I sobbed, "while you..."

"You have a good heart, Lente. And you have amazed me with your ingenuity," he said. "The trick you pulled in Holešovice on Wednesday with that police officer and the tram... I really did not see that coming."

I laughed through my tears.

"Still, I mean what I say. I have been a tough teacher towards you, that is true, but those skills of yours you have acquired independently of me and you'll be able to put them to good use in the future. You've come a long way, Lente."

"Not far enough, I'm afraid," I said a little sadly. "You know that he has proposed to me?"

"Yes."

I began to chew my lip – shitty habit. Could we not just talk about something else? So I asked, "But how are you doing, anyway? What have you been up to lately?"

"Working. The usual stuff. And I've gone on vacation."

"What?! Where? When?"

"I was in the U.S. for four days, right before you came to Prague."

"Wow, holidays in America. What state?"

"Oklahoma."

"What's in Oklahoma?"

"Strong winds and thunder storms. I joined a group of storm chasers."

"Tornado Alley... man, so you finally went and did it! And how did you like it?"

"Flipping the switch was not an easy thing to do."

"Oh, you'll get there with some practice," I said ironically.

He reacted in a stoic tone. "Indeed, going on vacation takes some practice."

A shiver ran through me. I said: "Are you sure you're doing okay? I mean, you don't have any long-lasting effects from last night, do you?"

"I'm doing alright. At most, I need a new track suit. I only had two of them."

I laughed, by myself. "Once a dryasdust, always a dryasdust, huh," I said. And a little raspy I added to that: "Lucas, it may sound strange, but I have missed you. I mean, the real you, like in those chat conversations."

"I'm sure we'll see each other again in future."

"But for now you think we need some space."

"You're worried about him and me."

"Yes..."

"You won't have to, anymore. Things will be just fine between us."

"Okay…"

"And things will be alright between you and him as well. You know that his love for you runs deep, don't you?"

"Yes," I replied with a tiny voice.

"And you realize that you have what it takes?"

"I don't know, Lucas, I honestly don't know."

"Rhona – Lente. Give yourself some time. He won't leave any time soon. And should you decide to say 'yes', know that I will be proud to call you my daughter-in-law."

For a moment it was silent. A minute to catch my breath during this strange conversation. But all interaction with Lucas was surrealistic. That would probably always stay that way.

After a while I asked: "What are those noises I keep hearing in the background? You're not anywhere in this area, I think…" Involuntarily I took a glance out of the kitchen window, which overlooked the hostel's inner garden, but Lucas answered: "No, I'm at the train station. I'm leaving for Dresden shortly."

"Not for Leipzig?" I asked smiling.

"Not for Leipzig."

"And will you be gone for long?"

"Why, Lente? Do you have a crush on me then?" was his counter question.

We laughed, together now. Then he said: "Listen. I want you to do something for me. There's a parcel for you at the reception desk of your hostel. Pick it up and open it. I have something to ask you about its content."

"Hold on, then…" I walked out of the kitchen, down the stairs. At the reception desk I received a soft, flexible something, wrapped in brown paper and taped with, typical for him, way too much adhesive tape. I sat down on the stairs and began to pick at it with one hand. With my other hand I held my cell phone up to my ear.

"When will you return to the Netherlands?" Lucas asked.

"Uh… Wednesday evening. We're going together, with his car, and then he will continue by ferry and so on. Wait, I have to put you aside for a minute. This isn't working."

With two hands the unpacking was only a matter of seconds. From the parcel a black T-shirt emerged.

"Have you unpacked it yet?" I heard him ask from the other end of the line.

"Don't rush me," I muttered, while I unfolded the piece of clothing and looked at the lilac print. It had a twister on it that was loosely drawn by hand with underneath it the words: *Tornadoes suck.* I chuckled.

"So this is humor, Lente?" it sounded from my cell phone that was on the step of the stairs beside me. I brought the device to my ear again and replied: "Yes, Lucas, this is humor."

## 75

EPILOGUE

Sometimes things can go very fast. Then a new insight presents itself totally unexpectedly, and the pros and cons that initially made you roll around with indecision in your bed for nights, give way to a clarity that is as clear as flawless crystal. And there is nothing that will be able to change your mind anymore...
I now knew what answer to give to the marriage proposal of Raphaël. Finally.

On the Tuesday evening, my final night in Prague for now, it happened.
It had all started out very romantically: I had just finished my meal, he had finished another drawing and the dishes were in the washer. After having lit a couple of candles he settled on the couch beside me. For a while we had then listened to one of my recently acquired Dvořak CDs, my head against his shoulders, his hand folded into mine. Between the moments of silent satisfaction we said sweet nothings to each other and every now and then he gave me a little kiss on the crown of my head.

At a certain point I had turned toward him and we kissed with a bit stronger intensity and then I had draped my right leg over his legs. I crawled into his lap and for a moment we just sat there, staring at each other.
And whether it was because of what I had just done or because of whatever – Raphaël suddenly had a different look in his eyes. His gaze drifted downward to my neck and he asked: "Did you know, *mon coeur*, that AB positive has the sweetest taste of all the blood types?" With the back of his hand he stroked my carotid artery. In an impulse I had then slid off his lap, stood up and exclaimed something along the lines of: "No, not *this* again! Why do you always have to let this type of nonsense come between us? I am so sick and tired of that dramatic bullshit of yours!"
With a lightly arrogant amazement he had protested: "But surely I can't help it, *cherie*, that you smell so delicious and that your life essence flows this temptingly visible through your veins? What else would you advise me to do?"
Indifferently I then had muttered, as I walked in the direction of the kitchen: "How should I know what you should do when that happens. Just bite your teeth, or something."

I had not yet left the room or his voice had sounded, now completely normal and human again. He said: "I'm sorry, Lente, you're absolutely right."

From that moment I knew that I had found what I had missed until then in my feelings: I had moved beyond the fear.
And the beast inside Raphaël was ready to be tamed.


END

## Lente's PHOTO ART

In this novel you were a witness of how Lente, the main character, was in the process of assembling photos for an art book.

*This art book really exists!*

It came out in 2013 and can be ordered via Amazon.com.

Name of the book: Love & Decay

Author: Lente van 't Zand (her actual, Dutch name)

ISBN: 9781482072822

Printed in Great Britain
by Amazon

57591407R00216